The
Bad
Muslim
Discount

The
Bad
Muslim
Discount

A Novel

Syed M. Masood

Doubleday New York

Copyright © 2021 by Syed M. Masood

All rights reserved. Published in the United States by Doubleday, a division of Penguin Random House LLC, New York, and distributed in Canada by Penguin Random House Canada Limited, Toronto.

www.doubleday.com

DOUBLEDAY and the portrayal of an anchor with a dolphin are registered trademarks of Penguin Random House LLC.

Book design by Michael Collica
Jacket artwork by Samya Arif
Jacket design by Emily Mahon

Library of Congress Cataloging-in-Publication Data
Names: Masood, Syed, author.
Title: The bad Muslim discount : a novel / Syed Masood.
Description: First edition. | New York : Doubleday, 2021.
Identifiers: LCCN 2019058987 | ISBN 9780385545259 (hardcover) | ISBN 9780385545235 (ebook)
Subjects: LCSH: Pakistani Americans—Fiction. | Iraqi Americans—Fiction. | Muslim families—United States—Fiction. | Immigrants—United States—Fiction. | Immigrant families—United States—Fiction. | Domestic fiction.
Classification: LCC PS3613.A8187 B33 2020 | DDC 813/.6—dc23
LC record available at https://lccn.loc.gov/2019058987

MANUFACTURED IN THE UNITED STATES OF AMERICA

1 3 5 7 9 10 8 6 4 2
First Edition

For my mother,
Hajra Masood,
who taught me how to talk,
&
my father,
Syed Manzar Masood,
who asked me to speak

THE OPENING

1995–2005

How you begin things is important. This is true in checkers and in life, because at the beginning of things you are freer than you will ever be again. Once the game starts, every move you make is influenced by what someone else has done. The longer the game goes, the messier the board becomes, the more that influence grows. But the opening, Anvar, belongs to you.

—Naani Jaan

ANVAR

I killed Mikey.

It sounds worse than it actually was. You have to understand that I didn't kill Mikey because I wanted to do it. I killed him because God told me to do it.

I don't suppose that sounds much better.

It helps, I think, to know that Mikey was a goat. He had bored brown eyes with rectangular pupils that made him seem a little creepy. Loud and obnoxious, he shat tiny round pellets all over the cramped garage he shared with three of his brethren. He was probably the only one of them who had a name. I know my parents didn't name their goats, and my brother, Aamir, said that naming animals was stupid.

Mikey was the only pet I ever had. He was mine for about a week. I fed him dry straw, brought him buckets of water and asked him if he really wanted to be slaughtered for the sake of Allah at the upcoming Eid because, quite frankly, that seemed like a poor career choice. He remained stoic in the face of his grim fate, at least so far as I could tell.

Eid al-Adha marks the end of the Hajj pilgrimage in Mecca. The name of the celebration translates to "the Festival of Sacrifice."

Yes, Islam has a marketing problem.

The festival commemorates Prophet Abraham's willingness to sacrifice his son, either Isaac or Ishmael depending on what you believe or disbelieve, to God. Muslims all over the world purchase and slaughter rams, goats, cows or camels in memory of the moment when God saved Abraham's son from God's own command.

Mikey was my sacrifice to Allah. Since I was only ten, his purchase was financed by my parents.

I remember that Eid well. I was forced to wake up a little after dawn and shower. My parents gave me a brand-new, bright white shalwar kameez and a matching woven skullcap. Then they took me to a mosque to pray.

When we got home, butchers my father had hired were waiting for us, carrying the sinister tools of their trade. Eventually, these men would skin the animals, gut them and chop their carcasses up into manageable bits to be cooked, frozen or given away as gifts or charity.

Mikey was the first one they led out of the garage. He didn't resist.

My father handed me a long, sharp knife and instructed me to be careful. He said that the butchers would hold the goat and expose its neck. All I had to do was slice open the carotid artery and Mikey's blood would flow out. One clean motion would be enough. He clapped a heavy hand on my shoulder.

"Be brave," he said.

I did not feel the need to be brave. I wasn't scared. I felt something else entirely. I didn't say anything to my father. I could've told him I didn't want to do this. I don't know what he would have said. Instead of speaking, however, I gripped the knife. I held on tight because the plastic handle felt slick and slippery in my hand.

The men tripped Mikey to bring him to the ground. Now he resisted. He kicked, trying to struggle to his feet, but was restrained.

I walked up to him. I think he saw me, recognized me, because he seemed to relax a little. I heard my brother say, "Allah hu Akbar."

God is Great.

Aamir told me later that he'd said those words, necessary for the ritual to be properly completed, out loud because he knew I would forget to say them. Aamir had almost forgotten them himself when he had done this for the first time a few years ago.

What I haven't forgotten are Mikey's unattractive eyes full of unshed tears once the deed was done.

I haven't forgotten his blood. It was everywhere.

I didn't move away from him in time and his blood, it didn't seep out. It gushed out in a wild torrent, a flood, a fountain that soaked my hands and my clothes with all the force of a panicked, dying, still beating heart, and I stepped back and there was so much red and I was the cause of it.

I ran. I showered. I wept.

Once I'd changed, my father came to speak to me.

"You know, Anvar, people don't understand these days," he told me, "the real sacrifice. They think their offering is the money they spend on the animal. Or they think it is the life of the animal. But it isn't. You are the sacrifice. What you are feeling now? That is your sacrifice. The lives of other creatures are not yours to take. Life is precious and to end one is final. Remember to never take more from the world than you can give back to it."

Then he told me to come have breakfast. My mother had fried up Mikey's liver and it was, apparently, delicious.

Unfortunately, Mikey's death may have been in vain. Four months after he died, I was informed that my soul was damned to eternal torment.

My mother, a self-proclaimed authority on all things religious, told me so.

It was an appropriately hot day for such a revelation. Of course, we lived in Karachi then, so most days were hot days.

Karachi, the city that spat me out into this world, is perpetually under siege by its own climate. The Indian Ocean does not sit placidly at the edge of the massive metropolitan port. It invades. It pours in through the air. It conspires with the dense smog of modern life and collective breath of fifteen million souls to oppress you. Under the gaze of an indifferent sun you sweat and the world sweats with you.

It's probably not as hot as hell but it is definitely as bad as the sketchier neighborhoods of purgatory, the kinds of places you are just a little reluctant to wander after dark.

When I was growing up, Karachi was a place caught between ages, grasping at modernity while still clutching at the fading relics of an inglorious past. It was a city of skyscrapers and small, squat shanties. It had modern highways but was still pockmarked with peddlers wheeling vegetables over narrow dirt lanes on wooden carts. Imported luxury cars, rumbling, shining and glimmering in marvelous mechanical glory, were not uncommon, though neither was the pitifully obnoxious braying of overladen donkeys hitched to rickety wagons.

After a bad day at school, all I wanted was to go home. However, we were stuck in traffic and the air conditioner in our temperamental old Beetle was malfunctioning.

Trouble started, as it often does, because my mother decided to speak. "When we get home, you are going to have to take a shower."

I ignored her and rolled down my window, hoping to alleviate the heat in the car a little. It was a mistake. There was no breeze and, in the vain hope for one, I had let the city in. As usual, Karachi was screaming at its inhabitants and they were screaming right back.

People were leaning on their horns, though the traffic light was red and there was nowhere to go. Hawkers carrying various goods yelled out a litany of prices in hoarse, worn voices. They sold information in newspapers and romance in strings of fresh jasmine. Divine protection, that is to say cheap pieces of plastic etched with verses of the Quran, could also be purchased for a modest price.

My mother raised her voice over the din. "Did you hear me?"

"Yes." I folded my slick, thin arms across my chest. "Why do I have to shower?"

"Because you need one," she said, her tone sharp. She didn't like questions. After taking a deep breath, she went on in a more conciliatory manner. "Besides, showers are fun."

"No, they aren't."

"But you will feel nice and cool afterward."

"I'll feel nice and cool when you get the AC fixed."

My mother preferred morality to rationality because it put God on her side. When God was on her side, she won arguments against most right-minded people. I'm not such a person but she didn't know that then and, truth be told, neither did I. So, she played what had long been her trump card, her divine ace. "Taking showers is good."

"It's good?"

"It is most certainly good. The Prophet, May Peace Be Upon Him, and his Companions used to take showers each and every day."

I thought about that for a moment. "That's not true."

"What?"

"That can't be true. They were in the middle of a desert. They didn't have any water."

My mother's lips disappeared. She was a gaunt woman, sort of like an exceptionally thin chapati. Her lips shared this quality. When she was angry and pressed them together, they vanished entirely from view. It was one of her more frequent expressions.

"Anvar Faris! How dare you?"

"I didn't—"

"Where did you get the courage from? How dare you say those great men were not clean?"

"I didn't—"

"You will pray for forgiveness, Anvar. It was an insult to the Prophet."

"It wasn't—"

"It was an insult to his Companions. They were the greatest of all men. And you dare. You dare? The first thing you will do when you get back home is get on your knees and beg Allah for forgiveness for having said such a vile thing. Or you will go to hell. Do you understand me? You will roast in hell for what you dare."

"Dare," by the way, was her favorite word. She relished saying it. Whenever the opportunity to deploy it in conversation presented itself, she took it. She was careful to enunciate it fully, drawing it out, emphasizing it by using the most piercing voice she could manage. Hearing her speak about someone, an uninformed observer was likely to mistake the meekest of men for Prometheus.

I was old enough to know that once sacrilege had been invoked, there was no way to win the argument. Any response other than silence would only intensify the wrath raining down upon me. So, I sat there, stewing in Karachi, until we got home. Once there, I went to my room, closed the door, kicked a few scattered action figures out of the way and laid out a prayer mat.

I knelt but did not pray.

That was the day the hold of the sacred upon me was broken forever.

It was the day that made me who I am.

The day I was first told I was damned was the day I felt I had been blessed.

All deaths are inconvenient, in one way or another, but the death of a car can be uniquely so. When our little Beetle died, for example, it left me stranded in the middle of a brand-new river.

It was the heart of the monsoon season, and as usual it felt like an ocean was being poured onto the Earth through a sieve of pregnant clouds. It was the kind of ceaseless, relentless rain that was designed to make one believe the story of Noah.

Karachi is one of those places that feels like it just happened. I'm sure it must have been planned out to some degree, like all the great cities in the world. However, either it was designed so artfully that the hand of the artist has become invisible, like the hand of God, or it was done so poorly that there might as well not have been a design at all.

For example, though Karachi gets annual monsoons, it wasn't constructed to withstand them. So, every year, the city drowns a little. The streets, lacking proper drainage, flood. Cars float along roads like rudderless boats, carried off the ground by the irresistible force of accumulating water.

It was on this water that our Beetle choked one day as we were coming back from school. Our father went looking for help, and I was left to bob along in a makeshift river in the middle of the street, alone with my brother, Aamir, who was then, and remains to this day, a stinking little turd muncher.

Before I go on, I should mention that I am the lone skeptic when it comes to Aamir Faris. He has gone through his life checking all the right boxes that a model desi boy should check. He maintained a perfect GPA throughout high school and college, never dating, never drinking or even so much as going to a party where everyone's parents weren't invited. He never snuck out of the house at night or got any detention and never, ever missed an extra-credit assignment. Then he went to medical school and graduated near the top of his class. When he gets married, around nine months or so after his honeymoon, he will probably have an infant for everyone to coo over and a mortgage to pay off.

Did I mention he was an easy baby, willing to eat anything, and that he never cried? Even labor was allegedly painless with him. Not like the eighteen-hour ordeal I put my mother through, or so the story goes.

Somehow he's always been popular too. Aamir is well liked at the mosque because he volunteers there. He organizes community events for young kids, all while praying five times a day and banking every optional prostration he can manage along the way. He does all this with a smile and it is a glorious smile. Five out of five dentists would recommend the toothpaste he uses.

Aamir Faris, in short, uses dull crayons but he is relentlessly fastidious about coloring inside the lines.

Anyway, there we were, I think I was twelve then, so he must have been fifteen, trapped together in the skeleton of a metallic bug. The radio was, of course, silent and there seemed to be nothing to say. The only noise in the car was the plastic rustling of the bag of chili chips Aamir was holding and the occasional forlorn rumble of my stomach. I waited patiently for him to open the bag and offer me some. When he didn't, I resorted to telling him that I hoped we would get home soon because I needed to eat lunch. When that did not work either, I clutched my stomach and groaned dramatically, muttering about how hungry I felt. Still nothing. Finally, I just flat-out asked him for the chips.

He looked at me in that imperious way of his and said, "Not yet."

"I'm hungry," I protested.

"Wait for Dad to get back."

"Why?"

"Because otherwise no one will know that I shared my chips with you."

"So what? I'll know."

"But you won't tell anyone. You never tell anyone when I do nice things. What is the point of being good if no one knows about it?"

I stared at him. His wide, bullish face was set with that rigid, stony determination I knew so well. It made him look a little older than his age.

"That's why we're going to starve?"

"He'll be back in a second."

I considered trying to snatch away the chips, but he was thick and heavy, while I, taking after my mother, have always been wiry and lean. I didn't think I could manage it. So, instead, trying to keep a straight face, I said, "Allah is here. He'll know what you did. Isn't that what's important?"

Aamir opened his mouth to argue but then closed it again. He had been raised by the same woman who had raised me. He knew he was trapped. With a scowl, he handed me the spicy spoils of my victory, which I proceeded to devour.

Back then there was only one person in the world who I knew preferred me to Aamir, and I know that because she told me so. I'm pretty sure Naani Jaan, our mother's mother, told Aamir so too. She didn't give a damn about anyone's feelings. As far as she was concerned, if someone was a pedantic little son of an owl—the insult loses something in translation—they ought to be informed of that fact. After all, if you didn't do people the service of pointing out their flaws, how could you reasonably expect them to improve themselves?

Naani Jaan was a severe-looking woman who rarely smiled and almost never laughed. With narrow, serious eyes she surveyed the world as she found it and, generally speaking, found it wanting. I loved her because she loved me, of course, but also because she never changed, and it is comforting to have constants in your life. Her gray hair was always pulled up in a tight, painful-looking bun, and she only wore a plain white saris, which she said was the appropriate dress for a widow.

My mother, appalled by Naani's adherence to what she considered a non-Islamic custom, lavished Naani with saris of every color imaginable, but the old woman wouldn't even try them on. When she died, Naani left behind a rainbow of never-worn, out-of-fashion clothes in her cupboard.

When you are young everything seems eternal, even if you've killed more than your fair share of goats. I thought the days of sitting by Naani Jaan's window watching the rain come down and playing checkers while spearing sweet slices of Chaunsa mango with her dull silver forks would never end.

I was twelve when I got good at checkers, but I never got good enough to beat Naani Jaan, who refused to teach me all her tricks because that was her way.

"I'm like a cat," she said. "And you're a young lion."

"What?"

"I'll teach you everything I know," Naani said, "except how to climb a tree. That way, I can always get away when I need to."

I shook my head. "I'm pretty sure lions can climb trees, Naani Jaan."

"But how high can they go?" she asked, a rare, broad smile on her frown-lined face as she plucked my final piece off the board and left me, once again, at a loss in her favorite game.

I groaned.

"Another one?" Naani asked.

"What's the point? I always lose."

"Losing is good for the soul."

"What about your soul?"

Another smile. "My soul is not your concern. Set up the board."

I started placing the red and black pieces on the board, which I'd been told was a task beneath the dignity of a winner. "I wish I was better."

"I wish you were better too."

I grumbled under my breath but didn't dare complain further. Naani was the only person I couldn't beat at checkers. She really had taught me well. Aamir wouldn't even play me anymore, and none of my friends were any threat. I didn't want to offend Naani Jaan and lose the only worthy opponent the game still had left to offer me.

"At least I'm getting better," I said, mostly to console myself, as I put the last piece in place, the board ready for another round.

"You aren't."

I looked up at her. "I'm not?"

"Not really."

"But Ma says that practice makes perfect."

"Don't listen to your mother. She doesn't know anything." After a moment, Naani added, "Don't tell her I said that."

"Tell me why I'm not getting better and I won't."

"Cheeky and irreverent." She didn't sound upset about it.

"Yes, Naani. The game?"

The old woman scratched at her left eyebrow with her pinkie finger, which I knew was something she did when she was thinking. Just now she was probably trying to decide if the secret of my weakness was something she wanted to share with me or if it was an advantage worth keeping. Finally, she plucked a round, red disk from the board and held it up for me.

"Checkers is the game of life," she said. "Idiots will tell you that chess is, but it isn't. That's a game of war. Real life is like checkers. You try to make your way to where you need to go and to do it you've got to jump over people while they're trying to jump over you and everyone is in each other's way."

"Okay, I guess. But—"

"I'm getting to it, boy," Naani Jaan snapped, and I ducked my head to show that I'd been suitably chastised. "Now, as I was saying, just like in life, right when you think you've got victory in your grasp, people screw with you by stalling the end as long as possible and generally making a nuisance of themselves."

"Not helpful, Naani Jaan."

"Life," she went on, as if I hadn't spoken, "requires risk. It requires that you sacrifice safety. You have to have courage, Anvar, to get what you want. You have to be bold. You have to, not to sound like your know-nothing mother, dare."

"I'm not brave enough? In checkers?"

She nodded. "You play like a wet cat."

"I thought I was a lion . . ."

Naani sounded weary. "Just play like you've still got your dangly bits. Stop being defensive. You never move the last row until you have no choice. It's too late. You think that makes you safe. It doesn't. It just makes you weak."

I eyed my rear guard, the wall they formed my only defense against Naani's men transforming into kings, and tried to figure out if my grandmother was just making all this up to ensure easier, faster victories. Her advice could be a ploy. She was not at all a trustworthy person when it came to important things like games.

Then I shrugged, and began to play, for the first time in my life using all the pieces at my disposal.

I still lost.

"What was that?"

"What?" Naani asked, the very heart of innocence itself.

"You still beat me."

"Of course. I've been playing the game properly for a lot longer than you have. You just started. You know, someone really wise once said, practice makes perfect . . ."

While we played the game of life, the games of death went on around us. Karachi became a casualty of the Kalashnikov effect, a geopolitical twist on chaos theory principles through which an automatic rifle fired in Afghanistan during a Soviet invasion can dramatically alter the character and destiny of the largest city in Pakistan, thousands of kilometers away.

The Kalashnikov effect created the Taliban. It brought down the Twin Towers. It maimed Iraq and Syria and Yemen, and unleashed a wave of terror on the world it was unprepared to deal with.

Let's not blame butterflies is what I'm saying.

The Soviet invasion of Afghanistan created a new front in the Cold War. In response, American money and arms flooded into Pakistan, and from there were smuggled north, across the border, to supply the resistance.

Money and arms alone, however, have never won a fight for freedom. A resistance requires fighters. To boost recruitment, campaigning against the Soviets was advertised as a jihad, a holy struggle. It was billed not as a simple annexation of one country by another, but rather as an invasion of Muslim lands by foreign nonbelievers. Taxpayer dollars, along with Saudi oil money, were used to push this narrative. Madrassas were built to create warriors willing to take up arms for what was declared a holy struggle.

Islam was weaponized for the Cold War.

It probably seemed like a good idea at the time.

The hard-line version of Islam taught by these madrassas, largely foreign to the subcontinent, metastasized. It fed on anxiety and fear created by the Muslim world's modern decline. It argued that this decline was a direct result of moral decay in society, Allah's punishment for deviation from the true path. In order to improve their fortunes, Muslims needed to regain God's favor, and they could do that only by practicing the faith as it had been practiced by the Prophet and his Companions in medieval times.

A return to the way things were done before would surely bring a return to the glory that had come before. It was how, preachers claimed, Muslims could make Islam great again.

Hijabs started appearing in middle-class social circles more often than before. Preachers became icons. I started hearing arguments that music was a forbidden thing. It was even said that miswak, a twig from an arak tree, was better for dental hygiene than toothpaste. After all, miswak was what the Prophet had used. What chemical formula could compete with such a divine endorsement?

When my mother tried to get us to use miswak sticks, my father asked her if she wanted to sell our car and buy a camel instead. After all, he said, a camel was what the Prophet had used to get around.

Simply put, sexy was not back. Islam was back. It was rejuvenated. Tossing out fourteen hundred years of history and progress will do that to a religion, I guess.

Through the early part of the nineties, violence and unrest became common in Karachi, as weapons and returning jihadists flooded in, taking over industries, and bringing with them a gun culture that shifted the tectonic plates of sectarianism the city was built on. The sounds of distant Kalashnikovs being fired became the lullabies I fell asleep to at night.

My mother had always been religiously inclined, but usually reasonable. Unfortunately, as parties where society women would get together to listen to preachers became common, she discovered that what she'd thought was Islam was not Islam at all. She became reeducated and recommitted. It was around this time that she became convinced that wearing a head scarf was an obligation, not an option, after a peddler of piety told her that angels would drag women who did not cover their hair into hellfire by their exposed locks on the Day of Judgment.

My father was different, immune somehow to religiosity and chaos. I always felt safe, despite the growing lawlessness around us, because I knew he was there. He was not physically strong, but he was ideologically sound. The spirit of the age would never possess him.

His appearance was reassuring as well. Imtiaz Faris looked and sounded like a brown Santa Claus, with a deep voice and a big laugh. His presence served as a reminder that there were still solid, pleasant things in the world.

My earliest memories of my father are tied to music. He loved old, classical ghazals—short, poignant poems, usually about love and loss, set to music and sung in crooning, mournful voices. He would sit listening to them on his creaking, discolored teak rocking chair, parked next to an old gramophone, eyes closed, a wistful smile on his face. Sometimes I would sit by his feet. We would not speak, but every once in a while he would ruffle my hair with an affectionate hand.

He had a few English records as well, but broke those out only on special occasions, like a birthday or an anniversary. Then, with Dean Martin or Elvis singing in the background, he would rouse his heavy, pudgy body into a sort of comic jig, shaking his wide hips and wagging his eyebrows up and down, skipping and hopping, occasionally tipping an imaginary top hat to my mother, who often sat by, rolling her eyes but also, I think, trying not to laugh.

I last saw him dance in Pakistan while celebrating New Year's Eve and the coming dawn of 'ninety-six. It was almost midnight. Louis Armstrong and Ella Fitzgerald were belting out "Let's Call the Whole Thing Off." I was singing along. My mother was knitting something and Aamir was shaking his head as my father twirled around the room with a goofy grin on his face.

Shouting erupted nearby. It took me a moment to realize that it was directed at our house. I looked out from a nearby window and . . . well, I don't know how many people constitute a mob, but there were ten, maybe fifteen men outside our house. They were young, probably in their twenties, and they were loud. A few of them were carrying field hockey sticks with ill-disguised ill intent, and chanting, as if at a rally, demanding that we turn off the music. My father came to stand beside me, the smile struck off his face.

"What's their problem?" I asked.

My mother answered. "New Year's is a holiday made up by infidels. We are forbidden to celebrate it. Also, music is the instrument of Shaitan. Those are pious young men."

Aamir hurried over to the gramophone and turned it off.

My father stood by the window until the mob, satisfied with the silence they had forced upon our home, moved on to shepherd other straying believers back into the fold they were creating.

Once the last of them disappeared from view, he whispered, maybe to me, maybe to himself, "I can't breathe here anymore."

Almost no one took my father seriously when he said he wanted to leave Pakistan. For one thing, Imtiaz Faris was simply not the kind of man whose resolutions people believed. For another, leaving the country of one's birth isn't an easy thing. Not only do you have to leave everything you've ever known—family, friends, streets littered with memories of your childhood and homes that have walls imbued with memories of generations—behind, you also have to find a place willing to take you.

It is a difficult business, uprooting yourself from the soil in which you've been planted. Few trees try it and more than a few never bloom again when they do. Everyone, especially my mother, knew that Imtiaz Faris was likely to wither in the face of such emotional, financial and filial trauma. So, she only nodded complacently as he explained that he had a school friend in California, a man he called Shah, who had his own business and who might be interested in hiring my father on a work visa.

"Do whatever you think is best," she said for perhaps the last time in her life.

When the process of immigration first began, with nothing more alarming than new passport-sized photographs, the only person taking it seriously aside from my father was Aamir. I didn't realize he was actually worried about the prospect of moving until he brought it up while we were waiting our turn to bat in an impromptu cricket match boys in the neighborhood had put together at Kokan Park.

Kokan Park wasn't much of a park at all. In fact, we called it Kokan Ground, which was a much more accurate description of the barren, grassless piece of empty land surrounded by a wall a few feet high. There was a concrete patch in the middle of the property, which served as a cricket pitch, but the rough, sand-covered lot had little else to recommend it as a playing surface.

Of course, since our only other choice was to play on the street and stop the game every few minutes to allow cars to pass, we were happy to claim it for our own when older kids weren't monopolizing it.

Just then, we were definitely not supposed to be there. A paiyya jam had been called by the opposition party, probably because of some outrage or slight committed by the government. It was, essentially, a cross between a traffic jam and a general strike. No tires were allowed to roll—they were jammed, hence the name—which meant that the powers calling for these demonstrations didn't want anyone on the roads.

Obedience to these calls for civil disobedience was secured, at times, in the most uncivil of ways, that is to say, with violence.

These strikes had become ridiculously common over the last few years. We missed a lot of school because our parents didn't want to risk sending us out into the world when a hartal was in effect. They wanted to keep us safe, but we still snuck out to play cricket because being safe was boring.

I was next up to bat, so I was paying pretty close attention to the game when my brother started talking. "Aren't you going to miss cricket?" Aamir asked.

I looked back at him. He was leaning against the rusted gate that let visitors onto the ground. It had probably never ever had occasion to actually be locked. "What?"

"They don't have cricket in America, do they? They've got baseball." He made a grimace. "That's like cricket, I guess, for people who don't know what cricket is."

"What are you talking about?"

"California, Anvar. What do you think I'm talking about?"

I shrugged. "I never know. Anyway, don't worry about it."

"Why not?"

"Because it is like the time Dad wanted to start changing the oil in his own car, or when he decided to learn how to make proper Hyderabadi biryani. It isn't going to happen. Remember when he thought carrying a cane made him look like Charlie Chaplin?"

"Like Fred Astaire, I think," Aamir said.

"Doesn't matter. My point is that he'll be tired of it in a month. In two months he'll forget all about it."

"It's been six months now."

"Fine. Worry if you want." I picked up one of the spare balls that was lying next to me. It wasn't made for cricket. It was a tennis ball covered with white electrical tape. The tape was meant to dull the bounce of the ball on a concrete pitch, letting it mimic how a proper cork ball acted on grass. It was almost as good as the real thing, except it didn't sound right when you played your shots and the weight was wrong, so you always knew that you weren't playing with the genuine article.

I rotated the ball in my hands, looking for flaws in the way it had been wrapped, or for cracks in the tape, which often broke down after the ball was thrashed around the park by a good batsman. This one looked pristine. I dropped it back to the ground. "But I think everything will be fine. Then again, I'm a total optimist."

Aamir snorted. "You are not. You just don't care about anything."

"Whatever. Stop worrying so much about Dad. Even if he's serious and we really leave, we get to go to California. Do you know what they have in California that they don't have here?"

Aamir shook his head.

"Blondes. There are a lot more blondes in California than there are in Karachi."

"Astaghfirullah. You've got such base thoughts."

I rolled my eyes. "Sure. Because I'm the one who watches *Baywatch* when Ma and Dad aren't home."

"That was one time," Aamir said. "I thought it was a show about exploding boats."

"Uh-huh."

Aamir glowered at my disbelief. Then, displaying that widely praised maturity of his, he changed the subject. "You can pretend it doesn't bother you, but there are things you'd miss if we left Karachi."

"Like what?"

He gave the triumphant smile of someone who is about to win an argument. "Like Naani Jaan."

"True," I said. "I'd get over it though. Because blondes."

"I'm telling Naani Jaan you said that."

"Of course you are, you—"

A cry of "how's that?" went up in the field before I could make things worse for myself. The batsman playing had been given out, and I was called to take my place at the center of the field.

Aamir had a bad habit of doing what he said.

The next time we visited Naani Jaan, he told on me. He was good at telling. It was the one thing that was true about him. He was obedient because he was taught to be obedient, and he studied hard because he was supposed to. Yes, he prayed a bunch and liked to spend time at the mosque, but if he'd been born in another part of the world, or even in a different family here, he'd have gone to temple or to a gurdwara or anywhere else he was supposed to go. Everything Aamir did, he did because people wanted him to do it.

Except being a tattletale. That he did all by himself, despite having been told that it was a bad habit. It was just who he was. It was almost hard to be angry with him when he told on you, if you knew him, because he couldn't help himself. You don't get angry at the desert for making you thirsty. That's just its nature.

Naani Jaan stared at Aamir in silence with unblinking, sharp eyes after he was done complaining. It was as if she was expecting him to go on. Aamir, with nothing more to say, stammered out a closing argument. "He really said that. That he wouldn't miss you because there'd be blond girls around. That . . . I mean, he'd forget you for something like that."

Still Naani said nothing.

"I . . . I thought you should know."

Finally, the old woman took a deep breath, held it for a long time, and let it out in a barely audible whistle. "How wonderfully religious you are."

That was precisely the right thing to say to cut Aamir. He looked down.

"How does the flesh of your brother taste?"

According to Naani Jaan, in the Muslim version of hell, that was the punishment backbiters got—they had to eat their own brothers for eternity. That didn't make sense to me. It sounded a lot worse for the brother being eaten than the brother doing the actual backbiting. Aamir bought it though. He never had the luxury of doubt. He didn't even bother pointing out that, technically, he wasn't backbiting at all, because I was right there.

"I'm pretty sure I'd be delicious," I said, just to help out. When Naani's baleful attention turned on me, I held up my hands in surrender. "Sorry."

"Tell me, Aamir," she said, deciding to ignore me. "What would make you forget me?"

"Nothing," he said quickly.

"You would forget me for nothing?" Naani asked.

Aamir stumbled around for an answer long enough for me to take pity on him.

"I didn't really mean it," I said. "I was just trying to make Aamir feel better."

"And why did you need to make him feel better?"

"He's worried that we might move to America."

Naani tilted her head a little, regarding Aamir more closely, as if she'd just noticed something interesting about him for the first time. Then she sat down on her favorite plush chair and reached for her dainty silver purse, which usually carried precisely one thousand and one rupees, three lighters and one pack of cigarettes. She'd taken up smoking when she'd given up colors.

"I thought you'd want to leave." She lit up and took a long draw. "You like religion. You follow the prophets and messengers, don't you? None of them stayed where they were from. Even Adam and Eve were immigrants. The first man and woman, the first ones to leave the place they were born."

"Hazrat Adam, May Peace Be Upon Him, wasn't an immigrant," Aamir said. "He was an exile."

"It's the same thing."

Aamir opened his mouth to argue, but our grandmother gestured for him to be silent.

"My point," she said, "is that all your heroes were wanderers upon this earth. Moses, Jesus, Abraham, Jacob, Joseph, Ishmael, Muhammad . . . The history of the world is the history of people who went places. People who walked to the horizon. If you get the chance, you should be glad to be one of them."

"Not that we're going anywhere," I said.

Our grandmother chuckled, looking past us, through the open window behind me, and through time perhaps at a land she had left fifty years ago, when she'd been young, probably around my age, to make her home in a new country. "You'll be surprised," she told me, "at how many people have said that to me in my life. My children, how wrong they've all been . . ."

The first time anyone ever touched my balls, so far as I can remember, was at the behest of the United States government. It turns out that one doesn't simply get on an airplane and start a new life in America. It's much more complicated than that. You have to go to a doctor, who makes you take off your pants, cups your testicles in a cold, clinical hand and asks you to cough. Then you get to go on a plane and start a new life in America.

The moment I was asked to take my pants off was the moment I realized that we were actually going to move to the States. This was in part because that directive—to take off your pants—is always a prologue to whatever is about to come next. It brings with it the certainty that something is about to happen.

More important, I was convinced that my father wouldn't have subjected me or Aamir or himself, for that matter, to such a rude medical exam if he wasn't absolutely committed to fulfilling all the onerous requirements of the United States Immigration and Naturalization Service.

I think Aamir knew that as well. Neither one of us spoke much on the drive back from the doctor's office, each looking out our window, looking at Karachi with eyes that suddenly had goodbyes in them.

I don't really know much about the paperwork my father had to complete to get us out of Karachi. My involvement was limited to being fondled, fingerprinted and photographed. I saw his late nights sitting at the dinner table, filling in forms. I overheard him speaking long-distance to his friend Mr. Shah about a job and a visa. He took me once to an attorney's office in Saddar, where I had nothing to do but wait in an empty room full of the sound of typewriters.

It was strange. We were home and yet about to head home at the same time.

—

They say that the wife is always the last to know.

To be fair to my father, he'd told his wife precisely what he was about to do before he went chasing after a new country. She simply hadn't believed him. The one thing Bariah Faris knew was that Bariah Faris knew everything, and she certainly knew the capabilities of her husband, who I think she'd always assumed to be a man of rather limited ambitions.

When you're young, you don't often think about the relationship between your parents. You see them existing together but never touching, not even talking to each other that much, and you assume that is the natural order of things. Now I recognize that maybe my parents should've never been paired off with each other, that their marriage should never have been arranged, because they were so different.

Yet, even though I doubt there was much passion or even love in their relationship, there was a fondness and understanding that comes with time. So maybe my mother can be forgiven for thinking that, even if she didn't always admire the round, jolly man her knot had been tied to, she at least knew what he was.

Then he surprised her.

Was she truly devastated about leaving Pakistan or was she just angry that Imtiaz Faris could still manage to shock her, after she was so sure she'd figured him out?

I haven't asked. I wouldn't dare. Back then all I knew was that my mother didn't want to move. I never actually saw her weep, but I could tell, from her puffy, red eyes, that she did and did so often.

Some nights, I could hear her screaming at my father, even though their room was clear down the hall from mine. It was a sin, she claimed, to move from a Muslim land to a country of infidels. She worried that Aamir and I would go astray, start drinking, dancing and doing drugs before marrying white girls, forever and irrevocably ruining the family tree.

She wanted to be buried next to her parents, where she already had a piece of land waiting for her shrouded body, not in a wooden box that would rot, and not next to strangers.

On and on her concerns went, like a monsoon of rage and fear and anxiety, but, uncharacteristically, my father remained unmoved by all that rained down upon him.

I was there when her crusade ended, as most crusades in the history of the world have ended, in failure. That morning, we sat at the breakfast table. A kettle whistled on the gas stove, signaling that the water for my parents' tea was ready. I was struggling to finish a greasy, overcooked omelet Ma had made for me. It smelled eggier than normal, as if it had stayed inside the chicken longer than actually necessary. I felt a little queasy. My mother stood up to fetch the kettle and some tea bags and, out of the blue, said, "You know, Anvar, you'll always be a second-class citizen in America. They will always think of you as different from themselves. Inferior."

My father set down the newspaper he was reading and looked in her direction. She wasn't meeting his gaze, focusing her complete attention on the tea she was preparing. In a quiet voice, he said, "You're bringing the children into this now? That's it. The water is over my head. I can't take any more. So that's enough."

And just like that, somehow, it was enough. I don't understand why but, after that moment, my mother didn't complain or try to argue against our pending immigration. She remained unhappy, but she remained unhappy in silence.

To me, my father said, "All men are equal."

"What?"

He picked up a piece of toast and began to butter it. "The Americans. They say that. All men are created equal. You won't be bloody second-class."

I thought about that. "Everyone was made equal," I agreed. "Except for Aamir. He was made special. With a stick up his butt."

My mother pursed her lips in stern disapproval, but Imtiaz Faris laughed that huge laugh of his and went back to the news of the day.

About a week later, from somewhere, my father brought me the only book I actually owned while I was in Pakistan. It was a thin, unmarked text, bound in worn blue leather. I opened the first page and saw from the title that it was *The Declaration of Independence and the Constitution of the United States of America.*

—

In our house, there was never music that wasn't mine unless, of course, my father was home. Except for one day, when I heard the soft, mournful words of a poem I'd heard often, but never managed to remember, coming from my parents' room. I was going somewhere, doing something, but I stopped. It was singing. My mother was singing.

I tiptoed to the master bedroom's door like I was approaching a wisp that might flit away at the sound of my steps, and I listened.

Bariah Faris could *sing*.

I don't remember the words. I don't think it was Urdu at all. It was Punjabi, maybe, or perhaps Sindhi. Whatever the language, I knew instinctively that the song was very old, and it echoed around the almost barren room like a ghost seeking something it could not find.

My mother's voice was gentle and melodic, like I'd never heard it. She'd always recited nursery rhymes in a monotone, like she was reading out of a cookbook, and had never indulged us with lullabies. Until that moment, I hadn't considered it possible that the woman would even be able to carry a tune.

Yet now she was doing justice to a song that seemed to reach back centuries, into the heart of the place she was about to leave.

I didn't want her to stop, but I knew that she would if she found me here. So, I tried to step away, and in doing so I must have made some noise, because as unexpectedly as I'd found the song, I found it gone, leaving behind a silence that seemed to remember it.

My mother wiped at her eyes, though I saw no tears there, and cleared her throat. "Music," she said, her manner as stern as ever, "is different from poetry."

"Okay," I said.

"The Prophet liked poetry. The human voice, you know, it is used in the—"

"Do you really not want to go?" I asked, and not just because I wanted an answer, but because I wanted to cut off the lecture I could sense coming for something that I hadn't even been doing.

She smiled a little. "Life is not about what we want."

"Why not?"

"Because if you do what you want—if you get what you want—then there is no one to blame if things go wrong. Your world, if you make it what you want it to be, becomes your responsibility."

I shook my head, not because I disagreed, but because I had no idea what she was talking about.

"You're too young to understand," my mother said. "Think what would happen if I got your father to stay here."

"Well . . . we'd keep living here."

"And with everything that is going on in this city, in this country, what if one day something happens to Aamir? Every house on this block has had burglars break in, hold the families at gunpoint. The Grace of Allah has kept us safe, but what if it happens to you? Who would your father blame? Who would I blame?"

"Well," I said, perhaps not entirely helpfully, "there is always God."

"Always you have to talk nonsense," she snapped. "Who would dare blame God?"

It seemed perfectly reasonable that if you were going to thank God when good things happened, you could blame Him if bad things did, but I knew better than to say that out loud.

"We have to be careful in this world, Anvar. The things we do— and the things we don't do—we pay for them all."

"Like checkers," I said.

"Uff. Yes. Fine. Like checkers. You spend too much time with your grandmother. I worry that she will fill your head with too much nonsense."

"You shouldn't talk about your mother like that," I said.

Bariah Faris glared at me, though her shoulders shook a little, with suppressed laughter, perhaps. "You want to get out of my sight now, unless you want me to show you what I mean when I say that actions have consequences you can regret."

My father thought we should each choose one last place to visit in Karachi before we left—a quick little goodbye tour to the places that meant the most to us. Ma declined to make a pick. Aamir thought going to visit our deceased grandparents' graves would be a fun time, I guess because that was the kind of thought that won him praise from grown-ups. I wanted to go to the beach.

The sea speaks to you when you're born by the ocean. It sings to you. If you stand still, just out of reach of the water for long enough, you begin to sense a small echo of the infinite inside your-self, and in the violent crashing and breaking of waves you begin to feel at peace. It was something I would miss.

Aamir said that was silly because there were plenty of beaches in California, and this is true, but I've yet to find one like Clifton Beach, where you can buy a ride on a camel or horse and walk back over their hoofprints barefoot in the black, tarry sand.

Anyway, since my parents agreed with Aamir that the beaches in California were better, I said that I'd like to go to Naani's house earlier than we had planned, so I could get in a few extra games of checkers. I was fairly certain that on this last day, of all days, my grandmother would let me win once.

She did not.

I did get close though, bringing Naani down to her final piece, a single solitary king, before she started counting. Then she moved that infuriating little monarch all over the familiar board with practiced ease, until she got to the magic number of twenty and the draw that came with it.

The look on my face when victory slipped away from me must have been something because my grandmother started to laugh. "I told you," she said. "Checkers is like life. Just when you think you've got everything you wanted, it all slips from your fingers."

We were sitting on her takht—a large, low wood bench covered with a bedsheet that was, in my opinion, only marginally more comfortable than the ground—and we were alone for the moment. The family had gone to look through the house again one last time. I stayed behind. I didn't care about the house.

She looked at me with something sad in her eyes.

"What?" I asked.

"It would be better for you, my child, if you were more like your brother."

I rolled my eyes. I'd heard that one before.

Naani chuckled. "I mean it. The world is difficult sometimes for restless minds and imaginative hearts. Things go easier for you if you do what you're told, when you're told, and never ask any questions."

"Sounds boring."

"There are worse things in life than being bored," she told me.

"No. There aren't."

Naani laughed just as my mother led the rest of the family back in. Bariah Faris smiled at the scene and shook her head. "You laugh more with him than I've ever seen you laugh in my life."

"She didn't used to," I said before I could think to stop myself, "until she started wearing white."

That killed my mother's smile, because nothing can kill a smile faster than the truth, and my father winced. Everyone started looking at anything except my grandmother, who just nodded, not at me, but at the checkers board.

"I know that your parents will want me to impart some wisdom to you, Anvar, before you leave, so . . . You're going to meet all kinds of girls there in America, I think." She leaned over and swatted my arm when I grinned widely at that. "Be careful. More than anything else, falling in love with the right person will bring you happiness. Failing to do that . . ." She took a deep breath. "Love is blind, beta, but be careful."

I wanted to ask Naani what she meant, but my mother spoke instead.

"He wasn't a bad man, Amma."

"No," Naani agreed. "He wasn't a bad man."

Aamir stepped forward, all eagerness. "What about me, Naani Jaan?"

"What about you?" Naani asked.

"Any advice for me?"

"Oh." She seemed to think about it for a while and then shrugged. "No. You I don't worry about."

Aamir grinned. It was the nicest thing Naani had ever said to him.

As frustrating as delayed flights and security checks can be, it would be a better world if more of the human experience was like being at the airport. People move around looking for things—loved ones, bags, boarding gates—and generally find them. Those who are lost are easily guided, directed to where they are supposed to be by people who sit behind counters and peer over eyeglasses and usually know the answers to the most pressing questions presented to them.

Airports are places of certainty and purpose. Those things are difficult to find.

Of course, when you're leaving behind the only country you've ever known, walking away from a caravan of first cousins and second cousins and close friends who have gathered to see you off, possibly forever, it is hard to appreciate that. I didn't feel very certain of much that day at Jinnah International.

"We'll meet again soon," Naani Jaan promised, as I pulled away from her embrace. She smelled like stale perfume, smoke and time. "All separations are temporary."

"I know," I said.

"Then smile."

I tried.

"When you're walking away," Naani said, "remember not to look back. If you look back, you turn to stone."

She was talking about Lot's wife, the woman who had looked back at the city she was leaving when she wasn't supposed to, and who had been punished for her disobedience by being turned to stone.

I felt something like kinship with her then, that woman centuries removed from me, abandoning her city in distress, leaving her home to its perilous fate. How could she have been expected to resist a glance back, and why had her punishment, for so small a transgression, been so severe?

My mother was standing by me, so I knew not to give voice to the question. It is one thing to relate to sinners. It is another thing to say that out loud. One must, after all, pretend virtue whenever possible.

I'll admit that I shared in the weakness of Lot's wife—Edith, they say her name was—because I couldn't keep myself from glancing back either, at my extended family, at the sun-soaked city where I'd been born, at the frail old woman who always played to win. Was there a chance that looking back could have turned me to stone? I didn't think it mattered. Anyone who didn't look back, I realized then, was stone already.

SAFWA

I didn't kill Fahd.

It's not my fault my brother's dead.

Back when I was a different person, when I was still called Safwa, I did leave him alone in Baghdad. This is true. Maybe it's also true that if I'd stayed with him, Fahd would have lived longer than he did. But he still would've died. There was no way to save him, so I saved myself.

For that, our father never forgave me.

He never blamed me, not out loud. With words, he only ever blamed Dr. Yousef.

Dr. Yousef Ganni was a small, thin man with little hair who always smelled of rosewater. He had a crooked nose and a bad limp. His being small wasn't my father's fault and neither was the sweet perfume he used too much of. The limp and the broken nose, those Abu had given him.

They were best friends. People said they were like brothers. Sometimes, Dr. Yousef came to our house when Abu wasn't there and didn't tell Abu. My mother didn't want Abu to know she was sick.

I was ten and still Safwa when I managed to fake a fever convincingly enough for Mama to let me stay home from school. I wasn't enjoying my day off. School was boring but staying home and pretending to be ill was boring too. There was nothing to do, so I sat in front of our small television, watching my mom's videotapes of the American show *Full House*. It was her obsession. She could quote passages of dialogue from some episodes word for word. She hummed the theme song all the time, sometimes without even realizing it, which irritated Abu.

Abu said it was all nonsense, that the kind, caring American characters of the show, full of love and empathy and compromise, existed only on screens. Abu had seen plenty of Americans during the Soviet invasion of Afghanistan, when he'd fought on their side against the Russians.

"I know how they really are," he told my mother.

Abu was a tall, powerful man who did that kind of thing—went off to fight other people's wars. Of course, to him, Afghans were not other people. They were Muslims.

If it hadn't been for his willingness to go to war, Abu wouldn't have been Abu at all. At the very least, we would've called him something else. Abati or Abba or perhaps Baba. In Pakistan he'd heard children call their fathers Abu. The name we called him by was a souvenir he'd brought back from battlefields he'd left behind.

"You can't judge a people by how they act in war," my mother had said.

"That's the only way to judge a people," Abu told her.

My mother hadn't argued. That wasn't her way. She was a wilting flower of a woman, and she should've married a kind, caring gardener. Instead, she had married the blazing sun.

Mama rarely gave voice to her opinions, and when she did, Abu would get upset. I don't think he understood how his wife could disagree with him about anything. He must have known that she couldn't help but have her own thoughts. He just didn't see why he, or anyone else, should be burdened with them.

When my mother did speak, and was told she was wrong, she offered no defense. It kept peace in the house, and some peace, as those who remember fondly the days of Saddam will tell you, is better than war.

I found it hard to believe that Dr. Yousef and my father had ever fought over Mama, and so viciously that Abu left his rival with a hip broken in three places. Maybe she'd been beautiful once. Any hint of that beauty was gone though. All that was left was a lean face, hungry for what I do not know, and dull dark eyes that had no spark I could see.

It would've been nice to have a picture of her from when she was young, to see what she had looked like, to get an idea of what she had been, but my father had burned all our family photographs after he came home from Afghanistan. He'd been taught there that pictures were not permitted in Islam.

Anyway, I was watching *Full House* when the doorbell rang. As I got up to see who it was, I reached for the niqab Abu made me wear. I was young enough that no one thought I needed it, but Abu insisted that habit was character, and made me put it on whenever I stepped outside.

I decided it wasn't necessary. The visitor was probably one of the women in the neighborhood, coming to chat with my mother or to ask to borrow some sugar or salt.

I walked out into the sharp sunlight and crossed a small courtyard to our iron gate. "Who is it?"

There was a moment of silence, as if the visitor hasn't been expecting an answer. Then a man cleared his throat, and a familiar voice said, "It is I. Let me in, Safwa."

"Dr. Yousef?" I asked, undoing a heavy, lightly rusted bolt. It screeched in protest at being disturbed. "Is something wrong?"

"I am sure many things are wrong, dear child. They always are, in this wonderful and terrible world."

I let out a sigh, which probably made him think I agreed with him. The truth was that I just hated the flowery way he spoke.

"Aren't you growing up to be a lovely creature? I've never understood why you Muslims hide what little beauty there is in the world."

I wanted to tell him that I wasn't a "creature" but instead I said, "How do nuns dress again?"

He chuckled at that and patted my cheek with one of his delicate, soft hands. "Clever too. Where do you get that from, I wonder."

I shrugged.

"Maybe the same place you get your eyes?"

I shrugged again. No one else in my family had my pale green eyes. In fact, no one I knew had eyes like mine . . . well, except for Dr. Yousef, of course, but his eyes were different than mine were. They were calm and old, the eyes of a man who had learned to accept his place in the world.

"Did you need something?"

"Your mother called me. She said she wasn't feeling well."

I frowned. My mother was always unwell, often in bed or complaining of pain in her back. "Is it worse than usual? She will be better soon?"

"We shall see, my dear. I must examine the patient before I can give you a diagnosis, much less a prognosis. I do not believe that is at all unreasonable."

"Sorry, Dr. Yousef."

"Not at all, I am sure," he said, with a deep bow of his head.

"It's just that she didn't seem all that sick this morning."

"The weather can change quickly, Safwa."

I wanted to tell him that wasn't really true, not in Baghdad, where the heat could seem unending, but I knew what a metaphor was, even if it was a bad one. "I'll go tell—"

"No need. She is expecting me, and I know perfectly well where her bedroom is."

About an hour after Dr. Yousef left without saying goodbye, my mother called me to her room. It was dark, with thick, maroon curtains drawn against the light, but even so my mother was lying in bed with a pillow over her head. I felt my heart beat a little faster as I walked in. Seeing her lying there, unable to bear even a little bit of the sun, worried me. Then I reminded myself that she'd been fine—well, almost like herself anyway—in the morning. It was probably just a bad headache.

She reached out for my hand when I sat down on the mattress beside her. She didn't uncover her face.

"I'm okay," she said, her voice muffled. When I took her hand in mine, it felt cold. "Don't tell you father Yousef was here."

"Do you need anything? I can make some tea or—"

"I don't want your father to know I'm not feeling well," she said. "He'll worry."

I raised my eyebrows at that. Abu wasn't the worrying sort.

"Safwa, promise me you won't tell your father Yousef was here."

"I promise," I said. I knew Abu wouldn't react well to a man being in the house, even someone harmless like Dr. Yousef, when neither he nor Fahd was home. It wasn't proper. "But if you're sick—"

"I'll be fine, light of my eyes, I'll be fine, if Allah permits it. Don't worry. It's nothing at all. I'll be fine. That much I promise."

My mother didn't keep her promise. Allah didn't permit it.

She died.

It was sudden. Thyroid cancer that became metastatic bone cancer. Change gone wrong upon change gone wrong until there could be no more change. Three days after I promised to keep her secret.

Three days.

"It was too late when I saw her," Yousef Ganni told me at her funeral, speaking in a whisper, keeping a secret the subject of which was beyond caring. He looked worse than Abu or Fahd or I did. His eyes were swollen and red, and he smelled so strongly of mint that I wondered what smell on his breath he was trying to cover up. I noticed his hands were trembling as he spoke, and his gaze was wet with tears. Somehow, he kept his voice steady. "I am so sorry, dear girl, but she must have been very ill for a long time. She hid it well."

I nodded but I knew it wasn't true. She hadn't hidden it well. She'd always been in pain, always weak, always having to lie down. None of us had worried about her. I think that Abu was used to it, and Fahd and I . . . well, I don't know about Fahd, but I'd never truly believed my parents were mortal. I knew, of course, that they would die one day, because everyone dies, but in my mind it wasn't real. I think maybe that awful knowledge isn't truly real for anyone, until it is real forever.

On the fourth day after my mother died, there was a knock on my bedroom door. It was Abu. I knew because of the way he knocked. Two quick, hard raps on the wood frame with his knuckles, and then silence. He wouldn't try again.

I hadn't spoken to anyone since the funeral. I'd said things, of course, because a lot of people had visited, all of them offering words of condolence that made nothing better. I'd responded to them all properly because I'd been brought up to say the right things at the right times, but all I wanted was to be left alone.

I didn't feel like talking to Abu either. I wanted to stay in my dark room, thinking my dark thoughts, and remembering. I thought about pretending to be asleep. He wouldn't enter until I told him he could. That was his way.

I sat up in bed.

"Come in."

Abu opened the door slowly, carefully, as if he might break it, and then stepped inside. He looked down at the mess in the room and the mess that was me, at the unmade bed, the clothes on the floor, the tearstains still on my face, the uncombed state of my hair, and scowled.

A wild part of me almost hoped he would dare to say something, so that I would have an excuse to yell at him, to scream at him, because that's all I'd wanted to do since he'd told me what had happened, and had held me as I broke into little pieces that fell from my eyes.

She wouldn't have died if you'd kept her happier. She wouldn't have died if you'd known her enough to know she was sick.

When Abu finally spoke, he said, "There is nothing to eat."

I frowned. "What?"

"People were bringing food for the past few days, but now there is nothing to eat in the house."

"So?"

"You're the woman of the house, Safwa. The kitchen is yours. The days of mourning are over. Time to go back to living now."

I laughed, a shrill sound laced with disbelief. "It's only been three days."

Was that how grief worked? Three days for three days?

"You are forbidden to mourn more than three days for the loss of anyone. That is what the Prophet said."

"How long do you think the Prophet mourned when his mother died?"

Abu actually gasped. "*Safwa!* Such words about the Prophet? Such disrespect! I cannot believe it came from a daughter of mine. You must beg Allah for forgiveness."

"Fine," I said just to make him go away, collapsing back onto my bed. "I will."

Abu didn't leave though.

"The kitchen, Safwa."

Maybe I should have gotten up like he wanted and just made something for him. That's what my mother would've done. She would have kept the peace.

But I wasn't my mother.

And I didn't want to be my mother. I wanted to be nothing like her. I definitely didn't want to live like she had lived, or to die like she had died, in silent pain. I wouldn't do it.

So I said what my mother hadn't said to Abu in years, if ever.

"No."

I saw anger in his eyes, and even as I shrank back from him, I wondered if his heart was as raw as mine was. Abu stepped toward me, and I was sure he would hit me, which he'd never done before, when out of the corner of my eye I saw Fahd at the door.

"I'll make something, Abu," my brother said.

Abu stopped where he was, but he didn't look away from me. "That is not work meant for you. She has to learn to do it."

"Maybe not today," Fahd suggested, his voice measured and reasonable.

"The permitted period of grieving is over."

"True," my brother said, "but she is a child. Remember that those who do not show mercy will have no mercy shown to them."

Those were the Prophet's words Fahd had used. Abu backed down before them, his head slightly bowed. "So it is. Remember to pray for forgiveness, Safwa."

"I will," I promised.

Despite my resolution to not be like my mother, however, I was still her daughter.

I did not keep my word.

Hours later there was another knock on my door. It was softer and most insistent. Fahd. I asked him to come in, and he stumbled through, carrying a plate of food covered with some flatbread. It smelled of burnt meat. I wrinkled my nose.

"Thanks," I said, "for earlier. Quoting the Prophet was very smart."

"Baiting a wounded lion was not very smart though," he said, but he said it without judgment. Fahd was one of those men who was surprisingly gentle. At seventeen, he was as tall as my father, which meant that he towered over most people. In fact, with his wide shoulders and thick neck, with his square face and high brow, he looked like a younger version of Abu.

Except that he never raised his voice and was more interested in science than in war. He was smart and always knew the right thing to say, like he had done with our father earlier, but he never cut anyone with his words.

"What?" Fahd asked, smiling at me as he sat across from me, folding his legs underneath himself.

"I was just thinking about how much I like you."

His smile widened. "Come on, eat."

I reached for the bread and uncovered the plate. Timman ou keema. I think that is what it was supposed to be anyway. To say that the minced meat was hopelessly charred would have been . . . generous, but I was feeling pretty generous toward my brother just then.

"Go on," he said.

I took a deep breath and took a bite.

I managed to swallow it.

Fahd was looking at me, obviously trying to gauge my reaction.

"Have you heard the saying 'When the mother dies, the house dies'?" I asked him, knowing full well that he had. When he nodded, I said, "Do you think that's because they all starve?"

"It isn't *that* bad."

"I really shouldn't complain."

"You really shouldn't," Fahd said. His smile faded as he regarded me. "You know that we're going to be fine, right? We'll be okay."

I know you've been running the water in the bathroom when you can't help crying, I almost told him, *so no one will hear your sobs.* He was trying to be strong though and I let him be what he thought he needed to be.

"I know," I said. "We'll be fine."

ANVAR

In California, I met Zuha Shah. She was pretty, but she wasn't the most beautiful girl I'd ever seen. There was something about her, however, that demanded and captured my attention. I was always aware of her presence, always conscious of where her slender form was in a room, always listening for her voice, always looking for her flashy, swift, capricious smile.

I spent days trying to think of clever things to say to her but, as sometimes happens with fourteen-year-old boys around fourteen-year-old girls, when the chance to speak came, I promptly forgot all the topics of conversation I had so meticulously mapped out.

I was more aware of myself when Zuha was around. I was aware of the awkward, lanky nature of my frame and the fact that my voice had not quite broken. For the first time in my life, I worried about how my hair looked and how my outfits were put together.

Being young is easy until you begin to worry about the opinions of other people.

On a humid summer afternoon, I found myself alone with Zuha in her parents' living room. Everyone else was in the backyard, attempting to barbecue burgers. The smoky smell of overcooked, heavily spiced beef patties and charcoal filled the house. Zuha was curled up on a black leather couch, her gaze fixed on a book, her heart-shaped face partially veiled by her rich brown hair.

I sat across from her, pretending to be enchanted by the soulless, hotel-lobby-caliber art decorating the Shah home. Every few minutes, I let out a dramatic sigh, and then glanced over at Zuha, wondering when she would ask me what was wrong.

She kept reading as if I didn't exist. I allowed myself one final, defeated, deep breath and started to rise from my chair, when I realized that her sublime eyes, lined with kohl, were fixed on me.

I hovered in place, caught between standing and sitting. Why wasn't she saying anything? I should say something. But what? My chest tightened. Her gaze, which I had so desired a moment ago, was heavy with crushing expectation.

I glanced over the room, searching for something to talk about. Love the artificial flowers on the mantel. Did you pick them yourself? No, that was stupid. Had I always been stupid? Seemed like something I would remember.

The cover of the book in her hands caught my eye and I let myself collapse back into the chair. "Harry Potter? Isn't that for little kids?"

Zuha flicked her hair over her shoulder and fixed me with a withering glare that nearly wilted my soul. "What are you reading these days?"

I shrugged. I'd never actually read a novel. I'd been to our neighborhood library in Karachi, the Shalimar Library. It hadn't been what you would call highbrow; doubling as a Bollywood movie rental store, it stocked only Archie Comics and Mills & Boons.

"Nothing."

"Nothing?" She adopted a horrid fresh-off-the-boat Indian accent. "Isn't that for . . . like, morons?"

My face felt warm. "I don't sound like that."

"No." Zuha set her book aside and leaned forward a little, offering me a small, conciliatory smile. "You don't. I'm sorry. You don't like to read, huh?"

"Never tried it."

"How's that possible?"

"All I've ever had are textbooks."

She stared, eyes wide. "Really? Your parents don't buy you books?"

My mother was very much a woman of one book and my father didn't care to read anything but newspapers. I shrugged.

Zuha leapt to her feet. "Come with me."

I followed her as she bounded up a flight of stairs. Her blue jeans looked *so* good. Had Shaitan himself dropped by to whisper filthy, scandalous desires to my agitated heart? I knew the right thing to do, the Muslim thing to do, was to avert my eyes. There was no way in hell I was going to do that.

When Zuha walked into her room, my step faltered. I'd never been in a girl's room before, and Zuha probably hadn't known she'd invite anyone into her private sanctum today. If her room was anything like mine, it would be a mess. I might see a bra lying around. Ya Allah, please let there be a bra lying around.

"Come on." Zuha waved for me to enter.

Her room was a lot less pink than I'd imagined a girl's room would be. No stuffed animals and, sadly, no stray underwear to be seen anywhere. The air smelled of peaches or nectarines, and the curtains were pulled back to let the day's warm sunshine filter in. The double bed was neatly made. I was careful not to look at it for more than an instant. I didn't want her thinking that I was thinking of her on the bed or, worse, of us on the bed together.

My father had once given me the "birds and the bees" talk. It had been brief. He'd asked me if I was studying biology in school.

"I am, Dad."

"All of it?"

"Yes?"

He'd nodded, apparently satisfied that his work in this regard was done. Despite my father's casual parenting in this area, I knew things. I had internet access. I knew what beds were for, and I was sure that Zuha knew what they were for as well.

Aside from the bed, the most noticeable thing in the room was the massive oak shelf that ran the entire length of the far wall. It overflowed with books of every description. I'd never seen anything like it before. I stepped up to it and, without realizing what I was doing, I ran my fingers over a section that housed classics bound in soft leather, their spines glittering with golden lettering. When I finally looked away, I saw Zuha studying me.

"Well?" she asked.

"Beautiful. The books. I meant the books. The books. Your books are beautiful."

Zuha flashed a brilliant smile that gripped me like exposed, live electric wiring. "I know." She walked over to stand near me. She was closer than she had ever been before. Parched, I would've asked for a glass of water, if it hadn't meant she would step away.

Reaching past me to pluck a book off the shelf, she smelled as sweet as caramel and white roses. As she handed over the volume she had selected, her manner was nearly reverent. "The first Harry Potter. It isn't for little kids. Well, it's a little for kids but . . . Will you trust me and read it?"

I did. She could have asked me for anything and I couldn't have refused her request.

When I was done, we talked about the book. I finally had something to say I knew she was interested in hearing. Then she lent me another book and another one after that. Our conversations, most of them on the phone, were hours long and, though initially focused on books, slowly came to be about everything. We became friends, though I pretended to barely know her when my parents were around. My mother was of the opinion that Islam prohibited intercourse between the sexes, in every sense of the word. Her view of the world would simply not allow her to believe that I could be just friends with Zuha Shah, or any girl for that matter, without serious moral peril.

Rather than enduring endless Bariah Faris lectures about my friendship with Zuha, I chose to keep it a secret. What my family didn't know, after all, couldn't hurt me.

"You were reading. Again?" Naani Jaan asked. Her voice was thin and marred by the static of a bad connection, but the suspicion in it came through just fine.

I sat up in bed, setting aside Tolkien for a minute, and pressed the phone to my ear a little harder to hear her better. "You don't believe me?"

"I don't need to believe you," my grandmother said. "Your father was talking my ear off about how you're finally taking an interest in your studies."

"I'm not reading for school. I'm just reading for fun."

"And there is no other reason?"

"Does there have to be another reason?"

"There doesn't have to be," Naani conceded, "but there usually is when young men make drastic changes to the way they live their lives. For the last few months, every time I've called, you've been reading something or other." I started to protest but she cut me off. "You. Who never met a book before. Now, we don't have to talk about it if you don't want to, but something is most certainly going on."

I definitely did not want to talk about it. Not that there was anything to talk about.

"Nothing is going on," I said.

"Fine." Naani harrumphed. "So, how is California?"

I looked outside my bedroom window. When my father had said we were moving to San Francisco, he'd been exaggerating quite a bit. We had moved to Fremont, the suburbiest suburbia in history. It was a very horizontal city, with a lot fewer people than there were in Karachi. The streets were quieter and cleaner, and the weather was nicer, but life was, surprisingly, not all that different.

In a way I'd been in training to become an American all my life. I spoke the language, and I knew all the cultural touch points—the movies other kids spoke about, the video games they played, the sports they followed, the music they listened to—none of it was foreign to me. I belonged here as much as I belonged anywhere, even if I didn't know many people or needed to print directions off MapQuest to get anywhere.

There was no culture shock—though I may have gawked a little at the first short skirt I saw . . . and maybe the second one too—because even though I'd never stepped foot on U.S. soil, I knew this place. I'd seen it on screens my entire life.

"It's nice. Dad's been trying to find a good desi restaurant."

Getting used to the food was the hardest part of the move. Everything tasted a little off. White bread was too sweet, and the frozen naan from Indian stores smelled like stale masalas. Fruits and vegetables were dull, like mere approximations of what they were supposed to be, maybe because the soil was different, or maybe it was the water.

Worst of all, the tea was atrocious. Fortunately, Mrs. Shah had hooked Ma up with a Tetley smuggling operation local aunties ran with a network of relatives and friends who snuck orange pekoe across the border from Canada. Demand was high and the supply chain unreliable, so what little of the good stuff we got was reserved for grown-ups.

"I trust your sweet potato of a father will find something to his liking soon," Naani said dismissively. "Tell me about the girl."

"What girl?"

"Anvar."

"Naani Jaan. You said we didn't have to talk about it."

"I lied. I do that sometimes. I don't see why you can't tell me. You know I won't tell anyone," my grandmother assured me. "I just need to know."

"Why?"

"So that I will know more than everyone else, of course."

I shook my head.

"So there is a girl?" Naani prompted into the silence.

"Maybe."

"Does she have a name?"

"No," I said with a laugh.

"She already sounds like a very strange young woman," Naani said. "I approve of strange young women. Just don't do anything stupid."

"Me? I would never."

Oddly enough, Ma had the easiest time finding her place in California. Her hijab attracted other Muslim women of a similar age into her orbit like a beacon. Without saying anything at all, Bariah Faris managed to tell the world what her values were and found like-minded individuals eager for new society. Within a few months, she was a regular at the parties and religious halaqas that the really quite secure housewives of Fremont hosted every other week.

Aamir should've had trouble fitting in at college, with his pants above his ankles and his wispy beard untouched by a razor of any kind, but he found a niche with the Muslim Students Association at Berkeley.

It was Imtiaz Faris who had the hardest time finding his place in the States. He didn't feel like he could go to the mosque and talk to people there about music or classic Hollywood movies. So he sulked his way through the playdates Ma set up for him with the husbands of her new acquaintances. I heard him sigh a lot through discussions about stock markets, old cricket matches and theological conundrums, none of which he had any interest in.

I was the beneficiary—victim, really—of his loneliness. He dragged me out on long walks through quiet neighborhoods adjoining our own. During these tame excursions, he spoke at length about all kinds of things, telling me stories from his childhood on some nights and reviewing for me in detail Bollywood blockbusters on others.

"I don't understand why everything has to be so . . ."

"What?" I asked.

"There is no variety in the life here. It is all planned. Look at these houses. They're all the same. A couple of facades that they build over and over again. Everywhere you go, there is a Target, a Wal-Mart, a McDonald's. Everywhere there is First Street and Main Street. Some of the most imaginative people in the world, Americans, and still their world is so same to same."

He did have a point. Karachi didn't feel this manufactured. Almost all homes, especially in older neighborhoods, looked different. There were no big chain stores to speak of, so depending on where you went to shop, you'd have a different experience.

We had McDonald's and Pizza Hut but only one location of each in one of the largest cities in the world. It was a little weird to see the same golden arches at every other freeway exit.

"People like familiar things, I guess."

"It isn't familiar to me," my father said. "It makes me miss home. All this order. I'm not used to it."

"Ma likes it."

"Of course Bariah likes it," he grumbled. "This is probably what she thinks paradise is like. Every road has street signs and all the trains run on time and there are no gunshots anywhere to be heard."

I grinned. "It sounds horrible when you put it like that."

"You know what I mean. Now come on. Let's go farther down this way. Maybe we'll find something new."

We didn't find anything new that night. It was several months, in fact, before he spotted A Pretty Good Ice Cream Parlor. Actually, he heard it before he saw it because the mournful guitar notes coming from the little shop clashed hopelessly with the jaunty Bollywood song he'd been humming.

"What's that?" he asked, looking around. Then, without waiting for an answer, he began following the music, drawn to it like a child of Hamelin.

A bell tinkled overhead as we walked into a cramped store with a very old man sitting behind a display of rather limited ice cream flavors.

"Come in, please," the man said with a quick smile, urging us forward with a wave of his hand. Grabbing a cane, he struggled to his feet. "Always nice to see new faces. Now we have a few fun flavors this week, and—"

My father held up a hand, stopping him midsentence, and then pointed up, like he was pointing to God. The shopkeeper frowned and looked at me for an explanation.

"The music," I said softly, trying to squeeze as much of an apology as I could into my tone.

That earned us a wide grin. "Of course," the man said, as if it was the most natural thing in the world for someone to wander into his business just to listen to what the radio was playing.

I stepped up to the display and was struggling to choose between Ginger Lemon Snaps and Dark Chocolate, when the song that had caught my dad's attention ended. He let out a great big sigh, then with a sheepish shrug said, "Sorry."

"I understand," the storekeeper said, "I really do. I'm Good."

"I also am fine," Dad said.

"No, that's my name. Joseph Good."

Dad held out a hand. "What was that?"

"That," Joseph said, "was Johnson. You never heard Blind Willie Johnson? 'Dark Was the Night'?"

"Never."

"Then you haven't lived, have you? What kind of music do you listen to?"

It was a question that started a friendship which completely altered my father's experience of America. Joseph Good introduced him to all kinds of music he'd never heard of or given a chance to before.

"You've heard of rap?" Dad asked a few weeks later, popping his head into my room. "There is cursing in the songs, Anvar. They just say the words and no one stops them. It's incredible. Don't tell your mother."

That little ice cream parlor rescued me from the long walks I'd been dragooned into taking. It made my father happier than he'd been since leaving his home and gave him a place to belong. It also made him diabetic, but I suppose nothing worth having comes without a price.

"Did I tell you that Sam asked me to prom?" Zuha asked.

I shifted uncomfortably on the cheap plastic chairs that were standard in our spartan school cafeteria. I'd known Sammy Chang was going to ask Zuha out. He'd told me—asked me, actually, if it was okay for him to do so, because Zuha and I were together all the time and everyone assumed we were sort of a couple, and he didn't want to get in the middle of anything.

I'd said it was fine, of course, because I knew that she'd shoot him down. Besides, it wasn't like Zuha and I were really together. We couldn't be. Muslim kids aren't allowed to date.

Even so, I had the sudden urge to give Sam the stink eye. I looked around for him but couldn't spot him in the rush of other students lining up to buy their lunch. I contented myself with a grimace aimed at no one in particular.

As usual, the cafeteria smelled of reheated meatloaf and aging lettuce. The constant clatter of silverware around me and the loud, enthusiastic conversations of the other students made this one of my least favorite places to eat.

"Did you hear me? Sam asked me to prom."

"He left it a little late, don't you think?" I said.

"He asked me weeks ago."

"Whatever. He's still an ass."

"Other boys asked me too. Josh and Mark and Alejandro."

"Dick. Turd. Douchebag."

Zuha chuckled, picking at her garden salad. "Aren't we charming today?"

I glowered in response, first at my soggy peanut butter and jelly sandwich and then at the student body of my school as a whole. No one seemed to notice my discontent, so I bit into my lunch viciously and ate in silence.

After a moment, Zuha said, "I've decided to go."

"You can't!" My voice was loud enough to cause silence to descend on the large room. Everyone turned to stare at our table. I ducked my head and ignored them as best I could.

"I can," she said, perfectly calm. "And I think you should ask me to go with you."

I stared at her. "What . . . wait—you want to go to prom? With me?"

"No. *You* want to go to prom with *me*."

This was true. I hadn't considered going to prom because of the miniature apocalypse that would ensue should my mother find out that I was even thinking about it. However, now that I did think about it, there was nothing else in the world that I wanted to do more, nothing else on which all my happiness depended, except taking Zuha to prom.

There was, of course, the possibility that my mother would kill me, but that seemed like an acceptable risk. After all, if I didn't take her, Zuha might actually go with someone else.

"I really do," I said. Incredibly, my voice didn't tremble.

"Fine." Zuha appeared focused entirely on her salad, as if going on our very first date was no big deal. "We'll just meet here then."

Zuha made it sound simple. It wasn't. I had committed myself to a complicated, dangerous mission against a formidable opponent, and now my life was at stake.

I didn't really know what my parents would do if they found out what I was planning, but the vague dread that kept me in line through my childhood had firm roots in fact. Years ago, there had been a Muslim kid in our neighborhood who had fallen in love with a non-Muslim girl. He'd gotten careless. He'd written her indiscreet notes, which had been discovered.

When his parents found out, they packed all of his belongings and put him on a flight back to Pakistan. Last I heard of him, he was enrolled in a medical school in Rawalpindi or Quetta or something.

I suppose that boy deserved his fate because he failed to take the one precaution that should be gospel for both white-collar criminals and naughty brown-skinned children—never, ever, under any circumstances, leave a paper trail. Even so, I felt sorry for him and was pretty certain that, given the approval with which Ma spoke of the remedial actions taken by his parents, I too could end up on a plane, exiled from the United States, if I was not very careful about how I lived my life.

Ma was an effective, skilled dictator, who seemed to hear everything and know everything going on under her roof. To understand what it was like to be her child, imagine Oceania from Orwell's *1984*, with a head of state called Big Mother.

To dress up, to escape the house unchallenged without providing a detailed itinerary, I needed my mother to be distracted by something else or, as it turned out, someone else.

I needed a plan.

Aamir was in the living room, watching *Charlie and the Chocolate Factory* for what must have been the hundredth time. The large bowl of popcorn he'd made had the entire house smelling of buttery, seductive goodness.

The VHS tape on which the movie was recorded had started to wear thin and warp from constant use. The print was getting worse every time Aamir sat through the film, with lines of static appearing and disappearing randomly at the top and bottom of the screen.

Surly-looking orange dwarfs with green hair were pouring sugar into a river of chocolate as I walked up to Aamir and said, "Can I borrow your laptop? I need it for homework."

He frowned up at me. "Desktop isn't working?"

"The monitor is acting up."

This was true. My brother could've walked up to the study and seen the malfunction for himself. Had he done so, he would have realized the problem was ridiculously easy to fix. The VGA cable, which connected the CPU to the display, had somehow gotten a bit loose.

I knew he wasn't going to do that though. *Charlie and the Chocolate Factory* was on.

"Fine," Aamir said with a dismissive wave of his hand. "It's in my room."

"Thank you."

I bounded up the stairs, nearly tripping in my hurry, and retrieved the laptop that was so necessary to my scheme. It was a thick, bulky unit made of cheap plastic. I carried it and the massive power brick it came with to the study, to plug the machine into the modem.

My plan to get to prom involved taking some of the shadier exits on the information superhighway. I glanced around the small, cramped room. It was not decorated, like most of our home, in an ostentatiously Islamic fashion but, even so, an elaborate prayer rug, made of some kind of soft, faux velvet material, lay on my right. There was a black painting with silver Arabic calligraphy on the wall directly in front of me, the sweeping and curving characters imbued, somehow, with a sense of being divine.

I fixed my eyes on the computer screen and prepared to wander into forbidden virtual spaces. I wanted to get this done quickly, and not just because I was afraid of getting caught looking at pornography.

I was never comfortable with porn. The prospect of having nudity, and more, available at the click of a mouse should have been enchanting to a teenager, and I know it was for some of my friends. For me, the experience involved too much prayer to be very exciting.

Aamir's chunky laptop hissed, shrieked and beeped its mechanical anxiety as the dial-up connection attempted to link it to the internet. The panicked sound a computer made in the early days of the internet, before cable and before wi-fi, was the swan song of solitude.

Dial-up internet was slow. This meant that pictures took forever to load. While computers across the world were chattering away, describing models to each other in binary code, I was a sitting duck, tethered to the study, unable to escape or hide from the prying gaze of an apparently omniscient mother. It was an enterprise so perilous that I could not help but pray constantly to Allah that I wouldn't be discovered doing what I was doing, which felt like the kind of thing you weren't supposed to ask of the Almighty. By the time the women on the screen had toes, all I felt was guilt.

I used the most popular of all search engines, AltaVista, and typed in the dirtiest words I knew. I clicked the first site that popped up and was immediately faced with a choice of genre. I went with the most vanilla stuff I could find, not just because Aamir was a vanilla kind of guy but also because I was trying to frame him, not get him killed.

Once I had downloaded enough images to be damning, I hid them deep within folders Aamir was unlikely to ever look through. I returned the laptop to him just as Willy Wonka was telling Charlie, "Don't forget what happened to the man who suddenly got every-thing he always wanted."

Aamir gave a sigh of satisfaction as the credits began to roll.

I smiled at him. "Why do you like that movie so much?"

He shrugged. "I like the way it ends."

"When Wonka lies to Charlie?"

"What are you talking about?" Aamir asked, suddenly sitting up with a frown. "Charlie lived happily ever after."

"Trapped in a job that Wonka hated? I mean, he gave away a magic chocolate factory just so that he could change careers."

My brother stared at me, eyes wide with horror. "That isn't what the movie is about. Why do you have to ruin everything?"

I shrugged. "What do you think it is about?"

"It's about justice," Aamir said. "About how if you're good, if you withstand the tests put before you, you'll end up winning."

"That isn't how the world works."

"You're in high school. You don't know anything about how the world works. Look at me, Anvar. I follow all the rules and, alham-dulillah, nothing bad happens to me."

I was careful not to look at the laptop I had set on the coffee table before him. "I wouldn't count my chickens," I whispered, more to myself than to him. He didn't hear me. He was already rewinding the tape before putting it back in its case, as he always did without fail to every video he ever watched.

A few hours before prom, Ma was in her kitchen, where the air was thick with the cozy, comforting smell of beefy stew. Something must have been off, because she was scowling at the nihari she had bubbling away in an oversized steel pot, as if she could glare the ingredients into proper proportions.

I cleared my throat as I walked in. "I need to talk to you about something, Ma."

Bariah Faris turned her threatening gaze—and her irritation—away from the nihari and fixed it on me. "What?"

"I . . . well, my computer wasn't working—"

"Talk to your father about it."

I laced my fingers together, unlaced them and then scratched the back of my head. "No, I'm saying, my computer wasn't working, so I borrowed Aamir's laptop and . . . I found some things, Ma."

My mother carefully covered the steaming metal pot with a lid and stepped toward me, her long neck craning forward as she peered into my face. "What things?"

"Pictures."

"What kind of pictures?"

"Um . . . dirty pictures," I said, hoping that I was coming across as truthful. "I just thought you should know. Anyway, I'm going to go to the library to return some—"

"These pictures," Ma hissed, her tone low and venomous, her dark eyes wide, "they were of women?"

"And men?"

"*Men!*" Her shriek was like the end of the world. "Aamir is looking at dirty pictures of men?"

"No. I mean, yes . . . I mean, the men and the women, they're not, you know, alone. They're together doing . . ."

"What?"

I started to speak, then stopped myself. I hadn't realized that I might have to use the word "sex." That would not go over well. Desi kids grow up around sanitized marriages, with little or no physical intimacy. I'd seen my parents hug each other once, and that was after my grandfather had died. Other than that, there had been a concerted effort to ensure that we never saw the genders touch. It was inevitable in the States, of course, to see couples kiss in malls or even in lines at the grocery store, but my mother was always sure to clear her throat loudly and disapprovingly at such times, making it known that what these other people were doing was not appropriate for us to do.

After an upbringing like that, one doesn't simply say the word "sex" to one's mother. The more graphic variations were, obviously, out for the same reason. In fact, I eliminated the letter "f" from consideration entirely, just to be safe, as I tried to find some way to express what I wanted to say, some phrase that was innocuous but had the right cadence to describe the act.

"Well?"

I tried to think of how Aamir would say what I needed to say, because he'd know the right words to use. All I could think about in that moment, however, was a song I'd recently heard him listening to. One phrase sounded just about right for what I needed to describe.

"Oompa loompa."

"*Oompa*," Ma thundered, as if I had said the worst words in the English language. She understood perfectly well what I meant. "*Loompa?*" She stepped past me, calling at the top of her voice, "Aamir. Aamir Faris, get down here right now. Right now. *Aamir?*"

I ran up the stairs past her at full speed, my mother calling out after me to send Aamir down. I nearly ran into my brother when I got to the top of the stairs.

"What's going on?" Aamir asked.

"No idea," I replied without slowing my pace. I ran to my room and grabbed the backpack I had prepared minutes ago. It contained one of my own belts and a tie I'd stolen from my father's wardrobe the day before. There was no time to lose. As soon as Aamir began offering explanations, my scheme would start to unravel.

I went to Aamir's room. The moment of truth. I tried the doorknob and it turned easily in my hand. I smiled. It had worked.

A few years ago, when Aamir had decided it was his duty to wake me up for Fajr prayers at dawn every morning, I'd gotten back at him by hiding fourteen alarm clocks in his room, set to go off at thirty-minute intervals after midnight. He'd responded to that long night by getting a lock for his bedroom door, which he religiously utilized whenever he was out of the house. The only way to get into this room, therefore, was to do it while he was around.

I went to his closet and threw open the doors. I saw my prize, the reason for all the plotting, the object of my mission—the cheap black wool suit my parents had purchased for Aamir for his college interviews.

Going to prom meant getting a tux. I simply didn't have the money for one of those, so Aamir's suit would have to do. I couldn't just ask him for it though. He would've wanted to know what I needed it for. I didn't trust him enough to tell him the truth. Unable to think up a satisfactory lie, I'd done the only thing I could do. I had found a way to occupy him while he was home, so that the door to his room was unlocked, and I could borrow his suit without being reported to Ma.

Without bothering to take the suit off the hanger, I zipped open the backpack and stuffed it inside. Then I raced downstairs, where the forest fire I had set was just starting to catch.

"I'm going to the library," I called out as I rushed through the front door. Given how loudly my mother was demanding Aamir show her what was on his laptop, I don't think they heard me. I didn't entirely catch what she was saying, but it sounded like Aamir was trying to explain to her that oompa loompas were not perverts. My heart, the part of it that was not cheering at the prospect of dancing with Zuha, wished him luck and wondered how I would make this up to him.

For now, the necessary mischief had been managed, and rather neatly at that. I ran almost the entire way to school and went straight into a bathroom to change.

As I began to dress, I realized there were a few minor flaws in my plan. A worsted wool suit is apparently not meant to be roughly shoved into a backpack. It came out horribly wrinkled. I had forgotten to grab a button-down shirt, which was unfortunate, or dress shoes, which was worse. I put the oversized, disheveled suit on top of my worn T-shirt and wore my white sneakers with the outfit. I did put on the tie because . . . well, I don't really know why. It seemed like the thing to do.

I emerged from the bathroom and, within moments, someone began to point and laugh. The laughter became an epidemic, spreading to everyone around me. I knew how I looked, so I told myself to be good-natured about the whole thing, but still I felt my ears grow hot.

Before I could snap at someone, I saw Zuha, and somehow forgot to feel humiliated.

She too was ridiculously underdressed. Instead of taffeta or silk, she was wearing a simple white cotton dress, just long enough to cover her knees.

No one was making fun of her though.

Incredibly, when she looked at me with those bewitching eyes of hers, she did not laugh. Instead, she took my hand and guided me into the gym, which pulsed with music.

I got to hold her close for the first time as we prepared to dance. Her body was soft against mine, her slender arms light around my neck. Her perfume made her smell like wild roses. I placed my hand at the small of her back. Heat radiated off her through the thin, textured fabric of her outfit.

I cleared my throat. "You look nice."

"I like your devastatingly eloquent compliments. They sweep a girl right off her feet."

I tried to think of something clever to say but all I could think about was how her lip gloss seemed to shine in the dim light. "I like how you make me forget all my words."

She rolled her eyes, but I could tell she was pleased. "Whatever, Romeo. Let's dance."

I hadn't ever danced before but how hard could it be?

With my most gallant smile, I began to move and promptly stepped on Zuha's toes. She yelped, I hoped more in surprise than in pain, and I hurried to apologize, before stepping on her feet again.

"*Ow.* Anvar, didn't you learn how to dance?"

"I was a little busy planning a covert mission against a brutal and oppressive regime."

"Fine. I'll lead."

I shrugged. "Sure. You know how to dance then?"

"Well . . . no."

We stood there, staring at each other, while everyone we knew twirled around us. After a moment, she began to giggle and then I started to laugh. We just held each other for the rest of the night, swaying clumsily in one place.

It was the best time.

When the last song ended, Zuha pulled away from me. I grabbed her girlish wrist. She looked back at me, surprise in her bright eyes.

"Mistletoe," I lied, pointing up at a garishly bright green streamer hanging overhead. Before she could say anything, before my own mind could protest my daring, I pulled her close and kissed her and kissed her and kissed her again.

The raspberry and youth of those kisses have forever been fresh on my lips.

"You should totally fall in love with me," I told her as I walked her home.

Her laughter echoed across the empty, dark street of the sleepy neighborhood. "That sounds like a bad idea."

"It's not. It's the best thing you'll ever do."

A ghazal was playing when I got home. Haunting notes of an old song filtered out from an open window into the night's pleasantly perfumed air, scented by Ma's precious jasmines. It told me that my father, at the very least, was waiting up to discipline me. His discipline always came with a soundtrack. I paused at the front door. I recognized the song he had chosen, because I'd heard it before, many times. It was one of his favorites. Farida Khanum was singing "Aaj Jaane Ki Zid Na Karo." She'd just gotten to the most beautiful lines, which mourned the fact that life is forever imprisoned by time.

With a sigh, I let myself into the house. It looked like my father was waiting for me alone. I would be spared, therefore, the loud recriminations of my mother and the just, righteous fury of Aamir, at least for now. I'd get only Imtiaz Faris, a little less censored than usual.

"There he is." My father set aside the newspaper he was reading, headlined by the fall of Saddam Hussein's Firdos Square statue in Iraq, and clapped his beefy hands together as I walked into the living room. "My bloody stupid clown prince."

"It's crown prince, Dad."

"No, you small-brained monkey, it's clown prince. You look like a stupid joke."

That was hard to dispute.

"You went to the filthy dance, haan, to watch girls wiggle around half-naked?"

"Yeah, Dad." I rolled my eyes. "That's what happens at prom."

"Abay, are you looking to die, Anvar? Show some respect. How come you're always so damn smart, my little sweet donkey, except when you're so goddamn bloody stupid that I can't quite convince myself you're my own child? No. Not another word. You hear me?" There was a long silence, then my father said, "Well? Answer my question. Did you go to the dance?"

"You did say not another word, so—"

My father grabbed a throw pillow with both hands and launched it at my head. I ducked unnecessarily. The soft projectile would've sailed over my head by a good meter or so anyway.

I raised my arms in mock surrender. "Yes. I went to the dance."

"Did you go like a neutered goat or was it with a girl?"

"A girl."

"Who?"

"No one you know."

My father leaned forward on the couch to get a better angle from which to peer up the stairs. After making certain that my mother was not eavesdropping, in a quieter voice, he asked, "Did you have fun?"

I grinned at him and whispered back, "It was kind of great."

In his normal voice, he said, "Doesn't matter who it was. You're grounded, you understand? Grounded from now until Israfil blows the horn and the world ends and the dead come back to life, so you can explain to your ancestors why you felt it necessary to heap this shame upon our family."

"That sounds fair."

"You will also apologize to your mother and to your brother. Aamir was very angry. And you don't even know how hard it was to convince your mother not to throw his laptop into the dishwasher."

I nodded and my dad got to his feet.

"I hope you regret what you've done."

I didn't dare say anything out loud but I mouthed "no" at him. He smiled at me in response but whacked me upside the head just the same as he walked past me to go to bed.

It was a month before my internet privileges were restored. During that time, despite my assurances that there was nothing objectionable on it, Ma took my desktop into a shop and asked them to format the hard drive twice in order to purify it of any potential filth I might have downloaded. When I was finally allowed to touch a keyboard again, I had to reinstall the operating system. It was an interminable process.

Maybe it just felt that way because the study, redesigned to prevent the perusal of pornographic material, now made me uncomfortable. The décor in the small room had been redone. A massive poster of the Kaaba in Mecca, the black square at the center of the Islamic faith, was pinned to the wall over the monitor. From the opposite wall, the Prophet's mosque in Medina, with its iconic green dome, peered over my shoulder to see what I was doing.

Black-and-white pictures of my grandparents were taped to the computer tower, just above color photos of our family. On the bookshelf, a plastic bottle filled with water from Zamzam, a well sanctified by the feet of the Prophet Ishmael, sat in judgment of my online activities. Ma had even thought to change the nature of the very air in the room. A few slender sticks of agarwood smoldered on the windowsill, the musky, sweet fragrance of their smoke making it a little hard to breathe.

I sat glaring at the Microsoft Windows 2000 symbol fluttering on my screen, willing it, without success, to take over my computer posthaste.

The door to the study opened and Aamir marched in. He didn't seem at all put out by changes in the surroundings. He'd probably helped plan them.

He hadn't spoken to me since the porn incident, so the fact that he walked up to me now, albeit with a pinched expression, like he had been munching on a bitter almond, was surprising. There was a carefully wrapped gift in his hand. I could tell it was a book, because you can always tell when it is a book. He handed it to me without ceremony and gruffly said, "For your graduation."

I tore into the packaging, which made him cringe. It was a battered, obviously used hardcover copy of *The Remains of the Day*. I flipped it open to a random page and the thick stench of strong tobacco wafted up from the pages.

"Sorry. I got it online." He offered me a sheepish grin. "It was supposed to be in better condition. Look at the front."

I opened the book gently to the title page. It was a first edition. A signed first edition. Kazuo Ishiguro himself had scrawled his name on the book in deep black ink. I gasped.

"Aamir, this is my favorite book. He's my favorite author."

"I know."

"How?"

He shrugged. "It takes me a while, sometimes, to tune you out when you're talking."

I was still examining the book, careful not to stress its shaky, unreliable spine, when I saw an inscription in fresh ink and in Aamir's sprawling, extravagant hand. It read: "He lived happily ever after."

A frenzy of shame clutched at my heart, not really for downloading porn onto his laptop, but because I had been too proud to apologize for it. "Thank you," I said. I didn't manage to say it as loudly as I wanted. "And I'm sorry for what I did."

Aamir heard me. He looked over my head, at the poster of the Grand Mosque, and perhaps it reminded him that forgiveness was a virtue because he reached over and mussed up my hair, like our father often did, and left me alone with the modest treasure he'd bestowed upon me.

"So that strange young woman of yours finally got you into trouble, didn't she?"

I made desperate shushing sounds as I turned down the sound on the desktop's speakers. The transition from phone calls to speaking to Naani Jaan over the internet was fraught with danger, but she didn't seem to understand that. We no longer enjoyed the same privacy we once had. Sure, everyone saved money on long distance, but it also meant that anyone walking past could hear both sides of our conversations.

Not being able to use the computer had meant no long chats with Naani Jaan, and that had been as much part of my punishment as anything else.

"She didn't twist my arm or anything."

"Twist your arm?" Naani asked. "Is that what young people are calling it nowadays?"

"It is an expression."

"Yes, yes." Naani paused to cough. "I was born under the British Raj. You think I don't know about twisting arms? It was a joke, Anvar. You're not the only act in town, you know."

"Sorry," I said. I'd gotten into the habit of explaining things to my parents—Ma in particular—and it was a little hard to know when to stop. In their defense, the language they heard wasn't consistent with the one they'd been taught. My mother didn't, for example, understand how something being sick or wicked was positive. Being "the bomb" was a good thing but "bombing" something was bad. None of this was in accord with her experience.

"Chalo, at least you aren't denying her existence anymore. That's progress. You remember what I told you before you left, yes? You're being careful?"

"I'm definitely being careful."

"It doesn't sound like you're being careful."

"I'm not very good at it."

Naani Jaan laughed and then was seized by a fit of coughing.

"You okay?" I asked.

"Fine, fine. Just need water. I'll go get it soon. Before I do, you know, I heard all about your adventure from your brother—"

I rolled my eyes. "Of course you did."

"And there is a part of the story I don't understand."

"It's not that complicated, Naani Jaan."

"Yes. I'm not saying it wasn't a simpleton's plan but what I don't understand is this: What is porn?"

SAFWA

I don't remember the first time the Americans went to war with Iraq, but I was born during that Desert Storm.

Americans are so good at naming things.

I don't remember that war, but I do remember my mother telling me that I'd been born under the shadow of two flags. One red, white and black; the other red, white and blue. It was, she thought, a small difference.

My father overheard her and laughed—he still knew how to laugh then—and said that it was a great difference indeed.

If my mother had lived to see me turn twelve, when the Americans returned, I think she would've learned to agree with my father, but the cancer that robbed her of her life spared her the indignity of being wrong.

Of course, if she had lived to see me turn twelve, she would've lived to see Fahd dying on the same bed that she had died on. She wouldn't have cared about being wrong then. Nothing improves one's perspective faster than a bit of death.

I sat next to Fahd as he slept, holding his hand. I was supposed to be praying, but if I believed that praying for my brother would save his life, I would've been more like Abu, standing in salah for hours upon hours during the night, desperate tears streaming down my face, holy words silently dancing on my dry lips, until my feet swelled.

I hadn't knelt before Allah since Abu commanded me to stop grieving for my mother. I'd felt guilty about not praying then. When had that feeling gone away?

Maybe when Fahd's body had turned on itself. Dr. Yousef said that a series of small clots had formed inside Fahd, robbing his heart and kidneys of oxygen. He was breathing, but not getting enough air. He was on dialysis now, and damage I couldn't see would end him soon.

"A rare and lethal condition," Dr. Yousef said, "but perhaps not rare enough."

Or maybe I stopped believing with the second coming of the Americans. How much of God's power had these men taken for themselves? They rained fire from the sky, made the earth shake, and could spare life and take it whenever they desired, without consequence. They elevated those they liked to power and then took that power away when they wished. Their word was sent to everyone around the world, streamed from the heavens into every home through their electronic messengers, television and radio.

All men are created equal.

Except not really, because some men are created American. Other men are created rich. Some men are created American and rich and are still not content with the world they inherit, so they try to change it. They try to make it more to their liking by painting it with blood and flame.

A rare and lethal condition, but perhaps not rare enough.

God wouldn't give up so much of his power to men, and certainly not to men such as these. At least, no God I would bow before.

I sat with Fahd for around ten minutes, which was enough time to fool Abu, and then made my way to the kitchen. Abu was sitting at our small table, waiting for his dinner, his face buried in his hands.

There wasn't much to give him. I put a handful of olives on a plate, along with bread that had aged into a cracker and some hummus. I served his dessert, a couple of hard dates stuffed with almonds, at the same time, which made it seem like we had more food than we did.

In the three years since Mama had passed, I'd become an adequate cook through trial and error and by looking up recipes on the internet, but there was nothing I could make if there was nothing to cook with. There hadn't been much in the house since Abu lost his job. The factory he'd worked at once was rubble now.

Duty done, I started to walk out of the kitchen when Abu said, "Sit with me, Safwa."

I hesitated, then did as he asked.

He didn't say anything for a while. He just stared at what little food I'd been able to give him without touching it. I glanced at the clock over his head, struggling not to fidget in my chair.

Six and a half minutes passed before he spoke again.

"I feel like we do not know each other's minds, you and I."

I crossed my arms over my chest. Where had that come from? It was true, but it had always been true. It had never seemed to bother him before.

He nodded when he saw me struggling for an answer, as if that was exactly what he expected. "Have you eaten?"

"Yes," I lied.

"People say that tragedy brings family together. We've had our share of tragedy, you and I."

"We have."

More silence.

"It is a mother's place to be the friend of her children. A father provides for them." Abu picked at his bread. It snapped between his fingers. A small smile touched his lips. "I fear that Allah has not given me the capacity to be a mother to you . . . or much of a father, at least these days."

"It's not your fault."

Abu let out a deep breath. "I will go out to look for work again tomorrow."

And I will probably return with nothing to show for it, he didn't say, *just like thousands upon thousands of others.* I didn't say that either because it would've been cruel. A small hope is better than no hope at all.

"Where will you go?"

With a pained twist of his lips, Abu said, "The Americans have work. People line up for it. I can clean their toilets and their floors for them if I am lucky." I jumped as he pushed back from the table, getting to his feet with more speed than I was used to seeing him move with. "I can see no other way, Safwa. The world is closed to me. We must have money for Fahd's treatment."

I nodded. Space in the hospital was dear, but Fahd needed regular dialysis treatments to live. If that meant cleaning up American shit, then it meant cleaning up American shit. Was Abu ashamed to do it or did he think that I'd be ashamed of him if he did?

I watched him pace the length of his small kitchen, obviously agitated. "Okay," I said. "That sounds good."

"Good?" Abu said, snarling more than speaking as he whirled to face me. "Good? There is no good in this, foolish girl. There is only what is."

If Fahd had been awake, he probably would have quoted the Prophet and said, "Wondrous is the affair of the Believer for there is good for him in every matter." He wasn't awake though, so Abu was stuck with me and I didn't know the right things to say. I never have. He would have preferred it, I think, if I'd been the one with the rare blood disease, inhaling and exhaling and yet not really breathing at all.

I tried to imagine what it must be like for Abu, having fought with the Americans for the freedom of Afghanistan, to now face the prospect of serving them as they invaded his own country. I could see in his dark eyes that it bothered him. It hurt his pride.

I wanted to say something reassuring, but all I could offer him was my truth.

"I'd do it in a heartbeat," I said, "if you'd let me."

He thought about that for a minute, frowning, then said, "Is that supposed to make me feel better?"

I shrugged.

"Well," Abu said, "it does, a little. It does."

It wasn't surprising that Abu couldn't find a job. With the Iraqi army disbanded, there were many men desperate for work, some with more mouths to feed than Abu had. Getting the privilege of serving the occupying force was like winning the lottery, and Abu had never been a lucky man.

He joined a political party. I'm not sure what Abu did for them, but they paid him a little. I heard him tell Dr. Yousef that he knew people said they were funded by the Iranians, but in our situation it didn't matter which country the money came from.

It was strange. There was so much happening around me, and yet my life, my world, was smaller than it had ever been. I couldn't leave home. Abu said it wasn't safe, and we couldn't leave Fahd alone. School was out of the question. We'd lost the internet because we couldn't pay for it. When there was electricity, I got to watch some TV, but I didn't want to hear about violence breaking out or statues being pulled down. It was prettier to just watch my mother's *Full House* tapes and wonder at lives so different from mine.

"At least things can't get worse," Fahd said one day. "Remember what the Quran says, Safwa. After hardship, there is ease. It is a promise from Allah. After hardship, there is ease. Take comfort in that."

I smiled and didn't point out that Allah didn't say how much hardship would have to be endured before the promised ease came or what kind of ease it would be. Death too was ease of a kind. Maybe those weren't verses of solace at all. Maybe they were just the truth about the human condition: you will suffer and then, one day, you will suffer no more.

"You've handled all this so well. Mama would be proud of you," Fahd told me. "You've become so much like her."

I pulled my hand away from his.

My brother frowned, unsure of what he had said wrong. "You're so good at managing everything around the house. You do every-thing she did. You stay home, just like she did. You don't waste your time with friends or fashion or pointless things." He laughed, not unkindly. "You even watch that American television show she loved so much."

I stared at him for a while, then looked away, first out the window at the city forbidden to me and then down at my hands. I didn't say a thing.

"What's wrong?" Fahd asked, straining to sit up in bed.

"Nothing. Nothing at all. I just never thought about . . . myself. I'm just doing what I have to with the world as I find it. Just trying to live."

My brother let out a deep, shuddering sigh. "Yeah. Tell me about it."

"Very funny," I said, getting to my feet.

Fahd was right. The life I was living now was indistinguishable from the one my mother had led. Would it end differently for me? Would it be the same? Four walls and a door that I rarely stepped through. Groceries. The stove. The prayer mat. A bed and in it a husband who cared about everything more than he did about me.

"Safwa?"

"Yes?" I said, turning to face my brother, a static smile on my face. "Sorry. I didn't realize that time was passing. That's all. I know it's stupid."

Fahd didn't say it was stupid, but then he wouldn't. That wasn't his way. Instead, he said, "She was a good woman, you know. It is not such a bad thing to be like her."

"I know she was good," I said. "But was she happy?"

"One is more important than the other, don't you agree?"

"Yes."

"I know you don't like talking about what is happening to me," Fahd said. "But what the books and scholars tell us is true. What the sermons tell us is true. The life of this world is like water held in a fist. Too soon it is gone and nothing remains. So bear your thirst now, and you will drink from the lakes of paradise one day."

I shook my head.

"What?" Fahd asked. He sounded self-conscious, like he'd tried out something new and was afraid I'd mock him for it. These flights of religiosity were new. They'd started shortly after he'd been diagnosed, when he'd realized how little time he had left. I didn't particularly care for them. He didn't sound like the Fahd I'd known my entire life when he spoke like that. He sounded more like a nicer, kinder, more eloquent Abu. Beneath the pretty words, however, the thoughts were the same.

What if there is no heaven and no hell? I wanted to ask him. What if there is no majestic reward at the end of this journey of pain and hurt that you want me to call a life? What if the time Mama had in this world was all the time she had, and she wasted it tied to a kitchen chair, yearning for the fictional lives of characters from a television series?

Maybe those aren't questions you can ask anyone ever. They definitely aren't questions you ask a dying man.

"You're right," I said.

It was what he wanted to hear, so he smiled when he heard it.

But I threw away all the *Full House* tapes in the house after I left his room. I never saw Mama's dream ever again.

—

I prefer bombs to goats. Bombs explode more often, this is true, and they're louder, but at least everything is over in a flash. A goat isn't like that. It goes on and on, bleating and chewing and peeing until its life is ended. Shock and awe is better than slow torment.

I realized this around the first Eid al-Adha after the fall of Baghdad. Our next-door neighbor, Baba Adam, bought a goat to sacrifice and tied the beast up on his roof. This meant that the goat spent all day, and all night, staring right into my bedroom window, chewing hay and looking a little threatening. My only sanctuary in my father's home began to smell, and the constant, nasty smacking of the goat's lips became the soundtrack to my life.

It wouldn't shut up no matter how much I yelled at it. When I drew the curtains to make its glowering face go away, it resorted to head-butting the windowpane.

I've never looked forward to an Eid as much as I did that one.

Baba Adam was a wiry, cranky man who lived alone in a building where he'd once housed three supercranky sons. I begged Abu to speak to Baba Adam about moving the goat, but Abu said the old man wouldn't do it, which was probably true.

Baba Adam had never been nice, but recently, after his three missing sons had been found in a mass grave in Mahaweel, he'd started picking fights with everyone around him—family members, friends, even strangers on the street. Abu didn't want to start anything with him. My father thought, in fact, that our neighbor had put the goat there on purpose, so his thirst for conflict could be sated.

Baba's boys had probably been killed during the intifada, when Saddam had been trying to suppress a Shia rebellion. The boys had Shia names, given to them by their Shia mother, and that was probably what had caused their deaths. It was important, Abu said, what we called people and what we called things. It was a matter of life and death.

"Baba's sons were missing for years," I said. "Everyone already thought they were dead. Shouldn't finding them and knowing for sure bring him peace?"

"There is no peace anymore," Abu said as Dr. Yousef, who had come to check on Fahd, nodded along. "You should feel sorry for the poor animal. And you should envy it. It is giving its life for the sake of Allah. It is making a great sacrifice."

This wasn't true. The goat wasn't noble. It wasn't making a sacrifice. It was being sacrificed. Those were very different things. The only reason to feel sorry for the animal, aside from the fact that it was going to die, was that it didn't have any control over what was happening to it. But then neither did we.

I spent a lot more time with Abu in those weeks before Eid. His company was more comfortable than the company of the goat. Mostly.

I could say that my father was an angry man, and it would be true. He was severe and rigid. He could be unkind, as he so often was to Mama. With me, he was a little more lenient, at least back then, though I had to always be doing something when he was around, because he disapproved of being idle.

One morning, having been driven out of my room, I was just lying on a sofa and watching a ceiling fan spin when he said, "Are you daydreaming again?"

I couldn't help but wince at the irritation in his tone. "No, Abu. What use are dreams to a girl like me?"

He stumbled over what he was going to say. The sting drained from his voice. "You've given Fahd his medicine? He's resting?"

I nodded.

"And have you no housework to do?"

I could've been dusting, I guess. In this city you could always be dusting, forever and ever into the arms of God if you wanted. Even so, I said, "None."

"Then you should be thanking Allah."

"That's what I was doing."

Abu let his head loll back, looking up at the same ceiling I was looking at. "Not like this. Damaghsiz. Properly with nose touching the ground. You know the Prophet said that you should keep your tongue wet with the remembrance of Allah."

I bit back my response, got up and went to sit by Baba Adam's goat.

Abu cleared his throat. Twice. Then again. Shaking my head, I looked up from the shirt button of his that I was mending. That shirt was the best piece of clothing he owned, and he wanted to wear it for Eid.

"What, Abu? I don't want to mess this up."

"Remember when for Eid we used to have new clothes," he said.

I smiled and went back to my task. "That wasn't so long ago."

"There was laughter in this house then. You and your mama would sit right there, at that table, and make kleecha, and she'd have to keep telling Fahd not to eat the dates she was baking with."

I didn't say anything. I did not want to be asked to make kleecha. I'd tried once, after Mama had died, and had burned all the little cookies, and had broken down into such tears that poor Fahd, alarmed, had gone to buy some from the store. I'd refused to eat them, and now wished I had.

"You know that it is a tradition of the Prophet Muhammad to wear new clothes on Eid, don't you?"

Yes, I thought, I'm not five years old.

"You taught me that, Abu," I said.

"That is at least one way in which I have not failed you."

"Is this about clothes? Abu, really, it's fine. I swear. I don't care that we couldn't get new clothes this year. It isn't important."

"It is important." Abu's voice rose a little. "The Prophet said—"

"You're right. I didn't mean it isn't important. I meant we need to take care of Fahd first."

He nodded but continued to hover over me.

I looked up again. "It'll be fixed soon."

"I have given some thought to what you said." Abu stuck his big hands into his pockets, looking like a sheepish schoolboy more than a war veteran.

I returned my eyes to the needle as it pierced the shirt again and again, hurting it and healing it at the same time.

"I wish you'd been born into a better world, habibti." He fished around in his pockets and pulled out a small, baby pink hair clip. It was shaped like a bow, the kind of thing I used to wear when I was a child. "It isn't a new dress or even something you'll use now, I know, but it made me think of you in happier times, when you would sit by your mother and listen to all the stories she knew how to tell and your eyes . . . they were full of stars."

He patted my cheek. The skin on his palm was rough, his fingers callused.

"I pray Allah wills that one day you find yourself facing a better destiny than you do now. You should remember who you were, before the dark times came, so you are ready in case you get to see the dawn."

Baba Adam's goat didn't seem to understand the significance of the knife in his owner's trembling hand. It stood where it was, chewing cud as the old man untied it. When he turned to head back downstairs, the goat in tow, he seemed to realize, for the first time, that I was watching them through the window.

He stared at me for a long moment, a scowl slowly growing on his face, until finally he said, "It is the will of Allah."

I almost asked him what he was talking about, but then realized he was defending his murderous intentions toward the animal.

"I know," I said.

"Then don't look at me like that."

"Like what?"

Baba Adam let go of the rope he'd been using to guide his sacrifice to its end and pointed in my direction. The sun's light reflected off the steel blade he held and somehow became brighter. Blinding.

"Don't look at me with those eyes."

"These are the only eyes I've got."

"I don't like them," Baba Adam groused. "They're strange."

"Unique," I said.

"Go beat your head on a wall. What is to happen to this creature"—he swung the blade to point toward the goat—"has already been written in the Book of Fate and the Pen has been lifted. Go on then."

I started to argue. I didn't have to go anywhere. I was, after all, in my own room. Besides, the old man was leaving himself, so his ordering me to go made no sense. Then I stopped, remembering what my father had said. Baba Adam wanted to fight. I wouldn't give him the satisfaction.

I stepped toward the window to draw the curtains when a familiar roar blasted through the air and the ground shook. I stumbled but caught myself. Even as I did so, I knew that we were safe. I could guess with some accuracy how far away an explosion was, and this was close, but not dangerously so.

There was a scream. I looked up just in time to see Baba Adam lying on his roof, a hand outstretched in the direction of his goat. It was running around in a frenzy, its eyes rolled back in its head, its panicked bleating piteous.

It was the only resident of Baghdad not used to bombs going off.

As Baba Adam screeched for the animal to calm down, he struggled to his feet. But the force of a second explosion made him fall again.

The goat was not having it. It let out a final, wild complaint, turned its head first to the right and then to the left, and then took a magnificent leap of faith into the air, toward the waiting concrete below.

Moments after it dropped out of view, I heard the sick slap of its body hitting the street, along with the alarmed cries of pedestrians, who may have just shrugged off the two explosions, but who hadn't yet become accustomed to the sight of livestock falling from the sky.

Baba Adam finally regained his feet. He turned to look back at me, eyes wide, arms held out as his knife clattered to the ground. His entire slack expression was a question. He was asking me if I'd just seen that. If I could believe it.

"But it was the will of Allah," he said in the voice of a lost soul.

"No," I said, "I don't think it was."

Fahd thought the story of the goat was hilarious. The goat had not, it turned out, been sacrificed that day. It had been put down, having shattered its hip in the fall, but a wounded animal doesn't count as a sacrifice for Eid. So, all that had happened was that Baba Adam was out some money and suicide bombers had killed people in the explosions that scared the goat.

"The question," Fahd said, "is why the goat jumped."

"That's the question?"

"Goats live on mountains and things, right? It must have thought—"

"Isn't the question why two men walked into a crowd of people and blew themselves up on Eid?"

Fahd shrugged. "They thought they were doing what Allah wanted."

That's what Abraham thought too, I almost said, but caught myself in time.

The Festival of Sacrifice was a celebration of Abraham's absolute obedience to God. So obedient was the great prophet that he was willing to sacrifice his own son when commanded to do so.

It occurred to me that day that Abraham's story was about more than obedience. It was a story about human ignorance too. Here was a man who spoke with the divine, and thought he understood what Allah wanted of him. Because of that misplaced certainty in his understanding of God's will, he'd almost slit open the throat of his own child.

Abu had taught me that Abraham's was an inspirational tale. I thought, maybe, it was also a cautionary one.

Yet two men today had killed themselves and many innocents because they thought they understood what Allah wanted, and they'd done it on a day celebrating Abraham.

"It had to have thought it would escape," Fahd said.

"What?"

"The goat, Safwa. When it jumped. It must have thought it would manage to get free."

I looked through one of Fahd's windows at the street below. At what point during the fall had the animal realized it had made a mistake? It must have, moments after jumping, recognized that what it had mistaken for safety was actually doom.

"It was free," I said, talking more to myself than Fahd, "for a while there. Right when it jumped, before it knew it had been wrong. There was a moment when it was free."

"I guess. It still didn't escape its destiny. I mean, it still died. Instead of a peaceful death as an honored sacrifice to Allah, it ended up on the road, in pain, and got a bad end. What was its struggle for?"

My brother was right. The goat hadn't escaped its destiny. It had, however, managed to change it. That was not, in my mind, nothing.

Clocks cannot measure time.

They can count seconds, minutes and hours, but those are not accurate measures of our experience of time. A day of hunger is longer than a day when you've eaten. How quickly time passes isn't constant. An hour can stretch out and seem unending. A year can pass you by before you know it.

Abu was late coming home from the mosque that Eid. At first, I barely noticed. Then the sun began to sink, and my fears began to rise with the coming dark. I thought of those two explosions I'd heard earlier and wondered where he'd been when they happened.

I walked through the house and did all the small chores I had been putting off. I fussed over Fahd until he shooed me away. I did everything I could not to look at the time because it was running away, faster and faster, and Abu still wasn't home.

My feet were aching when finally the bell rang. I ran out to the gate barefoot, head and face uncovered, and without wondering why my father didn't just let himself in, called out, "Abu?"

A moment of hesitation. Then a familiar voice said, "No, my dear girl. It is I, Dr. Yousef. Let me in, Safwa."

I hurried to open the gate, and before he could speak, I said, "Abu?"

It was still a question. Just a different one.

Dr. Yousef cast his eyes to the ground and said nothing.

"Abu?" I asked again, more desperately this time.

"He's gone, Safwa."

The words hit me with the force of the explosions I had heard but been spared earlier. I stepped back.

Dr. Yousef's next words were a balm and a toxin. "I heard they took him."

He was alive. At least he was alive. I took a deep breath.

"They?" I asked. There were so many "they" nowadays. Too many.

"The Americans. My dear girl, the Americans took your father."

"Where?"

Dr. Yousef shook his head. Of course, he didn't know. The

Americans did what they wanted, and they answered no questions. They had arrested many people. The families of the disappeared had no idea where their loved ones had been taken. There was no one they could ask. No one who would even say that they were alive.

Most of these disappearances had happened right after the invasion. Some were released. Others were not.

A few of those who returned told stories about what they'd seen, what they'd heard, that would make the desert sun go cold. These were only whispers though, and I'd only heard them in passing through Abu and Dr. Yousef. I wished, at that moment, that I knew more about the world, that I was more a part of it, so I would know what to do.

"What happens now?" I asked.

Dr. Yousef glanced up at the sky, at the moon becoming visible in it yet again. "Now," he said, "a long night begins."

ANVAR

It was only natural that Zuha and I planned on attending San Francisco State to major in English literature. It was, after all, the first thing we loved together. Of course, I had to convince my parents to let me waste my life by pursuing a liberal arts education.

Every kid from the subcontinent knows that there are three acceptable career paths you can walk down. You can become a doctor, you can become an engineer or, if you are painfully slow, you can study economics or finance.

Being an English major is not on the menu and, just in case it wasn't clear, you can't order anything that isn't on the menu.

I went to my father and said, "Isn't this why we are here?"

"So that you can open an English clinic and correct people's spelling mistakes?"

"No." I pulled out the thin book he had given me in Karachi, all those years ago, and showed it to him. I could see that he recognized it. "We came here for Jefferson, didn't we? We came for the pursuit of happiness. This is what I want to do, Dad. This is what makes me happy."

"That's world-class emotional blackmail," my father said. "You're sure you don't want to be a lawyer or something decent like that?"

"Positive."

"Then who am I to stand in the way of Thomas Jefferson?"

Bariah Faris didn't have any patience for talk of happiness. She continued to protest but, eventually, finding no support from her husband, lapsed into a scowling, disapproving silence.

—

I was in love with San Francisco. In love with the not-really-golden bridge and the water it sat on and the sight of Alcatraz on the horizon. I was in love with my classes and in love with the libraries those classes made me seek out. I was in love with the paths that led up to those libraries, and with the trees lining those paths, and the leaves on those trees, and the birds in the branches that carried those leaves singing their unimaginably beautiful songs into the heart of the wind.

I was in love with the world because Zuha Shah was in it.

And, of course, I was also in love with Zuha Shah.

We were hopeless book nerds with few friends because we were so immersed in each other, and in the minds we could experience through the words they had left behind. Together we were befriended by the Romantics and colonized by the Victorians. We spent days upon days, sometimes skipping classes entirely, with Milton and Shakespeare and Goethe and Wilde. We got drunk with Ghalib and were elevated by Rumi and Hafiz.

There may have also been some kissing. Or a lot of kissing. I hear a gentleman does not tell.

Besides, not telling was a bit of a habit of ours. We were friends in public and nothing more, because the desi aunty spy network had informants everywhere, and neither one of us wanted to deal with the family drama that would ensue if our romance became known within the community. Our reputations would be tarnished forever. We'd always be *those* kids who'd done *that* thing . . . though we hadn't actually done *that* thing yet. We hadn't even discussed it.

Our dorm rooms, where we had both been blessed with non-Muslim, non-desi roommates, were our refuges. The only places we could be what we were to each other.

It was in those dorms that I first learned how to love someone. I mean, sure, obviously I loved Naani Jaan, my parents and, to some extent, Aamir, but it was Zuha who taught me how to be in a relationship.

Turned out that being with someone is an acquired skill. There is an art to it. Basically, you have to watch your partner take a chisel—or a war hammer, depending on the day—and chip away at the ideal version of them that you've created in your mind. The person you fall in love with is always slightly different from the person you need to stay in love with. More real and more flawed, but also more complex and better defined.

There were a few things about Zuha that bothered me. I adored that she was smarter than I was, but she could slice me to pieces with her wit whenever she wanted. I'd always known this about her, but her words when they were sharp—whether because she was in a mood or because she was just being careless—now cut deep when before they'd just stung. I could also be carelessly mean. It was something we were learning to live with.

She was surprisingly human in other ways too. Her hands were bitterly cold, her pretty long hair somehow got everywhere, and her incurable lust for shawarma wasn't ideal. Garlic breath is real, after all.

The thing about being in love is that if you can endure the sight of the idol you've fallen for crumbling before you, and learn to love the truth of who your partner is as you discover it, then you'll have someone to take your hand as she's reading, and who'll lean over and whisper in your ear, "Let us be true to one another . . ."

My first thought when I opened the door to my dorm room for Aamir was relief. If Zuha were here, it would've been hard to explain. Fortunately, Aamir had showed up at my door drenched in rain at one o'clock in the morning.

What was he doing there this late? I stared at his unsmiling face and saw the lost sleep and sorrow in his eyes, and I knew something was wrong. Very wrong.

"Who?" I asked.

"Naani Jaan got sick . . ."

"Is she going to be okay?"

Aamir looked past me at Nico, my roommate, who'd paused the second Knights of the Old Republic game he was playing. They nodded to each other.

"You need to pack. I came to get you. You need to be home."

"What hospital did they take her to? Agha Khan? What's wrong with—"

"Anvar." Aamir placed a hand on my shoulder. "She's gone."

I remember being unable to respond as Aamir pulled me into

a bear hug. His clothes were wet and his eyes were wet and I did nothing because nothing was all I could do.

"You should sit down," my brother said, as Nico got me a glass of water and asked me if I was okay. I nodded. I'm not sure why.

They threw some of my stuff into a duffel bag, and Aamir guided me out of the room holding my arm. Nico followed us to the exit of the building and said to let him know if I needed anything, because that is what people say when these things happen.

A slow, even drizzle was falling on us as we walked to our father's silver Camry. It was an ugly night and it made the city seem ugly and I hated it. I couldn't imagine that I'd ever thought San Francisco beautiful. It was a place of wealth and privilege that still had streets that reeked of urine. Homeless, forgotten, broken souls shuffled past us, and I wondered why, in one of the greatest cities in the world, they could find no solace and no aid. It was a cold night for them. It was a cold night for me too, and I should have worn a jacket, but I didn't care about being comfortable now.

"You haven't said anything," Aamir said, once he'd taken the driver's seat and turned on the heat in the car at full blast.

"What is there to say?" I asked.

"Inna lillahi wa inna ilayhi raji'un," my brother reminded me.

From Allah we come, and to Allah we return.

It was what you were supposed to say when someone died, a reminder that death was expected, that your grief was not unique, and that the departed were where they truly belonged.

They were good words. Prescribed words. Ultimately, however, they were just words, and they were not enough. Not for this. Not for me.

It was just after dawn when I learned that I couldn't go to Naani Jaan's funeral. My parents were going to fly out in the evening. It was too expensive for all of us to go on such short notice. My father looked nervous when he told me, like he'd been asked to defuse a bomb. I understood. It was the way things were. There was nothing he or I could do to change that.

Friends and family had descended upon the house, bringing food and sorrowful smiles, nods designed to convey empathy and understanding, and old words of wisdom that had been vetted by generations. It is easy, in a way, to know what to say when someone dies. Humanity, as a whole, has a lot of practice in dealing with death. Only individuals struggle with it.

"So sorry for your loss."

"She was such a wonderful woman."

"Celebrate her life more than you mourn her death."

"Here if you need anything."

"Inna lillahi wa inna ilayhi raji'un."

"You'll see her again soon in heaven."

I have to admit that the last one was my favorite. Not only was it a stunning mix of piety and audacity, but it also sounded like a threat. Naani Jaan would've approved.

They floated through the house, dressed either in black or in white, depending on where they were from, what traditions they'd grown up with, and gave us their condolences.

There was only one face that I wanted to see, that I needed to see. Eventually, I heard my father open the door and greet Mr. Shah.

Zuha was there. She looked at me and in those bright brown eyes of hers, I could see she desperately wished she could embrace me, gather me up, pull me together. She couldn't. Not here.

She crossed her arms behind her back, bowed her head a little, and asked softly, "How are you?"

"Like . . . this world that lies before us like a field of dreams, so beautiful and so new, has really neither joy nor help for pain."

My father gave a little sigh. "Incredible, isn't it, how loss turns everyone into a poet?"

"It's Matthew Arnold," Zuha said.

My father looked around, frowning, searching for the long-dead Victorian. "Who? Where?"

"No, Dad, it's who I was quoting."

"Misquoting," Zuha whispered, and though moments before I'd been convinced that it would never happen ever again, entirely without meaning to, I smiled.

My parents left for Karachi, and Aamir went to Davis, drawn away by some medical school test or exam that couldn't wait. I was alone.

After I dropped my parents off at the airport, I came home and wandered through the house. I wasn't really looking for anything, I don't think. I just didn't want to sit still in the dark silence. I flipped switches wherever I went and soon every room was bathed in light. It was the kind of waste that would've typically had my mother screaming at me, but I didn't think she would mind tonight. Eventually, I lay down on my own bed, staring up at the ceiling fan, hands behind my head.

Ma had been quiet, somber and obviously moved by her mother's passing, but everyone treated me like they expected me to be the broken one. I suppose I was closer to Naani Jaan than she had been and that thought was a little terrible. I wondered what had happened between them, and when, to make them . . . not estranged, exactly, but soul strangers—people too different to connect, to ever understand each other. Would it be the same for me when Ma died? Everyone would assume, probably correctly, that Aamir was the one most in need of comfort.

I'd never learn more about the relationship between Bariah Faris and Naani Jaan. It was not a story my mother would ever tell, and maybe it wasn't a story for me to hear.

The high-pitched chime of the doorbell went off. I considered ignoring it and pretending I wasn't home. However, I had just turned on every single light in the house, so that wasn't really going to be a believable excuse.

I trudged downstairs and opened the door. Zuha stood there, holding a large, unmarked cardboard box.

"Hi," she said.

I looked past her at her car to see if anyone else was with her. "You're here alone?"

"Yes. I'm scandalous like that. Got you pizza."

"I can see that."

"Let me in before someone we know sees me and I get branded with the scarlet letter, will you?"

"The scarlet letter wasn't a brand. It was—"

"Shut up," Zuha snapped when I closed the door behind her. I raised my eyebrows. "How could you not call me?"

"I didn't have the chance."

"You could have texted. How long does that take?"

I took the pizza from her. The smell of the baked crust made me realize how hungry I was. "Sorry. You're not actually mad, are you?"

Zuha shook her head as she walked to the kitchen. "No. I just wish I could've been there for you."

"You're here now."

She turned around and glared at me, but I could see the mischief in her eyes.

"What?" I asked.

"I hate it when you say exactly the right thing. A girl likes to have the last word, you know. So . . . what can I do to make you feel better?"

"You can tell me there is no pineapple on this pizza."

"If I did, it would only be half the truth," Zuha said. As I started reaching for plates, she walked over to me and took my hands. Her eyes were serious now, as she reached up and ran a hand through my hair. "Hey."

"Hi?"

"I'm sorry I never got to meet your Naani Jaan. I think I would've liked her."

"You would have."

Zuha took a deep breath. "I don't know what else to say, Anvar."

"You don't have to say anything."

She stood on tiptoe and kissed me lightly on the lips. Then, drawing back, she said, "Now that I'm here, what do you want to do?"

Zuha growled as I took the last three of her pieces in one elegant move. "You're ridiculously good at this."

"Thank you. I know."

"I'm not sure that was a compliment."

I folded my arms and nodded at the checkers board between us. She rolled her eyes and tossed one of the small plastic disks at me. It bounced off my nose before I could react, and then off the bed. Zuha smothered a laugh as she hopped down to pick it up off the carpet.

"Hey," I said. "Respect the game."

"You're taking this way too seriously."

"It's the game of life."

She frowned. "I thought that was chess."

I shook my head, as if profoundly disappointed by her ignorance.

"How'd you get so good?"

"Practice," I said. "And Naani Jaan taught me."

That turned her tone serious. "Really?"

"Yeah. She was the best at the game. Checkers, I mean. Not life."

Zuha started to arrange the board for another round.

"I don't even know why she liked it so much. It wasn't like she loved board games or something. She never really played anything else. This was it. I never got to beat her, you know. She never let me win."

"That's kind of awesome."

I nodded. I'd always thought so.

She picked up a piece as if to make her first move, seemed to reconsider and put it back down. "Can I ask you something?" Then, without waiting for me to answer, she said, "What's bothering you?"

"Well, my grandmother just died—"

"It won't kill you to not be funny for like ten minutes," Zuha said. "That's not what I meant. And you knew that. It's something else."

I got up off the bed and went to stand by a window. The moon was low and glorious, not silver that night but a pale gold, as if it had been touched by an alchemist. I stared at its bruised face, a chronicle of millennia, and said nothing for a long time. Eventually, Zuha came to stand next to me. She didn't speak either. She just took my hand and squeezed it.

"I haven't cried," I said, like a man seeking absolution from a priest at a confessional. "Everyone else did. But, somehow, I can't. Is it because distance made her less real to me? I think I would've cried if I'd been there with her, but when you leave people behind, when you can't see them . . ."

She didn't say anything. She just stood by me, looking up at the starless sky.

"I don't know. Maybe part of me just doesn't believe it? She loved me, Zuha. It was a given in my life. I could do anything. I could be anyone. I knew that her love would never change. That's what is gone from my world. That is why I thought Arnold was appropriate. There is no certainty anymore."

"You left out the best lines though. 'Love, let us be true to one another. . . .' He wrote it on his honeymoon for his wife. These aren't verses of loss and despair. They're verses asking for a promise. Asking for a constant."

"My point is that there is no one left I can ask that of anymore."

"You can ask me," Zuha said.

I turned to look at her.

"I don't want you to be alone tonight, Anvar."

"I'll be fine," I said.

"No. I want to stay with you. You should ask me to stay with you."

I stared down at her. That wasn't something we had ever done—not that she had said we'd *do* anything, of course, but spending the night together was a very significant line to cross. I glanced in the direction of the bed. That made Zuha blush and look away from me.

She tucked a strand of hair that didn't need rearranging back behind an ear. "I mean . . . you know, if you don't want . . ."

I wasn't looking at the bed. I was looking at the checkers board sitting on it, all the pieces perfectly in place.

Life requires risk. . . . You have to have courage, Anvar, to get what you want. You have to be bold. You have to, not to sound like your know-nothing mother, dare . . .

"No," I said. "I mean, yes. That would be . . . that . . . Yes. Stay with me. Please."

Later, when she turned off the light and closed the door to my room, even though we were alone together, and closed the distance between us . . . in those secret, holy, forbidden moments I learned that even if there was no cure for pain in the world, as long as I was with Zuha, there was relief from it.

And later still, just before the rising of the sun, when she woke to find that I was not in our . . . my bed, she came to find me, and when she found me weeping, she kissed my forehead, stayed with me and let me cry.

SAFWA

I sat staring at a clock in Fahd's room. That seemed like all I did these days. Dr. Yousef insisted it was too dangerous for me to work, and there was no work to be had anyway, certainly not for a young girl with no experience and little education.

Rude laughter from outside the house broke the silence. I shivered, though it wasn't cold. I no longer dared go to the window. Strangers had been coming to the neighborhood. They were armed and they were not pleasant. When Baba Adam, the old man next door, had tried to pick a fight with them, like he did with everyone, one of them hit him repeatedly in the face with the butt end of a rifle. He wasn't expected to recover.

Another had seen me on the roof a few days before and shouted something, and I'd hurried away. He'd banged at our gate a couple of times, yelling for me to come down, until his giggling friends had taken him away.

He'd been back every day since, calling out lewd comments, singing romantic songs and threatening to break in.

There was fighting too. I hadn't slept more than a couple of hours in the last few nights. The songs of bullets and mortar shells kept me awake.

Dr. Yousef was worried. He'd been informed by a patient that these men had spoken at the local mosque. They wanted to take our country back from the Americans and the British. They said they wanted to restore the glory of the caliphate.

Dr. Yousef had insisted that I keep a bag packed with essentials in case I had to run. I'd told him I couldn't leave. I couldn't leave Fahd.

I looked over at my brother's sleeping form. His breathing was shallow now, though I knew that could change any minute. Sometimes he'd start panting, gasping for breath. Other times I'd be tempted to check on him, to see if he were still alive.

He'd missed his last few dialysis treatments. I couldn't afford them. It had been months now, and there was no word on Abu at all. I'd already asked Dr. Yousef to sell all of Mama's jewelry, and anything else of value in the house. The computer, our phones, the microwave, the television. This home was emptying out around me. Soon it might not be around me at all. We were two months behind on the rent.

Dr. Yousef had been helping us, but he had his own troubles. He'd been reduced to sleeping in his clinic. It didn't make sense to me, how a doctor could be so poor, but I'd always heard Abu say Dr. Yousef was a truly Christian man. He worked in desperate areas, barely charging his patients and often giving them free care. Maybe he'd just been too generous.

Still he came by every night, bringing food. I was waiting for him now. It was all I ever did. Wait for someone to save me. It was worse than hunger.

I turned away from Fahd and went back to staring at the clock. It was the easier thing to do.

I wondered what Dr. Yousef would say about Fahd's symptoms today. For the first time, he hadn't recognized me. Were his body's own poisons really going to kill him? It seemed like they were reaching his mind.

I got to my feet and walked to the kitchen. I checked the cabinets and the fridge. There was nothing there. I'm not sure why I bothered. Still I went from room to room. Everything was clean, every surface recently dusted. There was nothing to do.

I felt like my own mother's ghost sometimes, cursed to haunting this place.

A bullet rang out. Then another. There was the sound of breaking glass. I rushed toward it, running back into Fahd's room. A window was shattered. There was a bullet hole in the ceiling. There were men yelling downstairs. I tiptoed around the shards of glass and dared to peek outside.

Dr. Yousef's car sped away as the same armed man who had been screaming at me a few days ago was shouting at him, asking him if the girl inside the house was his mistress and if he'd share. Obviously, he'd also shot into the house. There were other men around him, laughing either at him or with him.

I had to clean up the mess in Fahd's room. I went to get a broom and was surprised to find that my hands were trembling. I left the broken glass where it was.

I packed a bag.

Sunlight stung my eyes. I hadn't been outside in a while, and they were raw from a lack of sleep. I'd spent the night weeping by Fahd's side. I opened the gate to let Dr. Yousef in. He looked worse than he had when Mama died. His green eyes, bloodshot and swollen, underlined with dark bags, looked more like mine than they ever had. His head was drooped forward, his shoulders were hunched.

There was a short, slender, middle-aged man with him who gave me the kind of smile one gives to a scared animal. The pity with which he looked at me made me feel exposed. I wished I'd put on my niqab. I was getting careless with it. Abu would've been upset.

"This is Hasan al-Qurayshi," Dr. Yousef said, his manner subdued but his voice firm. "You are going with him, my dear girl. I have spoken to your mother's sister in Basra. You can stay with her. Your filial piety is most commendable, but your decision to leave is the correct one. It isn't safe here anymore. When the Americans come, and they will come for these fools, it'll be a war zone."

"You're sure Fahd can't come with me?" I asked, unable to stop the tears that were suddenly falling from my eyes again.

"We've already spoken of this. The journey will be impossible for him. Besides, with no money, who will give him medical care? I am here. I will see to him."

"You must," I said. "You must."

"I promise."

I wiped my tears away. He might try, I knew, but he would only be able to stop by once, maybe twice a day, if that. I was abandoning my brother. I could pretend I was leaving him in a doctor's care, and Yousef Ganni could do the same, but we both knew the truth.

"Is there any chance he'll live?" I asked, finally giving voice to the one question I'd been too scared to ask since Fahd had taken ill.

Dr. Yousef shook his head.

"I don't want to die with him," I whispered. "Or worse."

Our old family friend put a hand on my shoulder. "This is a good decision."

Except it wasn't.

It was mean and selfish and cruel. It might have been smart, but it wasn't good.

Then again, as Abu had once said to me, there is no good. There is only what is.

I turned toward the man that Dr. Yousef had brought with him. Hasan. He was still looking at me with those sad eyes I did not like.

"He'll get you to Basra safe," Yousef Ganni said.

Hasan gave a little bow, as if that somehow demonstrated he was reliable.

I glanced at Dr. Yousef and the question must have been obvious on my face.

"I trust him with you. You've always been like a daughter to me, Safwa. Go on. Get your things. It is time."

Hasan al-Qurayshi didn't speak to me as he drove me through Baghdad for the last time. That was fine with me. We passed the People's Stadium and the graveyard where Mama was buried. It was only when we were outside the city that he finally decided to say something.

"You're a pretty girl."

I didn't reply. That was not the kind of comment I wanted to invite.

"How old are you? Come on. No harm telling me. Fifteen? Sixteen? It's a sweet age."

"Just drive." I said it like an order, with confidence I didn't feel.

He laughed. It was an inappropriately happy sound, and it unsettled my heart. "I like you. I've always liked serrated knives."

I didn't know what that meant, exactly, and I didn't want to encourage him to talk by asking him questions. Instead, I looked out of the window, at the roads broken under the weight of tanks, at the desolate landscape spotted with a few green shrubs, scattered palm trees and not much else.

"Yousef Ganni said your father was taken. What did he do?"

"Nothing," I said.

"That's enough to get in trouble these days," Hasan said. "You think he's still alive?"

"I don't know."

"Do you hope he's still alive? You know if he is and they release him one day, he'll find you. And you'll have to tell him about how you left your brother behind. If it were my father, that isn't a conversation that would go well."

"Can you stop talking please?"

He shrugged. "We're traveling for five hundred kilometers. We have to pass the time somehow."

"My father says the Prophet said to keep the name of Allah on your tongue always."

Hasan seemed to think this was uproariously funny. Abu had told me once he didn't care for men who laughed too much. I was beginning to see why.

"I like you. Did I say that I like you?"

"Yes."

"It's true, you know. I hope my daughter is like you. Brave."

"Brave?" That was a ridiculous thing to say. I was anything but brave. I was running away from my home, leaving a sick, dying Fahd behind to suffer alone. I was a coward.

"You don't think so?" He turned to look at me, as if to make sure, then shrugged. "I think it's brave to know when to live and when to die. Pretty brave to understand that sometimes a drowning man has to grab ahold of a snake. Pretty brave to get in this car with a man you don't know."

"Dr. Yousef said I could trust you."

"Trust is always a bad idea. Your family, your friends and, if you ever get married, your husband—always assume they're going to hurt you because they probably will."

He waited for me to respond.

When I didn't, he went on. "My pregnant wife is at Yousef Ganni's clinic. He'll be delivering our daughter. That's why he believes I'll deliver you. Besides, he's known my family forever."

"You know it's a girl?"

His laugh wasn't so annoying this time. "My wife couldn't

wait to find out. No patience in that woman. It's better to know what you're getting, I think. This way, we have a name ready and everything."

"What are you going to call her?"

"Azza," he said. "It means gazelle. I want her to be like that, you know. Free. A little wild. Alert, always, and fast enough to escape when the predators of the world come chasing after her."

"That's a good name," I said.

"We think so." He paused, then said, "It's difficult, you know, having a child in these times. I just pray that she has a good life." His eyes flicked up to the mirror again, and he added, "I hope you do as well."

THE ZUGZWANG

2005–2010

You're caught in a zugzwang, Anvar. You have to take your turn, but anything you do will cost you pieces. There are no good options. This happens. Sometimes all you get are dark clouds. Sometimes there are no silver linings. Just make the best move you can and hope the weather will turn.

—Naani Jaan

ANVAR

Aamir was running to be the treasurer of his school's Muslim Students Association. I was blacklisted from mine.

My relationship with the MSA—there is one in almost every college and university in the United States—got off to a poor start. I only went to their first meeting in my freshman year because Zuha dragged me there.

"It's a cult."

Zuha laughed. "You're insane. It's a social club."

"Isn't that what all cults call themselves?"

"You'll have fun." She pinched my arm for no reason at all. "Come on. Don't you want to meet other people like you?"

"There's no one else like me."

She rolled her eyes. "Thank God for that. We're going."

So, of course, we went. It didn't exactly go well. I mean, it started out fine, but then most things do. The president, an earnest senior with a pleasant smile and entirely too much energy, was babbling on about something or another. I wasn't paying attention. I'd picked up the MSA newsletter and was skimming through it. There was an article on the life of Bilal, one of the Prophet's Companions, extolling the man's many virtues. A few reminders about why prayers were important, a calendar of upcoming events and a humor section.

That was where the trouble started. The first few jokes were barely jokes at all, but it is hard to be funny when you're also trying to preach, so that wasn't necessarily unexpected. As I read on, however, I came across one that, after wasting a paragraph on the setup, had a punch line that called atheists fools.

I didn't say anything right away. No point in making a scene. I waited for the president to be done speaking, and while everyone else rushed to the spread of finger foods that the MSA had laid out, I pulled him aside. I showed him the newsletter.

"You guys really shouldn't print stuff like that. It's offensive."

"But funny," the president replied with a disarming grin.

"Not really. You're mocking another creed." That was something even I knew Muslims weren't supposed to do. "Isn't there something about not making fun of other people's gods?"

"The Prophet did say that," he said. "But they're atheists. They don't have gods. It's different. Hey, where are you going?"

"I'm out," I said, probably a little louder than was absolutely necessary, as I backed away. "I don't agree with your underlying philosophy."

He looked genuinely confused. "But we don't have an underlying philosophy. It's just a newsletter. Nobody even reads it." I was walking away now, and Zuha, having noticed the commotion, was scrambling after me while balancing the snacks she had picked out on a paper plate.

The president, his stunned disbelief at this turn of events evident in his voice, called out after me. "We have samosas."

"Got one," I heard Zuha say as she hurried past him. "They look lovely. Thank you."

"Wait. At least sign up for our mailing list!"

It is surely to the MSA's credit that almost all of their members continued to be irritatingly nice to me after that little kerfuffle. I never went to another meeting, though Zuha did. She told me I'd become famous among the Muslim students at the school for not having a sense of humor, which was hilarious.

Anyway, it was fine that Zuha wanted to hang out with them. Really. We didn't have to do everything together. She had the MSA, and I had the school newspaper. Apparently, I had a tendency to take things no one read seriously.

I didn't like Zuha's new friends though. One girl in particular, Shabana Wassay, had latched on to her like a leech. She followed her everywhere, significantly cutting into our alone time.

"She thinks you don't like her because she wears the hijab," Zuha said.

"Ma wears the hijab."

"True. And you don't like your mother much either."

That was difficult to argue with. "I don't like Shabana," I said, "because she thinks everyone should be wearing a hijab. I bet that if she could wrap one around my head she would."

Zuha giggled. "She's not that bad."

"Every time you talk to me in public, she looks like she's having a stroke."

"She probably is."

"Anyway, that's why I don't like her."

"Fine." Zuha shrugged. "I'll let her know."

"You do that," I said. Then, after a moment, "Except don't do that. You're not going to do that, are you?"

I was happy enough to be ignored by the MSA, and they'd probably all but forgotten I existed by the time our second year started, and Shabana became president. Though I didn't have anything to do with her in her official capacity, she continued to annoy me as an individual. She'd convinced Zuha that it was worthwhile to at least try to pray five times a day, which meant that whenever we managed to get a night together, an alarm went off at five or six in the morning for the predawn prayer. I was tempted to get up and pray myself a couple of times, if only to ask Allah to rain down misery, pestilence and maybe boils, if He was so inclined, onto Zuha's religious friend for these ridiculously early mornings.

I never did, of course. Somehow it didn't seem like the kind of request God would seriously entertain.

I'm not sure what would have happened if the universe hadn't intervened. Maybe life would have unfolded exactly as it did. Zuha changed. I didn't. It is an old story when it comes to young love. People drift apart. So even without the whole pregnancy thing, it is possible that we were heading in different directions.

It started when Professor Herman asked Zuha and me to stay behind after class. He told us that he wanted to teach Salman Rushdie's *The Satanic Verses* the following semester. We were the only two Muslim students registered for his course, and he wanted to know if we would object.

"It is, of course, not my intention to assign any reading that is offensive to your religion. However, I believe that certain noncontroversial sections of the book will be very useful in illuminating the themes of the course. Those are all you will be required to read. Do either of you have any objections to my proceeding in this manner?"

We didn't, and that should have been an end to the matter. Except it wasn't, because Shabana Wassay and the MSA were about to get involved.

"This is ridiculous. Unacceptable. We have to call him out."

I looked up from my lunch—a sandwich made up of perfectly sliced pastrami—to find Shabana Wassay standing over me, her voice raised loud enough to be heard by everyone in the cafeteria. Her eyes were wide, her skin flushed and her nostrils flaring. Zuha followed in her wake, clutching a copy of *A Fine Balance* to her chest and looking like she'd rather be anywhere else right now.

"You're frothing, Madam President." I slid my plate toward them. "Fries?"

The leader of the MSA fairly snarled at me and turned to Zuha. "Is he ever serious?"

Zuha shook her head, and I wondered, not for the first time, how much about our relationship she had shared with her friend. Barely anyone knew we were a couple. It was classified information, and we always discussed whom we might disclose it to before we did so.

"What outrage has you so outrageously outraged today, Shabana?"

"Did you know that one of the English professors at this school is teaching *The Satanic Verses*?"

I glanced at Zuha, who didn't meet my gaze. Instead, she chose the moment to grab three fries and shove them into her mouth, clearly not wanting to speak.

"I did," I said, deciding to leave her out of it. For now.

Shabana gasped and gaped at me. "You did? And you didn't tell me?"

"I didn't realize you were in the class."

"I'm not."

"Then there is no reason you should know."

"But it's *offensive*."

I told her that the professor had spoken to me about it, and he wasn't going to assign anything that insulted the Prophet. "Besides, you don't have to read any of it. Zuha and I are the only Muslims in that class."

"I'm . . . not," Zuha said. "In the class."

"What?"

"I dropped it."

I sat back in my chair. "Really?"

"It isn't a big deal," my secret girlfriend said airily. "I was going to tell you. Can I have some of your sandwich?"

I slowly pulled my plate closer to myself.

"Jerk," Zuha muttered under her breath.

"What matters," Shabana said, "is that it is offensive for me to even see that book around. It is horrible."

"Okay," I said. "Let's try it this way. What, specifically, offends you about the book?"

"I don't know. I haven't read it."

"You see where I'm going with this, right?"

The president of the MSA drew herself up to her not very considerable full height. "I don't have to read it. I've been told by people whom I trust that it is offensive."

"Who do you know that's read the book?"

"My sister's husband's cousin read it."

I folded my arms across my chest. "And what did this hopelessly removed cousin of yours find objectionable?"

"The parts about the Prophet, of course. Look, you're missing the point. This needs to stop. The Muslim students here are being oppressed—"

I snorted at that, which earned me a glare from Zuha.

"We're being disrespected," Shabana insisted. "It is offensive to us to have to see that filthy book on the bookstore shelves and our voices deserve to be heard. So, since you are part of the school newspaper, and you're the best writer we know, we need you to write an article denouncing the professor. It is the absolute least you can do for your Muslim brothers and sisters."

"You really thought coming to me with this was a good idea?"

"I told you," Zuha said. "He's not going to do it."

"Because it absolutely was. You want me to write about this? Sure, I'll write about it."

"Really?" Zuha asked, all skepticism.

"Really?" Shabana asked, all hope and excitement.

"Of course. I'm a big fan of doing the absolute least I can do for my Muslim brothers and sisters. Didn't you know?"

"Don't do it."

I watched as Zuha barged into my room, stalked to the closet and picked out my green and silver Slytherin tie.

"Hi," I said.

She ignored me and marched back to the entrance, looping the tie on the doorknob. This was usually a sign meant to keep my roommate out during extracurricular activities, but somehow I didn't think those were in the cards just then.

"Promise me you won't do it."

I tried out my very best look of angelic innocence. I doubt it was at all convincing. "What are you talking about?"

"Whatever stupid thing you're going to do to the MSA. Don't do it, Anvar. These people are my friends."

"You should get better friends. In fact"—I swiveled around in my chair and held out my hands in a grand gesture, which was only slightly spoiled by the fact that I bumped my left wrist pretty painfully against my desk—"you already have one."

"I'm not kidding."

"Neither am I. I can't believe you're on Shabana's side on this one."

"We're on the same side, Anvar. If you would stop thinking about yourself for like five minutes, maybe you'd see that."

"What the hell does that mean?"

Zuha held out a warning finger toward me. Then she exhaled and turned her back to me, before spinning around again. "Just promise me you won't do anything I wouldn't do."

"Apparently, I don't know what you would or wouldn't do. Why'd you drop the class?"

She gave a dismissive wave. "Who cares?"

"You do, obviously, or you wouldn't have done it. Why are you so desperate to be liked by those people?"

"Anvar, they're *our* people." She shook her head, cutting off my response. "Just tell me. Are you going to do what I say or not?"

I wanted to just say no because she was being ridiculous. Besides, banning books or stifling discussion about them was the beginning of the end. I wasn't going to kneel at the altar of the perpetually offended. I didn't believe that was right and Zuha agreed with me. That's why the way she was acting made no sense.

To prevent a full-blown fight more than anything else I said, "I'll think about it."

"Fine. You do that."

"Babe?"

That single word seemed to draw some of the tension out of her. "What?"

I got to my feet and walked up to her. "You want to tell me what this is about?"

Zuha bit her lip and looked down at the floor. "You're not as smart as you think you are."

"That is a truth universally acknowledged, I think."

The reference to Austen didn't manage to draw even a small smile from her. "We aren't smart. We're stupid, Anvar. We did something really stupid." When I didn't say anything, she whispered, "I'm late."

I almost asked her what she was late for, exactly.

Then it hit me.

"Oh." I sat back down. "That's . . . You're sure?"

Zuha hugged her arms to her body. "Yes."

I sank back farther into my chair. The breath wasn't knocked out of me or anything, but it felt like it. It was as if the world was a race, and my mind was suddenly struggling to keep up. The implications of what she was telling me were . . . like . . . Ma was going to kill me. She was going to literally take a rolling pin and bash my head in. She'd sell tickets, make it a cautionary tale for naughty little brown children everywhere.

I looked at Zuha, at this woman I loved, and even though she was only a few feet away from me, she seemed hopelessly alone standing there. I wanted to get to my feet. I wanted to say something smart and funny and profound. I just couldn't think of anything. Then I realized what she'd said, or more important, what she hadn't said.

"Have you . . . you know . . ." I gestured vaguely toward the lower half of her body.

She knew me well enough to know what I was asking. Of course, she did. That is who we were. "No. Not yet."

I was about to ask her why, when I noticed the tears she was holding back, and realized that she was scared too. I went to her and took her hands in mine. "Okay. It's okay. We'll find out together. You and me."

"It's just . . . you look down on Shabana and the MSA. You think you're better than them. More evolved. I don't think that's true. You're just different. The lives they lead . . . they're honorable lives, Anvar. They're good people. They live by a code, and they would never find themselves in the situation we are in. There are reasons for Allah's commands, and we shouldn't be—"

"Let me just go get a pregnancy test," I said. "Are you ready?"

"Yes. As long as you're with me."

"Always," I said, relieved to have finally found a promise I was able to truthfully give her.

There are times when strangers are better than acquaintances and even friends. When you are buying a pregnancy test for your distraught girlfriend along with a few different brands of condoms, having lost faith in your current one, it would be nice to have a cashier who has absolutely no idea who you are.

"Hey, Anvar. How's it going?" Cindy Chui asked, sounding cheerful before she saw the merchandise I was carrying. "Um . . . congratulations, maybe?"

I shook my head. "No."

"Wow. Straight people problems, huh?"

"Possibly."

"Heavy." Cindy, who'd been in a couple of my classes last year, gave me a sympathetic smile. "By the way, not to state the obvious or anything, but I've heard that these"—she held up the boxes of condoms, and then pointed to the pregnancy test—"are best purchased before you have to buy that."

"Thanks for the pro tip. Listen, Cindy, could you not mention this to anyone?"

"Cross my heart. Are you sure you only want to buy one of these tests?"

"Why?"

"They're not a hundred percent accurate. And some of them can be wrong. I mean, that's what I've seen on TV, so it must be true."

I went back and got two of every single brand of pregnancy test that the store had available. I plunked all eight of them before Cindy.

"So who'd you get in trouble?"

"No one is in trouble yet."

Cindy didn't press me further and, after admonishing me to be a man, finally checked me out. I added her to a list of people I'd have to avoid forever.

Walking back to the dorm, I found it impossible not to worry. I'd heard once, probably in an Islamiyat class in Pakistan, that the human soul has two wings—hope and fear—and that we can only ascend if we find a balance between them.

Had Zuha and I hoped too much and thought too little of the consequences of what we were doing? On our first night together, I'd remembered my grandmother's advice not to play it safe, but maybe I should have reached for her advice to be careful instead. Had Zuha and I done something irrevocable together? I'd been warned about doing things that could not be undone, on that Eid long ago, when there had been a knife in my hands and blood on my clothes.

None of that mattered now. I had to appear calm for Zuha, no matter what happened. I paused with my hand on the doorknob, closed my eyes, centered myself and then walked in. Zuha wiped quickly at her eyes. When she saw the contents of the bag I handed her, she shook her head. "You're an idiot."

I was not in a position to argue the point, so I just shrugged. Zuha grabbed her purse, hid two of the tests inside and went to the bathroom.

I waited.

She was gone an infinity but returned a few minutes later. We sat down together, holding hands, waiting for the results on the two sticks she held.

"Maybe we should pray," she said.

"Seems a little late for that."

"It's never too late."

I grimaced at the tired cliché, but I didn't want to argue with her. Not then. I loved her more than enough to do what she asked, and so, for the first time in forever, I raised my hands, and asked God for help.

It was a glorious day. The sun high and bright in the sky, proof beyond all doubt that the world had not ended. Zuha was not pregnant. Ragnarok had been avoided. Life was incredible.

It was, at the very least, great. I was a little nervous waiting outside Professor Herman's office. My article on the *Satanic Verses* fiasco had come out and it was brilliant. I had absolutely eviscerated the MSA, accusing them of trying to make themselves feel better by fighting small, pedantic, pointless battles, while they did absolutely nothing for the suffering of Muslims in Afghanistan and Iraq. They took no action at all to relieve the pain of Muslims in Kashmir, Somalia or Bosnia. They were small-minded and their decision to pick a fight over a book two decades old, the author of which was living in England and married to a supermodel despite the fatwas against him, was merely emblematic of the pathetic, impotent state of their organization and the Muslim World in general.

Life was good. Zuha and I hadn't spoken much after the scare. I'd called her a couple of times, and though she'd always answered, she'd also had reasons, good reasons to be sure, to get off the phone quickly. She'd also missed a few classes. I'd thought about dropping by her dorm room but Nico, whom I'd brought up to speed on everything, had advised against it.

Everything was fine. Perfectly fine.

When the professor ushered me in, he gestured for me to take a seat. "Sorry for not letting you in right away, Mr. Faris. I wanted to take a look at your article one more time before I spoke to you."

"No worries," I said. "What did you think?"

He cleared his throat, looked down at a yellow legal notepad in front of him that was covered in illegible chicken scratch and looked back up. "First of all, I have to say that I wish you had shown this to me before publishing it. If you had, I would've had the opportunity to tell you that I am no longer teaching *The Satanic Verses*."

I stared at him. "What? Professor, you can't give in to these philistines—"

"Mr. Faris, do you have any idea how many emails I have received about this issue in the last few days? No fewer than three hundred and thirty-one."

"You're kidding."

He shook his head. "I am not, though I certainly wish I were. Apparently, word of my decision to have my students read parts of Rushdie's book spread to a local mosque and then beyond. A lot of people, it seems, have rather vociferous objections. I've decided, in deference to their feelings, not to teach the book until I can convince them that I mean no harm."

"You realize that you will die before that happens."

"Be that as it may," Professor Herman said, his tone infuriatingly calm.

"They could've been picketing outside my door and I would've still taught it, if I were you."

"I understand if you are disappointed in me."

I prepared to speak a polite lie. "I'm not disappointed—"

"Certainly, I am disappointed in you."

"Me?" I'd done nothing, except for writing in his defense.

"I read your work." He picked up his copy of the school newspaper. My story was visible and covered in red marks. He tossed it in my direction and it landed on his desk in front of me. "It is my opinion that it was a cohesive, commendable and well-constructed argument for the free discussion of ideas. I thought that part was very well done."

"But?"

"However, the manner in which you took on the Muslim Students Association—the MSA, is it?—was rather merciless."

I couldn't help but grin. "That was exactly what I was going for."

"So I assumed. Tell me, Mr. Faris," the professor said, taking off his glasses and setting them aside before regarding me from over steepled hands. "Do you think the article was effective?"

"What do you mean?"

"Let me ask you this instead. What was it that you hoped to accomplish?"

I shrugged. "I wanted the MSA to see that they were being—"

"You were looking to change their minds and their behavior then?"

"Of course."

"And do you think you succeeded? I suspect you've offended them. I know you've shamed them in public. However, I would be astounded if you've actually managed to convince any of them that you are right. All in all, therefore, are you not forced to agree that whatever the merits of your argument, you failed to effectively present it?"

My ears felt warm, my face hot. I wasn't sure if it was anger or embarrassment or a mix of both.

"Anvar," Professor Herman said, his voice kind, "you're a bright and winning man. You're also very young. I know this all seems like a big deal to you now but—"

"But I was right. Wasn't I right? Nothing I wrote was untrue."

"It isn't enough to be right. When you raise your voice to speak, you must speak the truth, but you should speak it in the most persuasive way possible. You could make a difference in your community, Anvar. You could be a leader. You have all the gifts. People will follow someone like you, if you stand for something."

"I did." My voice was louder than it should have been. "I stood for you."

"What you wrote was not about me. It was about showing everyone how very smart you are. It was about how you are morally superior to your peers, despite all their religion. It was petty. I expect better from you."

I should've said something clever. Actually, I could have just repeated his last sentence back to him. That would have worked. Instead, I think I managed to nod at him, grabbed my backpack and rushed out of his office.

Within the hour, I'd dropped his class too.

—

Zuha was waiting for me when I got back to the dorm. She had a couple of pieces of paper in her hand, and she was reading them when I walked in. She looked up. She didn't smile. Beside her, on my bed, lay a copy of the school paper.

"You couldn't help yourself, could you? You just had to go after Shabana and the others. I asked you—I begged you—to do one thing for me."

"Technically, you asked me not to do one thing, just so—"

"Shut up."

I started to say something I would have instantly regretted, took a deep breath, then held up a hand to stop her. "Can we talk about this later please?"

She didn't reply. Instead she shoved the papers she'd been holding up at me. I took them. ". . . with his poisonous pen, Mr. Faris spits venom at those who believe, perhaps to mask the reality that he truly has no beliefs himself. His self-satisfied, smug sneering . . ." I read out loud. I was about to ask her what this was, when I realized that she'd handed me the second sheet first. Looking at the first page, I realized it was a letter to the editor. "The alliteration is a bit much. You wrote this?"

Quietly she said, "The MSA leadership asked me—"

"You mean, Shabana asked you. At least have the courage to—"

"I'm here showing this to you before the world sees it, which is more of a courtesy than you gave anyone, Anvar, so don't lecture me about courage."

"How can you be on their side? You don't believe what they believe."

"Stop telling me what I believe." She shook her head, as if trying to shake loose her own thoughts so that they would make sense. "I'm figuring that out. I'll tell you what I don't believe though. I don't believe in stabbing my friends in the back and doing it in public."

I held up the letter she'd just handed me. "Could've fooled me."

"That's a cheap shot."

I crumpled up her pages and tossed them at the wastebasket in the corner of the room. They sailed wide. "Anyway, they're not my friends."

"I am. And I'm one of them. Why can't you get that through your head?"

"You're *not* one of them. You get up from my bed in the middle of the night to pray? Does that make you pious now? What kind of Islam is that? What do you think your MSA friends would say if they knew—"

"Stop. Stop. Stop talking. I don't want this to be how I remember us. Please."

Then it hit me. It was a heart punch. I sat down across from her, on Nico's bed.

"You're breaking up with me. This is you breaking up with me."

She nodded, her eyes barely holding on to tears. She whispered, "Yes."

"No. No, Zuha. I'm sorry. I'm sorry." I hated the desperation in my own voice, but I couldn't keep it out. I didn't know my world without Zuha Shah in it. I wouldn't recognize it. She was so intertwined with my sense of being that to lose her was unthinkable. "I'll tell Shabana I'm sorry. I'll write it in the paper. I'll—"

"Anvar, it isn't about the MSA."

"Then what is it? What did I do? Tell me what I did."

"It isn't about you either. The pregnancy scare was a sign from God. I've been thinking about it a lot. For a while, I haven't felt good about us. I don't feel good about being in a relationship. The more I study what Allah wants, the more I realize that I don't want to sin anymore. I want to be a better Muslim. It's nothing you did, Anvar. You're the same as you ever were, but I'm not. I'm still becoming who I'm going to be."

I don't know how long we sat there together, in silence, her tears falling at a distance from mine, until eventually she walked over, kissed my forehead and was gone.

SAFWA

Khalti Rabia's garden outside of Basra was an unlikely little thing. Getting that many flowers to consistently bloom in that heat, with the salt-tinged waters of Shatt al-Arab, was difficult for a poor woman with few resources.

My mother once said that her parents had made a mistake in naming their youngest daughter Rabia, after one of the most famous women in Islam's history. Like Rabia Basri, the holy woman of old, my aunt had little use for things from the world of men or for men themselves. She'd never married, never even bothered to hope for love from what I'd heard. She seemed content to draw colorful miracles from the earth, which seemed happy to give her what her gardener's heart desired.

Like my mother, Khalti Rabia didn't talk much, but you could tell it was because she didn't have much to say, not because she was being silenced. She was rarely interested in what I was doing, or why, and never asked me to do anything at all. For the few months that I lived with her, I might as well have been alone.

So maybe it is not surprising that I miss her petunias more than I miss her, and that I miss how free I was then most of all. Still she was kind to me when the world was cruel and gave me refuge when I had no home. It is difficult not to love someone who does that for you, even if they are indifferent to your existence.

Khalti Rabia took me with her to Basra itself just once. She didn't tell me what her errand was, and I think she liked that I did not ask. I was more than happy to get a chance to walk along the city's canals, which my mother had recalled so fondly from her own childhood. Of course, my mother had described them full of flowing water, like the veins of a living, breathing thing. Now the water in the canals seemed still and filthy, with garbage floating on top.

The world of my mother's memories had not outlived her.

Dr. Yousef called three times while I was living with my aunt.

The first time he called to make sure I had arrived safely.

The second time he called to tell me my brother had died.

The third time he called, he told me he'd heard that Abu was free.

Abu was different than I remembered. It wasn't just that he had lost a lot of weight, or that his beard had grown long and wild. It wasn't just that the fingers on one of his hands were swollen, his fingernails gone. It wasn't even the fact that his eyes looked like the windows of an empty house, sad and haunted. It was his shoulders. He wasn't as tall as he had been once. He was hunched over, as if unable to stand up straight anymore.

And there was blood on his shirt.

I ran to him barefoot across the path leading up to Khalti Rabia's home, the sunbaked concrete searing my skin. I called out his name and wrapped my arms around his chest. He did not respond. He stood rigid, like stone, and I had to pull away, a sudden, surprising sadness rising in my heart.

"Abu?"

He was looking past me at Rabia, who had come to the door. "I've come to take this one with me."

In her usual soft manner, and as if she was only mildly interested, my aunt asked, "Is that your blood, Abu Fahd?"

I could hear his teeth grinding at the name. Father of Fahd. Father of a boy who no longer was. I stepped away from him.

"No."

"Then whose blood is it?"

"The blood on this shirt is the blood of Yousef."

I gasped, stepping back again, and nearly stumbling. "What did you do?"

Still Abu did not look at me. "Men will come asking about me."

Rabia nodded once.

"What happened to Dr. Yousef?" I spoke louder this time.

My father looked down at his big hands. I noticed not just the missing fingernails, but the bloody, skinned, bruised knuckles. "He left Fahd to die. My son died alone, in the dark, and no one was with him." Abu did look at me then, with dark eyes that had become lifeless—no, not lifeless . . . wilted, like Khalti Rabia's plants that could not bear the heat to which they were exposed. "No one. For that there is no forgiveness."

"Abu, I had no choice."

"You had a choice. You made a choice."

"I would've died there too."

"Then," he roared like a sandstorm, his voice somehow seeming to echo all around me, and through me, "You. Should. Have. *Died*."

Something like a whimper came to my lips, and I felt my tears, and I stepped back again, and this time I did lose my balance, and I did fall. Abu didn't move to help me. He turned back to Rabia, speaking normally again. "She is my daughter. I'm taking her with me."

"If she decides to go with you," my aunt said, "then she is yours."

Abu looked down at me. "Get your things."

I scrambled to my feet and ran inside.

I've thought a great deal about that moment over the years. I think, maybe, my aunt had offered me something I could not then recognize. A chance to live my own life. I think that if I had said I did not want to go with my father, she would have stood up for me. I'm not sure if it would've done any good. I'm not sure if Abu was capable of listening to reason then. He would've probably tried to take me anyway.

As it was, I simply obeyed Abu's command, and I left the garden behind.

I was lost. Abu wouldn't talk to me, wouldn't tell me where we were or where we were going. He just drove his rusting pickup in silence. We went through deserts I cannot name, past rivers I do not know and mountains I did not recognize. We went through cities and, occasionally, villages, and when we were stopped or asked questions, he seemed to always know what to say and how to say it.

I realized then that he had made this journey before. Abu was taking me to a place he was familiar with, on a road he had walked before.

He was going back to an old battlefield, a place where he'd fought a war, and had emerged, at least in his own mind, unbroken.

We were in Pakistan or Afghanistan, but I don't know the name of the village we went to. Not just because I didn't care to find out, but also because I couldn't speak the local language and very few people had any English or Arabic except for the Quran they'd memorized.

We lived in a small hut of bricks, with oil lamps for light and a stove on the floor for a kitchen. There was nothing for me to do there. An old woman had mimed that she could teach me how to knit, but I'd turned her away by shaking my head. At least, I think she was old, because of the wrinkles around her eyes. Women rarely left their homes there, and when they did, it was never without their niqabs.

It was a land of serious men, who sometimes rode out with weapons, and who often prayed when there were explosions close by.

When Abu was home, he wouldn't say a word to me, no matter how I begged, even though he was all that was left of the world I'd once known.

One day I said, "This is not what Fahd would've wanted."

Abu struck my right cheek with the back of his hand, and my head twisted sharply. This had never happened before. Shame and anger and pain and humiliation made my eyes water, and I saw it then, though it was only there for a moment. I saw the horrible smile that flickered across Abu's face. And I knew. I knew he was going to hit me again.

And he did, though he didn't hit my face. He struck my back, and he punched my stomach, and when I went down he kicked me and kicked me and kept kicking me and screaming for me to be silent, to never say his son's name again, until I could hear the words but make no sense of them.

Until I could hear nothing at all.

—

I think I woke, for a moment, and heard Abu weeping. Weeping as if he were Job himself, afflicted with all the sorrows of the world, through no fault of his own. Or, maybe, it was a dream. I can't be sure.

It is difficult to measure time when you cannot stay awake, and when pain is always there. I didn't speak Fahd's name again, but it didn't matter. Abu would hit me for any reason at all, for things I did, for things I failed to do, until I stopped speaking when he was home, until I was afraid to move at all around him.

And then he hit me for my silence, screaming at me to speak, and it would have been easy to speak, to say something, to beg some more.

It would have been easy. It would have been so easy.

I did what was hard.

"Keep at this, Abu Fahd, and you will kill the girl. Most excellent. A model father you are. I think that indeed Allah must be most satisfied with you." It was a woman's voice, a very old voice, and it was somehow full of both laughter and sorrow. "You know, in Arabia, before the Prophet Muhammad, they used to bury baby girls alive when they were born. Allah sent a messenger to put a stop to it. If you are looking to bring the practice back—"

"Enough. Please. It is enough, Bibi Warda." It was Abu. "You cannot make me feel worse than I already do."

"I am willing to try. One never knows until one tries, you know."

A great, shuddering breath came from Abu. "I don't know what happens to me, Bibi. I just . . . when I hit her, it makes me feel . . ."

A long quiet. I felt a cold, wet cloth being laid on my forehead, and realized that I was burning up and that it hurt to breathe. It hurt to be awake.

"I don't know what they did to me, bibi. I didn't know you could hurt a man's body and change his heart. They would strip . . . people, bibi, and bend them over, take a tube and . . ."

They ran out of words again. A gentle, light hand caressed my hair.

Who was this Bibi Warda I was with? It was incredible that Abu would speak of these things to her. Even if he knew her well from a life I'd never seen him live, it wasn't like him to tell stories like this to anyone, especially a woman.

Then again, Mama used to tell me a fairy tale about a servant girl who was suffering under a cruel master. She had no one to complain to, so she would go tell her sorrows to a statue. Maybe there was a limit to how much pain a human being could carry around before they had to share it. Unlike the servant, who'd been overheard by a prince and rescued, I didn't think Abu would find any help here.

"They put diapers on us and laughed when we pissed and shat ourselves. They would cut off our clothes, drag us through the halls and beat us. They kept us standing, wouldn't let us sleep. The things they did to me, bibi, I am ashamed to say that I endured them. Better that I had died."

"Certainly better for your daughter, I think," she said from beside me. "Abu Fahd, I've known you a long time. You fought with my son when the Soviets came. I haven't forgotten. No one here has forgotten who you are. So why have you forgotten?"

"I have spoken to an imam. He has said that I must fast and that I must pray. I will go to Mecca for Hajj. At the door of my Lord, I will beg for forgiveness and restraint."

"Mecca is a long way away, and you have wandered far on the Earth, Abu Fahd. There is forgiveness to be found here, I suspect, if you would but seek it."

Hesitation from Abu. "Will you keep her safe, bibi? For the sake of days gone by."

"I will do what I can."

"Shukran."

"I hope you find peace in the holy city. Tell me, please, that you will not leave until you have a chance to say goodbye to young Safwa here. You should stay until she is awake."

I did not let them know that I was already awake.

And Abu did not stay.

—

I wondered if Abu was coming back at all. He was gone for over a year, too long for it to have been just for Hajj. I stayed with Bibi Warda. There was nowhere else to go.

The village was a difficult place to breathe in, though the air was fine. Bibi Warda told me we were in Pakistan, but in a part of it where boundaries mattered little. Men carried weapons and drove out in beat-up jeeps to use them. If she knew where they went, she did not tell me, and I did not ask. I didn't want to know why gunfire echoed across the ragged, rocky, broken horizon, or why the sounds of planes passing overhead made the old woman pale.

None of the girls here went out unless they were fully covered. It was not like back home, where it had been a choice—not a choice Abu let me make, of course, but still a choice. Here it was a requirement.

I don't know why that bothered me. I hadn't been permitted to leave home in Baghdad without my niqab. Nothing had changed. It shouldn't have mattered to me that I was being commanded to wear it not by Abu but by strangers. Except, for reasons I cannot explain to myself, it mattered a great deal.

Maybe I'd just gotten too used to doing what I wanted, being who I wanted, in my aunt's garden in Basra. Maybe freedom is addictive, like the fruit of a poppy.

Bibi was being kind, I think, in not saying anything to warn or scold me when I began stepping out of the house with my hair and face bare. It was brash, but not too brash. Her little home was near the edge of the village, and it was unlikely I'd be seen since I stayed within a foot or so of the back wall. Besides, I only went out right after dawn, just after Fajr prayers, when the village was waking up. She probably thought it was safe.

Months went by and I was never disturbed. For ten minutes, maybe fifteen, I got to stand alone, looking up at the rising dawn, with only birdsong interrupting the quiet of my rebellion. There were no gardens, no flowers here. It was a wild place that either no one had tried to tame or, if they'd tried, they'd failed.

Then one day I saw him. I later learned that his name was Qais, but just then he was a stranger, leaning against the wall of a neighbor's house, his eyes fixed upon me. It reminded me of the way a hawk or eagle might look at a little mouse.

I jumped and he gave me a smile, which did nothing to calm my startled, suddenly racing heart. I turned to hurry back inside when he said, "You're a beautiful girl."

I stopped. It wasn't because of the compliment. That I did not want. It was because he'd spoken in English, and the pull of words I could understand was impossible to resist, so I turned to face him. "Stop staring at me."

His smile widened to reveal perfectly white but hopelessly crooked teeth. "No."

I glared at him for a moment. Then, realizing how improper it was to be out there with him, at that hour, and what people might think and, worse, what they might say, I ran inside.

He was there the next morning. I'd known he would be. I put on my niqab for that very reason. I should've just stayed inside, hoping that he would get bored after a few days, and give up on . . . whatever it was that he was doing standing there in the fading dark. I couldn't. I was tired of having only Bibi Warda to speak with. The thought of being able to speak to someone else, anyone else really, was too tempting to resist.

He was standing closer to Bibi Warda's house this time than he had yesterday, but his smile was the same as before. "Your beauty is in your eyes. It is Allah's will that it remain unveiled. He has protected you from being covered by his own command."

I made a disgusted sound at the back of my throat. No matter how comforting the language, it couldn't make up for words that were trash. I moved to leave.

"No. Wait. Don't go," he said. "I didn't realize the truth would offend."

I hesitated, then asked, "Where did you learn to speak English?"

"From my father. He was an educated man, a translator for the Americans during the war." He took a breath and added, "Before the face of the enemy changed."

I nodded and studied him more closely. He was broad and looked strong, like he'd be good in a fight. Maybe he was. He had a pointed chin and a pointed nose and angular eyes. He was drawn with harsh lines, but his manner was soft and pleasant.

Something felt wrong about him, though. It was easy to see that he wanted to be liked, so everything he said felt too eager and a little insincere.

"I should go back inside."

"I'll be here tomorrow," he said.

"I know," I told him.

It was only later that I realized he could tell the villagers I'd been sneaking out of the house without my niqab, that I'd been alone talking to a man I didn't know.

He probably wouldn't. After all, he'd done the same thing. He had spoken to me, looked at me when he could have looked away. I knew, of course, that such things almost always went worse for women than they did for men, and so the doubt remained. Every time I thought I was rid of it, it returned, until I could not wait for the next sunrise, so that I could find out what his intentions were.

We became friends of a sort. I looked forward to speaking to him. Being heard is a rare and powerful thing. Few were the days when I parted from Qais Badami without wishing that we had time to share more words.

I learned that he didn't like to go outside during the day unless it was absolutely necessary. The light, he told me, belonged to the Americans. They'd left us darkness.

"There are Americans here?"

"There is no escaping Americans," he said. "They are like the air. Everywhere."

He said he hadn't always been this way. After a drone had burned away his grandmother, however, he'd become afraid to leave home. His father, he said, was impatient with him. He was staying with his grandfather, a pious man who spent his nights standing in prayer. Qais stood next to him, praying, not out of hope that he would be saved, but because of a more mortal fear.

He listened to the stories I had to tell in silence, and if he thought I'd been cruel to Fahd, he didn't say so out loud. It was a strange thing for two cowards to meet in a land carved up by war.

"I know a place where we can be safe from the Americans," he said.

"The grave?"

He laughed, then, realizing his voice had become too loud and might attract attention, whispered. "Two places then. But in this world, there is one place they will never burn."

"What place is that?"

"America, of course. No man sets fire to his own house."

I smiled, though he could not see it. "We should go there as soon as we can."

"Yes," he said. "We must."

He was not smiling.

Again my father looked different when he returned home. He had shaved his head and he actually smiled when he saw me. It wasn't like the smile I remembered from my childhood. It was cautious and guarded and it did not reach his eyes.

"As-salamu alaykum, Safwa," he said.

I didn't say anything. I did not run up to Abu this time, and I did not wait for him to tell me to go pack my things. I just got up from next to Bibi Warda and walked out of the room. I knew what I had to do without being instructed.

I heard Bibi Warda chuckling as I left. "There is a price to pay, Abu Fahd, for the things we do in this world."

"Doesn't your tongue get bitter," he said, "from all the truth you speak?"

The old woman laughed, then followed after me. She kissed both my cheeks, then taking my hands, kissed them as well. "Come back whenever you want."

I nodded, and didn't say anything, because there was nothing to say. As I was heading out the door, however, the old woman added, "And be careful in the morning hours."

Abu frowned as he took my light bag. "What did she mean by that?"

I didn't answer him. I couldn't answer that question, and I didn't want to talk to him at all. I had stopped speaking to him before he left home. Just because he'd gone for Hajj, just because God had forgiven him all of his sins, didn't mean that I would.

He tried to speak to me again, a few times, when we were home. I kept silent.

It was a foolish thing to do. He had beaten me for less, and he was one of the few people in my world with whom I shared a language. I could, however, not understand him, and so I had decided that nothing he had to say would mean anything to me.

The days of silence went on, and for a time, it seemed that they would have no end.

ANVAR

Months after Zuha broke me, Aamir walked into my room without knocking, searching for his laptop, and found me in bed in the dark. My face was buried in a pillow, my shoulders shaking.

He hesitated in the doorway for a moment, then came to sit down next to me. The old box spring creaked uncomfortably under his weight. He smelled, because of his overpowering, outdated cologne, like an old man. For a while, Aamir didn't say anything. Then he put his heavy arms around me. It was an awkward gesture, unfamiliar to us both. His voice was gentler than I had ever heard it before. "What's wrong?"

I shook my head. I couldn't tell him. I'm not sure I would have told him, even if the secret were mine alone.

"I might be able to help you if you tell me. Did you fail a class?"

I couldn't help but chuckle at that assumption. Aamir couldn't imagine a worse fate than flunking a test. "No," I said, raising my head and wiping at my eyes, "I just lost something important."

"Expensive?"

"Invaluable, I think."

"I don't have a lot of money, Anvar, but I'll lend you everything I can and—"

"Don't worry about it," I told him. "I'll be fine."

I wasn't.

I couldn't escape Zuha, and she could not escape me. We saw each other at parties our parents threw when we could not beg our way out of attending, and we smiled at each other as we had in front of other people in the past, as if we were strangers. The difference was that we actually were strangers now, as much as former lovers can ever truly be strangers. Those familiar smiles lacking familiarity, designed once to deceive, became horribly genuine.

Attending San Francisco State became difficult. Zuha was still there and so every moment was consumed with thoughts of her. I constantly wondered when I might see her walking down a corridor, how I would react, what she might say or do.

I transferred to Boston University for my third year. It was there that I learned to believe in God.

It was an intellectual decision, not a spiritual one. I met people in Boston who encouraged me to question dogma. Their influence, combined with the many hours I spent at libraries, immersed me in a river of doubt and ambiguity.

I no longer enjoyed reading like I once had. Maybe because I wasn't used to doing it alone. Maybe because I found myself reaching for my phone to call Zuha after finishing a book, desperate to share with her some artful line I'd found or some beautiful sentence I'd uncovered. For once in my life, I managed to resist temptation and leave her in peace.

I still wandered through the stacks of the library aimlessly. It was, Zuha claimed, a way to let the universe guide you to the next world you would spend time in.

In this way, toward the beginning of my senior year, a black book caught my eye. It was a collection of essays written under pseudonyms by various authors, historians allegedly, who sought to discredit the traditional version of Islam's narrative. Their arguments were factual, not theological. They weren't asking whether or not there was a God but rather, for example, if Mecca had ever really been a stop on a trade route over which caravans passed. The goal was a simple one. Early Islamic history and theology were oral, not written traditions. The Quran itself had lived only in the memories of those who heard it, until years after the Prophet passed. If it could be established that initial Muslim sources had lied about one thing, doubt could be cast on everything they had said and taught. Like Peter was the Rock of the Church, the veracity of Muhammad's Companions was the foundation on which all of Islam stood. This was what these authors sought to break.

They used false names to hide their identities. It was an understandable precaution, in case their scholarship made them targets for people eager to take offense, but it undermined their own credibility. Trained by now to question everything, I did not trust the black book. However, truth be told, it did affect my soul. I no longer trusted conventional Islam any more than I trusted anything else.

I walked out of the library and looked at the world for the first time—with its vast sky, its cold buildings and its fall-plagued trees—as if there were no God.

Never before and never since have I felt my own insignificance as keenly as I did then.

The greatest reassurance of religion is the promise that there is someone out there—someone with all the power in the universe—who cares about you. He records your life, listens to your prayers and wants to ease your pain. The moment that I took God out of the equation, the world became too large, too cruel and too indifferent for me to live in.

I decided then that there was a God. There had to be. I needed Him.

Whether or not he was the same God that I had been taught about since I was a child was a different matter entirely. It was a strange spiritual state to be in. I no longer believed that I believed, though I did have faith without knowing what I had faith in.

I did what any reasonable person who is faced with such a terrible epiphany would do.

I went and bought myself a television.

Muslims have always been a thread, albeit a subdued one, in the tapestry of America. We fought against the Confederacy in the Civil War, so our presence in the States is not exactly a new phenomenon. Before September 11, 2001, however, no one talked about us because, despite our facial hair and head coverings and odd prayer routines, we were like everyone else. We lived our lives in peace and were, though noticeable, generally unnoticed.

After the fall of the Twin Towers, there was no anonymity to be had. Some people saw the thread that represented Islam in the United States and began furiously yanking at it, hoping to rip it away from the idea of America, not realizing that doing so would change the very fabric they sought to preserve. The message was clear. We no longer belonged where we had always been.

I never had to face overt hatred or bigotry. Clean shaven, dressed in Western clothes, blessed by television with more or less the right accent, I thought I blended in.

Bariah Faris, however, did not. In her hijab, she stood out, which was fine. People are allowed to stand out in California. It is, in fact, encouraged. As the years went by, my mother didn't face any discrimination that she felt worth mentioning.

On the sixth anniversary of 9/11, however, my father called.

"You will hear from Bariah soon," he said. He sounded exhausted. "So she can yell at you."

"Why?"

"All your life you've been crooked like a dog's tail. I expect she'll try to straighten you out today. She needs someone else to be angry with. I've taken all I can. Now it is your turn."

I sighed. "Let me guess. You did something to piss off Ma and found a way to use me as a human shield."

Imtiaz Faris shrugged. I couldn't see it, of course, but I could imagine it perfectly in the pause that followed.

"She's not angry with me," he said. "Not really. She's angry with America."

Apparently, Ma had gone to get bread from a grocery store she'd shopped at for years. When her turn came to be checked out, the cashier held out a hand for her to stay where she was, pointed at the customer behind her to come forward and served him instead.

She was made to wait while five people skipped ahead of her, until she was the only one remaining.

"All he said was 'Never forget.'"

"Dad, what the—"

"Don't you start raising your voice as well, okay? I've been getting the business here all day. 'I told you it was a lie. You said all men are created equal but no one believes that. Not really.' So, yes, I moved us here. How long—"

"Did you call the store?" I asked. "You need to speak to the manager."

"That's exactly what I said we should do. I told Bariah, I'll call over and give them a piece of my mind. She wouldn't let me. You don't have the brains to spare, she says." He said, "Anyway, it took a long time, but I've finally convinced her that this is your fault."

"How?"

"If you'd gone to law school, like all the cool kids are doing, instead of reading useless novels all day, maybe this wouldn't have happened."

"That's completely illogical."

"Well, your mother agrees with me. Expect a call soon, okay? I'd say I'm sorry, but you know, Anvar, this kind of situation is pretty much the only reason I had kids. So, in a way, you're fulfilling your purpose in the world. That should make you happy."

"Thanks, Dad."

He ignored the lethal dose of sarcasm in my response entirely. "You're welcome. Don't say I never did anything for you."

When my father said that all the cool kids were going to law school, he meant that the law had become a popular career choice for young Muslims after 9/11. Uncertainty and the fear of oppression breed lawyers. One would think that knowing this would be enough to make people be nicer to one another.

The call of the times played some part in my decision to go to William and Mary and become an attorney. What had happened to Ma in that store—although it didn't, on the scale of injustices committed in American history, even warrant a footnote to a footnote—pushed me in that direction as well.

Mostly, however, it seemed like something I ought to do at a time when I had no idea what I wanted to do and a choice was demanded of me. I'd spent my life pursuing my own dreams, and I had nothing to show for it but heartbreak. It was, perhaps, time to fulfill the dreams of other people.

I went to school in sleepy little Williamsburg, Virginia, in part because I knew it would make my father happy. He wandered around Colonial Williamsburg and then Monticello with a dazed smile on his face, blissfully unaware of the people looking at him strangely, as if he was going to burst into a Bollywood dance routine at any moment. It's easy to forget, somehow, that for being pretty far north, Virginia can still be pretty far south.

"Thomas Jefferson had a Quran, you know," my father told me, an excited gleam in his eye.

"I've heard."

"Do you think they have it on display? Can we see it?"

"I doubt it, Dad."

His shoulders drooped a little at that, but his spirit recovered quickly enough when he went to use a public restroom. "Imagine it," he said, unaware of the fact the zipper on his slacks was still open when he returned. "How many great men have peed in the same spot where I just peed. It's humbling if you think about it."

I shook my head. "I'm pretty sure that bathroom wasn't around back then."

"Those great men didn't need bathrooms. The world was their bathroom, yaar."

My mother, overhearing the comment, made a disgusted sound.

"I'm telling you." Noticing that his fly was undone, my father zipped it up. "History is made by men who aren't afraid to shit all over everything. Anyway, I'm very happy you decided to come here. It's a big accomplishment. You know what, I almost forgot, that Shah girl, what's her name?"

"Zuha," my mother said.

"Right. We saw Zuha Shah the other day. She said to tell you congratulations on getting in here. You remember her, right?"

SAFWA

Three years after I'd left Basra, my world was smaller than it had ever been. Old age had put Bibi Warda in the ground. Abu and I were like ghosts to each other, existing together and not existing at all, and Qais was gone. Months ago, he'd said he would be back, but I knew that was a promise he might not be able to keep.

I shouldn't have wanted him to come back, not after telling him to leave me alone, but he was the only relief from my claustrophobic life. I had done it to myself. I could've made an effort to belong with the people I was living with. I could've tried to learn the language and pretended to be interested in the small details of their lives, so that I was not always so alone.

I never did. I knew where that would lead. I would become entangled in this place, and some well-meaning woman would want me to marry her son, and maybe I would agree, and then there would be children and a little house and then I too would be in the ground, like my mother, like Bibi Warda and the countless others who had lived and died in these mountains. That was not how I would end.

A few months after Abu returned, he stopped trying to draw words from me. He didn't hit me. He came close, a few times, I think, but he held himself in check. The silence wasn't as bad for him as it was for me. He could go out into the world, engage people, build relationships and have a purpose.

In fact, before Qais left, he'd befriended Abu, despite the many years that separated them. I wasn't sure why Qais spent so much time being religious for my father's sake. My father had nothing that Qais wanted, and yet he was at our home often, the two men speaking for many hours about the fine points of theology or the rise and fall of empires. I asked Qais once why he did this, and he just laughed, and gave no reply.

Abu's life was not as quiet as mine and he knew it. He was the center of my life. He provided me food, shelter and protection. I needed him a lot more than he needed me.

He'd use that against me, leaving without notice for a city or another village, and then returning with a cold smile and a question. "Did I not tell you I was leaving? It is hard to remember you are here sometimes."

Before Qais left, sneaking out to speak to him had been the highlight of my life. We traded dawn for midnight and met under the moon. I wore my niqab, until he asked me not to, and then I didn't, because he said he wouldn't come by anymore if I did, and that I could not bear. I did not like his smile when he got what he wanted.

The pull of America had latched on to him like a fever that would not drop. There were no drones there, he insisted. There was peace. It was said, he told me, that you could be whatever you wanted in America. It was the land of opportunity. The land of the free.

It was a nice dream. I began to dream it with him, not just because he would talk about it so often, but also because it spoke to my soul. I began to list for him the things that I wanted there. I would go to school. I would get a job. I would make my own money and have my own place and no one would tell me what to do and how to live.

These were not the things he wanted. He wanted a big house and fast cars and security guards. He made fun of me sometimes for having such modest desires.

Qais had friends who had promised that they could get him there, if he did a few things for them. What these were he wouldn't tell me. All he would say was that it would be good for us.

The "us" should have given me pause. He had joined his hopes and mine, though they were not at all the same. He had other hopes too, hopes that forced me to tell him to leave me alone.

"I'm going soon," he said one night. "And when I return, we will go to America."

I laughed as quietly as I could. We were outside. Given where the crescent moon was in the sky, I thought it had to be a little after one. Voices carried in the night. My mother used to say that the whisper of a woman can travel farther than the roar of a lion. I never understood what that meant until I started meeting Qais this way.

We were sitting across from each other on the ground behind Abu's house. I was, as always, leaning my back against the wall. It was somehow pleasantly cool in the middle of a warm night.

"I know we will," I said. "And George Bush will come pick us up at the airport."

"I like it when you laugh. It's such a lovely sound."

I made a face. "You know I don't like it when you talk like that."

He nodded. Still he looked at me like he had the first day, like I was something he would devour. He got that look sometimes and I always ignored it, because there was nothing else to do.

That night there was something else written on his face though, something between sadness and anger and frustration. "Have I not been patient with you, Safwa? I have been more patient than any other man would've been."

"What are you talking about?"

"You know what I mean. You know what I want."

I did.

Of course, I did.

I'd known from the first time we met. It was easy, necessary, to pretend otherwise. A great tiredness descended upon me. Now that he'd said it, it was impossible to pretend anymore.

I got to my feet. "Good night, Qais."

He stood as well, grabbing my wrist as he did so. I gasped and pulled away from him. "Don't touch me."

He stepped closer. I'd never realized how much taller he was than me until just then. He stepped closer still. I tried to move back, but the wall was there, and though it had been a comfort a moment ago, now, suddenly, it betrayed me. There was a fleeting thought, a thought that I could call for help, but no matter what Abu would do to him, what he would do to me would be worse.

Qais smirked as if he knew exactly what I was thinking. He reached up and with a single finger started to trace a line down my jaw. I slapped his hand away, and he sighed. "You'll let me touch you when I come back. I'll come back with proof that I can take you to America. Then I'll have something you want, and you'll let me have you."

"Get away from me." My voice somehow sounded strong, like the wall behind me, unwilling to yield. *"Now."*

He held up his hands. "I'm making a trade, Safwa. Stay trapped here, with your legs closed, if you want. Or you can be a little more flexible and you'll have a chance to live the life you want. Up to you."

"You should fear Allah."

"He sent you here. He sent me here. This was meant to happen. You know," he said in a perfectly calm voice, as if he were in the mosque, or engaged in a philosophical debate with Abu, "scholars say that the future has already been written. I wasn't the one who wrote it. Neither were you. So how can we be responsible for what happens next?"

Three months passed. It was too much time. My days were empty, and at night I barely slept. Often the sound of Abu shouting out in his sleep in the other room would wake me, and sometimes, though he tried to be quiet, the sounds of him weeping kept me up.

There was nothing to do except think, and I couldn't help but think of what Qais had said.

If Qais could get me to America, he could get Abu there as well. Maybe getting to a place of safety would help calm the demons that haunted my father.

Or maybe it'd be better to just run away with Qais, leaving Abu behind. That would be easiest. There would be nothing holding me back in America then. I would, for the first time ever, be free.

I felt tears come to my eyes when I thought of leaving Abu behind. He was hurt so badly, broken in worse ways, perhaps, than Fahd had been broken, and I knew what had happened when I abandoned my brother. I was not prepared to wonder, for the rest of my life, about what had become of my father.

Besides, I would need him. I didn't know what Qais's plan was, but going with him alone would mean trusting him completely. I wasn't prepared to do that. What had that man who drove me from

Baghdad to Basra, the one who wanted to name his daughter after a gazelle, said?

Trust is always a bad idea.

No. I needed Abu. If Qais tossed me aside or left me alone in some strange land, I wouldn't know how to protect myself. Besides, despite everything, Abu was still family. There was no real question of leaving him behind.

It was only after I'd thought all of these things that I realized some part of me was considering Qais's bargain.

That was all it was to him. Like I was a thing to be bought and sold in the marketplace. My fingernails left deep marks on the palms of my hands when I remembered what he'd said.

Everything I'd been taught, everything I knew about myself, told me that what he was proposing was wrong. It was against the will of Allah. It was a thing beneath me. Mama used to tell me that the most important things a woman has are honor and virtue. Qais was asking for both.

Had Mama been right? It was easy to say yes, but maybe the easy answer was the wrong one. A small portion of one night could make the rest of my existence worth living. It would let me out of this barzakh—this purgatory—and into either heaven or hell. Was the cost not worth the prize?

Qais came back and he didn't seem at all surprised when, in the small hours, I snuck out to meet him, just as always. The knowing sneer on his face told me that he had been expecting me.

Wordlessly, he handed me proof that he could make America a reality. Not a guarantee, but a hope at least. It was a Pakistani passport—his Pakistani passport, though he hadn't been born in Pakistan. It was fake.

Qais took the little green book from my hands carefully, like it was precious beyond words, and maybe it was in a way. He flipped through it until he came to the page he wanted to show me. A visa for Mexico.

"We can cross the border there," he said, "into America. I've heard people cross all the time. It is all over their news. My friends—"

"Who are these friends? What did you do for them?"

"The only question you should ask," he said, "is what you will do for me." He held up the passport. "To get you one of these."

I looked away, from him, from the prize he offered. In the dim silver light of a fading moon, a small animal scurried across the sand and disappeared into the dark. I wondered what it had been. A mouse, maybe, maybe a rat. In the distance, an owl cried out and then everything was still again.

I looked back at him. "Two."

He frowned. "What?"

"My father will come with us. I want two passports. Two visas."

"You're haggling? This isn't—"

"It's a trade." I stood up as tall as I could, though my heart was mired in quicksand. "You said it yourself. That is what I want in exchange . . . in exchange for what you want."

"Expensive." His voice was steeped in contempt.

I didn't say anything. I just kept looking at him, until finally, he nodded and smiled, his hands going to his belt.

"Wait." There was panic in my voice now, but I ignored it and he ignored it too. "I'll do this one time, and then . . . Just . . . promise me."

"I promise," he said, "that I'll get you the two passports you need."

Then he shoved his lips against mine. His breath was damp and sour and sweet, like curdled milk with honey in it. His hands were soft, but he was rough. Sharp rocks on the ground cut into the skin on my back. I closed my eyes. I let him do what he wanted, and when pain brought tears, I did not open my eyes to allow them to fall. Not in front of him.

Never in front of him.

A few minutes later, when he pulled away just before he was finished, I left him lying there.

I ran. I bathed. I wept.

I wept into a pillow so that no one would hear me. Not Abu and not God.

—

Qais came by the house the next evening and spoke to Abu. Their conversation was, as always, about religion.

"Adam was made so that he would sin," Qais said. "His disobedience of Allah was necessary for the world, for all human beings, to exist. From the seed of that first sin, everything in the world has grown. God knew this when He made the first man, Adam, and the first woman, Hawwah. It was all His plan for the fall to happen."

"So no blame falls on Adam?" Abu sipped thoughtfully at a glass full of weak tea he was holding. "My young friend, if you believe that, then we are no better than characters in a book or a play. Nothing we do has any meaning."

"Does that thought never occur to you?"

"Stand up," Abu said, setting his drink aside. As Qais did what he asked, Abu said, "Now balance yourself on one leg."

Qais glanced over at the corner where I was standing, wrapped in my niqab, of course. Then he shrugged and did what he was asked.

"That," Abu told him, "is free will. Now you keep standing as you are but lift up your other leg as well."

"I can't," Qais told him. "I'll fall."

"And that," my father said with a satisfied smile, "is destiny."

Qais laughed. "You're a wise man, Abu Fahd."

"Ali, May Allah Be Pleased with Him, was a wise man. I've just stolen a drop from the ocean of his knowledge. Tell me, Badami, why the interest today in destiny all of a sudden?"

"I was in Peshawar the last few months," Qais said, "and I heard a saying there. On every grain of rice is written the name of the person who will eat it. They mean to say that you will go where you are meant to go, take from the world what Allah has written for you, and you will die where you are meant to die."

Abu, who'd been nodding along, said, "Yes, but—"

"I'm going to America, Abu Fahd. I've found a way to go. That is what is written for me."

My father raised his eyebrows. "I suppose that is good news?"

"It is a chance for a good life."

"A man can live a good life wherever he finds himself, I think."

"But not an easy one."

For the first time in forever, I actually heard Abu laugh. It was a sharp, cutting sound. "Now you have spoken the truth. Very well, my friend, it will be a sad thing to lose your company but—"

"I want you to come with me. You and your daughter. We can all go together. I will arrange everything, all the papers, everything."

Abu stared at Qais as if he were completely insane.

"Think about the life you and your daughter are living. You know there is no peace here. There is only war. Tomorrow, it may touch this village. Even if it doesn't, a drone may come, or just a bomb that falls where it isn't supposed to fall—"

Abu's voice was somehow stern and weak at the same time. "I am not afraid."

"Not for yourself, but think of your child—"

"No."

"Abu Fahd, you must—"

"I will not go," my father said, "to the land of those . . . men. I will not be their neighbor. I will not—"

There it was. The old steel forming in his voice. I recognized it right away. He would talk and talk, convincing himself of his own argument, and would stand for no disagreement.

I had to stop that from happening. I didn't want to stay here. I wouldn't. Not after the price I'd paid for this chance. I wouldn't let Abu make it all for nothing.

"We should go," I said.

My father turned to look at me, his lips parted. It had been years since I had last said a word to him. In his stunned expression, I could see the earthquake shaking his soul at the sound of my quiet voice.

"I don't want to live here. Abu. Abu, please. We must go. I'm begging you. Take me from this place."

He didn't say anything. I'm not sure that, at that moment, he was capable of saying anything. He was blinking fast, his breathing was uneven.

"Please," I pressed. "I'll do whatever you want. I won't ask you for anything ever again. I swear it, but please . . . *Please*. We must take this chance. It is a gift from Allah."

Abu looked down at the ground, taking deep breaths, until he seemed to regain some control over himself. It was to Qais that he spoke again. "Why would you do this for us?"

"It is the bride price I offer. When we are in America, when my best friend and cousin who lives there can attend, I want to marry your daughter. She just said she would do anything. Have her marry me."

I must have made some kind of noise because they both turned to look at me. I tried to speak but I couldn't figure out what to say, or how to say it. What treachery was this?

Then, very slowly, my father smiled. "I see now why you spoke of destiny. Very well, Badami, you shall both have what you want from me. My word is given, and my word is fate."

"I'm not going to marry you."

I spat the words at Qais. It was another night, another dark meeting between us. He'd taken me completely by surprise by asking Abu for my hand. He'd gone on about how a virtuous father could only have a virtuous daughter, and how lucky he was to have secured for himself a bride raised by a good man.

"Do you really think I'd want to marry you?" he asked. "After what you agreed to last night, you're not worthy of it."

"Then why'd you lie to him? Why tell him—"

"I want to make sure you don't escape, Safwa. Do you think I haven't come to know you in all this time? You're a vile little thing. You'd break your promise to me the first chance you got. I was sure that when I got you to the States, the first thing you would do is run. I'd lose you."

"I don't owe you anything anymore. You got what you wanted."

He shrugged, an easy, casual gesture. "I want more."

"You promised it was one time."

"No," Qais said. "What I promised you, you're going to get. I keep my promises. I'm a man of honor, just like your father."

I tried to think of something to say, anything to say, that would make this right. I'd given Qais too much. There was nothing I could do to stop what he was doing.

His chin jutted out, and he looked down at me. "You're mine now, Safwa, until I don't want you anymore. Don't forget it. Now that you are promised to me, Abu Fahd won't try to marry you off.

He won't let you move far from me. He'll keep his word. You'll always be available for me, when I want you."

"That isn't going to happen."

Qais spread his arms wide and stepped back. "As you wish. I'll walk away then. No passport. No visa. Stay here and rot. Is that what you desire?"

I didn't answer him. We both knew he'd won.

THE CROWNING

2011–2016

A single piece, by itself, is predictable. It can only go in one direction. When two pieces come together—when one of your men leaves home and travels the length of the board to earn a crown and becomes a king—it becomes harder to know what will happen next. Experience, you see, can be lethal to certainty.

—Naani Jaan

ANVAR

My mother expected me to use my newly acquired attorney powers for "good." She told me that there were some people in the Muslim community who, in her opinion, were due for a reckoning. She said, "You need to make these wrongdoers chew chickpeas of steel."

"That sounds very unpleasant, Ma."

"They are very unpleasant people and you need to go after them. Like the Rajas. Do you know what they did?" I didn't say anything because, obviously, she was about to tell me all about the Rajas. "They named names."

"You've been watching *Seinfeld* reruns again?"

"This isn't a joke," my mother said. "Some people are like camels. There isn't a straight bone in their body."

"The Rajas are gay?"

My mom slapped the back of my head. "What is wrong with you? Just listen. The Rajas had a dispute with their neighbors over the property line between their homes. Now two Muslim families, you would think they would work it out."

"Would you think that?"

"Anyway, the fight grew worse and worse and then, suddenly, the FBI came and started asking the neighbors all these questions, as if they were terrorists. Can you believe it? It was the Rajas who made the accusation, I am sure of it. Only they would dare do such a thing."

"You have no way of knowing that."

"Everybody knows. It is happening all over. Don't like a family member? Report them to the FBI. Say they are a terrorist and, with one phone call, all your problems are gone."

"Tempting."

This time my mother grabbed my left ear and twisted it painfully. I winced and, through years of practice, managed not to curse. After a few seconds, she released me from her hold. "Anyway, it is becoming a big problem. White people on the television say Muslims don't report on other Muslims. I've been hearing things at the mosque and sometimes it's the opposite. There is too much reporting going on, all for personal gain, and you, my son, you are going to stop it."

"How?"

"Sue these people. Sue them and then sue them some more. Make them chew . . ."

"Chickpeas of steel. Yes, Ma, I got it, but you can't go around suing people just because you don't like what they are doing. You need to have standing." I realized, as she opened her mouth to object, that she had no idea what that was, so I added, "You have to have a personal stake in the lawsuit. I mean, someone has to have done something wrong to you, not just to other people."

"Have you not heard that the Prophet said that all the Muslim ummah is like one body? That if even one little finger is hurting, then the whole of the body is in distress? What happens to my Muslim sisters and brothers does have an effect on me. Therefore, I think I have standing."

"By that logic, what you're saying is that the Rajas were really just hurting themselves?"

My mother seemed to have not considered that. She thought about it for a minute and then said, "You're my least favorite child."

I leaned forward and kissed her cheek. "Yes, Ma. I know."

For the next few years, Ma got to see me stand up for the cause of a wronged Muslim. I took on the defense of Taleb Mansoor. I've never seen her so proud.

It was a strange case, one in which I never got to meet my client. I learned a valuable lesson by taking it on though, a lesson they should teach you in law school. I learned that you should never represent a man who might be innocent.

They didn't teach me that at William and Mary. There, they taught me to be a citizen lawyer, a "Jefferson lawyer." They taught me to believe in the ideals of our legal system, in the sacrosanct nature of the United States Constitution.

"It is easy to be a lawyer," they said. "We'd rather be role models."

Except it isn't easy to be a lawyer. It is certainly not easy to be a lawyer when you come across someone accused of a crime they did not commit.

I have spoken to other attorneys who've represented clients they believed with fierce certainty were innocent, and most of them fear ever encountering that certainty, that innocence, again. They have learned the hard way that the weight of innocence can crush you. The thought that you will lose when you should not, when you must not, can break you. It can shatter your soul. It can make you ask, again and again and again and again, that question most fatal to a litigator: "What if I make a mistake?"

The case that broke me was different, I suppose, in that it didn't end up being about my client's innocence. It ended up being about mine.

I don't know if Taleb Mansoor was guilty or not. He never got a trial.

I shouldn't have taken his case. I had recently passed the bar and had only a few cases under my belt when a college classmate contacted me. She'd heard I was a lawyer now and she was calling because her brother, Taleb, needed help. Apparently, he was in "a shitload of trouble."

That was a bit of an understatement.

Taleb Mansoor was an American citizen, born of Yemeni parents. A perfectly innocuous young man, apparently, until he was radicalized by Islamic State propaganda on the internet. At least, that's how the story went. The government claimed he'd then moved to Syria and started shaping the very propaganda machine that had perverted his own worldview. This made him a high-value target. The United States made it clear he was being hunted—"targeted" is the word they used—for assassination.

Actually, they called it an "extrajudicial killing," which is different only in that it seems cleaner and so doesn't need as much detergent when it gets thrown into the news cycle.

Taleb's family told me that he'd become deeply religious and that he'd gone to Syria to study Islam. They wanted me to file a lawsuit to stop the manhunt, to plead for a trial, for an actual determination from a legal tribunal that their son, their brother, their loved one, was truly guilty of something.

Like I said, there was no trial.

One day, probably a Tuesday, the President of the United States decided, based on secret evidence to which I never had access, that a drone should execute this man. There was no due process, no court of appeal, no jury of Taleb Mansoor's peers to judge him. The White House had marked him for death and the decree of the White House was final.

Taleb Mansoor died in a ball of fire somewhere, murdered by his president.

I was his attorney and he died defenseless.

I stopped practicing then, at least in any meaningful sense of the word. I still made money doing document review and legal research for big firms and took on odd jobs, but I simply could not bring myself to stand up in a court and argue, despite the pleas of my family to continue what should've been a lucrative career.

This was not a sacrifice or a grand statement of superiority. It was an admission of my own weakness. The women and men who continued to fight for truth and justice and the American Way, who continued to challenge oppression when they encountered it, they had my admiration and my awe.

As for me, I decided that I would not spend my life fighting for a lost cause. I would leave the battlefield and live a quiet life.

There was no heroism in such desertion. There was only cowardice.

I became something of a local celebrity after the Taleb Mansoor case. It seemed like everyone at the mosque knew that I'd represented him. They probably did, now that I think about it. My mother, having finally discovered an achievement of mine she felt she could justifiably boast about, told everyone who would listen that I, her lawyer son, had valiantly tried to save an innocent man. She embellished the details, I'm sure. People were under the impression that

I had made a brilliant, passionate argument in court, as if I were Clarence Darrow with a really good tan.

I'm not complaining. It was nice to be known for a little while as something other than just the black sheep of a proper and respectable family. In fact, my newly burnished reputation helped me find an affordable apartment in San Francisco.

My landlord was Hafeez Bhatti, or Hafeez Bhai as he liked to be called. He was chewing noisily on a stale paan when I first walked into his office to sign a lease, orange-red betel nut juice dribbling from the corners of his wide mouth. He looked like he had just been through a passionate make-out session with a clumsy, twisted clown. In fact, if his toupee had been red instead of jet black, he would've passed for Ronald McDonald's morbidly obese Indian half brother.

"As-salamu alaykum, Mr. Anvar Faris Barrister Sir," he said with extravagant, false enthusiasm. "What a pleasure to see you. I was just now expecting you. Welcome. Welcome. We spoke on the phone, yes? You are here for 221?" He pointed to the wobbly chair across from him. "Sit down. Sit. Some forms for you to fill out."

He beamed at me from across his large desk as I sat down and slid a thick stack of documents over toward me. "All formality, of course. I would never turn you away, my friend, for I know you are a good Muslim."

As I did not know that myself, I was surprised to hear it. "Really?"

"Most certainly. You are the one who defended Taleb Mansoor, are you not?"

I nodded. "Not very effectively, I'm afraid."

Bhatti made a dismissive sound at the back of his throat. "The fight matters more than the outcome."

My former client would have probably disagreed with that statement, but I decided not to say so. "You give low-rent housing to . . ."

"Good Muslims exclusively." He smacked his lips and continued to chew on the thick wad of spices, wrapped in a betel nut leaf that was held together with slaked lime. I'm not sure how he managed to speak with that thing stuffed in his mouth. He'd obviously had years of practice. Unfortunately, he hadn't entirely managed to learn how to keep the red juice of the concoction from escaping his mouth as he spoke, so he was forced to be diligent in his use of a handkerchief. "Everyone else pays standard rate."

I hesitated, out of self-interest more than anything else, before saying, "I'm not an expert on housing law, but I'm pretty sure that's massively illegal."

Hafeez Bhai snorted in response and then coughed as he choked on a piece of areca nut from this paan. "What do I care for man's law?" he managed to croak out, once he had recovered a little. "It is unjust. Look at what they did to you."

"They? Did to me?"

"Yes, sir. Brilliant young lawyer like you. Coming up. Now see, they won't give you job. You're stuck doing small-time projects because they won't give you jobs."

"Right," I said slowly, deciding not to tell him that the pitiable state of my legal career was a result of my own decisions, not a nefarious plot by some unknown, mysterious "they." I really wanted to live in the city. "Anyway, can we go look at the apartment?"

"Why?"

"To see if I like it."

"What does it matter? You have no other options, yes?"

I sighed. "Yes."

"Excellent," Hafeez Bhai chirped, dabbing at his mouth with his ratty, stained handkerchief. "Here is a pen. You fill out the forms. Now just for your information, there is a small problem with this particular unit. Not to worry, for it is temporary only and I will fix it soon. You see, I had some difficulties with the last tenant. Don't stop writing, Barrister Sir, keep writing."

I complied, and he went on.

"The last one in there was a finicky sort. Complaining of mold in the wall. He complained, you see, and I don't like complaints. Now, the tenant is gone but the mold is still there. I wanted you to know that in case you have any asthma issues or something. You grew up in Pakistan, yes? You'll be fine. We all have iron lungs. Not like these white folk, panicking over a few little black spots."

"But you're going to deal with the mold, right?"

"Sure. No problem," Bhatti replied. "I will shortly have this fixed for you. Rest easy."

"How many days do you think—"

"No problem. Soon, okay, everything will be fine. Don't you worry, sir, you just trust me. You can fill the rest of the forms later. Don't forget the Eid al-Adha disclaimer. Best to make sure you're aware that the killing of animals in the courtyard is very much frowned upon."

"Is that a problem here?"

"It never hurts just to be clear is all I am saying. I'm sure for you, it won't be a problem. It's a very nice place to be living. Don't look so worried." He peered at me intently, as if trying to figure out if I had bought his assurances. Apparently, he decided that I hadn't because with a grimace, he went on. "Fine, so one time it happened that a guy got a dumba, what they call a lamb, yes? One time someone did the sacrifice right here in the courtyard. Since then, I like to be clear about the whole business for when that time of the year rolls around. There will even be a reminder on the notice board when Eid comes around. Don't worry."

I paused a little over the final signature line. I had known, of course, before I ever called Hafeez, that the apartments were terrible. However, I could afford nothing else in San Francisco. This place was within my budget only due to the accident of my religion and the bigoted largesse of Hafeez Bhatti.

I executed the lease not knowing what taking up residence in Trinity Gardens would mean for my life.

AZZA

Abu and I had to change our names when we left for Mexico hoping to cross the border into the United States. Qais was worried that the Americans, when they had captured Abu, had entered his information into one of their all-knowing computer systems. It was necessary for us, therefore, to become new people.

It was strange. We got to choose who we would be. Abu became Saqr ibn Jameel, though everyone would still call him Abu Fahd—the Father of Fahd—as that was his title. Qais didn't think Abu needed to change that. I don't think he would have. I certainly wouldn't have asked him to do it.

I'd expected Abu to just pick a name out for me, like he'd done when I was born, but he turned to me instead and asked, "And you, my daughter, what name will you take for yourself?"

I'd been taught that names have power. The Prophet said that. There is destiny in a name. It isn't a small thing to pick one. I would have liked some time before deciding, but I'd been asked as if I'd have one at the ready, as if what I wanted to be called, instead of what I was called, was something I would just know.

I'd been thinking about trust a lot then, and what the man who had driven me to Basra, who'd been expecting a daughter, had said. *Trust is always a bad idea.*

He'd also told me what he was going to name his daughter. He was going to call her a gazelle, because he wanted her to be like one. *Free. A little wild. Alert, always, and fast enough to escape when the predators of the world come chasing after her.*

"Azza," I said. "You can call me Azza."

—

We came to San Francisco, because that was where Abu wanted to go. I never asked him why he picked it, but I wanted to think it was in memory of Mama. If she could've come to any city in America, she would've come here. It was where she would've built her own little full house.

One of the first things we heard when we got here was that there was an election for president, and one of the people running wanted to build a wall to keep Mexicans out. Qais said we'd made it just in time.

Anyway, though it was nice to pretend that Abu had chosen San Francisco for our home because of Mama, the fact was that he knew someone here. There was a man who had fought with him against the Soviets, a Yemeni man, who Abu thought would be helpful.

We went to this friend's, and I sat with his wife and two of her sisters while the men planned what we would do next. I overheard them speaking of where to get cash jobs, of a doughnut place that sold social security numbers, and a landlord in the city who might be able to give us a place we could afford to live.

I couldn't tell the women apart. They seemed to be one person at three different stages of her life, that's how much they resembled one another. The middle one was very pregnant and all of them were knitting away furiously, using gender-neutral-colored yarn— yellow, green and orange—to make hats, sweaters and socks for the expected child.

They didn't seem to mind having me there. In fact, it felt like they'd forgotten I was there at all after a few minutes. Once I was offered food and drink, they seemed to pick up their conversation exactly where it had been before I'd come.

"So, as I was just telling them," the eldest of the three, and also the wife of Abu's friend, said, "I got a call from Bariah Faris yesterday. The woman wants all the Bay Area mosques to get together and organize a program—"

"What kind of program?"

The youngest sister got an irritated look for speaking up. "A lecture or something. Something about mosque crawlers. Who cares?"

"Mosque what?" I asked.

"It's nothing, dear. Just informants inside mosques, you know. It's started after 9/11. I don't know why it gets to Bariah. Anyway"—she turned back to her sisters—"the real question is why Queen Faris thinks she should be involved with teaching anyone anything about Islam at our mosque. She didn't teach her son much—"

"I think Anvar is brilliant," the youngest said.

"He's smart. But is he Muslim? Roshni Badree told me she overheard him order a ham sandwich in a restaurant."

"Roshni Badree will say anything about anyone."

"Please," the eldest said with a roll of her eyes. "There is too much smoke around that boy for there to be no fire. I know all you young people like him—"

"I heard he still checks in on Taleb Mansoor's family every once in a while," the middle one broke in, resting her knitting on her lap. "How many lawyers do you think do that? It's been a while now."

"He took that case all the way to the Supreme Court," the youngest one said. "He even went to the White House to talk to Obama, but he spoke the truth with such fury—not that the Drone King didn't deserve it—that he's not allowed to practice law anymore."

"I didn't know that is how things work in America," I said.

The women all smiled at my innocence the way I'd seen married women smile at a bride they thought was a virgin before her wedding night. "When you've been here long enough, dear girl, you will see that everywhere in the world, men are the same."

"A woman will be president soon though and things will change," the youngest one said, and the middle one disagreed with that, saying that there was a primacy or something to get through first, and they started in on a discussion about politics that I could not follow.

"My point was," the eldest said, "that all the noise around Anvar Faris about drinking and dating girls paints a picture of a bad mother. So I don't know where Bariah Faris gets off trying to educate the rest of the world, when she couldn't educate her own sons. She's always getting involved, that woman. What an involved woman she is. I think she should remain confined to her mosque and leave us alone."

"Maybe she isn't a bad mother. The one who is a doctor turned out fine," the middle one said. "Though it is a little strange he isn't married yet. You don't think he's . . . different, do you?"

"I think he's not married because of who his mother is. No one is going to give their daughter into that household. Can you imagine having Bariah Faris as your mother-in-law?"

All three women simultaneously shuddered.

"Well," the youngest said, "I heard that there is something in the works for the doctor. I don't think he'll be single much longer."

"Really? You're such a gossip. Such a horrible gossip. It's a sin, gossiping. Very much a sin." The eldest stopped to consider her sweater, and then pulled at the yarn, undoing the work she'd done over the last few minutes. "Dropped one," she muttered, then looked back up. "Anyway, do tell. Who is the poor girl?"

"Some other Fremont family," the youngest said with an air of disdain that made it clear Fremont families were not as good as San Francisco families.

"Barely matters then, does it? It isn't like we'd get invited. Anyway, I told Imam Sama that I'm not dealing with Queen Faris. If he wants to go along with her nonsense, he'll have to find someone else to help him."

By this time, I felt I wasn't really part of the conversation, so I was surprised when the middle one turned to me. "You might even see her soon."

"Who?"

"Bariah Faris, of course," the lady of the house broke in. "That is who we were talking about, you know. Anyway, I'm sure my husband will send you to Trinity Gardens. That is where Anvar—the lawyer—lives, so Bariah probably visits him. That's where all the discounted people live."

"What?"

"The landlord, Hafeez Bhatti, he rents apartments out for cheap, but only to broken people. People who are damaged or dented or bruised. People no one would pay full price for, I mean . . . though I guess that's not a nice way to put it."

"It really isn't," one of the sisters confirmed.

"I am sorry, my dear. I'm sure you would go for full price if you were for sale."

"Thank you?"

"Anyway, if you want Hafeez Bhatti's help," she went on, "tell him a sad story. He likes sad stories, that one."

"Also wouldn't hurt to take some food," the youngest one said, snickering.

"Now there's no reason to be rude, my dear, though he has gotten bigger somehow. I saw him at the mosque the other day and . . . Anyway, no, I don't think food is good. Too obvious. One mustn't be obvious, you know, when trying to get people to do things." She took a moment to consider me, then said, "It might help if you could cry though. Can you cry when you need to, Azza?"

I shook my head. I'd never had reason to try such a thing. I'd decided, alone and in the dark, that I'd never shed tears in front of Qais. As for Abu, it didn't seem like my weeping had any effect on him at all.

"But why not? It's very useful. My husband says that I'm the YouTube of tears. Always streaming, you know." She stopped to chuckle at the joke. "You just have to think of something really sad, maybe something from the past that still hurts a bit. Given where you're from, something like that has happened to you I'm sure?"

They looked at me expectantly, waiting for me to speak. When I said nothing, they looked disappointed, and moved on to other topics of conversation I cared nothing about.

While Abu was saying his goodbyes, Qais stepped up behind me. Low enough so that only I could hear, he said, "This guy is getting your father a job as a security guard. Abu Fahd will be out all night, and I'll be right next door. We'll have a lot of time to ourselves, Safwa."

I tried to ignore him. He knew that there was nothing that I could do except say mean, powerless things to him. Trying to get me angry, calling me by my old name when I'd asked him not to anymore, all of it was just a show of his strength.

The thought of having him next door, having to spend entire nights with him . . . I took a deep breath and felt like I got no air. Was this how Fahd had felt when he'd gotten sick? I hoped not.

Abu, who had come out to join us, gave me a worried look. "Are you all right?"

"Fine." I did not look at Qais.

Trinity Gardens was not a very nice complex. It was in an area of the city with garbage on the streets and with painted writing on the walls, and it smelled more human than I would've liked. Our neighborhood in Baghdad had once been nicer than this place.

"Just like Hollywood," Qais said to the driver, who laughed and said that it depended on the kinds of movies you watched.

It was definitely not the kind of pretty place the home from *Full House* had been. There were no happy, shining, smiling faces here.

Well, except for Hafeez Bhatti, the landlord, who smiled enough for everyone in the world as he led us to his office. Abu walked in front of us, and Qais kept trying to walk near me. I stayed as far away from him as possible, but we were all going to the same place, and I could drift only so far from the group without making it seem strange.

As Bhatti explained the various lease terms to Abu, Qais leaned close to me and whispered, "I think we'll start using your father's bed. Just to make it interesting for you."

I wrapped my arms around myself and studied a crack in the wall. It had probably started as a small thing and had gotten larger and larger until it now dominated that part of the room.

When Qais finally moved away, I glanced toward the paperwork my father was filling out and saw that Mr. Bhatti was looking at me, a curious expression on his face. I nodded my head, because it was something to do, but the old man did not look away, his mouth working as he chewed on something and considered my existence, as if from a great distance.

Once my father was done, Qais took his seat and reached for a pen. Bhatti leaned over and plucked it from his fingers. "Not you."

"What?"

"I am very sorry to say, young man, that your living here is not a possibility. There are no more apartments available."

Qais frowned. "But you said you had room when we got here."

"Did I? So sorry, I spoke without checking, you see. No, there is no place for you here. I wish it were not so, but you'll have to make other arrangements."

"You should have said something before Abu Fahd agreed to rent here."

Mr. Bhatti nodded. "Most correct you are. Once more, I say sorry to you."

"I guess I'll have to stay with you," Qais said, looking up at Abu, "until—"

"Not possible. No, no. That won't do at all," Mr. Bhatti said. "First of all, it would negate all the price breaks I've given Abu Fahd, wouldn't it? The obviously good Muslim discount. The long beard discount. The niqabi daughter discount. None of these could be given if two unwed young peoples were cohabitating in a place. Astaghfirullah. I'm sure that Abu Fahd, being a pious man, would never allow it."

Abu, who I'm sure was prepared to accept Qais into our house—after all, we'd been with him constantly for our long journey, and I was sure having Qais around was becoming a habit for him—nodded uncertainly. It is hard to disagree with someone who praises you for being religious.

"Second of all, that unit is to be occupied by two people only." Mr. Bhatti jabbed his right index and middle fingers into the air emphatically. "It is a government rule, and in this country, they care about these things very much. So, young man, you'll have to go elsewhere. Not to worry. No problem. Let me make some phone calls. I will put you in your place."

It was a tiny apartment with dim lighting and little sunlight and a bathroom that smelled faintly of mildew, and it was wonderful because I was farther from Qais than I had been in years. I was still in his grip. I knew that. However, to be rid of him, even temporarily, was a blessing. I did a little twirl around the empty living area, and when I stopped Abu was looking at me.

"It's a little horrible," he said. "But we've lived in worse places."

"Much worse." I went to the biggest window to see what the view was like and found myself staring at the wall of the building next door. I laughed.

"You're not angry with Hafeez Bhatti?" Abu asked.

"Angry? Why would I— Oh, because of Qais? He just made a mistake. Everyone makes mistakes."

"I'd feel better about leaving you alone all night," Abu said, "if I knew your intended was nearby to protect you." He walked over to the window where I was standing, shook his head and turned to face me. "Has Qais talked to you about when he wants to marry? He keeps changing the topic whenever I mention his cousin—"

"Can we please just . . ." I waved my arms to take in everything—the lack of everything actually—around me. "It's a good day, Abu."

"It is."

"Then let's not think. Thinking makes it impossible to be happy. We're here. After everything. It's a miracle."

He smiled, but it was a flickering, fading thing that was gone quickly. "It is good that you are happy, Saf— Azza."

"You're not happy though?"

He turned back to look at the wall that blocked our view of the city and the world. "I'm tired. The lands Allah has made are vast, and I've traveled far and seen too much of them. Once I have delivered you safely to the home of your husband, I hope that Allah will not leave me too long on the earth anymore."

"You're so much fun, Abu. It is easy to see why Mama agreed to marry you."

This time his smile caught and lit up his face. "It is different when you are young. The world seems like a simple place, and you can go from desire to desire without worrying yourself about consequences. I fear I've gotten old before my time."

"Fifty isn't old here," I said. "And you still have today."

"Yes," Abu agreed, patting my hair with his heavy hand. "We still have today. Come then. We should talk about how we are going to make this place home."

That awful knock on the door came every night after Abu went to work guarding strangers. Every night, I ignored it.

Mama used to read me a book of English stories when I was a child, and one of the stories was about this wolf trying to get into the houses of three pigs. That was my life. There was a wolf at my door.

He hadn't bothered me for the first few nights, but I hadn't dared to hope. I'd been right. He'd come for me soon enough. He always went away cursing, swearing revenge for my broken oath. Always, he came back, pleading at first, then threatening.

I'll huff and I'll puff and I'll blow your house in.

The days were better, especially after I went back to school.

One day, I'd asked Mr. Bhatti where to get started, and he had me call the local library, which gave me information about adult education programs. I'd have classes again for the first time in a decade.

I worried that Abu would object. He was so used to me staying at home that he might not like my leaving the house. That was how he'd kept his wife. If I'd been more charitable, I would've remembered how upset he'd been when the violence around us had forced him to pull me out of school.

"If the mother is educated," he now told me, "then her children also end up educated. For my grandchildren's sake it is most important for you to do this thing."

What about for my own sake, Abu?

What if I want no children?

And what if I want no husband?

I didn't ask him.

The number of things that went unsaid between us had been growing since before Mama died. They made room for themselves by pushing us further away from each other, until sometimes it seemed like a miracle that he could see me and I could see him.

For the first time in forever, my world began to get bigger again. How amazing a thing a book is. How wonderful a piece of paper and a pen. A lot of things about religion do not make sense to me, it is true, but I understand why, in that desert mountain cave, when the history of man was about to change, God's first command to His last prophet was one simple word.

Read.

It was no easy thing to start studying again, after all this time. One of my teachers, a woman with a kind smile and hair that shone like silver, said to me, "You know that you're a long way from getting a GED, my dear?"

"Yes," I said.

"That's a good start then."

I liked going to class, even though it meant walking in a wet cold that made me shiver, despite the ridiculously oversized coat that Abu had bought for me from Goodwill. I liked that San Francisco was a tall place, and everyone was busy, and seemed to know exactly where they were going, unless they had cameras in their hands and were pointing all around them. I loved watching those people. They were so happy even though they seemed to barely know where they were.

I saw plenty of new things. I walked past a restaurant once and I watched as a car went up to a box, the driver poked his head out, and started speaking. The box answered back, and then the car rolled forward to a window, where a person was waiting to exchange money for food. Why couldn't the person at the window have just taken the order?

I went up to the box to ask why its existence was necessary, but the box told me I could only use the "drive through" if I had a car, which made sense, and asked me to go inside if I wanted something. So I did.

It was warm and everything smelled of baked things and coffee. I asked a man in an apron about the box, and he laughed at me but not unkindly, and he asked me what I would like to drink, but when I saw how much everything was, I told him I couldn't afford it. He smiled and said it was "on the house," which for some reason meant that I didn't have to pay.

Sometimes I got strange looks because of the niqab, but I also had people who were probably not Muslim smile and nod and say "As-salamu alaykum." They almost always stumbled over it so much that it barely had any meaning, but they seemed so proud of themselves that I never thought of correcting them. I didn't even correct the guy who, instead of saying "May Peace Be Upon You," ended up saying "May Death Be Upon You." After all it is, as the Americans say, the thought that counts.

A few people even came up to tell me how glad they were that I was in the country, and that the idea of a "Muslim Ban" was un-American, and that I should let them know if anyone ever bothered me. I didn't know how I was to contact these strangers if I did end up having trouble, but it seemed impolite to ask, so I simply nodded gravely and thanked them for their kindness.

I never walked too far from home. Abu had forbidden it and, also, I didn't want to get lost. I'm sure it would've been no problem if I had. There were always plenty of people to ask for directions. However, I didn't want to ask anyone for anything. I wanted to belong here. I wanted to be home.

Qais was waiting for me as I left the building one day, heading for a math class. He grabbed my shoulders and tried to pull me toward him. I struggled. He laughed. I took the keys I was holding and drove one into his left arm, and he yelped and let go. His hand came up to strike me.

"I'll scream," I said.

"There is no one here."

"Not out here, but there are people inside their apartments. They'll come to help."

He glowered at me, his lean face so close that his thin nose was almost touching mine. There was a moment of doubt, and then he stepped back, arms raised. "I'm owed a debt."

I thought about going back inside but decided against it. If I retreated, he'd see it as a victory. Any sign that he could control me would make him bolder.

I should've been scared. My mind was telling me that, but my heart wasn't. What I felt was not fear. It was a hot coal at the pit of my stomach that lit my blood on fire, and all that was left inside me was the desire to set the world alight.

Even when I'd been furious with Abu, even when he had hurt me, I had never wanted to hurt him. I had wanted to punish him. I'd done that with silence. This, however, was more than that. I didn't want to just punish Qais. I wanted to burn him to ash.

"Touch me again," I said, "and I will end you."

He laughed. "How?"

"I'll call the police."

Qais folded his arms across his chest and leaned against a parked car. "And then what? If you do that, I'll tell them that you're here illegally, that Abu Fahd is too. I might go away, but no matter where I go, you both are coming with me."

I looked away from him, and when I looked back, he was grinning.

"Why are you being so unreasonable, Safwa—"

"Azza."

He rolled his eyes. "Why are you treating me like I'm a bad person? You're the one who broke our deal. I'm owed payment. I'm just trying to collect. Nothing wrong with that. It is only fair. Doesn't Islam teach us to keep our promises?"

"Don't you dare—"

He shook his head, like a man wronged showing great forbearance. When he spoke again, he spoke slowly, as if he was speaking a language I had difficulty following. "You know I can win whenever I want, yes? All I have to do is go to Abu Fahd and tell him I'm ready to marry. Then all this nonsense of leaving the house will stop. You'll be mine to use, mine to keep."

"You don't want to marry me."

"I don't," he said, "but I will. If you make me. So don't try my patience by making empty threats. Otherwise"—he held up a warning finger—"I'll take your life from you. Whatever it is you're trying to build, I'll knock it down. So . . ." He stepped forward and grabbed my arm so hard that I knew I would bruise. "When I come knocking on your door tonight, you open the door. Do you understand?"

I tried to pull away from him, but he just held on tighter, his grip a ring of pain. Then he pushed me and I stumbled back, my shoulder hitting the gate I'd just walked out of. As Qais left, his promise to return that night heavy in my heart, I decided not to go to class after all. My hands were trembling too much to take notes, and I didn't think I could learn anything at all.

Qais was done knocking. Instead, he'd been slapping his hand against the door as hard as he could, again and again, screaming my name. I sat on the ground in the kitchen, leaning against the old green fridge that came with the place, my head between my knees. The hum of the machine, so routine, so disinterested, was comforting somehow.

He'd go away soon. He'd go away. Soon.

When? It felt like he'd been out there forever.

For a moment the strikes stopped, and then there was a heavy, strong thud, and a muffled grunt from outside. Still Qais. Throwing his shoulder against the door now, as if he could break it down. Could he? No. It wasn't possible. Not—

Again he slammed into the door. If there had been any pictures on the walls, they would have fallen.

The door would hold. Let the door hold. Of course, it would. Even still, because I had nothing else I could do, I prayed.

Then I heard a new voice. A shouted warning, and Qais's assault stopped. Arguing. I got to my feet and stepped closer. I heard Hafeez Bhatti's voice.

"You need to leave here. All the people are calling and complaining about your noise. What is it that you're doing here exactly?"

"I need to get in there."

"And why are you needing so badly to get in there?"

"I left something I own in there."

"Very good. Most excellent," Hafeez Bhatti said. "And trying to get what you own, you'll ruin what I own, will you? This is my building. Mine. It is no place for loafers and thugs. If you need something, you come back in the morning, when Abu Fahd is here. You understand?"

Qais slapped his hand against the door again, and I jumped back.

"Abay, what in the heck do you think you're doing, you . . . you . . . rough person. You think I'm messing around with you? I will count to three, and if you're not gone from here, I'll call the police, you understand?"

"No, Mr. Bhatti," Qais said, suddenly sounding calmer now. "There is no need for that."

"One."

"This is a personal matter between me and my fiancée and—"

"Two."

"If you will just let me explain—"

"And the last one," Bhatti said, "is going to be number . . . that's right. You better run, you no good piece of . . . this and that. If I ever see you in the building without Abu Fahd, I'll call the police on you. I swear by Allah I will." He heaved a great sigh, and after a long moment of silence said in a calmer tone, "He's gone."

I bit my lip, trying to decide what to do, and then I unlocked the door. The landlord, armed with a cricket bat, was red in the face.

If he was surprised to see what I looked like without my niqab, he didn't let on. Instead, he reached over to pat my head awkwardly.

The gesture was so much like something I imagined Abu would've once done for me but couldn't now because I was caught in a web of secrets, that it threatened to break a vital part of the dam I had built within myself, and for a moment I was worried that I might break down and cry.

"Thank you," I managed.

"Bad apple that one." Bhatti waved his bat in the general direction Qais had walked off in. "You'll be having more trouble with him in coming days, I'm afraid. Tonight, I think, you'll be fine." He peered at me closely, then said, "Still, if you're not very much against it, I would like to talk to you. Will you come to my office?"

"You could just come in."

Bhatti bobbed his head up and down, but I think he meant to shake it. "I don't think your father would be liking that very much. I'm old but not old enough, I think, to visit a young woman alone in her home at this time. Come down when you've gathered yourself. Besides, I must return this bat to Mr. Sethi. He's very much attached to it."

When I got to Mr. Bhatti's office fifteen minutes later, he offered me a styrofoam cup with steam rising from it. "My thinking is," he said, "that you are in desperate need for some tea. A good Indian chai is the cure for everything in the world."

"I'm sure that isn't true," I said. I took the cup from him though.

"It won't work if you don't have faith. Belief is a must for things to turn out the way you want," he said. "The universe is magic. Tell me, is the Heisenberg principle something you know anything about?"

"No, I'm—"

"Once upon a time, there was a man called Heisenberg." He frowned, took a sip of his tea and smacked his lips together in appreciation. "He found out . . . So the universe is made up of atoms, right, and these atoms are having protons and electrons in them. You understand this?"

I nodded and tentatively tried the milky tea he had given me. It was nice, but it didn't make anything about my life better at all. Except, I guess, for the few moments I was having it.

"Good. I wasn't sure if you'd been to school. Your English is most surprisingly good for a refugee. I myself have lived here many years of my life, which is why my English, also, is very excellent."

I had no idea what to say to that. Bhatti didn't wait long for a response.

"Anyway, what was I saying? Yes, Heisenberg. So, he realized that human beings can't ever know the location of an electron and the velocity of that electron at the same time. We can know where it is, or we can know how fast it is going to where it is going, but we can't know both. Are you seeing how that's magic?"

"I'm sorry, I don't—"

Bhatti threw his arms up in the air and slowly brought them back down to put them on his head. "The power of the human mind, don't you see? We focus on this tiny thing, and the power of our focus makes it move. It's magic."

I blinked. I didn't know anything about this Heisenberg, but I doubted that he had discovered proof that magic was real. If he had, he'd be famous. Anyway, even if Bhatti was right, and human beings could move tiny particles with our minds, it seemed like a pretty useless trick. If that was the extent of magic in the world, then it was a sad thing.

"The point," Bhatti said, "being only that in order to achieve any change in the world, the human mind must act on it. Simple, no? And, as you must already be knowing, they say that two minds are better than one. So, Azza bint Saqr, tell me your story, and I will put my most considerable mind to trying to solve your problem, and like magic we will find you a solution."

"It isn't a very happy story," I said.

"How many happy stories do you think I'm getting to hear in this office?" he asked.

I wanted to tell this man my secrets. There was something about Mr. Bhatti. His eyes seemed to shine out from his round face with a light that was soft and warm. And it would've been a relief to just talk to someone.

But I didn't. I barely knew him, nice as he seemed. The risk that he would tell Abu was too high.

I shook my head.

"There it is," he said.

"What?"

"The Heisenberg principle as applied to human beings. Can we call it the Azza principle? I'm allowed to know where you are, but the knowledge of where you have been and where you will go is not for me. Human beings, I'm thinking, are not so different from the electrons."

"I know you're trying to help, Mr. Bhatti." I sat up in my chair, leaning forward a little to convey my earnestness. "But I just—"

He waved off my explanation. "It is your story. Tell it. Don't tell it. That is for you. I can, being myself keen and sharp, guess that you're having trouble with this Qais Badami character, no?"

I nodded.

"Your father wants you to marry him. You don't want to marry him. In point of fact, you see, I got this much from the very first time you were here with him in my office. That is why I didn't give him a home here." He smiled and sat back, nodding appreciatively at his past self. "You need to be rid of him. Tell me, Azza— No, no, for this part only, I must insist that you look at me. Look me in the face and tell me only the truth. Has he hurt you?"

I met his eyes. "Yes."

"Have you told your father?"

"I can't."

"And you can't or won't go to the police."

I nodded.

"And this man, Qais, in your opinion, he won't stop?"

"He told me he would take my life from me."

Bhatti drew a deep breath. "I believe it. I saw his face. I saw how much anger he's got. You very much need to be ready to protect yourself. I'll be doing what I can to keep him away from the building, but . . ."

"I understand. And thank you for tonight. I—"

He gave a dismissive flick of his wrist. "Not at all. It is most unfortunate that I can do so little for you." Then he paused and seemed to consider something. "Actually, there is a lawyer who lives here. He could maybe help somehow."

"A lawyer? I don't need a lawyer."

"Most people who end up having to say that out loud," he chuckled, "find out they were very wrong. Listen, there is a youth group at the mosque. College children and the sort. Imam Sama himself told me my lawyer friend is going to be a special guest there next week. I want you to go."

"Why?"

"Indulge me. Just go and be sure to speak to the speaker. You don't have to tell him anything about Qais. Not unless you want to. I just think that he's the kind of person that . . . Let's just say I suspect knowing him will be making a difference in your life. He's a good man. Well, okay, so maybe not a *good* man. But he's not a bad man. Not really. He's tried to help people."

I frowned, skeptical and more than a little confused by what he thought speaking to some stranger would do for me.

Bhatti held out his palms, as if to show that he had nothing up his sleeve. "It is just a feeling that I'm having. My hair, you know, I haven't bleached it white in the sun. I know a thing or two. Besides, what I ask is but a small thing, no?"

ANVAR

Allegations that I had defamed the Imam of our mosque quickly caused any goodwill I had accumulated with the Muslim community here to evaporate. For the record, I would like to state that I never actually said that the Imam had a venereal disease. That should be absolutely clear from the outset.

I probably wouldn't have bothered going to the mosque on Fridays if it weren't for my mother's spy network. I was certain that she'd had the masjid uncles tracking my attendance, because if I missed a couple of services, I started getting calls.

Debt collectors are relentless, but they've got nothing on Bariah Faris.

When I missed more than a couple of prayers in a row, Ma started sending Aamir, who worked near my apartment and attended the same mosque as I did, to pick me up. This was enough to ensure that I showed up for Friday services regularly. I'll torture myself voluntarily, thank you, before I let Aamir do it.

The Imam, Ahmed Sama, was an earnest and cheerful man of about forty from Burkina Faso. He usually walked around San Francisco in a skullcap and thobe, his beatific smile bright and unwavering. He had this manner of making you feel welcome and wanted, as if he had been waiting a long time for the exquisite pleasure of your conversation.

Last Friday, he came up to me after the service was done and said that he needed a favor. He had organized a youth group and was hoping I could come talk to them. He wanted to give them an idea of what it was like to work—or in my case, not work—as a lawyer.

"They should have role models in the real world. Not just movie stars and rappers and sports guys."

"You've got the wrong person, Sheikh. I can't give a talk at a mosque to inspire people. I'm a remedial Muslim."

"You stood for Taleb Mansoor."

"Who, as I keep having to point out, died in rather gruesome fashion."

"You tried," the Imam reassured me. "What happened was Allah's will."

"That's really more your department than mine."

"It's just a few college kids," he said. "No reason to feel intimidated."

"Easy for you to say. I practice Islam at a fourth-grade level."

He patted my shoulder and smiled, obviously mistaking the truth for self-deprecation. "You'll do fine. I appreciate it. I always have to find new ways to engage them. Every time I believe I am making progress, something happens to distract them from the True Path. Americans like to keep you entertained. It keeps kids from thinking. There is always a big game or a playoff, new music or a new show they just have to watch. Every time I feel like they're starting to focus on spiritual matters, the material world seduces them again."

"You must feel like Sisyphus."

The Imam was not familiar with the Greek myth, so I had to explain it to him before taking my leave, promising to return next week at six for his youth group.

I was a little early for my talk and found myself alone in the mosque.

An empty mosque is a strange place. You can be alone there and yet, somehow, you cannot be alone. There are no icons, no idols or images. There are no visible, tangible signs of any divine presence. This absence, however, is a lingering challenge to the soul, a question as to whether human beings can find nothing where they see nothing.

It was disconcerting, but I was not alone long. Soon the first student, a woman, arrived. She entered the prayer hall wearing a full niqab, a black, flowing garment with a veil that covered everything but her pale green eyes. It was meant to protect her modesty.

Her exposed eyes, however, were not modest. They were bold and alive, yet there was something about them that was either more than human or less than human. It was a light, or perhaps a shadow, that was a little sorcerous, and a little wild.

I stared at her and she stared right back.

For a moment, I forgot where I was and then, within seconds, I think, the spell was broken as a few other students walked in, chatting amiably. None of them approached or spoke to the girl in the niqab, who sat aloof and inscrutable. I introduced myself and we waited for the Imam. Ten minutes passed, then fifteen. It was clear that Imam Sama was not going to attend. "Maybe he's sick," someone finally suggested.

"He's probably just tired," I said. "He's got a touch of Sisyphus."

No laughter followed my joke. Instead, frantic whispering ensued. Ignoring it, I launched into an impromptu talk. I decided not to discuss the experience of being an attorney, despite the Imam's instructions. His absence meant that I could say anything I wanted and, on that particular subject, I had nothing to say that would inspire my audience.

I told them, instead, about Mikey the goat, because Eid was coming soon and they, having grown up in nice American neighborhoods, had inhabited a world where slaughtering livestock in one's front yard was generally not a done thing.

I also told them of my paternal uncle who never actually managed to dispatch the animals himself. He was, as he freely admitted, too disturbed by killing and too nauseated by the sight of blood to participate in the ritual Eid sacrifice. This was remarkable because he had served in two wars against India, where he had been charged with operating a tank.

"But you killed people in 'sixty-five and 'seventy-one," I had said, sensible even as a child to the inconsistent nature of his claimed revulsion for violence.

"Well, all I was required to do was push a button, see?" my uncle had replied, jabbing his index finger at my forehead. "I would push a button, just like so"—this was punctuated with another poke— "when I was ordered to and then, far away, somewhere, there was an explosion. That's all it was."

No one seemed particularly impressed or even amused. In fact, some of the students were visibly disappointed. I'm not sure what they'd been expecting but, whatever it was, I hadn't managed to deliver it. Fortunately, my life had left me uniquely prepared for vague disapproval. I shrugged it off.

When the group dispersed, the woman with the striking eyes came up to me.

"I'm Azza."

"Anvar."

"Yes. I've heard of you. From a lot of people. Everybody talks about you."

I gave a self-deprecating shrug. "Not everybody, I'm sure."

"People say you're a bad person," she said in a soft, hoarse voice.

The unexpected nature of the remark threw me off a little. "Well . . . I didn't know that. They don't say it to my face."

"Word among the young women is that you drink. You've had girlfriends. That you don't pray. That you smoke. That you eat pork."

"Well, that's simply not true. I don't eat pork."

"You admit the rest then?"

"Do I admit to being a bad person? No. I will, however, admit to being a bad Muslim, which is an entirely different thing."

Her light eyes narrowed and seemed to get more intense somehow. I ran a hand through my hair, glancing at the door. I nodded at Azza and began to move away.

"Wait," she said. "We live in the same apartment complex. Trinity Gardens. Tell me which unit you are in."

"Why?"

"Because I am a bad person and a bad Muslim. I'd like to be worse."

"This is a calamity, Anvar Faris, Barrister Sahib," Hafeez Bhatti screamed, his voice shrill, spittle stained with paan juice spraying from his lips as he rushed toward me. "A disaster of the very first order. Is it true? Why would you say it if it isn't true? However, if it is true, sir, then why would you say it? And say it to such impressionable young minds at that. You must make sense of it for me."

"What are you talking about? I just got back from the mosque."

"I am knowing that, Faris. Sirji, my nephew, was there at the talk you gave. Why would you say to him—" Hafeez dropped his voice to a small, barely audible whisper. "Why would you say that Imam Sama is infected with the gonorrhea?"

"I never said anything about gonorrhea."

"My nephew was there."

"I was there too. I was the one speaking, remember?"

Confronted with my indignation, Bhatti hesitated, then tried to snap his fingers but produced no sound. "Absolutely right you are. Not gonorrhea. Syphilis."

"I never said anything about . . . Oh. Come on. Really? I didn't say he had syphilis. I said he *was* Sisyphus. The Greek guy who pushes the boulder up the mountain."

"You think Imam Sama is Greek?"

"No. Jesus Christ . . ."

It went downhill from there.

Two hours later, I was on the phone with my mother, still trying to explain myself.

"Would you like to tell me how you ended up giving the Imam syphilis?"

"I was talking about Sisyphus. It isn't a disease. It is a myth. You can't catch Sisyphus, Mom."

She gave one of her patented Bariah Faris sniffs of disdain. "You can if you're not careful."

"I honestly can't even tell if you're joking right now."

"Just stay away from the mosque. Muslims have enough problems without you adding to them. The Board of Directors will probably have to start an inquiry just to clear all this up. Poor Ahmed Sama will be humiliated. How many times have I told you to stop being so clever?"

"Too many times."

"You never listen, that's your problem, Anvar. I wish you were more like your brother. He is such a good boy. When I told him who I had picked for him to marry, he didn't object at all. Didn't have any problems with it. I don't really know where we went wrong with you. You should come over this weekend. We're going to the girl's house . . ."

"What girl?"

"The girl I picked for Aamir to marry, of course. She's so sweet. I've always liked her. And what a fantastic family. You remember . . ."

Someone knocked on my door.

"I have to go, Mom."

"What is this 'Mom' nonsense you've started like we're some white family?"

"Fine, Ma. I have to go. There's someone here."

"Who is it? If it's Imam Sama, tell him you're—"

"Sure. Bye, Mom." I hung up on my mother and opened the door to my apartment.

It was the niqabi woman from the mosque.

I moved aside, and she started to walk in. Then she paused, hesitating at my threshold.

"Azza?" I asked.

She frowned, as if confused or disoriented for a moment, like I'd called her by someone else's name. "Sorry. I just haven't . . ." She shook her head, stopped speaking for a moment, took a deep, bracing breath, then looked at me with those haunting and haunted green eyes of hers. "I shouldn't be here."

I didn't know what to say to that, so I just told her the obvious truth. "You don't have to come in. You're free to do what you want."

"Exactly."

Before I could ask her what she meant by that, she made her decision, and stepped inside.

She came the next day, and the day after that, and then after two days when I didn't hear from her, she came again.

"I feel like we don't talk anymore."

Azza, who'd been coming back to bed, paused in the bathroom doorway. "What?"

"You heard me."

"What do you mean 'anymore'? We've never talked."

"We should. I'm an extremely accomplished conversationalist."

"That's not why I come here."

I placed a hand over my heart. "Ouch."

She pulled open the loose ponytail her hair was tied in, and though it had looked perfectly fine, started to redo it, her eyes never leaving me. When she was done, instead of coming closer, she chose to lean against the doorframe. "What do you want to talk about?"

"The weather? I could tell you what Mark Twain said about San Francisco. Or maybe something more interesting. Like why Hafeez Bhatti sent you to the mosque to talk to me, maybe."

She let out a sharp breath.

"He didn't tell me anything," I assured her. "He just asked me if I'd been able to help you."

"He should mind his own business."

"He's from Pakistan. We're incapable of doing that. Are you in some kind of trouble?"

She shook her head. "I said I don't want to talk about it."

I held up my hands in the universal gesture of surrender. "Fine."

Azza stalked over to the chair on which the rest of her clothes, and her niqab, were draped. She began to dress.

"You don't have to leave."

"Don't tell me what I have to do," she snapped.

I didn't respond. You can really surrender only so often. Do it too much, and it loses all meaning.

"This"—she pointed a finger at me and then to herself—"isn't a relationship. I don't need anything from you."

"I'm sorry."

"And don't talk to other people about me."

"I wasn't like—"

It was no use. She was already walking out of the room.

It was a while before she returned, and when she did, things went back to the way they had started, as if nothing had happened. It went on that way for weeks. I never knew when she'd knock on my door, or why she suddenly wouldn't for days. I asked for no explanations. I'd been taught in school the story of Moses and Khidr and the futility of asking questions when you're not supposed to. Also, I'd been raised by Bariah Faris, and in her house curiosity was generally frowned upon.

Then one night she came by and said, "We can't tonight. It's my time of the month."

"Okay."

Azza looked at me like she expected me to say something else. When I didn't, she went on. "I wanted some tea. You said you made good tea."

I'd never said anything of the sort, and I made horrible tea, but I nodded. "Absolutely."

"What kind of tea do you have?"

"There's more than one kind?"

She paused taking off her niqab.

"That was a joke."

"Was it?"

I went over to the kitchen and opened the coffee cabinet. "I have some Moroccan mint."

"What makes it Moroccan?"

"I don't know. It's green."

"Fine," Azza said, and headed to sit down in the living room for the first time.

My phone buzzed. It was Ma.

"You aren't going to answer it?"

I shook my head. "Just my mother. It's either still about Imam Sama or it is about the talk she wants to give at the mosque about mosque crawlers. She's been trying to get me to help with the research. She emails me something new every day."

"I've heard about those. Mosque crawlers, I mean."

"Yeah. Anyway, Ma had these friends, the 'chickpeas of steel' people—"

"What?"

"She lost some friends because a family here, the Rajas, allegedly, falsely reported them for terrorism. The FBI came and interrogated Ma's friends, and they got so freaked out, they moved back to Pakistan. Anyway, it's been a thing for Ma ever since."

"But your mother's friends never really got in any trouble?"

I shrugged. "There must've been no evidence against them. Anyway, Ma thinks that it's a way of making people you don't like disappear. I think she's just worried Dad is going to report her one day."

The joke didn't land with Azza because she didn't know them. Without replying, she picked up the remote and turned the TV on. The news was about the election.

It should have been boring, like a race between a tortoise and a hare, the outcome evident. There should have been a lack of suspense, with the victory of the Democratic Party candidate and former Secretary of State obvious. However, Nero was in town and he was putting on a show you couldn't look away from. An anti-immigrant, anti-Muslim, far-right fervor had gripped the Republican Party, and their candidate was leading a nationalist movement that promised to "Make America Great Again."

After a few seconds Azza made an irritated sound and turned the screen off. I smiled. "I wouldn't worry. He isn't going to win."

"It doesn't matter."

I looked at her. "Of course it matters."

"They're all the same."

"They're really not."

"No?" Azza asked. "Abu told me that when that Secretary of State woman came to Afghanistan, and the bunch of cars that went to pick her up—"

"A motorcade?"

"Okay." Azza swatted at the air, as if my vocabulary was an irritating fly, getting in her face. "Anyway, as Americans were going to pick her up, they ran over a woman crossing the street. They didn't stop. They hit her and left her in the middle of the road."

"That's horrible."

"They come to our countries and they pretend to care, and they run us over and they don't stop to see how bad they've hurt us. They never stop, which is what they're supposed to do. It's American policy, according to the rules someone wrote down and all of them agreed to follow." Azza tossed the remote aside. "It doesn't matter who wins. They'll still be running us over. So who cares?"

That was the most I'd ever heard Azza say, and I liked hearing her voice, so I let it stand for a while. When the tea was done brewing, I carried it to her. "I understand what you're saying but—"

"Do you think they wonder if the woman they ran over survived? If she had children? Do they wonder what might have happened to those children if they didn't have anyone else?"

"I don't know," I said.

"I hope they do," Azza said, her voice quiet. "I hope they can't ever sleep at night."

I put the tea she still hadn't taken from me on a table beside her and sat down across from her. We were quiet for a long time. I held my cup in both hands for warmth and watched steam rise from it.

"Go ahead," she finally said. "Ask me. Ask me what you're thinking."

I glanced up at her, at the pain on her face, and said, "What happened to you?"

She looked away and didn't answer.

I cleared my throat. "Let's not talk about politics. Let's talk about something light and fun like—"

"I'm engaged," she said.

"Or we could talk about that . . ."

Azza was engaged to Qais Badami. I'd met him at the mosque a couple of times. He tried hard to be pleasant, but came off as so intensely friendly that it was a little uncomfortable.

"You're not going to ask me why, if he thinks he has spoken for me, I come here?"

"Do you want to tell me?" I asked.

She shook her head.

"Then I'm not going to ask you."

It was the right thing to say, I think, because we started talking a little more after that. I learned that her father was a man called Abu Fahd, a security guard who worked nights, which was why she had to return home by dawn, before his shift ended.

I told her about Dad and Ma and Aamir.

We played checkers, and I didn't let her win once. She came close to beating me a couple of times though. She played with a reckless-ness that would have impressed Naani Jaan, I think.

When we weren't sleeping together, we talked most about mundane things, like homework she was having trouble with or how ridiculous Hafeez Bhatti's toupee looked. I was glad for these conversations, shallow though they were, because I was ducking my family's calls, certain that the whole Imam Sama saga was still ongoing.

Besides, despite the fact that Ma's society would've expected me to be involved as the younger brother, I was determined to recuse myself from having anything to do with Aamir's arranged marriage. I had no interest in watching my brother paraded around like a prize pony at a fair as a litany of his virtues was recited for a prospective mate. Aamir would be enjoying himself too much for such a scene to be bearable.

The lunar calendar sometimes has interesting interactions with its solar counterpart. That year Eid al-Adha, the Festival of Sacrifice, was set to fall on September 11. At the last moment, it was decided—allegedly by the cycle of the moon, though I believe it was really just the Saudis—that Eid would, instead, fall on the next day. Whether this change was caused by cosmic or human forces, it was a fortunate development. The last thing Muslims in America needed was to be seen celebrating anything on the anniversary of the fall of the Twin Towers.

As was my personal tradition, I slept through the Eid prayer services. My father and Aamir always went to some remote farm outside of Sacramento, where the farmer let Muslims purchase and then slaughter livestock in the ritual manner. They usually made their way to the farm directly after the service was over, and so if I was not at the mosque, I was not required to kill anything I would normally be inclined to pet.

When I eventually did wake up, I saw that I had missed five calls from my mother. Groaning, I plucked my phone from the nightstand, yanked it free from the charger and dialed home. I wasn't crazy enough to dodge Ma's calls on Eid.

She answered on the third ring but did not immediately address me. She was screaming at someone else in the background. I sat up.

"Mom, what's wrong?"

"He's got a chain saw, Anvar," my mother yelled into the phone. "A chain saw! There is blood everywhere. It's *everywhere*."

"What's happening? Are you all right?"

"Your father has a chain saw. He got a chain saw and now the garage is a mess and there are chips of bone in the meat and I can't cook in these conditions. I am telling you, Anvar, I have had it with this."

I may not have mentioned it before, but my father loves food. Point him to the best nihari in your state and he'll drive two or three hundred miles to get at it without hesitation. This accounts for his rather generous proportions.

What he loves more than anything else in the world, more than his wife and his sons and even music, is meat. If you were to offer him a choice between fresh meat and ambrosia, he would pick the meat and never have any doubts about his choice.

The problem is that you can't really get fresh, off-the-bone halal meat in the States. Even on Eid al-Adha, his favorite holiday, Imtiaz Faris has to leave his sacrificed goat with a farmer, who then has it skinned, gutted, cut into manageable pieces and nicely packaged over several days. My father has long railed against this process because, in his opinion, the wait alters the taste of the goat and ruins his Eid.

Ma told me to hold, shouted at my father some more, then returned to our call. "So, your father has the farmer skin and gut the goat, puts the carcass in the back of our Camry, and drives to a hardware store. He buys a chain saw. Then he lines the entire garage with old newspapers, unloads the goat and goes about trying to butcher it. What should I do?"

The real question was what my parents' neighbors would do if they saw my dad, dressed in his shalwar kameez and skullcap, sitting in a pool of blood, dicing up a dead body.

"Mom." I jumped to my feet. "I'm on my way. Listen carefully. Whatever happens, make sure the garage door remains closed. All right? Otherwise, people will freak out."

"I have to air it out," my mother said. "Everything smells like goat."

"I don't care. He'll end up on the news. Just contain the situation."

"Would serve him right if he got arrested." She sniffed and, in a more resigned voice, said, "Fine. I'll make sure no one finds out what is happening. Stop by a store on your way home. I really need an air freshener for the car."

Ma opened the door dressed in bloodied surgical scrubs. They obviously belonged to Aamir, as she fairly swam in them, but the menace in her dark eyes, visible over the surgeon's mask, was enough to keep me from laughing at her outfit. I couldn't help but point to the blue cap she was wearing though. "Nice hat, Mom."

She snarled and thrust a pair of clear plastic gloves at me. "Go put on old clothes and come down to help clean up your father's mess."

"I don't get scrubs?"

"If you wanted them, you should've become a doctor."

"You're not a doctor. Also, I *am* a doctor."

Ma sniffed to show her disdain for my juris doctorate and marched away in the direction of the garage. As I went up the stairs to my old room, I ran into Aamir hurrying down.

"Going down to help?"

"I can't. Emergency at the hospital. I got called in."

"Convenient."

"Anvar, a woman is dying. I might be able to save her life."

I hate physicians. They have the best excuses. "Sure. Whatever."

He gave me a wide grin that convinced me he was full of shit, the default human condition, and rushed past me. Grumbling to myself, I dressed and made my way down to help my parents.

A chain saw is not a precision instrument. That is why it isn't the first choice of world-renowned orthopedic surgeons but is the first choice of serial killers.

The inside of my parents' garage looked like the inside of Stephen King's head. Blood was splattered everywhere, shreds and chunks of meat and gristle clung to the walls and a giant pile of red-soaked newspapers sat in the middle.

Ma handed me a bucket of water and a large sponge, still wrapped in cellophane, as soon as I walked into the little house of horrors my father had created. "You clean the walls. I'll paint them. These spots of blood will never come out."

"Sure, Lady Macbeth."

My mother glared at me, though I was fairly sure she didn't get the reference. "Was that a joke?"

"Yes."

"Was it funny?"

"Not really, no."

She put her hands on her hips, still staring me down. "You don't joke with me, you understand? You and I don't have a fun relationship."

"It's definitely not a fun relationship."

I'd never thought it possible that someone could break a name in half. My mother did it and she made it seem effortless. "Anvar. Faris."

"Sorry, Ma."

As my mother stomped off toward the paint bucket at the opposite side of the garage, my father, who was sitting in a corner, trying to look as small as possible, hissed at me. "What you are doing, man? You'll get us both killed."

"This is all on you, Dad."

My father shrugged as he went back to using dental floss to try to get the last bits of his latest sacrifice to Allah out from the teeth of his otherwise new saw. "It seemed like a good idea at the time. Then again, so did having you."

"I don't have to be here, you know."

"Yes," Bariah Faris said from across the garage. "You do." She pointed to the wall nearest to her. "Start cleaning."

It was long, slow and, literally, bloody work. An hour in, I was only halfway done. My wrists were tired, my knees were tired, and my ears were tired.

". . . stupid man with his stupid goats and his stupid fried liver that he just plops on the table as if I don't have things to do myself, and then he expects me to drop everything and make biryani, but does he remember to bring yogurt? No, of course, the great king of kings doesn't remember to bring the yogurt and then, when he goes out for it, he calls from the store to ask if we use full fat or half fat and then he comes back with vanilla by mistake because he is a stupid man who loves stupid goats . . ."

For the last hour, my mother had been muttering to herself, while my father sat by the water heater, eyes downcast, shoulders slumped. This was something she did whenever she was extremely worked up.

Prophet Muhammad once said that the believer does not swear. Therefore, Bariah Faris does not swear. Ever. In her life she claims to have never said a three-, four-, five- or six-letter word. Her accounting may not be precise, but I can attest to the fact that I never heard her curse. Not being able to vent her frustrations in one forceful expletive, however, she was forced to gradually put her displeasure into words.

So, like a kettle letting off steam as it comes to a boil, my mother whispers her fury to the world. I was pretty good at tuning her out but had never been trapped in a room with her when she was in one of these moods for an extended period of time. It was exhausting. No wonder my father looked so defeated.

". . . so now my whole day is thrown off, you see, and does the maharaja care? No, of course he doesn't care because it doesn't really change his schedule. He isn't the one who has to get Zuha's Eid present together and make it look all nice and pretty. No, he'll just waddle along, pretending the whole while that he helped when, truth be told . . ."

"Wait, Ma, what did you say?"

Both my parents stared at me, their eyes wide. My father, I suspect, was afraid. My mother was just surprised. No one ever asked her to repeat herself when she was in this mood.

"I was saying there is so much to do. I have to finish getting Zuha's Eid present together." She paused and looked at me a moment, her expression odd. "You didn't know? I thought I told you we were going to see the Shahs when the whole fiasco with Imam Sama happened four weeks ago. I'm sure I asked you to come. This is what happens when you don't pick up your phone and don't take any interest in the affairs of the family. It really is your own fault if you're feeling left out now. Anyway, we finalized everything with the Shah family. Aamir will be getting engaged to their daughter, Zuha. Frankly, I can't believe we didn't think of it sooner. It is such a great match. And you, you who are supposed to be so smart about everything, how come you didn't suggest it?"

I begged off going to the Shahs', claiming that the fumes from the paint had given me a headache. Then I went home and proceeded to procure a headache by getting utterly and completely drunk.

THE TRAP

2016

This kind play, one that looks like it will help you but which ultimately causes you pain, is called a trap. And you, my son, are in one now.

—Naani Jaan

AZZA

Being with Anvar was a mistake. It was stupid, sinful, reckless, mad. I'd known all that before I'd gone to his home and his bed. I'd gone to him, again and again, despite knowing that if Abu or Qais found out, it'd be the end of me.

Maybe it was just the upcoming Eid. It had me thinking of Baba Adam's suicidal goat. What would it be like, just for a moment, to be completely free, even if it all ended badly?

And then there was Anvar. His quick half smile, the constant laughter in his brown eyes, and the way he could shape words, turning them in on themselves. He made the world seem easy. It was as if he'd managed to survive life without letting it bruise him. That was a miracle. I was used to being around shattered people. He was different.

Or not. I found him drunk one night, wrecked by the thought of a woman he had loved—probably still did love, given how broken the thought of her made him—marrying his brother.

There is no true measure of pain. Each hurt is unique, and even small wounds can bleed a lot. I should've laughed at Anvar Faris as he told me stories about Zuha Shah. The misery he'd experienced was so many shades lighter than mine. Still, as I sat there listening to him, I didn't feel like laughing. I felt wonder.

I led him to his bed, and held him as he found sleep, running my fingers through his hair and wondering what being in love actually was. What force it must have to completely shake a man who seemed to be so solid, who seemed to have an answer to everything, a smile for every moment.

What would it be like to have someone love you like that, over years, through separation and heartache? I didn't think I'd ever know, and somehow that seemed like the saddest thing in all creation.

So, I was able to feel sorry for him, even though the world had cut me much more deeply than it had cut him. He still had a scar and so he was entitled to sympathy, and it felt like I was as well.

I woke at home the next morning just as Abu got back from work. I'd overslept and felt groggy. I grimaced when I heard him call my name, but quickly ran my hands through my hair a couple of times, got to my feet and went to see him.

Abu smiled when he saw me, the kind of big broad smile he rarely gave anyone anymore. I started to smile back but then saw why he was happy. In his hands was a small, blue, velvety box. The kind of box you get from a jewelry store. I stepped back from it.

"Abu?"

"Mabruk," he said, "Alf mabruk. A thousand congratulations, yes, for my daughter. Qais has sent this for you." Abu held the box out to me. I looked at it, and then up at him. "We've agreed on a wedding date. He wanted it as soon as possible, but always it is like that with grooms. All this time, he told me, he'd only been patient because he was getting money together for a ring. Now, I told him, give me some time to raise some money, to do the wedding properly, so you'll both have to wait till the end of the year."

Qais had done it. He'd done exactly what he'd said he would do.

I took another step back. I couldn't cry in front of Abu. What would he think? What would he say? I'd promised. More important, he'd promised. He wouldn't go back on his word to Qais. He'd die first. He'd kill me first.

I tried to breathe deep and even breaths. I tried to stay together.

"Already so emotional?" Abu asked with a chuckle. "You haven't even seen the ring yet. Open it." He extended his hand farther and I had no choice but to take the box. I opened it. It was a thin slip of silver with a single, dull diamond set in it. It wasn't at all a glamorous thing, but it was still beautiful, in its own way.

"Put it on," Abu said. "A ring is prettiest when it is worn."

My fingers shook a little as I pried the ring loose from the box, and then, biting my lip, I slid it on.

"How does it feel?"

There had been a movie I'd caught the ending of on TV once, with these little creatures who had to fight monsters and run through war zones so that they could take a ring into a mountain of lava and throw it in there to destroy it before being rescued by a giant flying eagle. That's what it felt like.

"It's tight," I managed.

"That can be fixed," Abu said. "Wear it for now. It'll make Qais happy to see it. I'll take it to a store to have it resized for you later."

"I can wait to wear it until—"

"Don't be silly. What will Qais think? You don't want to hurt him."

No. I wanted to kill him.

I'll take your life from you.

I threw my hand out in the direction of my room. "Abu, I . . ."

"Yes, yes," he said, touching my cheek gently with his rough hand. "Go. Cry these tears. It is a great blessing from Allah to see tears of happiness in your eyes after so long a time."

I didn't let myself cry long. Mama had spent her life crying and hoping no one would notice. It had changed nothing for her, and being like her would change nothing for me.

Everything good that had happened to me was because I'd done something to try to get what I wanted. I'd survived Baghdad by going to Basra, I'd brought us to the States. Now it was time to do something again.

Except I had no idea what to do and everything that hurt in my life was also because of the things I'd done. My heart still ached over Fahd, and my promises to Qais, now wrapped painfully around my ring finger, digging into my skin, were also my own doing. I had to be careful. I didn't think my heart could survive too many more consequences.

There was nowhere to run. I had no money and no skills with which to find work. How would I support myself? And I didn't really want to leave Abu. He was the last of my family, the only thing left of the life I had been born into. He was the last person I loved, even if I did so bitterly.

And there was always the chance that Abu or Qais would find me.

Maybe if Qais could be made to want someone else, anyone else. Then he would leave me alone. But I knew no one, and marrying him was a cruel fate to thrust upon another girl.

I went to the kitchen to start on dinner, my mind a mess of hopes and thoughts. How happy would I be if Qais didn't exist? I couldn't imagine it.

I opened the cabinets above the stove and looked over the ingredients there, trying to figure out what I would make. It didn't matter what I'd make, I'd need salt, so I reached for it, but Abu had put it just out of my grasp.

Shaking my head, I stood on tiptoe. I stretched my fingers as far as I could, and managed to tip the container forward. As I pulled away, my hand hit the sumac, and suddenly a wave of plastic tumbled toward me. I covered my face with my arms as plastic bottles and jars fell around me.

I heard Abu shout a sleepy complaint from his room.

The lid came off a container full of chickpeas, which smashed into the ground, sending the little balls skittering out over the floor, with some of them rolling under the oven.

I stared at the mess around me, unable to move for a moment.

I could have gotten a broom and gathered the chickpeas together in a dustpan to toss away. I knew, however, that I could wash them and use them, so I knelt down and began picking them up one at a time.

ANVAR

I found things to do. Took on a few more document review jobs to keep busy. I paid more attention to the news. Misery, you may have heard, loves company, and there is no better chronicle of misery than the day-to-day experience of humanity as a whole.

The Republican bid to turn back time, led by Donald Quixote, went on. It had seemed funny when it started, but it wasn't funny anymore. My father was apoplectic about it on social media, where he'd once been mocking. It was sobering for him to realize that the nativist ideology he had laughed at as unworthy of a great nation had actually found an audience.

The growing fear and panic in my father's posts, and in the Muslim community as a whole, were due to the fact that tens of millions of Americans appeared convinced that we were an existential threat to their survival. It was a result of a rude epiphany that the people around us, our countrymen, viewed us as being inherently, unalterably, alien.

We'd thought we were home, only to learn that our family thought we were dangerous, unreliable strangers.

There was, perhaps, another dimension to Imtiaz Faris's fear. He already knew these people and had run from them before. The great intellectual plague on the Muslim World was the continuing belief that as a civilization our fortunes had declined because we had strayed from the Word of God. It was the call to Make Islam Great Again, to return to the strict religiosity that had reigned in the seventh and eighth centuries, that had made my father pack us up and leave the country of our birth.

That radical Islamists and "America First" nationalists had essentially the same worldview and the same desire to recapture a nostalgia-gilded past glory was proof, in my opinion, that God's sense of irony was simply divine.

Still, I wasn't worried. The common sense and decency of my fellow Americans would never allow xenophobia and hatred to come to power.

I started reading voraciously again, not a book here or there, as had become routine, but like I used to in college, going through five or six books at a time, switching from one to another when I needed a break.

For the next few weeks, I made myself busy enough that I had good and true reasons not to visit my family much or even speak to them at all.

None of it made any difference. Time continued to slip away, Aamir's engagement to Zuha drawing inexorably closer, until it was upon me. I wouldn't be able to avoid it, of course. I'd have to go. I'd have to be happy for them.

"What were you thinking about?"

I looked at Azza in time to see her reaching for her engagement ring, which lay on my nightstand. I hadn't said anything about the ring. I wasn't sure it was my place and I wasn't sure what I wanted to say. The cheap diamond struggled to sparkle under the California sun. It remained dutiful despite the fact that the promises it represented were hopelessly, irrevocably broken. Azza smiled at me, her typical skittish, fragile smile, and waited for a response.

I didn't particularly like the question, mostly because I didn't like the answer. I offered her an irritated shrug. "Nothing."

This was, apparently, the wrong thing to say, because though she leaned over and gave me a quick kiss on the lips, she also slid out of bed. As she stepped into the panties she had discarded the night before, I glanced at the clock. She didn't have to leave for a couple of hours yet.

"You still have time before your father gets home."

"Not much."

"Stay for a few more minutes."

"You just don't want to be alone because you'll be thinking about your brother's engagement."

"That's not true."

"Don't lie," Azza said. "Just say you don't want to talk about it."

"I don't want to talk about it."

She chuckled. "I know."

"Then why bring it up?"

"Because you should talk about it." She paused a moment, as if considering whether or not to say what she wanted to say. "Are you embarrassed?"

"About what?"

"About being . . . what's the word? It's not exactly original to be in love with your brother's fiancée."

"You think I'm a cliché?"

"No. You think you are one. I just think it upsets you. Challenges your self-image."

I wanted to tell her that I didn't need her pop psychology, but before I could, I remembered that she was pretty and the way the sunlight kissed her black hair was wonderful and I wanted her to come back that night.

I said, "That isn't until the day after tomorrow. I'll be here until the weekend."

"I might come by."

"Sure. Whenever you have time."

She finished dressing in silence. I watched her slender frame vanish behind the flowing, loose black robe that I now knew her father forced her to wear outside their home. A woman's body is sacred, I'd once heard an imam say, so Muslims cover it like they cover the Kaaba in Mecca. The hijab, the purdah, the abayah, the niqab, all of it, is reverence.

It was meant to be a profound thought, but ultimately it was barely a pretty one. The object of one's reverence is still just an object. It is a poor dervish who cares if and how the Kaaba is covered.

Soon I could see nothing of Azza except those remarkable pale green eyes. I knew her well enough by then, however, that even though I could not see her smile, I could hear it in her voice and picture it nearly perfectly.

"If I don't see you before you go, remember to try to have a good time."

"You know perfectly well that I'll do no such thing."

I showered and shaved after she left. I suppose, despite discovering that Zuha was destined to marry Aamir, I should've been grateful for small miracles, like Azza bint Saqr. There aren't a lot of women, I imagine, who would let you cry on their shoulders about being broken up over your high school sweetheart and still come back to your bed.

I was pathetic. People got over their first romances, they nursed their broken hearts back to some semblance of health, and they sought out other people to try to be happy with. That was what was expected of me, what would've been normal. Unfortunately, I'd made defying expectations a signature feature of my existence.

Azza hadn't thought I was pathetic, though, or at least that is how I remembered it. It was hard to know for sure. I'd been pretty drunk.

What was Azza's relationship with Qais Badami like for her to seek me out, to break promises she had only recently made? These were uncomfortable thoughts, so I abandoned them. Instead, I studied my phone for information on how the world had changed in the few hours I'd been distracted by the trivial pursuits of sex and sleep.

The world was much the same as it had always been. My news feed, however, insisted that there were urgent stories requiring my attention. Celebrities had broken up. Dunks had been thrown down and goals scored. Stooge One had insulted Stooge Two and retaliation was anticipated. The latest episode of the hottest television show was apparently epic.

An epic with commercial breaks. A trick Homer missed out on.

I skipped over my father's posts, scrolling past the flood of anxiety and fear that he was drowning in. He was sharing every piece of news he could get his hands on, credible or not, about how the ban on Muslims entering the United States would be implemented, about how hate crimes against Muslims were on the rise, and how a registry would go into effect, so that Muslims could be tracked by the government.

I didn't doubt that my father was concerned. It was going around. Even Imam Sama had started joking—half joking, really—about there being undercover federal agents in the congregation. Ma was probably getting to him.

As far as Dad was concerned, I suspected that a very real driving force behind his Chicken Little messages was their popularity. Everyone likes to be liked, and Imtiaz Faris had never felt quite liked enough in some quarters.

Speaking of my mother, her online persona was focused, predictably, on religion. "Glory Be to Allah," one image she shared read in bright red letters, next to a completely unrelated picture of Istanbul's famous Blue Mosque. "There are 114 chapters in the Quran. Subtract your age from this number and then add 2. This will give you the year of your birth. Miraculous!"

I considered pointing out this only worked because the year was 2016 but thought better of it. I never actually replied to anything posted for public consumption. I never shared, never tweeted or chirped or peeped anything online. I was antisocial on social media. I listened but never spoke. It was the way of sages and of brown boys seeking to avoid parental disapproval.

I was about to log off when a message popped up. I had a new "friend request."

The internet wanted to know if Zuha Shah and I were still friends.

I am not sure how long I sat there, just staring at Zuha's profile picture, before doing what was inevitable and letting her back into my world. Instantly, a message from her popped up.

Hi.

I thought for some time about what to say, so long, in fact, that she must have started to wonder if I'd respond at all. Finally, I wrote back. *For the record, we are not really friends.*

I see you haven't changed.

I'm virtually the same, I replied.

Can we meet?

I frowned at the screen, wondering if Zuha really hadn't caught my clever bit of wordplay. *Did you catch the pun?*

Yes and I ignored it, she replied. *Need to talk. Can we meet?*

Busy. Don't really have time.

I'll come to you. Address?

Zuha said she would be by after Friday prayers, so I went downtown as planned, walking to my favorite food truck. It was painted a garish neon orange and decorated with robin's-egg-blue graffiti, which shouted the name of my friend's business to the world: Junk in the Trunk.

Giant sesame seed buns loomed next to the words, in case anyone was dense enough to miss the joke. It was risqué for halal food, but that hadn't detracted from business.

Jason Backes, the truck's sole proprietor, was a client and a friend. He lacked certain talents necessary for running a business. Talents that would enable him to obtain state and city permits, for example, or get a food handler's certification. Jason only barely accepted that a food truck needed to meet the standards of the Department of Public Health. Actually, I think he barely believed the department existed. When it came to bureaucracy, Jason was a decided agnostic.

This, of course, meant that the amount of paperwork involved in running a food truck confounded him. I'd agreed to keep track of his insurance, manage his books and make sure the truck's paperwork was in order. In exchange, as long as I also helped him with advertising, I got a free lunch on Fridays. This weekly meal made Junk in the Trunk my highest-paying client.

Jason smiled when he saw me. "Yo, Faris."

I waved to him and took a place at the back of the line.

The first time I'd brought my father here, Imtiaz Faris had stared at the lean white man covered with tattoos. His gaze had lingered first on Jason's perpetually bloodshot eyes, then on the chef's scruffy beard and shaggy brown hair. "Pothead hippies can't make halal food."

This was, fortunately, not true. Jason made a mean burger, so much so that he could now honestly count my father as a regular.

I rarely got a burger though. Jason didn't take orders from me. Instead, he just gave me whatever happened to not be selling. San Francisco, as was too often the case, wasn't feeling his grilled chicken sandwich that day.

As always, my meal came with a side of bright pink flyers. I took them dutifully, intending to get to the mosque quickly, before the limited space on the console table by the front door was taken. That way, I could drop the flyers off and let people pick them up if they wanted, instead of handing them out one at a time.

My friend was apparently onto the trick. "Actually, give them to people this time. Don't just leave them lying around in a corner. I've heard that's what you've been doing."

"I wouldn't mind handing them out so much if you'd picked a better name for the truck. Something less offensive to delicate Muslim sensibilities."

"There are no better names. I have the best name. I have all the best names. Believe me."

"Don't do that."

"What?" Jason asked with a wicked grin. "Sound presidential?"

I snorted and picked up the pink stack of paper.

"If you just leave them lying around, I'll know."

"What? You have spies at the mosque now?"

Jason winked. "Doesn't everybody?"

I was too late to find a spot for Jason's flyers on the table by the mosque's entrance, so I hung on to them and sat on the ground at the back of the prayer hall, waiting for the service to begin.

Soon after Imam Sama took the pulpit and began speaking in his sonorous voice, I realized this was going to be a poor sermon, which wasn't particularly unusual. Ahmed Sama had many fine qualities, but he wasn't an organized orator. He jumped from topic to topic, often without any detectable pattern. Today, he started with the story of Adam, the Islamic version. Where the Bible said Adam had transgressed gravely, committing the original sin that would taint all of humankind, the Quran claimed that it was just a little slipup. It was a mistake for which Adam had begged for forgiveness and for which forgiveness had been granted.

I knew the exact words Adam had used to repent. My mother had forced me to memorize them when I was young. She'd predicted I would need them often.

Unfortunately, instead of discussing how this single shift in perspective had led to the development of two very different dogmas, Imam Sama somehow ended up lecturing the congregation on the importance of smiling at people when passing by them on the street.

He covered some of his favorite topics—cellphone etiquette, the importance of respecting your parents, making sure your breath doesn't stink—along the way. I'd heard him speak on all of this before, and I usually tuned him out after around five minutes.

His speech was uninspiring, but as the congregation rose to pray, I couldn't help but admire the friendly, practical religion that was California's Islam. I've either visited or been dragged to mosques in many parts of the world. There are thinly veiled politics in some mosques in Karachi and the severity of brimstone can be found in the mosques of Bradford, England. Islam in Toronto is sometimes shrill; I remember an imam there screeching at his audience, demanding that they go home and take hammers to their television sets, because the devil resides therein. In the mosques of California, however, a calm prevails.

I tried to focus on prayer but, as always, whatever I was supposed to feel in such moments eluded me.

The man praying next to me could have been from here or from Indonesia or Malaysia or China or Myanmar. Wherever he was from, the nuances of the religion he was raised with must have been different from the rather puritan upbringing my mother had given me. Yet as we stood together, our movements synchronized by prayer, we seemed for a moment to be and to believe exactly the same things.

It was, perhaps, understandable that the rest of the world saw us, labeled us, as being the same.

After all, we're told that is what God does.

Despite Qais Badami's desperate friendliness, I avoided his company. It was his ring Azza wore. It's not pleasant to be very long in the presence of the man you are actively cuckolding.

I didn't know why Azza objected to him. It probably wasn't because of his appearance. His features were sharp—perhaps a touch too sharp—and his skin fair. He was better looking than I was.

Granted, he was too polite, too solicitous and too generous with his honeyed smile, for my liking, but then I'd always preferred people with a little spice to them. Like Naani Jaan.

Or Zuha.

Fortunately, I didn't have much time to think about her, as Qais walked up to me, a cheerful grin pasted on his face. "Anvar. Good to see you. As-salamu alaykum."

I thrust a flyer at him before the other peddlers around me, all advertising their own restaurants, bookstores or charitable causes, could ambush him with their offerings. "Yeah," I said, struggling to sound sincere, "always good to see you too."

He looked down at Jason's ad. "Junk in the Trunk. Odd name."

"It's not ideal."

"You're working in a food truck?"

The second question had a small "I thought you were a lawyer" sneer to it.

"Just doing a favor for a client," I told him.

"Then you don't actually know anything about the business? You must know something if you are handing out flyers, I think. It is run by a non-Believer, isn't it?"

"Jason believes in a lot of things."

"I'm sure he does," Qais said after a small pause, during which I could almost see his mind working to decipher my comment. "But he doesn't believe in what we believe in." When I simply shrugged my shoulders, he went on. "Are you certain then that the meat is halal?"

"I've got no reason to doubt it."

Qais reached out and grabbed my forearm, his grip cold and strong. "You have to be sure." He moved closer, forcing me to step back to be comfortable. "You have to see that. If you're sending people from the mosque there, you have to know the details about the meat. You're responsible."

"I've never been accused of being responsible before."

He didn't think I was funny, which maybe explained why Azza didn't want to spend the rest of her life with him.

I tried to nod my farewell to him and tried to pull my arm back so that I could shove flyers at the other men exiting the mosque.

Qais didn't let go.

"I'm serious," he went on, as if I hadn't moved. "You must make sure that the meat is halal. Where does this non-Believer get the meat? You must find out. Are the cows slaughtered by hand? Or machine?

Are they stunned beforehand? Is there a tape recorder reciting the takbir or is a Muslim actually there speaking it out loud?"

I'd had all these questions put to me regarding Jason's food by other people, though never with such insistent zeal. Qais's behavior was strange, but not entirely bizarre by the standards of his community. If there is another group of people that sweats the small stuff as profusely as Muslims do, I have not come across them.

"I need my hand."

The sickly sweet smile was back in an instant as he released his grip on me. "Sorry. I'm just trying to make sure you don't endanger your soul."

"Don't worry about it. They made me give it up when I passed the bar."

He let that sit a few moments in silence. Then a broken mountain of a man came up behind Qais. He had broad, open features. His body radiated the memory of physical strength, and his face, through deep lines like cracks in stone, told of a difficult life. Qais turned to see what had captured my attention, then smiled broadly.

"Anvar Faris, this man will soon be my father-in-law. His name is Abu Fahd."

Of course, the older man's name wasn't really Abu Fahd. That was his kunya, a title that some Arabs took after they had a child. It indicated that he had a son. Azza had never mentioned a brother.

Abu Fahd gave me a wide, toothy smile and held out his right hand for me to shake. I noticed that he had no fingernails. "I have heard of you," he said. In response to my surprised look, he added, "From Hafeez Bhai."

"Wonderful."

"Yes." Abu Fahd beamed at the mention of our landlord. "Hafeez Bhai is wonderful. A generous man."

Qais gave a little snort of derision, then asked, "What did Bhatti say about Anvar?"

"Don't you know? This is the warrior who defended Taleb Mansoor."

I'd been called many things in my life, mostly by my father, but never a warrior. Qais turned that sharp gaze on me again, clearly reappraising my worth. "Really? Any interesting cases you're working on now?"

"No," Abu Fahd responded before I could. "They won't let him in court anymore. Hafeez told me."

I probably should've corrected them but I didn't. I just handed Abu Fahd a flyer. "I really need to give these out. Then I have a meeting, so . . ."

Qais seemed to be on the verge of turning away when a thought arrested him and brought him back to the conversation. "You know, we should hang out sometime. Let me get your number. I'll call you."

I tried not to look appalled, certain that this was the beginning of a terrible friendship.

"As-salamu alaykum, Barrister Faris," Hafeez Bhatti said as I walked past his office on my way back to my apartment. "I was only just now wondering what was keeping you." With a gesture for me to come closer, he lowered his voice, as if about to tell me something important and private. "A woman was at the office, asking about you."

I glanced at my watch. "When?"

"A few minutes ago, maybe." Hafeez Bhai raised grotesquely thick eyebrows at me and then dropped them back down. He did this three or four times. Somehow, he made this gesture convey a lewd subtext. "She's waiting for you outside your apartment." He finished off his facial contortions with a wink. "Have fun."

I checked the time on my phone. "Damn it. She came early."

"That's a good problem to have, Barrister Sahib. Most men have the opposite issue."

I spared a frown for my landlord, but Bhatti had adopted a perfectly innocent expression. Shaking my head, I rushed up the stairs as fast as I could. If I hadn't lost my breath running up several floors, I would've lost it when I saw Zuha. Despite everything that had happened, as soon as I saw her, I was caught up in the music of her again, caught up in the familiar melody of her slender form and her mischievous smile and her slightly wavy brown hair and the flirtatious hem of her short kameez.

"Hi." My greeting came out lame and broken.

"Hey."

Zuha stepped forward and held out her arms. Our embrace was brief and awkward. She smelled like white chocolate and vanilla and the vague memory of a flower I once knew. I cleared my throat and tried to think of something innocuous to say. She spoke first. "You look good."

"There have to be some constants in the universe, I suppose."

"You really haven't changed then."

"But you have." There was an edge to my voice. I had known it was there, but I hadn't meant to cut with it.

Her smile faded. "Are we going to do this here, in the hallway?"

"My apartment is depressing."

"Seems like just the right setting for this conversation then."

I reached into my pocket for my keys. "So, how's God?"

"Good, I'm sure."

"Let Him know I was asking after Him."

Zuha adjusted the strap of her white handbag, so that it rested more comfortably on her shoulder. "You realize that He didn't start magically speaking to me as soon as I stopped sleeping with you, right?"

"Hardly seems worth it then." I opened the door to the small unit of space I called home, and let her in. It was a cramped, run-down place with little to redeem it in the eyes of men—and even less in the eyes of women, if my mother was to be believed. The ceiling was low enough to touch, the appliances old, almost midcentury, and the gray carpet threadbare.

I'd seen but somehow also never really seen how inadequate the place was, how depressing and lightless, until Zuha walked in. She didn't belong here, in these drab surroundings.

She was thinking the same thing. I could see it in her eyes. She said, "It's—"

I didn't want to hear her polite lie. "Shit. It's shit." I gestured to a dilapidated old couch in a corner by the television. "Take a seat."

"I was going to say that it has character."

"What does that mean, exactly?"

Zuha shrugged her shoulders, eyes still looking my place over. "I don't know. It's something I've heard people say."

"What else do people say?"

"That you have five girlfriends. I'm just here to find out which one you're planning on bringing to the wedding."

"All of them, of course."

"Right." She smiled as she sat down, crossing her legs and perching her fingers on a knee. It was an old habit of hers. "Naturally."

I sat down in an armchair as far away from her as possible. I should've offered her something to drink. My hands were shaking though, and I didn't want her to know that. A teacup rattling in its saucer would betray the extent of my agitation.

I drew in a deep breath, closed my eyes for a moment and tried to channel the part of me that was still a lawyer, the part of me trained to be calm, distant and dispassionate. Appearing in control was one of my few professional strengths. I scripted a statement in my mind. I would let her off the hook, let her know that she meant nothing to me anymore, that I didn't care what she did with her life.

Before I could say anything, she asked, "You're tutoring?"

I was thrown for a second before realizing that Azza had left some of her homework lying on the coffee table. Not much got past Zuha Shah, even all these years later.

"No."

She raised her eyebrows. "Then you're dating a student?"

"I wouldn't call it dating."

Zuha reached over and picked up whatever Azza had been working on. "Is she in *high school?*"

"She's catching up," I said, in defense of Azza. And myself.

"Doesn't seem like someone you'd be interested in." When I gave her a confused look, she went on. "You've always looked down on people who weren't as smart as you."

"That's not true."

Zuha raised an eyebrow at me.

"It's not entirely true," I conceded. "Not anymore. You keep saying I haven't changed, but I have. It's been a long time."

She didn't respond.

"I'm sure you've changed too. I heard you tried on the hijab for a while."

"Yeah. That didn't take."

"So you're not religious anymore?"

So you left me for no reason is what I wanted to say, but didn't.

Zuha seemed to hear it anyway. "I'm probably still a lot more religious than you are."

"That's true for most people."

She smiled a little.

And just like that, as ridiculous as it may seem, it felt like there was nothing left to say. Or maybe there was so much to say that the enormity of it left us both speechless. The silence between us grew and got jagged, until finally I couldn't bear it anymore.

"Look, Zuha—"

"I'm sorry." Her interruption was quick. "That's what I came to say. I wanted a chance to say that before—"

"It's fine."

When I didn't say anything more, she shook her head, as if she couldn't believe what was happening. "That's it? 'Fine'? That's all you have to say to me?"

With a grimace, I rose to my feet and began to pace. This was not going the way it was supposed to go. I was doing the wrong things. You don't fidget, you don't walk around, when making an argument. It is bad form. You stand and you deliver, so that you project confidence.

I couldn't make myself do the things I knew I was supposed to do, couldn't be what I was supposed to be. I should have been gracious and dismissive, wounded but generous, contemptuous and yet, at the same time, polite.

Why did I never feel in possession of myself around Zuha? I still didn't know the answer. I shook my head at myself, but she misread the gesture. She seemed to think it was meant for her.

"Given everything . . . please, at least tell me how you feel."

"I can't tell you." I said it in a frustrated bark. "Because I don't know. The girl I had a crush on since forever, my first girlfriend, my first kiss—"

"You called mistletoe and—"

"I remember."

"I just meant it was—"

"A surprise. Just like it was a surprise when I heard you had agreed to marry my brother."

"A less pleasant one, I imagine," Zuha said.

"You're going to make jokes now?"

"I'm just trying to keep it . . . I just don't want us to fight."

"If you don't want us to fight, you should let me do all the jokes."

Zuha ran both her hands through her hair, holding back the flowing locks for a moment before letting them fall again and slumping into her seat. "Were you always this difficult?"

"Yes. It never used to bother you. You loved me once."

"Yes. I did."

"And you're going to marry a Faris now. Just, you know, the wrong brother." I stopped pacing and looked down at her. "I was going to let it go, you know. I was going to let you do whatever you wanted. I want you to be happy, so I was going to hold my tongue. But then you come here and ask me how I feel. How badly do you need me to lie to you, Zuha?"

"This isn't about me being happy." Her eyes were bright but in the wrong way, in the way that broken crystal sparkles. "Look, the proposal came from your parents. I thought you knew all about it. How could you not? I thought you didn't care, or you would've said something. That made me so angry that I—"

"You thought I was okay with it. Have we met?"

She didn't respond for a while and my words hung between us. Finally, she said, "Not for a long time. It isn't like you ever pursued me after we ended it."

"We didn't end it. It was you. You had a religious seizure, suddenly I wasn't good enough, or holy enough, for you, so you broke it off—"

"You didn't— You could've done something."

"Like what?"

"You could've proposed."

I threw out my arms to encompass the entirety of my apartment, like an addled magician unveiling a decapitated rabbit. "Look at my life, Zuha. I don't have anything to offer you. Would your parents have said yes if I had proposed? Would you have?"

She didn't say anything for a while, which I suppose was answer enough.

"So," Zuha asked eventually, "what happens now?"

"I'll see you at your engagement party, I guess."

She remained seated, looking up at me with an expression I couldn't identify. Finally, she sighed and wiped roughly at her brown eyes. I turned to head back to my chair, so I didn't have to see any tears fall.

"Fine," she said. "Listen, just so you know I haven't . . . I realized from my conversations with Aamir that you never . . . You haven't told him anything about the two of us, so—"

Realization smashed into my mind and I actually laughed as I turned back to face her. It did not, to my ears, sound like it usually does. "You haven't told Aamir about us? That's why you're really here."

"No." She pushed herself up out of her seat, her tone angry and indignant. "That's not true and you know that and you're an ass for saying it."

I held up my hands in surrender. "Fine. What about Aamir?"

She let herself glare at me for a few moments and then, more calmly, said, "I'm not sure if I should tell him now. It seems too late. What do you think?"

"I don't know. Do what you want."

"And what will you do?"

"I'll dance at your wedding."

"No," she said. "You won't."

"No." I was not sure if she was done with everything she had to say, but I walked to the door and, slowly, she followed. "I will not."

I glanced at the clock again. It was two in the morning and I was alone. If Azza had come over, I could have distracted myself. As it was, memories kept bleeding into my conscious mind, denying me sleep, and I was unable to stanch their flow. I could not replace, certainly not in a few hours, the years of careful bandaging that the mere sight of Zuha had effortlessly ripped away.

It is true what they say. Pain really is worse at night.

I could not believe that, all these years later, once again, the thought of her was keeping me up.

Then again, there have to be some constants in the universe.

I googled how much chamomile tea was safe to drink before

heading to the kitchen to brew my fourth cup. Somehow, while the tea bag was still fresh, I found myself staring at her picture on my phone again. When I studied her online profile, I noticed that she checked in at the same café on Embarcadero almost every morning. Then I had the worst idea.

The café was a typical cramped San Francisco spot, with low, close wood rafters. Real estate in the city was too precious to allow small businesses anything more than tiny spaces. I nursed my rapidly cooling cappuccino and hoped that Zuha would keep to her routine and come here for coffee.

And yes, I was aware that this was an ill-advised plan. I'd made peace with my own stupidity.

The ridiculous nature of one's own actions isn't pleasant to dwell upon, so I looked out the window, past the barista, past the eager customers lining up to pay more than anyone should have to pay for a latte, and noticed that the beauty of the day was fading. The sun was almost gone. Clouds were claiming dominion over the sky, and soon I knew they would become dark and ominous. Then it would rain.

The mutability of San Francisco never fails to surprise me, though the city has been unpredictable from the very first day I arrived. When I'd emerged from an underground BART train, the first thing I'd seen was a large, heavily tattooed white man in a mesh onesie waving around a Bible, screaming out urgent warnings about the end of times.

No matter how many independent bookstores I explored, how many protests I walked past, how many plays I attended, for me the most memorable thing about San Francisco would always be that giant, flaccid, Bible-thumping hobo. Some associations are indelible, no matter how much rain falls upon them.

The door opened and Zuha walked in.

There are those who would say that a Muslim has no business seeking the divine in the face of a woman. What they must not know is that there are moments and creatures of such exquisite, transcendent imperfection in this hollow, broken world that the hand of a great artist is evident in them. Let those who can look away look away if they wish.

She noticed me instantly. I had strategically chosen my location to ensure it. Her smile, swift and warm for one moment, became guarded and cautious as she walked over to me.

"Hey," Zuha said.

"Hi. Wow. This is . . . What a complete and utter coincidence that we should meet here."

"You're full of shit."

"Not at the moment. I just went—"

"Don't be gross."

"You used to like it when I was gross."

Zuha shook her head. "No. I really never did."

"Sit. I'll get your coffee."

"I can do it."

I got to my feet and gestured gallantly to the empty chair across from me. "Please."

"Sure. Okay. Cream and—"

"Two sugars. I remember."

As I walked back with her drink and an almond butter toast, I noticed she was texting. I tried not to wonder who, since there was a possibility it could be Aamir. Their engagement party was tomorrow. Still, I smiled at Zuha as she looked up from her phone and thanked me. "You come here often?"

"All the time."

"I would've thought they'd teach you to be a better liar in law school."

I leaned back in my chair and crossed my arms over my chest. Then, realizing my posture was intensely defensive, I tried to relax. Zuha had always been able to read me far too easily.

"I'm not sure you've heard, but I'm not a very good lawyer."

"Fair point. I've seen where you live."

"Nice."

She set her phone down on the table and looked at me, her eyes earnest. "Did you come here just to see me?"

I nodded.

"Why?"

"I don't know. I felt bad about yesterday and I was thinking . . . Actually, I have no idea why I am here. Not really. I'm sorry. I just couldn't sleep and there was all this herbal tea and—I don't know why, but this just seemed like what I should do."

Zuha nodded, accepting the explanation, such as it was, and sipped her coffee.

"I really am sorry," I told her, just to kill the growing silence, "about yesterday. I was rude."

She chuckled. "We've apologized to each other more in two days than we have in our entire lives."

"This is our new normal, I guess."

"I kind of hate it." She said it with the air of someone who had lost something important.

"It won't be so bad. We won't be around each other that much." She raised her eyebrows, so I explained. "Aamir and I still aren't that close."

"I gathered."

"Mostly because he remains a horse's ass."

"He is not."

"Is so. Always has been. Frankly, I can't believe you said yes to him."

"I guess I have a type, Anvar."

I placed a hand on my heart, both in jest and not in jest. "Now you're just being hurtful on purpose."

We drank our beverages quietly for a while. This was going much better than it had yesterday. She couldn't know, from the way I was behaving today, how erratic my heartbeat felt in her presence, how desperately an insane part of me had been hoping that our hands would touch, momentarily, when I handed her coffee to her.

"Are you going to your parents' place today?"

I looked up at her, startled by the question. "Tomorrow. I try to spend as little time with my family as possible."

"That's horrible."

"You only say that because you don't know them that well yet."

Zuha shook her head. "I'd forgotten how much I missed you."

"I never forgot."

She looked away from me, suddenly very interested in the pastry display across the room. Then she said, "You're going to stop talking like that soon, I hope."

"Of course."

"We were friends once." She looked back at me. "Right? We can be again."

I wanted to tell her that was impossible. I wanted to tell her that some associations are indelible and that the scars inflicted by love do not heal. At least for me.

"Sure," I told her. "Absolutely. I'd like that."

If she saw through my lie that time, she did not tell me.

AZZA

My niqab kept my scowl a secret as I served a smiling Qais and Abu tea. Qais picked up a cup from the plastic tray and I stepped away, wanting to hurry back to my room, to the journals I'd been writing since those chickpeas had rained down upon me. Qais stopped me.

"Your birthday is coming up, isn't it?"

I glanced at Abu, who nodded, obviously pleased that his future son-in-law had managed to remember his daughter's birthday. I couldn't remember Abu ever making a fuss over Mama's birthdays. There were never any flowers or any cards. I wondered why I'd never thought of it before.

Dr. Yousef had always come by.

"What present would you like for your birthday?" Qais asked.

"I want a gun," I said.

Both men stared at me.

"Look at what is happening," I said. "People hate Muslims, and a lot of *them* have weapons. If they have guns, we should have guns too."

I wouldn't have to argue with them. The lives they had led did that for me. Qais nodded once, thoughtfully, and said, "That is true. Maybe I should get one for myself as well."

"For Abu too," I said. "The more guns, the better. We are Americans now."

"I've got a moral question."

Anvar looked up from his laptop. He'd been reading the news a lot more lately. He'd been trying to get me to read it too, but it wasn't for me.

For Anvar and Americans like him, their election was the most important thing in the world—and maybe that was fair—but these people, who claimed to be leaders of the free world, didn't know the world at all. They didn't understand its nature or its size. They thought it was smaller than it was, and that they were bigger than they were.

"What?"

"A moral question," I said.

"I'm probably not the best person in the world to answer those."

"You're the best person I know," I told him.

"I'm flattered, I suppose. If you think about it, though, that's either really funny or really very sad."

I tucked a strand of hair that had been acting out all day behind my ear. "You want to make jokes, or do you want to help?"

He smiled in surrender. "What's the question?"

I glared at him, just to make sure he would take me seriously. He had a bad habit of thinking everything was funny.

"Should we be guided by our limits or our priorities?"

I was proud of the way I phrased that. I couldn't just come out and ask him how he felt about what I was planning to do. Unfortunately, he didn't seem to understand.

I tried to explain. "It's like your thing with your brother's fiancée."

"Zuha."

"Right. I mean, you could try to stop the engagement tomorrow. You could tell your parents about Zuha's past. Or tell your brother. Or just make a big scene at the party. You could make a mess of the whole thing if you wanted to. But you're not doing any of that. Is it because of your own personal limits? Society's limits? Or is it because of your priorities? Like family first or literally bros before hos, as they say on TV."

"Well, Zuha is not a 'ho,' so not really literally."

"Whatever. Well?"

"I haven't really thought about it," he said.

"Yes. You have. I've been thinking about this a lot. Every action we take is a balancing act between these two things, isn't it? How far are we willing to go to get what we want? You must have thought about it. You must have."

Anvar looked at me like I was odd. "I haven't. You know what they say, the examined life is not worth living."

I shook my head. I should've known better than to ask him. He took nothing seriously . . . and that was attractive sometimes, but it could also be really annoying.

"Hey," he said. "What is this about anyway?"

I'm going to end Qais Badami.

I'm going to make sure he can never hurt me again.

I just don't like what I have to do to make it happen.

I didn't say any of that.

"Just go back to doing whatever you were doing," I told him. "It isn't important."

ANVAR

The thing that surprises you when you enter a Pakistani home after a long absence is the smell. The aroma of desi food is a problem, mostly because of the amount of fried onions it requires. Some people simply do not bother to control the odor and are content to let it soak into their clothes. They sit beside innocent civilians on subways and buses and assault their noses with memories of old curry.

Most desis, however, take great pains to make sure that all traces of food remain confined to their kitchens. To this end they use air fresheners and scented candles; they leave windows open and light incense. The result is that their homes have a smell to them—it varies from household to household, depending on what scent has been used and how long ago—however, the constant is this perfume in the air, a gesture of care and courtesy, lingering just behind the door to welcome you in.

My parents' house always smells of saffron and lemons.

It is a small suburban home that still has an empty room set aside for me, as if my family is not sure when I will need to move back in. Aamir's room had been left similarly undisturbed, and he'd returned to it after his last residency, so my parents probably thought that my return was also inevitable.

I found Aamir in the living room, sitting cross-legged on a sofa. He was dressed in a white kurta over faded jeans, a small cap on his head. There was an ostentatiously large Quran nestled in his lap. He gently rocked back and forth as he read it out loud in an unnecessarily melodious manner. He gave no answer to my greeting, except that the volume of the recitation went up and the pitch rose an octave.

He could've recited the Quran in the privacy of his own room, of course, or sat quietly here and read it to himself, but that was not how Aamir did things.

"Stop glaring at your brother," my mother said, as she walked downstairs. I was struck by how much the world had changed, first becoming digital and now strangely virtual, while Bariah Faris remained the same. She was still that slender, severe woman I had always known. "Tell me why you are late."

I followed her into the modest kitchen. "Does he have to do that out there?"

"It's good to hear the Quran," she snapped, though her heart was not really in the admonishment. One of the benefits of a pending wedding in the family was how it preoccupied my mother. As she reached for a large wooden ladle, she whipped around, however, and asked, "When was the last time you even opened a Quran?"

"Yesterday." The lie came to my lips automatically, prompted more by muscle memory than by actual thought.

She regarded me with dark, narrowed eyes. "Really?"

"Absolutely. I'm pretty far in on my current reading." I hoped that the added detail made my story sound more convincing.

"You are reading with a translation, of course."

"I mean, yes, obviously," I said with a put-upon air. Something about that damn house always made me feel like a teenager again. "I have to understand what it is saying, after all. To better apply the teachings to my own life."

My mother made a noncommittal sound and then shrugged. "That's a good boy, then."

"Thank you. That makes me feel very validated."

She spared me an irritated look and then began to hunt around a cabinet for precisely the kind of pot she wanted. "By the way, what are you wearing?"

I glanced down at the battered, gray Barenaked Ladies T-shirt that I wore over faded blue jeans. My mother and I had fought a long and brutal jihad over the scandalous nature of the band's name, years ago. I won the right to wear their merchandise when I was a teenager and, over the years, had accumulated a closet full of shirts like this one in order to relish a rare victory over my mother's tyrannical will. For a horrible moment, I wondered if that old battle would once again have to be joined.

With some trepidation, I asked, "What's wrong with my clothes?"

"Not right now. What's bigger? Your brain or a cow?"

I've always been pretty sure that question, which my mother is fond of asking, loses something in the translation, but I've never bothered to ask for an explanation of what it might possibly mean. The answer is, one would think, self-evident.

After a moment, she said, "What are you wearing to Aamir's engagement party, I mean to ask."

"I hadn't thought about it."

"Were you planning on thinking about it?"

"Not for very long, no."

"How old are you? Do I still have to pick out your clothes for you? Are you a boy or a pajama?"

Another question that, I assumed, somehow made more sense in the original Urdu.

"You don't have to pick out my clothes for me."

She sniffed. "Wrong. I had to do it. Already picked out a nice shalwar kameez for you to wear."

"Thank you?"

"You really should do this yourself."

"I would've," I said as she turned her attention back to the cabinets, looking at the wide selection of lentils at her disposal.

"Well go change and show me how it fits. Aamir looks really good in the one I got for him. He couldn't stop talking about it for a whole day. He even had me take a picture and sent it to all his friends on Instantgram."

"Never heard of it. Is it like Instagram?"

"Why is it always the glib answer with you? Aamir isn't like that. How many times have I told you to try to be more like him?"

"Way too many times."

"Yet do you listen? You always have to be a smart donkey."

"Smart ass, you mean."

She whirled around to face me with impressive alacrity for a woman her age, her horrified eyes wide. "What did you say to me?"

"The expression. It's not 'smart donkey,' it's sm—"

I realized what I had done.

"Astaghfirullah. What is wrong with you, boy? Don't use filthy language in my kitchen. You know the Prophet, Peace Be Upon Him, said that a believer does not swear, don't you?"

I could have tried to explain I had not said a swear word. I could even have done a Google search to prove that "ass" is another way of saying "donkey," but I knew from long and exhausting experience that it wouldn't make any difference.

I hit my head lightly on the nearest wall for effect. "All right. I'm sorry. I'll go change."

As I turned to leave, though, she spoke up again. "What was the last thing you read?"

"What?"

"In the Quran. You remember what the last thing you read was about?"

I cast around desperately for an answer. I didn't even own a copy of the Quran. My mother drummed the ladle on her granite countertop expectantly.

"It was . . . about how there is no compulsion in religion," I said. That was one of the few parts I remembered. It had appealed to me, even when I was a child.

"Ah yes," she said, her voice dangerously low. "From Surah Baqarah. Very strange."

"Why?"

"The Chapter of the Cow is at the beginning of the Quran. As you well know, it is the second chapter."

"As I well know." I slowly backed out of the kitchen.

"I thought you said you were, how did you put it, 'pretty far in,' was it?"

Not for the first time in my life, I wondered if the wrong member of the family had gone to law school. "I meant I'm pretty far into the chapter, Ma."

"That makes sense. Because you wouldn't dare lie about something like that, would you? You wouldn't dare."

"Cross my heart and hope to die."

"May Allah forgive you. Don't you talk to me about crosses."

"Sorry."

"And you know that verse you're talking about only applies to non-Muslims, right? It means you can't force someone to accept the religion. Once you are in, a different set of rules applies. You have to do everything you're told or there is hell to pay."

I grinned at her. "It's a lot like this family then."

She sighed in the profoundly tired way that old people can sigh. "Go change, Anvar. Please change before it is too late."

I didn't manage to change in time. Guests had already started to arrive by the time I showered, shaved and donned the deep turquoise raw silk kurta and blood-red shalwar my mother had picked out. It wasn't something I would have worn if left to my own devices, but I had to admit that it suited me.

Aamir was freaking out a little about our running late and Ma was trying to calm him down by reminding him that no one was rude enough to show up to a Pakistani party on time.

Now that I was ready, the thirty-odd people who were squished into my parents' small house, decked out in fine clothes and sparkling like the shiny happy creatures they always pretended to be at these occasions, began dividing themselves into groups. They'd all assembled here and would travel in a procession to the hotel ballroom where the engagement was supposed to take place. There was mild chaos as they tried to decide which cars to take and who would drive.

"If we're so worried about being punctual," I told my father, "we should've all gone directly to the party."

That wasn't what Imtiaz Faris was concerned about. "Are you all right?"

"Me?" I cleared my throat and stood up to my full height. "Sure."

"You look like you're in pain."

"I mean, I have to be around Aamir, so I guess I am a little. No more than usual though."

My father sighed. "How is it that you both turned out to be such turds but, at the same time, turned out so different?"

"Awful parenting?"

"Well, I think Zuha will improve our family quite a bit. I just remembered the other day how kind she was when she came over after your Naani Jaan died. Remember? You two talked about poetry then."

"It's impossible to forget."

"Your naani would've liked her, I think."

"Yeah. I don't doubt it."

He paused, looking at me intently for a moment, and I tried to smile for him. After a moment, he clapped me on my shoulder. "Let's get this party started."

Zuha wore an off-white raw silk lehenga with silver embroidery. The choli, though sleeveless, was longer than it was meant to be, covering her midriff entirely, the demands of fashion giving some way to religion. It was a modest change, but it wasn't enough. I heard a few women whispering among themselves, scandalized, when she made her entrance. My mother's expression was grim but, at least as far as I could tell, she said nothing to Zuha or the Shahs. The guardians of orthodoxy, those desi aunties who'd never admit to any indiscretions, youthful or otherwise, would be talking about Zuha's bare arms for years.

Zuha wore a simple white-gold necklace cradling a pearl, with a matching bracelet on her left wrist. Her makeup highlighted the graceful line of her jaw, calling attention up to her brown eyes, which were darker today than usual.

My father startled me. I looked away from Zuha and the stage that had been set up at the front of the room, with two elaborately carved chairs for her and Aamir to sit on. In his life, this was the first time Imtiaz Faris had managed to sneak up on anybody.

"Don't stare. That dress is going to be trouble, but we should pretend everything is normal."

I cleared my throat, trying to compose my features into an expression both innocent and indignant at the same time. "You're right, Dad, of course. I'm just shocked, that's all."

"Your mother will be very upset. What kind of Pakistani bride wears white? Did nobody tell that girl it's the color of mourning?"

"To be fair, she is marrying Aamir, so maybe it's entirely appropriate."

"Repeat that in front of your mother and you'll be the one people are mourning for. Go and mingle."

I made a face. Surveying the large, gaudily decorated hall for innocuous, shallow conversation, I saw no one that I actually wanted to speak with—well, except for one person.

Zuha's gaze found mine and she gave a quick little wave with her fingers. I was about to wave back when I heard my mom call my name and jumped, caught staring for apparently the second time that night. I wondered how long I had been standing there. My ears felt warm. I straightened my shoulders and turned my attention to Bariah Faris, who was walking toward me, a pleasantly plump-looking aunty and a pretty young woman, obviously the aunty's daughter, in tow. I managed not to swear out loud, but just barely.

Ma laid a proprietary hand on my elbow, smiling at her companions. "Anvar, you remember Nusrat, yes? And this is her daughter, Aliyah Dzatil Himmah."

"Wow. Try saying that four times fast."

The girl blushed. "My friends call me Allie."

My mother tightened her grip on my arm. Her tone of voice, however, did not change at all. "This is my younger son, Anvar." She gave the women a smile loaded with significance and added, "The lawyer."

"The lapsed lawyer." I bowed in an exaggerated fashion, as if I were in a BBC period piece.

The middle-aged woman turned to her daughter, then to my mother and finally to myself with a look of confusion. "What does that mean?"

"Nothing at all," Ma said. Her cheerfulness sounded ridiculous to me, but then I knew her well. I knew that Bariah Faris was never really cheerful. "This one thinks he is funny." She trained her best death glare on me. "He's the only one who thinks so."

"My daughter," Nusrat Aunty said, "is also superfunny. Always with the jokes about everything. Except about school, of course. She's very serious about that. She's studying the sciences at Harvard, you know."

"All of them?"

My mother let out an exasperated sigh at my remark. Then, regaining her misleading sunny disposition, as if a sudden thought had dawned upon her, she said, "Nusrat, did I introduce you to Mrs. Shah? No? You must meet her, she's such a lovely woman. I'm sure these two can find something to talk about."

"Well," Allie said, after a moment of uncomfortable silence in which we watched our mothers disappear into the crowd. "That wasn't mortifying at all."

"They were very subtle."

We smiled at each other, her fingers playing with the edge of her shimmery dupatta, my hands clasped behind my back. Finally, she said, "Just get it out of the way now."

"What?"

"Whatever outrageous thing you're going to say to make me tell my mother I'm not interested."

"Is that something people do?"

She nodded. "Sure. At least, I hope that is what they're doing. If the guy who asked me, in our first conversation, if I was a virgin was genuinely trying . . . well, then I'd just feel bad for him." When I didn't reply, Allie said, "How do you drive unwanted prospects away?"

"Naturally, I guess."

Allie grinned. "That's actually funny. Too bad you're not at all interested in me. You might not have scared me away."

"How do you know I'm not interested?"

"Because I never understood the expression 'deer in the head-lights' until we met. So, should we get our stories straight about why this won't work?"

"Most girls just tell their mothers I'm a jerk."

Allie shook her head. "That's not true, though. I don't like to lie."

"It's a little true. Besides, you don't get to be a lawyer and still insist that people tell the truth."

"You're sure? It'll hurt your reputation with the aunties, you know."

"Somehow I think I'll manage to survive the disgrace. It was nice meeting you."

I wandered away, though not without offering an exaggerated bow, in case my mother was watching, drifting from group to group, until I noticed that Zuha had been left alone for a moment.

Everyone around her seemed occupied with something or other, so I had a small window of opportunity to speak to her. I drifted casually up to the stage and took Aamir's chair beside her.

"Saw you talking to Allie," Zuha said. "How'd that go?"

"She seemed nice."

"Very nice and much too good for you."

I ignored the comment. "So, your dress seems to have caused quite a stir."

"You like it though, right?"

I shrugged. "It's fine."

"Fine? I look great."

"I've seen you look a lot better in a lot less."

Zuha's breath caught and she glanced around us, as surreptitiously as she could manage while sitting on a stage in front of a crowd of a hundred people, to make sure no one had overheard. Then she hissed, "You can't say that. What the hell is wrong with you?"

"It's not one thing. It's more of a cascading malfunctions type of situation."

"I think the correct technical term is 'cascading failures.'" Aamir's voice broke in and I nearly leapt up in surprise. What was with my family and sneaking up on me tonight? I looked away from Zuha to see my brother standing before me. "Anvar, you're in my seat."

I considered telling him that I was exactly where I was supposed to be but thought better of it. Instead, I got to my feet, so Aamir could sit down next to Zuha. Smiling at his fiancée to be, and without bothering to look at me, he said, "Go get Mom. It's time to exchange rings."

I found myself standing with a crowd in a circle around the couple. Aamir held Zuha's hand. I was so intent on the sight that it took me a while to realize that everyone was looking at me. Aamir had asked me something and everyone was waiting for a response.

"The ring, Anvar," my brother said, with the air of someone unhappy at having to repeat himself. "Where did you put the ring?"

I shook my head, trying to clear the storm clouds that had suddenly gathered on the shore of my thoughts. I did not remember being in possession of a ring. It seemed like something I would recall.

Aamir grinned. "Just kidding. We wouldn't trust you with something that important."

There was silence.

Aamir's smile sank out of sight as he realized that the joke was a bad one, perhaps even a cruel one, and no one thought it was very funny.

I looked down at him. Then I glanced at Zuha, who was staring at me intently, with those quicksand eyes. She seemed to expect me to do something, so I laughed, to make the moment easier for Aamir, and everyone else laughed as well.

Laugh and the world laughs with you.

Except Zuha. She did not laugh. She did not even smile as my brother slipped his ring on her finger and let her hand go.

The next night my parents had a party at their place. Zuha's extended family had come to town for the engagement, and the rules of desi hospitality dictated that Bariah and Imtiaz Faris honor them by hosting dinner. I slipped out onto the porch when the music and pedantic conversation got to be too much. Making sure I was alone, I lit a cigarette and stared up at the starless night.

My jaw ached from forcing myself to smile and the effort of maintaining a happy, sunny disposition was exhausting. I couldn't wait to get away, get home and be alone, so I could begin to process what was happening.

"Not having fun?"

I fumbled with my lighter and almost dropped it. I turned. Zuha stood in the shadows. She walked up beside me, smiling at my surprise. A moment passed in silence, then she folded her thin arms below her chest and pointedly looked at my cigarette. "You're not going to offer me one?"

"When did you start smoking?"

"I don't," she said impishly. "But that does not give you license to be rude."

I shook my head and offered her a cigarette from my pack. She took one.

"You said you don't smoke."

"You offered. I didn't want to be rude either," Zuha replied, amusement still hiding in ambush in her tone. "You've got the fire?"

Wary and obviously out of my depth, I held out my lighter without comment. She plucked it from my hand with her delicate fingers and flicked it on after a few attempts. She lit her cigarette. She didn't smoke it though. She just watched it burn, her expression strangely intent, as the red embers ate away the pristine white paper, turning it into black ash. Then she dropped it to the ground and it went out.

"That was a waste of a perfectly good cigarette."

"Really?" She handed me back my lighter. "Strange. I didn't realize there was such a thing as a good cigarette."

"Clever. Did you come out here to give me a hard time? You realize that I am an adult? I've earned the right to slowly destroy myself."

"I came to talk."

"About what?"

"I'm going to tell Aamir everything that happened. It would be pretty shitty if he found out after we actually got married."

"It'll be pretty shitty either way. If you were going to do it—"

"Not everyone has your infuriating certainty about everything."

I took a long drag and blew smoke out forcefully, trying to exhale my frustration.

"You don't think I should?"

"I told you to do what you want." I shrugged. "I meant it."

"Also, I wanted to tell you that you have been laboring under a misapprehension."

"That's a nifty phrase. Austen?"

"Bridget Jones's Diary."

"Of course it is."

"Are you done being a snob? Can I go on now?" When she didn't get a response, Zuha continued, "I wanted to tell you that it wouldn't have been that way and you're a jerk for thinking so little of me."

"What are you talking about?"

"You said I would've turned you down because you aren't successful, because you think you have nothing to offer, because you don't have money. It's been bothering me. I wouldn't have cared where you lived or how much you made. You should know me better than that and it hurts that you don't."

"Really? Despite everything that I am—that I am not, I should say—you would have said yes if I had asked you to marry me?"

Someone called her name before she could respond. They wanted her back inside. Zuha gave me a tight smile and walked out of the black night.

My hangover the next day was a wounded tiger in its unrelenting and deranged fury. It seemed to claw and tear at the inside of my mind. I must have drifted off on my couch because I woke to the cruel sound of an insistent doorbell. Muttering under my breath, I stumbled to my feet, hurrying as best I could, to make sure that the chime wouldn't go off again. It irritated the predator in my mind.

It was Azza's father, Abu Fahd.

I stared at him.

"As-salamu alaykum," he said when I didn't speak, but the sudden panic of my heart made the greeting of peace seem ironic. What was he doing here? It was impossible that he'd found out Azza came here. Wasn't it? I knew enough to know he'd be furious if he found out about our relationship. That was true of most men who forced their daughters to wear the niqab.

"This is a bad time. You look ill."

"No, I'm fine." My voice was burnt, husky and hoarse. "Sorry. It's been a tough few days."

This seemed to amuse him. "I know something about tough days."

I glanced down at his hands, at the missing fingernails I remembered from the mosque. His meaning was clear. Whatever you're going through, I've been through worse. "Right. What can I do for you?"

"Where are you from?"

I frowned. "What do you—"

"I've been to Pakistan," he said. "And hospitality is not dead there."

I sighed and stepped back. "Come in. Pardon the mess. I wasn't expecting anyone."

As he stepped inside, his troubled eyes fell upon the discarded bottles of scotch I had not yet put away. "In a Muslim country, you'd be whipped for this. Seventy lashes."

"That's not how it works here."

He gave me a grim smile. "That is not really how it works anywhere. There are no Muslim countries anymore."

"Doesn't Saudi still have Sharia Law?"

Abu Fahd made a dismissive sound at the back of his throat. "The law is for the poor," he said grimly. "Money is the new furqan in this world."

Even I winced at the bitterness of that thought. Al-Furqan, "The Criterion," was a name of the Quran, as it decided between what was good and what was evil. He was saying that money, not justice, governed the world. It was true in Saudi Arabia, and it was true here.

"That is why I am here. I asked Hafeez for your apartment number because I need advice from a lawyer, and I have nothing to give you in return."

I exhaled sharply in relief, then gestured to the sofa. "What can I do for you?"

He glanced at the bottles of alcohol again, hesitated, then sat. "I don't mean to preach—"

"No, no. By all means, go ahead."

Either he missed the sarcasm or he ignored it. "Getting drunk is not the act of a good Muslim."

"I'm not a good Muslim. I am, at best, a remedial one."

"Do Americans think you are funny? It doesn't appear to me that you are."

"The jury is still out on that one."

I considered making some coffee. It would revitalize me but would also prolong Abu Fahd's visit. I decided it wasn't worth it. Best to end this quickly. "So do you want to tell me what's going on?"

He smiled at me, an unsettling expression. I don't really know what it looks like when tectonic plates shift, but I imagine it looks a little like Abu Fahd's smile.

"That is most kind. I need some information about this country's immigration system. Can you keep a secret?"

"If you have anything you can give me for a retainer, a fee, you'll be protected by attorney-client privilege."

Abu Fahd fished around in his pocket, pulled out an almost empty roll of Mentos and put it on the coffee table.

I really have to do something about my hourly rates.

"Just so you're clear, there are exceptions to what I can and cannot keep to myself. For example, if you tell me you are going to kill someone, then I'd have to report that to the police. You're not going to kill anyone, are you?"

"Not today."

I chuckled and then met his hard gaze and realized that Abu Fahd had been perfectly serious.

"Well, that's not at all terrifying."

He decided to get to the point. "I am here because I'm worried for my daughter. Her name is Safwa."

"Safwa? How many children do you have?"

"Just one now. You seem confused."

"I'd heard people call your daughter Azza."

"That is not her true name, just as Saqr is not mine. These are the names of the people we became in order to live in this country. I would not make it here otherwise."

I steepled my hands in front of my face and sank back into my seat. I couldn't afford to appear shocked. So far as Abu Fahd knew, there was no reason for me to care about that information. But Azza hadn't even told me her real name. We'd been sleeping together for months and I didn't even know who she really was. That was incomprehensible.

Abu Fahd was still talking. I tried to focus on what he was saying.

"Sorry, what?"

"We have no passports or visas. No certificates of birth."

"You're illegal immigrants."

"Yes," he said. "From Mexico."

"Mexico?"

"I'm from Iraq. I lived in Afghanistan during the Soviet jihad and then in Pakistan for a while. Then we came to Mexico and made our way here."

"Wow. That's incredible. Maybe they should build a wall."

"The three of us came through a tunnel."

"Brilliant. Wait. The three of you?"

"Myself, Safwa and Qais Badami. I want to know if there is a way to change that, to make us legal, because everywhere in the news, they say if the Republicans win, they're going to come after people like us. They'll build a wall, ban Muslims, throw us out of the country."

"That's not going to happen. Have some faith in Americans."

Abu Fahd's little smile was slow and pained, like that of an old man struggling to stand after falling to the ground. "I have not found that to be wise."

"Fair enough. Then let me say that for any kind of mass deportation to happen here, the government would have to come find you and everyone else who is out of status. We're talking about federal agents rounding up millions of people across the country. They don't have the time or resources for that."

"So, you are saying it is not possible."

"I'm saying I would be surprised if it happens. Very surprised."

"That is not as reassuring as you might think it sounds."

That too was fair.

"Is there a way for Safwa to become legal? It doesn't matter for me. I have grown old walking the face of this world. If they throw me out, I will find some other place to die."

I leaned forward, my elbows resting on my thighs. "If Azza married an American citizen—"

"I promised her to Qais."

"I understand. I'm just saying that, from a purely legal perspective, it might be best for her to break that particular promise."

"Impossible," Abu Fahd snapped, eyes wide. "What kind of man—what kind of Muslim—breaks a promise? Is your word, your honor, not iron?"

I sighed. Obviously, Abu Fahd had never heard of the theory of efficient breach.

"Look, I'm not an immigration lawyer. I can ask my friends if there is any potential relief to be had. Maybe some kind of refugee program or some other application process I am unaware of—"

"No," he said, rising to his feet. "No one else can know of this."

"I wouldn't disclose your name or identity."

He hesitated, then shook his head. "I am satisfied with the answers you have given me."

"I wish I had better news for you."

"It is as Allah wills," the large man replied with a shrug. "That has to be sufficient for me."

"It has never been sufficient for me."

The older man looked at me with an expression that reeked of pity. "I can tell. That is why I fear that when the Day of Judgment comes, I will not find you in the Garden."

I don't remember the punch. There was a knock on the door seconds after Abu Fahd left, so I assumed there was something else he wanted to ask me. I simply said, "It's open." The next thing I remember, albeit vaguely, is falling. Then I was lying there, on the gray linoleum floor, with Aamir peering down at me.

"Hit you harder than I thought." My brother waved his hand in front of my face. "How many fingers am I holding up?"

I held up a finger of my own.

"You're fine." Aamir reluctantly held out a hand to help me up. "And you deserved it."

Groaning, I got to my feet. The tiger from earlier had multiplied. Now there was a litter of feral cats in my head and everything felt scattered, blurred by pain and disorientation. Aamir held out a can of beer.

"It's the only cold thing you have here. Hold it against your left eye."

I took the can and popped it open. "Thanks."

"Astaghfirullah."

"Right." I took a sip and let out an exaggerated sigh of satisfaction. "Totally."

"You're going to hell for that."

"I'm hearing that a lot today."

"From Abu Fahd?"

I nodded. Aamir had probably seen him leaving, and most likely knew the man from the mosque. It didn't matter just then. Walking to the couch, I draped myself over it. "She told you then?"

He sat down across from me and placed a hand on his head in a way that made him appear very tired. The anger that had driven him to strike me was gone, and it had left him deflated. "That you slept with my fiancée. Yes. She told me."

"I'm not sure if this helps but I would like to say, in my defense, that she wasn't your anything back then."

"What was she to you, exactly?"

I stared out the nearest window and said nothing. It wasn't much of a view, but it was San Francisco. I loved this city because it reminded me of my childhood, of where I grew up. It vacillated between extremes, like Karachi, except in an entirely different way. In Karachi, politics had been unpredictable and volatile. In San Francisco, nature was. The weather here was capricious and whimsical. The chaos felt familiar. It felt like home.

Aamir's presence felt like home too. Even though I often didn't like him very much, he was part of where I belonged in the world and that was something.

"I should've told you."

"You think?"

"I can't explain myself if that's why you are here."

"I came here to punch you in the face."

I raised my drink to him. "Cheers then. Mission accomplished."

Aamir shook his head.

"It felt like it was her secret to tell," I said. "I felt like I couldn't say anything. Does that make sense?"

Aamir shrugged his wide, responsible shoulders. "Doesn't matter, I guess. You did what you did. What I want to know is what am I supposed to do now?"

"I don't know."

He got to his feet, looked around the cramped apartment, as if trying to decide which direction to pace in, then sat down again. "We already had this big party. Everyone knows we're engaged. Wedding invitations have gone out. What will people say if we have to cancel it?"

"I wouldn't worry about that."

"No," he said, his tone venomous, "you wouldn't. I'm serious. Tell me what to do. Every time the two of you are together, I'm going to wonder what she is thinking. Every time she is with me, I'll wonder if . . . I can't do it. You really messed me up."

Wincing, I sat up straight. I didn't want to be casual when I said what I wanted to say to him. I wanted him to know that I was serious. Certain to look him in the eye, I spoke more earnestly than I ever had in my life. "I really am sorry, for what it is worth."

He held my gaze for a moment, then looked away. "This isn't supposed to happen to me. I do everything right. Always. I resist temptation. Then you come along with whatever the heck it is that you do. It's like you're hacking my laptop again."

"It was hardly hacking. And will you let that go already?"

"You put porn on my computer, Anvar, and framed me for it."

"Yeah but . . . that was like one time."

"All you ever think about is yourself. You wanted to go to prom, so you . . ." He trailed off and I could almost see a piece of the puzzle of my past fall into place for him. "It was Zuha. You went to prom with Zuha."

I nodded.

He sighed and collapsed back into his chair, rubbing his eyes with the palms of his hands. "What happened?"

"We danced. Mostly."

"Not with prom. I meant with Zuha. What happened between you two?"

"You want details?"

"No. I really don't."

"It didn't work out. She heard a lecture by some famous imam, some Hamza Younis or something—"

"Sheikh Hamza Yusuf. How can you not know who he is? The man is an ocean of knowledge. How can you be a Muslim in California and not know who Hamza Yusuf is?"

"Whatever. She thought he was the bee's knees. She heard more and more of his lectures and became more and more religious. Started praying regularly and, you know, us Muslims are not big on the fornication."

"You don't say."

"She repented from all of it. Repented from me."

Aamir snorted in a fair imitation of our mother's favorite expression of contempt. "Mom's still asking for forgiveness for you too."

"That was that. Then after I went to law school—"

"Wait. You two dated through college?"

"The first two years, yeah."

He counted off the numbers on the squares of his fingers, trying to do that math.

"Ten years," I told him. "We dated a decade ago."

"How did none of us know?" When I shrugged, he sighed, defeated. "I don't understand. Why did she say yes when Ma asked her family about me?"

"You should ask her that."

"I did. I want to know what she told you," Aamir said.

"When we talked about it, it wasn't . . . We just argued, okay, and I didn't get to her reasons. Aside from spite, I guess. What did she tell you?"

He stared down at his hands. It took me a moment to realize he was looking at his ring. "She was angry that you let it happen. That you thought so little of your time together that you'd let Ma propose for me."

"I guess she didn't know this family doesn't tell me anything."

"You never ask. There was also all this pressure from her parents. She isn't twenty-five anymore, and she's turned down everyone they've introduced her to. She couldn't come up with a good reason to say no to me. She couldn't tell them about you. She says she's sorry."

"I'm sorry too," I said again.

There was a long silence, then Aamir grimaced, got to his feet and started clearing up the bottles and cans that were lying around. "This place is a mess."

"Leave it. I'll get to it."

"No. You won't."

Okay, so he was right about that.

"You haven't answered my question," he said. "What should I do?"

"Stop asking me that. I don't know. I can tell you that, despite the fact that . . . Despite this situation and whatever blame falls to her for it, Zuha is one of the most beautiful souls I've ever known. I wouldn't let her go."

"Except you did."

"She didn't want me anymore, Aamir. I didn't have a choice."

He shook his head. "Naani Jaan was right about you."

"What are you talking about?" I asked, more sharply than I had a right to just then.

"She said you play checkers without courage. But it's true about everything you do. You never stand up and fight for what you want or believe in."

"That's not true."

"Really? What kind of law do you practice again?"

"That's different," I snapped.

"No, Anvar. Think about your life. Think about how you went to prom—"

"Come on."

"Why'd you go all the way to Boston? It makes sense now. You ran away after breaking up with Zuha, right? It's your nature. Remember that goat you liked so much?"

"Mikey."

"I was ready to do it for you, to argue that you were too young. I was waiting for you to tell Dad you didn't want to kill Mikey. But you didn't stand up. You never do. That's the real reason you didn't tell me about Zuha. You're a coward."

I managed, somehow, to keep from telling him to shut up. I'd hurt him, and he was lashing out. But there wasn't much more of this I could take. "You should leave," I told him quietly, "before this gets worse."

He dropped the last can he'd picked up and it clattered onto the floor. "I have one more question."

"What?"

"Do you still have feelings for her?"

I held his gaze but didn't give him an answer.

Still, he nodded, like he heard the truth I couldn't bring myself to voice.

AZZA

When I got back from class, Abu was still awake. His face was pale. He looked older than he usually did, like the years had suddenly overtaken him. I took off my coat and greeted him. He replied in a tired voice.

"You should sleep," I told him. "You've got to be at work again soon."

And I have to write, I didn't tell him. He could, of course, never know what I had planned. He couldn't know that I was filling pages upon pages with half lies and incomplete truths.

"Qais managed to get the birthday present you wanted—"

"He found a gun?" I couldn't keep excitement out of my voice.

Abu didn't notice. "He came by with it and . . . I am afraid I have made him very angry with me."

I went to sit with him. "What happened?"

"There is a lawyer here that I met. Anvar Faris."

For a short moment, my heart started to race but then I remembered that Abu was not angry with me. If he'd found out the truth about Anvar, and what I did with Anvar, then we wouldn't be sitting here like this. That secret of mine was safe.

"Hafeez Bhatti was saying good things about him, so I went. I told him everything. I thought only to get some advice about . . ." Abu waved his hands around, trying to pull the word he was searching for out of the air. "Our situation with not being here legally. I thought maybe there was something to be done. When I told Qais of this, he got very upset, started screaming. He doesn't trust this lawyer with our secret. Doesn't trust anyone. He says it was a foolish thing to do."

"Who cares if he's upset? He shouldn't have raised his voice to you."

"I've never seen him this way before," Abu said. "Like he was barely in control of himself. When you marry him, my child, this side of him will cause you pain. I'd thought maybe he would make you happy, but after seeing his fury today . . ." Abu shook his head. "It will be your life's work to make sure he doesn't ever get upset."

I should've kept silent. Instead, I spoke. "Why?"

He frowned. "What?"

"After seeing what he really is, why would you still force me to marry him?"

Something in Abu's face shifted. I saw the tiredness of his eyes become confusion and then anger. "Force you? I asked you if you wanted to marry him. Did I not ask you? Have you forgotten?"

"No," I whispered. "You never did."

"Lies!" Abu said, the volume of his voice making me cringe. "You will marry him. I gave my word."

"But I didn't," I said, trying to speak as gently as I could. "I was silent."

Abu's manner was not gentle. "What is silence if not agreement? And you accepted his bride price, did you not?"

"I wanted what he could give us," I said. "I never wanted him."

Abu looked at me as if I were a stranger. "Immoral," he hissed. "Depraved. You are saying that you promised to marry a man for this?" He looked at the close walls surrounding us. "How are you better than a woman who sells herself?"

I closed my eyes, wondering how much harsher his words would be if he knew the whole truth.

"In the end," he whispered, "you turn out to be no less filthy than your mother."

"What? Abu—"

He slapped me hard across my face with the back of his hand.

I stared at him. He stared back. It seemed for a moment that we were equally dazed. He hadn't raised his hand to me in so long, I'd started to hope it would never happen again.

"No," Abu said. He said it in the way a man begs for something. "Don't call me that. If you do not understand honor, you are no child of mine. After everything I have done for you, your blood still belongs to Yousef Ganni."

The world shifted.

It was as if a veil that childhood had draped over memories of my own past was yanked off. I saw what was obvious for the first time.

Mama.

She had been more than the weak, broken, dying flower I'd known.

She had dared to seek happiness in the world, and she'd betrayed Abu to do it. It seemed impossible, given what I knew of her. I guess I hadn't really known her at all.

"I should've thrown you out when you were born. I should have killed your mother when I found out the truth," he said. "But I just pretended not to know. I loved her too much. This is the result. Only dishonor and misery comes from weakness."

"Abu—"

He hit me again.

"Don't make me do this, Safwa. Say you will marry Qais and I'll forgive you. Please. I'll be able to pretend again."

I should've said what he wanted to hear.

But I didn't.

I kept silent and he kept hitting me, until I wasn't able to talk anymore, and Abu was a fountain of tears.

ANVAR

The next morning, I had sixteen missed calls from my mother. I ignored them all. I tried to drown myself in my work, but the lingering pain from Aamir's strike kept me from focusing. The only thing I had to look forward to was a possible visit from Azza, but her father wouldn't go to work for hours.

My phone rang again, this time a call from an unknown number. It was possible that my mother either had purchased a new phone or was borrowing one from someone to trick me into speaking to her. Those were both things she would do. However, since it was much more probable that a client was calling, I answered. It was Qais Badami.

"I need to speak to you about the situation Abu Fahd discussed with you," he said, without waiting for me to say anything.

"I can't really talk to you about that."

"I also have my own questions. Can you meet me?"

I agreed because getting out of the apartment seemed like a good idea and any distraction from thoughts of Zuha and Aamir felt like a welcome one. Besides, somehow, my acquaintance with Qais had been the most uncomplicated relationship in my life. He gave me the name of an Egyptian restaurant on Jones Street and we agreed on a time.

I arrived ten minutes early and he was already there. The restaurant itself was fine. The sparse furniture and uninspired ambience were typical of the Tenderloin District.

Qais frowned when he saw me. The black eye I had forming was not pretty.

"I'm fine," I said.

"Were you attacked by racists?"

"What?"

"Islamophobia. It's everywhere these days."

"I've heard of it."

"Did they jump you near the mosque? Just tell me who it was, and I will take care of them, you better believe that."

"I didn't get hit because I'm Muslim. I got hit because I'm not Muslim enough."

"One of us did that?"

"Yeah."

"That's our problem right there. No unity among the ummah, you know. It's like brother against brother out there."

"That's precisely what it is like."

"Very sad."

"Sure. What did you want to talk about?"

"Let's get some food first."

He ordered something called hawawshy. I got the same thing without looking at the menu.

"Here is the thing," Qais said, leaning forward to whisper, though we were virtually alone in the restaurant. "I want to make sure you know not to repeat anything Abu Fahd told you."

"I couldn't repeat it even if I wanted to. He hired me as his attorney."

"He paid you?"

"Using breath mints."

Qais grinned. "You're great."

"I'm aware. It means everything he told me is confidential."

"Good. Very good. Very bad things could happen if people found out. He never should have told you. We agreed not to tell anyone."

"He was worried about his daughter."

Qais nodded. "It is still strange of him to go back on his word. Abu Fahd takes his honor very seriously. Once Azza ran out of the house without her niqab for some reason. I can't even remember why she did it. He locked her in a room and didn't feed her for three days. You're shocked? Yes. It is shocking, maybe, but not so surprising. All that grief, all that pain, it shifts the balance of the mind, no?"

I'd heard stories of women being abused, and been forced to sit through a couple of Pakistani television dramas where such violence was a theme, but it was foreign to my personal experience. Learning this about Azza was like coming home to find that someone had broken in and rearranged everything, so nothing was where it should've been.

I couldn't react much or even seem interested, of course. Qais couldn't know that I knew Azza. From his perspective, the only reason for me to care about his story was Abu Fahd. If I wanted to know more, I'd have to direct my inquiry through Azza's father. "What do you mean by grief and pain?"

As the waiter returned with water, Qais fell silent. When we were alone again, he changed the subject. "Since you are accepting food as payment these days . . ."

"I'm not."

"In exchange for this meal, can I ask you some questions?"

"You're already asking me questions and I can pay for my own lunch."

Qais hesitated, then seemed to decide to say what he wanted. "I want to know about the Second Commandment."

"You shall have no gods but me?"

He looked completely confused.

"That's the Second Commandment. At least, I'm pretty sure it is."

Qais scratched his head. "I'm talking about guns."

I couldn't help but laugh. "You mean the Second Amendment."

"Yes," he said, obviously irritated. "That one."

"It's the right to bear arms. What do you want to know?"

Our food arrived before he could answer. It turned out that I had ordered a toasted pita filled with ground beef mixed with lamb. It was greasy, but the perfectly cooked meat was deliciously spiced with coriander, cayenne pepper and garlic. I nodded my appreciation to Qais.

"Does it only apply to guns? You said the right to arms, right? Bombs are arms."

"Those are illegal though."

"Good. That's good. So," he went on between mouthfuls. "I heard that pretty much the only way illegals get deported is if they commit a crime. But the Second Amendment says that I can get a gun, right? So it isn't a crime for me to have one?"

"I don't know. You aren't a citizen, so the question of whether or not a constitutional provision applies to someone in your position would probably be based on a substantial connections test. If you have enough contact with the United States—"

"I'm here."

"What I'm saying is that I've seen that test applied for other amendments. I don't know if it applies to the Second."

"So, it could be different."

I shrugged. "Could be."

"These people just make this whole thing up as they go along, don't they?"

"It feels that way sometimes."

"How do you spend your life wading through their bullshit? It's all about using the right words against the wrong words. That's not justice."

"It's not that simple."

"It's not complicated. You're a Muslim, aren't you?" The way he asked the question made it seem more than rhetorical. "Then you should know that law comes from Allah. Right is right and wrong is wrong. We have an example before us. Just because Americans wrote a law allowing them to do what they did to Abu Fahd doesn't make it okay, right?"

"What did they do to Abu Fahd?"

"You've seen his right hand. Did you notice he has no fingernails? It was the Americans who took them." Qais paused, then laughed. "Sometimes I wonder if he is here only to get them back."

"You're saying that he was tortured?"

"It was a bad place he was held in. He was lucky to come out alive. Many were not so fortunate."

"What was he in prison for?"

"Americans don't need a reason. They do whatever they want. In Afghanistan, I know of men who disappeared because they wore Casio watches. Abu Fahd was just Iraqi at the wrong time."

"Hold on. So this man who we tortured—"

"You didn't torture anyone."

"America, I mean. How can he be here?"

There was pride on Qais's face now. "I arranged all of it."

"How?"

"That I cannot tell you. It is amazing though, isn't it? These people would shit their pants if they knew who Abu Fahd was. They are good at making demons for themselves, these Americans."

"And you're one of them now."

"No," Qais said. "They are making it very clear that I am not one of them. And neither are you."

I didn't really know what to say to that. So instead, I asked, "Why did you want to know about the Second Amendment?"

Leaning forward, he said quietly, "I got a gun. I just wanted to know if it is a crime, if I have to keep it a secret from my roommates or if they can know about it. Like I said, from what I've heard only criminals get deported."

We ate in silence for a few minutes and then he asked, "Do you have a gun?"

I shook my head.

"Get one," Qais said. "Bad men will come for you someday. You should be able to defend yourself."

"What makes you think they will come for me?"

"Only the fact that they have been coming for me my entire life."

As I walked back to my apartment, I passed Hafeez Bhatti's office. He called out to me, waving his betel-nut-juice-stained handkerchief wildly to get my attention.

"It may be wise for you not to go home just now, Barrister Sahib. Your mother is here."

I glanced at the stairs I'd been about to climb and stepped back, retreating toward my landlord's office. "That's not good."

"No indeed. She stopped by to ask where you were. Very much angry she was looking, I can tell you. Truth be told, even I was a little scared." He chortled happily at this, though it was unclear to me why he should find it at all funny. "So, tell me, what did you do?"

"I remained silent when I should have spoken."

The landlord gave a long, drawn-out sigh that emanated from the core of his being and seemed to leave his massive balloon of a body slightly deflated. "What living Muslim can't relate to that, Barrister Sahib? Come now, why don't you walk with me for a while."

"Where are you going?"

Hafeez shrugged. "What does it matter to you? It is away from here."

A fair point, given the circumstances. I fell in step next to him as he led me back outside, loudly chewing his paan. We were silent for a few blocks. It was a clear afternoon in the Tenderloin, the less-than-glamorous underbelly of San Francisco. I noticed things I wouldn't normally notice when moving at my own faster pace. A run-down hotel had dressed its doormen in bright, lemon-yellow overcoats. A new Chinese restaurant had opened and claimed to serve the perfect apple pie.

"You shouldn't avoid your mother," Bhatti finally told me. "No matter how much trouble you're having. I helped you in this one instance as a way to apologize."

"For what?"

"I shouldn't have sent Abu Fahd to your apartment. Shouldn't have told him where you lived."

"It's fine."

"Is it?" Bhatti asked, his beady eyes keen and shining. "And what if he had come and his daughter was there also?" I was so stunned that he knew about my relationship with Azza, I stopped walking.

Bhatti shot me a sideways glance when I caught up to him. "Of course, I was aware of your filthy hanky-panky. Everything that happens in that building, I know. I forgot momentarily is all. I should've been more careful. And you, you should be more careful, my young friend. You don't know what you're mixing yourself up in."

"He just had a few legal questions."

"He said as much," Hafeez said. "I've walked a long time on this world. I have seen a few things. I have learned how to tell one kind of man from another kind. Let's take you, for example. I know full well you are a man of conflict."

"All lawyers are."

"Maybe. But you are different. You don't fight others. You fight the Great Jihad. The Prophet said that the fight inside a man, the fight for his soul, is the greatest struggle of all, yes? The fight between the white brown man and the brown white man. The fight between the good bad man and the bad good man. I see it in you all the time. That is why I let you stay in my building for cheap. To see how it ends." He smiled at me. It was a kind expression. "Right now, I think it is not going so well."

After we'd been walking together silently for a while, he went on. "It's okay, you know, if things aren't going well. Even if you lose a hundred battles, perhaps Allah helps you, and you win the war."

"We were talking about Abu Fahd."

"Abu Fahd. The Father of the Lion. That one is a different man. Best keep your distance from him. Keep your distance from that Qais Badami also. Like a hyena that one. Did you know I had to kick him out of the building once? These are men of violence. Wallahi, were it not for what I saw in Azza's eyes, they would not have found a home with me."

"What did you see in her eyes?"

The old man gave me a sudden wide grin. "Better to ask what you have seen in her eyes. Or were you looking at other things? Secret things?" He smirked. "To be young again would be a blessing and a curse, I think. Young people are so silly. You think you know the whole world. You think you understand everything. The truth is that you read aloud the story of your life and don't realize that it is in first person. Each and every one of you tells their own life story to the soul of the world, all the while thinking you are the only one with a story to tell."

"I'm not sure what you are trying to say, Hafeez Bhai."

"I am saying that you should read everyone else's story with the same respect as you do your own. Think about that girl, Azza. Have you ever thought about why she really comes to you? You get the sexy times and are satisfied. What about her? Did you ever think what would happen to her if Abu Fahd found out about your fun-time activities? It is not beyond a man like that to hurt her very much. At the very least, he would kick her out of his home. She must know this. Still the girl is risking it. For you? Has she told you she loves you?"

I shook my head.

"Do you think she loves you?"

"No."

"Then why does she risk her life as she knows it? For a little rub-a-dub-dub only? Or does she get something else out of it?"

I frowned, trying to answer the question he posed, one that I had never bothered asking myself. Maybe her time with me was the only small measure of independence, of freedom, she found in her life. Maybe she was lonely, maybe just bored.

"What do you think she's getting out of it?"

Bhatti gave a little sigh, a forlorn, wistful thing. "A little stolen happiness, I think, or a little forgetfulness of what has not yet happened."

"I'm not sure what that means. But you're right. I don't understand Azza."

"Of course you don't. Only God understands people. My problem is that you young people don't even *try* to understand each other. You make no attempt. This is why there is so much less wisdom in the world. You try to understand one other person and you learn to love. You try to understand many people and you become wise."

"And if you try to understand everybody?"

"Then you become a poet, of course." He came to a stop and I realized that he had brought me to our mosque. "Come along," he said. "Pray with me and see what happens next."

Hafeez Bhatti was part of a study group at the mosque. After evening prayers, they gathered to discuss the life of the Prophet Muhammad. These halaqas, as they were called, were obviously not for me. Still, I was glad not to be alone just then. I didn't want to think about what Bhatti had said. How had I not considered Azza's motives for being with me before?

The answer was an uncomfortable mix of ego, selfishness and, as I'm sure Aamir would be happy to point out, cowardice. It takes courage of a kind to look at a friend or a lover and wonder if we are enough for them or if they are with us despite the fact that we are not. It was easier and prettier to let myself believe that Azza had come to me because of who I was than to wonder if I was just a diversion or escape from things she didn't want to even share with me.

Bhatti, who seemed to be looking at me more than he was looking at Imam Sama, leaned over after a few minutes and whispered, "Attention, please."

I nodded. The Imam was telling us about the time the Prophet fell asleep under a tree. For a refugee, a man persecuted and hunted for his religious beliefs, this was dangerous.

Indeed, when the Prophet awoke, one of his enemies was standing before him, sword drawn. As the Prophet rose to his feet, the man challenged Muhammad, saying, "Who will save you from me now?"

There was no fear in the Prophet's voice when he gave his reply. It was simple. He said that Allah would save him.

This conviction left the man so stunned that his grip on his blade weakened and it fell to the ground. The Prophet picked up the sword and asked the man who would save him from Muhammad. When the man said he had no one to help him, the Prophet spared his life.

"You're very quiet," Hafeez Bhatti noted, something like approval in his voice. "Imam Sama put you in a reflective mood, haan?"

"Actually, I was just wondering how a man who is all over the place in his sermon can be so eloquent and focused in a study group."

My landlord chortled. "The fewer people he is around, the better he seems to become at being an imam. And when he is giving one-on-one advice, he is brilliant. Just imagine how good he must be at this job when he is with himself only, looking into a mirror."

We walked through the early night in silence. The moon was bright but distant, withdrawn from our affairs. It was waning, diminishing, and would soon disappear from the sky for a time. On the days when it wasn't forced to hang in the sky, did it feel relieved, finally able to look away from the unending struggles, petty and terrific, that mark the lives of humankind, or did it just feel alone?

When Bhatti spoke again, he said, "So are you coming back for the study group next week?"

"Not unless Ma shows up at my door again."

"You're not curious to know what lesson to take from the hadith that was told to you?"

"The Imam wants us to think about the power of faith. The lesson is that if you have faith, God will reward you with His help."

"It is probable you are right," Hafeez said. "Did you also think it was a story about faith?"

"I thought it was about forgiveness."

"Could you find such forgiveness within yourself for a man set against you, you think?"

"I'm not sure," I admitted.

"Do you think Abu Fahd could?"

I did not know the answer to that question either, so I did not volunteer one. Instead, I asked a question of my own. "Did you give him the good Muslim discount too?"

Bhatti gave me a sidelong glance. "Something like that."

"How many of your tenants are getting discounts? And what kind? Most of them aren't Muslims."

He seemed to think about how to answer for a moment—or maybe he was thinking about if he was going to answer at all. "Everyone is getting some discount. Now that you've found that out, you're going to be wanting to know why I do it. All very predictable, Barrister Faris. No person understands why a man would not care about making lots and lots of money."

"Have you tried explaining it to them?"

Hafeez Bhai smiled. "No."

"Will you explain it to me?"

"Already I have given you so much rich wisdom today. Too much more and you'll be feeling like vomiting wisdom all over the street." After a long pause, he went on. "I am not like other people, sir. There is something wrong inside my heart."

"Are you ill?" I asked, constructing in my mind the story of his life. He was a rich man, perhaps, who discovered he had a fatal illness and was now being generous to make amends for his own perceived greed. Ebenezer Scrooge finally face-to-face with the specter of a mortal future that haunts us all and that, somehow, we usually manage to forget.

With his next words, Bhatti made it clear that I had gathered the pages of his life up all wrong.

"Not in my body. I am superhealthy, but I have not been able, in my life, to love anyone or to hate anyone or to have any junoon about anything. You know what is junoon?"

I nodded. "Passion."

"Mad passion, yes. Fire. I haven't ever had any part of it, though I have wanted it always. I married a nice woman, you know, and she was rich and I lived with her for many years. It was fine when she was there. It was fine when she died also. Actually, it was not so fine. I began to realize that I missed something when I was no longer around her, and it wasn't her, not really. It was being able to see that fire that I had been chasing in my life in someone's eyes, in someone's acts, in someone's talk. So, I purchased Trinity Gardens. It was not to make money. It was to meet people, to be around people, who had what Allah had never seen fit to give me."

"I don't know what to say to that."

"You don't always have to be saying something, Barrister Sahib," the old man said. "It is a modern disease this one, to always be speaking. Never have I told anyone these things. Do you know why I tell you? You are the opposite of myself. Very interesting. The fire inside you, Mr. Faris, I saw it from the first. You could set the world alight. Yet you choose to always try to put it out. You are afraid of being burned, yet to burn, to burn on and on and on until there is nothing left of me, that is all I've ever wanted."

"I am sorry," I said because that was the only thing I could think to say.

"Do not be sorry, my friend. Be brave."

When I saw Azza a few hours later, it was immediately clear that she'd been crying. Her eyes were swollen, her veil incapable of keeping their secret.

"What happened?" I stepped away from the door to let her into my apartment.

She didn't answer. She pushed past and headed to the bedroom. I followed her. Azza took off her niqab in silence, facing away from me. Her hands were shaking. She was wearing a tank top underneath. Her bare shoulders and arms had livid pink welts running across them.

"Jesus, Azza. What—"

"I'm fine," she whispered, her soft voice now so low that I could barely hear her. I was reaching for my phone to call for help when her words registered. "Come to bed."

"Don't be ridiculous. Azza, you need to go to the hospital. We need to report—"

"*Stop it!*" The shriek ripped from her small frame like the last scream of a tortured angel. "You don't tell me what to do." Her eyes turned to me now and I could see that they were drowning in wrath. "You have no right."

I stepped back. Azza's face was contorted with fury. She stared at me, but her gaze was strangely unfocused, almost as if she was looking through me, beyond me, at someone else. When she spoke, her voice was calm but her tone cold. "Just shut up," she said. "Please, do what I ask."

I stood there for a moment, trying to process how to deal with the flash flood of fury that poured out from her. My heart raced. It knew how to deal with anger and love and lust and fear, but what I was feeling then was something different entirely. Pity? No, not just pity. It was something else. Something I didn't know how to name, much less process.

Azza spoke again. "Please."

I turned off the light and, once she lay down, joined her on the bed. I wanted to hold her but I didn't want to hurt her, so I stroked her dark hair. Time passed. I am not certain how much. I am not certain it mattered. Her breathing slowed and became nearly even. She'd fall asleep soon.

"It was your father, wasn't it?" I finally dared to ask, remembering what Bhatti had said about Abu Fahd. I listened for a reply in the moonlit darkness and a second eternity passed, silent except for the muffled sounds of a drowsy city. When she didn't respond, I said, "I can help you."

There was a tainted, poisoned amusement in her voice when she spoke. "What makes you think you can help, or even that you should?"

"I know someone hurt you. It was either your father or it was Qais."

"Maybe I deserved it."

"That can't be true."

"You're very certain for a man who didn't know my real name until yesterday. You should know by now that you don't understand what's happening."

"I want to understand."

"You can't. The lives we've lived, the lives we live now, they're too different. You won't get it. What I've done, what I'm going to do . . . You belong to this place, Anvar. I am an alien."

I didn't respond. I didn't know how.

I thought about what Hafeez Bhatti had said about young people having a limited perspective.

They say there are over seven billion people on Earth. The stars are probably unable to count us, just as we are unable to count them. Each person has her or his own story. Not to mention the uncounted legions who are dust. Each one a protagonist. It is a scale beyond epic. It is past comprehension.

Amidst all of that, however, was this one woman next to me. Was it possible that she too was beyond comprehension?

I could try to uncover her past, to know where she came from, and maybe I could even find out who she was. I might be able to convince her to tell me what happened to her and I could probably compel her to inform the police. For a brief moment, I could change the course of her narrative.

I had no right to do that though. Her story was not mine. Her mind, her soul were indeed, as she'd said, alien to me. I could never experience the world as she experienced it. I was blind to the light in which she saw everything, including me and even herself.

The mystery of the universe is not just grand, it is also small. It is not just vast, but also particular.

Should I have tried to read those pages of her life she excluded me from?

Maybe.

I thought then that it was more respectful to read what I have been given and become comfortable with the knowledge that behind every truth I sought was another truth, and none of them, ultimately, led to understanding.

AZZA

Anvar didn't get up when I rose before dawn. His sleep was the sleep of a man who had never known true fear.

He must have stayed up longer than I had. There were pills and a covered glass of water on the nightstand beside me. I smiled, but these medicines were no cure for pain and I didn't take them. They didn't heal. They simply made people numb and let them forget, a little, how bad their hurts were. The name—painkillers—was a lie we told ourselves and nothing more.

It was important to call things what they really were. Abu told me how Allah had taught Adam the names of all things. It was the first thing human beings had been taught, according to the Quran. It was important knowledge. How had we become so careless with it?

I went to the living room and made my way to the bag I carried with me. I'd started using it to carry books for school, but I rarely managed to study these days. There would be time enough for that later, when Qais was gone.

I couldn't complain too much about false names. I was, after all, not really Azza. Was I?

And Abu wasn't Abu.

He wasn't my father.

Every small thing I'd missed or ignored over the years between Yousef Ganni and my mother taunted me now, asking me how I could have been so blind as to not see what was obvious.

If I could've been satisfied with the easy answer—that I'd been a naïve child—I don't think it would have hurt as much as it did.

But I knew the truth.

I'd never known my mother.

I'd thought her a weak woman, resigned to her fate, suffering in silence. The thought that she might rebel against destiny, that she might defy God to seek happiness, that she might risk everything she had for a few moments of freedom had never occurred to me. Even now, it seemed barely possible.

For the first time ever, I was seized by the desire to speak to her, to ask for her advice, to get her blessing for the horrible and necessary things I planned to do.

I'd had no use for her when I thought her a saint. I needed her now, when I knew she'd been a sinner. A sinner I could understand. A sinner would understand me.

From my backpack, I pulled out the notebooks that I'd been filling up with deception.

The idea for them had come to me a while back, when I'd tipped the jar of chickpeas onto myself. I'd remembered Anvar saying something about "chickpeas of steel," about how his mother's friends had been reported to the government as terrorists by mosque crawlers who didn't like them. Anvar's mother had lucky friends, because there had been nothing to prove their guilt. If there had been, they might have been disappeared by the government.

It was possible in this country to be rid of people one didn't like—people like Qais—if one reported them and produced evidence against them.

It was not required that the evidence be true. All that was required was that it be believable. Americans were credulous people, even though they lived in a world of lies and illusions. They took a lot of painkillers.

My notebooks called Qais a terrorist and recorded in detail how he'd told me his plans to kill as many innocent people as possible. They talked about the fact that he'd gotten his hands on guns to further his schemes and that he wanted to get many more. I'd gathered other information as well, like maps marked with "targets," the works of radical preachers from the internet. I had everything the Americans would need to put Qais away forever.

Some part of me—the part that was still Safwa—had feared I'd hesitate when the time came to actually contact Homeland Security and accuse Qais of what he hadn't done. That girl knew me no better than she'd known her mother though. As I took up my pen for the last time, my hand did not shake, my fingers did not tremble.

It was as Abu had said. Only misery comes from weakness.

The time for morning prayer came and went. I sat in place as the sun rose, eyes fixed on the thin, unmarked envelope that still sat on Anvar's coffee table. It was difficult to put away, difficult to look away from. It was a beautiful and terrible thing.

In that small, fragile piece of paper was all the power I'd ever held over anyone. I'd never decided anyone's fate before.

There was a sharp knock on the door. I was on my feet in an instant, my heart suddenly running though I was standing still. Was it Abu? That was impossible. Wasn't it?

I looked around for places to hide, thinking that I should wake Anvar, tell him what was happening . . . There was another knock, and then a third, more uncertain one followed. My breathing started to slow. It was almost certainly not my father. I'd never known him to knock more than once. Besides, if he thought I was here, he'd be hammering away at the door, not waiting patiently for a response.

Even so, I had every reason to be careful. I tiptoed to the door to see who was there, to make sure I was safe.

Through the peephole, I saw a woman.

I had no reason to recognize her. But I did.

I stood by the door, staring hard, struggling to study her face. I couldn't see her properly. I couldn't see any magic about her that made her so special to Anvar that he still bled from wounds she'd left him with a decade ago.

She knocked again, then looked at her phone. If she didn't get an answer, she would leave, and I'd never figure out why she deserved a life so much better than mine. Before I could think to stop myself, I moved to let Zuha Shah in.

THE BLITZ

2016

We're going to try something different now. Remember how I told you that checkers is the game of life? That's never more true than when you play a blitz, where the time you have to make your moves is limited. When the world starts spinning faster and faster around you, Anvar, you either learn to run or you fall.

—Naani Jaan

ANVAR

I woke to the buzzing of my phone, followed moments later by the sound of a voice I hadn't woken up to since college. Back then, Zuha's words had been either sweet or playful or chiding, but never as restrained, as cool, as they were now. Of course, she wasn't talking to me.

I jumped out of bed with more agility than I'd had occasion to call upon for some time, and in my rush to get out to the living room, I slammed my toes against the bed frame. I grimaced, hopped around but managed not to swear, all the while running my hands through my hair in a desperate attempt to make it seem like I hadn't just gotten up. I don't think I succeeded, but I'm not certain success would've improved my morning. After all, spending the night with Azza and not sleeping with her was certainly worse, in this situation, than spending the night with her by actually sleeping.

When I finally made it out of my bedroom, Zuha and Azza were speaking intently by the front door. When Zuha saw me, her warm brown eyes went a little arctic.

"Good morning?" I said.

Azza turned to face me, her brow furrowed. She looked somehow confused and frustrated and guilty and angry at the same time.

"Hi," I tried again, when I got no response from either of them. "What happened?"

It took me a moment to understand Zuha's question. Azza was still in her tank top, the vicious marks on her skin very much visible.

"I'm fine," Azza said in the tone of someone who was repeating herself. "I should go. I shouldn't have—"

"No. Please," Zuha assured her. "I just thought Anvar might want to get some breakfast. I didn't realize I'd be interrupting—"

I opened my mouth to say something, but all I could think to say was "This isn't what it looks like," which was beneath me. Not only was it untrue, it was also a cliché. If you're going to lie, you absolutely must have the courtesy to do so in a creative fashion.

"I'm his brother's fiancée," Zuha said, managing an exculpatory statement that was also honest.

Azza, who had grabbed her niqab and was rushing to put it on, answered with just a hint of venom: "I know exactly who you are."

Zuha raised a questioning eyebrow at me. I looked away from her, glancing around the room for anything remotely interesting that I could study, anything that would give me a plausible reason not to meet her gaze.

I noticed an envelope on the coffee table that I was pretty certain was not mine. Grateful to have something less than awkward to say, I walked over to it, took it and held it up. "Azza, is this yours?"

Her green eyes snapped toward me. She hesitated for a moment, then came and snatched her letter from my hand. Grabbing her backpack, she then rushed past Zuha, out into the morning.

Her departure was followed by a hard silence.

"Well," I said, "that didn't go as badly as it could have."

Zuha glared at me for a considerable fraction of an eternity, then spun around and stalked out of my apartment. The door slammed behind her.

"Or"—I was talking to myself at this point—"maybe it did."

AZZA

I'd imagined Zuha would be beautiful. A lot prettier than me. That would explain why Anvar was, after all the years they'd been apart, still crazy about her. It would explain why she had found love in this world.

But Zuha was nothing special. She was ordinary. I don't know why that upset me. I don't know why it made the world seem even more unfair than it had been before.

Why did she have so much? It was like God had painted her life with brighter, richer colors than he'd used on mine. She'd gone to school. She got to live life how she wanted, untouched by war, in safety.

It wasn't that she was unusually lovely or even all that kind. Agreeing to marry Anvar's brother had been a cruel thing to do, after all. So, if she wasn't exceptional, if she wasn't better than me in any way, then why did God love her more than He loved me?

What had I done wrong, before I'd even drawn breath, to be sent from heaven to Iraq, in this time, to Abu's house? Zuha Shah could've been me and I her. When we had started our lives, there must have been very little difference between us, except where we'd been born and whom we'd been born to.

"Slow down."

In the hallway, a few feet away from home, I spun around and saw that Zuha had come after me. I shook my head. Nothing this woman did made sense. I turned and kept walking away from her. When I got to the door and had to stop to pull out my keys, she caught up to me.

"I'm sorry I followed you."

"Then stop."

That drew a small smile from her. "I just wanted to apologize for . . . I don't want anyone to get hurt because of me—"

"Except for Anvar."

"I . . ." She shook her head, then took a deep breath. "I'm not talking about him. I don't know what you and Anvar have and—"

"We don't have anything. I don't have anything, which is how it's always been."

"You don't have to cover for him. Whatever he told you happened between us was a long time ago, and it doesn't matter anymore. It's the past."

I laughed. It came out sour. "He hasn't touched me—not in that way—since he saw you again. So, either you're lying to me, or to yourself, or you're stupid. And from everything he has told me about you, you're not stupid."

She looked overcome when I said that, like someone witnessing the vastness of the desert, or the vastness of the ocean, for the first time.

It made my voice softer than it had been before. "You don't have to worry about me."

It took a moment for Zuha to process what she wanted to say and, in that moment, I heard a familiar, heavy step on the stairs. Before she could speak, I reached over and gripped her wrist in a forceful, urgent warning.

"Even though class was canceled, and Abu isn't expecting me back, I never go anywhere without telling him where I'm going. We have to wait for him."

Zuha blinked. "What?"

"I know it seems strange to you, but it's one of his rules. Come in and sit. Can I make you some tea? Oh. There he is. As-salamu alaykum, Abu."

My father—the man who raised me, anyway—frowned at my cheerful tone. It must have seemed incredible to him after the painful way our last talk had ended, but then his gaze found Zuha and he seemed to understand that I was putting on a show.

"Who is your friend?"

"She's a teacher at my school," I said quickly, at the same time Zuha told him her name.

He studied her more closely then. "That is a Muslim name, is it not?"

She nodded.

"Yet you are not modest like a Muslim woman. Your dress betrays what is in your heart."

Zuha was wearing a simple long-sleeved shirt with dress pants. No one, except for Abu and his friends, could have had any objections. I was certain, however, that he thought her pants highlighted her legs too much, and her shirt emphasized her waist more than necessary.

I was still thinking about what to say when Zuha answered him. She spoke sweetly, but her words had the edge of a knife. "And your gaze betrays what is in yours."

I couldn't help myself. I gasped.

Abu looked like he'd just been slapped. For all that was made of how Muslim women had to dress, little was ever said of how Muslim men were supposed to look away when they saw what they weren't supposed to see.

For the first time in my life, I'd seen Abu's practice of his religion challenged.

His face flushed and he stepped toward Zuha, looming over her. She looked completely unconcerned. I understood then why Anvar liked her so much.

"How dare you speak to me that way!"

"I've got no reason to be afraid. You can't hit *me* and get away with it."

She said it with a glance in my direction, just to make sure Abu knew she knew. How did she know though? How had she figured out it was Abu who'd beat me after being around him for only a few seconds?

She wasn't stupid.

Abu hesitated, then stepped away from Zuha, toward our front door. He didn't turn away from her, however, before snarling "leave" in her direction, and waving for me to follow him. She was definitely not the kind of person he wanted his "daughter" to associate with.

ANVAR

I called Zuha to explain myself—actually, I called her to point out how completely absurd it was that I should have to explain myself to her, given that she was currently engaged to my brother—but she didn't answer. Perhaps that was fortunate. It wasn't a conversation that was going to go well.

At least Azza came back the next night, though she pretended that nothing unusual had happened. That seemed to be her preferred method of dealing with the world.

I too was in the conflict-dodging game, ducking all the calls my mom made to speak to me. When she stopped calling, I was initially relieved. Then I began to wonder if I had managed only to stave off the inevitable, and if her fury was now building toward an apocalyptic fallout. Just when I was becoming convinced that she was essentially the human equivalent of the San Andreas Fault, her agent, my father, came to find me. He insisted on taking me for a drive.

When the mafia wants you to take a ride with them, it's bad. When my father wants you to do it, it's worse. Imtiaz Faris, despite his deep voice and intimidating girth, has never really been comfortable with disciplining his children. Both Aamir and I recognized early that our mother was the stronger, more involved, dominant parent.

Every once in a while, however, when things were going so badly that he could not stomach it, my father would enter the parenting arena and take us for a drive. He would turn the volume up on the car's stereo and pop in the mixtape he had prepared for the occasion. The mishmash of songs he chose was somehow always topical, and our childhood featured a heavy dose of weepy old Indian music. As my father's tastes diversified, however, the songs got more eclectic. I got Michael Jackson's "Dangerous" after my first speeding ticket. Aamir swears that when he started gaining weight during the long nights of medical school, he got "Milkshake" by Kelis and "I Want Candy" from Bow Wow Wow.

That day, my lot consisted of a few emotional Indian songs including "Dost Dost Na Raha," followed by Dire Straits's "Brothers in Arms" and then Harry Chapin's "Cat's in the Cradle." When a song from the movie *Hum Saath—Saath Hain* began to play, I broke. "All right. I'm sorry, okay? I'm really sorry. Please make it stop."

My father turned off the music and drove, as he always did in these situations, to his friend's shop, A Pretty Good Ice Cream Parlor.

"Hi, Mr. Good." I greeted him in the same sullen fashion I'd been greeting him since I'd been a teenager. "How're you?"

"Won't complain," Joseph answered with a grin. "You staying out of trouble?"

"No," my father announced, "he is most certainly not staying out of trouble."

"Ah, it's one of those visits," the shopkeeper said, chuckling. "All right, all right. One bubble gum coming right up."

"Two scoops, Joseph," my father said, "and sprinkles."

Mr. Good whistled low. "Must have really messed up."

Dad nodded emphatically, and then ordered for himself.

This was another Imtiaz Faris punishment technique. He'd bring you for ice cream and get you the one flavor he knew you hated. For me that's always been bubble gum.

Joe heaped an ungodly amount of sprinkles on my unnaturally bright blue ice cream, then handed me the pureed Smurfs in a cone. "Don't worry, son," he said, like he'd done for decades, "this too shall pass."

Following his ritual to the letter, my father then ate his ice cream in the car, while I was made to stand outside in the chill wind until mine was finished. Finally, he unlocked the passenger door and I climbed into his beat-up Camry, which still smelled like dead goat.

"You ready to talk seriously now, you little pecker?"

"Yes, Dad. I . . ."

"What the constantly burning bloody hell, boy? Is your mind in your bum, you stupid donkey fellow?" He was shouting at me, his arms flailing around the car in wild, expansive gestures that were too big for the cramped space. "Did you shit out all your brains? No, I'm seriously asking you, yaar, what the what, man?"

"I made a mistake."

"A mistake? That wasn't a mistake. That was a goddamn mountain of stupidity you dropped on us. Why? Why couldn't you just come to me and say, Dad, Aamir shouldn't marry this girl. I stuck it in her pooch?"

"Cooch."

He frowned. "Really? I was pretty sure it was . . ."

"No. I'm right about this one."

"Fine. Be that as it may, you could have just told us. Of all the pigeon shit . . ."

"Chicken shit."

"Stop correcting me when I am correcting you."

"I said I was sorry. You guys didn't tell me until after everything had been agreed."

"That's fine, you stupid son of a rabid dog . . ."

"Dad."

"I know," he snapped. "Let me finish. We hadn't told Tom, Dick and Harry and their kuttya grandmother, haan? All this wasn't public knowledge. Now when we break it off, there will be a thousand and one questions. What if someone finds out what you and that girl did, haan? Since you were frolicking around for Allah knows how many years with each other, that isn't, you know, out of the question." When I didn't respond, he prompted me. "You had the chance to stop all this before it got this far. True or not true?"

"I didn't know what to do."

"That's when you come to me, you brain pedestrian. You come to me and ask me what to do. When did you stop doing that?"

"I never did that."

He sighed, glanced away and said gruffly, "I know. That is why I put the song about the cat and the cradle in there."

"I heard it."

"If ever there was truth in music, I tell you. . . . You want another ice cream? You can pick yourself."

I shuddered at the thought. "No. I'm done with ice cream for a while."

He turned on the ignition. Then he turned the car off again. This time he did not look at me when he spoke. "I never even realized I was going wrong with you. You were always so damn clever. Always smart. Smarter than me. I relaxed with you, and by the time I figured out that I did have things to teach you, it was too late. Time is a bitch. A real bitch." His voice was quiet. It made my eyes sting. "I just don't know when we got to the point that you think you can't even come to me to say, please, don't give this one away. I love this one. This one belongs to me."

"It would have been . . ." I paused and cleared my throat, forcing the words out in a steady fashion. "It isn't like that. It isn't that simple."

"That's because you are an evergreen fool," my father said gently. He held out a card. It had Zuha's number on it. I decided not to tell him that she wasn't taking my calls just then. That would require an explanation I most definitely did not want to give. "You call her. Speak to her and figure it out."

"What about Aamir?"

"This is your shit. Be a man and fix it." He turned to look at me again. "I'm serious, Anvar. Fix it."

"Yes, sir."

He started the engine up again.

"Is Mom really angry?"

"She is now. Since you've been avoiding her calls. She wasn't upset with you about not saying anything about the girl though."

"Really?"

"Somehow she thought you did the right thing. Something about how we have to conceal the sins of people who repent. It was the Muslim thing to do. She was proud of you."

I raised my eyebrows at that little revelation. I had never heard, to the best of my recollection, any such emotion attributed to my mother in my life. That she should be pleased with me in these particular circumstances was a little incredible.

"I guess that was a side effect of your shitty decisions, not your goal."

"Obviously."

"Now that I think about it, she was fine until the part about what you had actually done with Zuha sank in. Then she was furious. I'm not ashamed to say, it was a little scary."

"You think I should keep avoiding her?"

"That is what I would do." He sighed. "Unfortunately, that's never really been an option for me. Come on. Let's have one more song."

"I already said I was sorry."

"Trust me. It's a good one."

It was a good one. It was Farida Khanum singing "Aaj Jaane Ki Zid Na Karo."

"I remember this song. You played it for me once before, when you grounded me for sneaking in after curfew. Back in high school."

"Don't remember, but that makes sense. You say you were late and this is a song about time. Now, can you shut up, so we can listen?"

For once in my life, I was happy to do what I was told.

I listened to those old lyrics that had danced with many souls before mine. I listened to the lament of a poet begging his beloved to not insist on leaving, asking her to stay with him, to sit with him, because her talk of leaving was sufficient for his death and his ruin.

Our lives, I was reminded, are hostages held by time. We are free only for a few moments. What we choose to do in those moments, who we choose to spend them with, defines who we are.

I thought of Zuha.

I thought of Azza.

I let the song color my memories of them until the music ended and I was left wondering if the poet got what he so desperately desired.

AZZA

Days Abu was off work were miserable at the best of times. They meant that he was around to keep an eye on where I was going and for how long. Qais came over often when Abu was there, and stayed as long as he could, making the apartment seem even smaller than it was.

After Abu's revelation of who my father had been, things were tense. They were made a lot worse by Zuha Shah biting off a piece of Abu's pride and spitting it out into the mud. He spent his time fuming, warning me not to let my horrible teacher influence me and asking if the other Muslim women in the community here were as awful as Zuha had been.

It wasn't until Qais came over with the news that someone had ransacked the office of Hafeez Bhatti that Abu finally found something else to talk about.

"Who would do such a thing? All that man does is help everyone."

"I think," Qais said, a smirk on his face, his gaze fixed on me, "maybe he helped the wrong person. Some people are in trouble they cannot ever escape, no matter who protects them."

"Except for God," Abu said, earnestly pious.

"Yes," Qais said. "But not everyone finds protection with Him, do they? Some people are too vile to be saved."

"For all of our sakes, my friend," Abu said quietly, "we should hope that is not true."

Qais didn't answer, but there was joy in his eyes that day, like he'd won a great victory. I knew he'd try to speak to me alone soon, to gloat properly and openly, to remind me how much power he possessed. He liked tormenting me too much to stay away.

The next morning, as I was locking up the apartment before heading out, I heard his footsteps behind me.

"Leave. Me. *Alone.*" It came out louder than I'd intended, almost like a scream, but I didn't regret it. I wanted to scream it, over and over, until it finally sank into Qais's shriveled soul and took root.

There was a pause.

Zuha Shah said, "Okay. That's fair. Harsh, certainly but—"

I whirled around to face her. "What are you doing here?"

"I came to see Anvar, but then I thought I should see how you were instead. Me pissing off your father probably did not do you any favors."

"I'm fine," I told her. She didn't seem convinced, but she didn't say anything more either. She just kept looking at me, expecting me to go on. I hesitated, then, partly to have something to fill the silence she had created and partly because I was curious, asked, "So you haven't seen Anvar?"

She shook her head.

"Okay."

"You think I should?"

"I don't care."

My answer seemed to amuse Zuha, which I found irrationally aggravating.

"What?"

"Are you seriously telling me you don't care about Anvar Faris? That seems impossible."

I made a face. "Sounds like something he would say."

Zuha grinned. "It is."

For a second, I smiled back, not that she could see it through my veil. Then I shook my head and started to walk past her. "Excuse me. I've got to go pretty far and Abu always wants me back for lunch—"

"Let me drive you," she volunteered.

I narrowed my eyes. "Why? You know we're not friends, yes? We will never be friends."

"Because of Anvar?"

"We can't be friends because I don't understand you," I told her. It was the truth. I hadn't really been around girls and women my own age since Baghdad. The last person I'd been close to who hadn't been a man had been Bibi Warda, and it felt like she had died so long ago that it might as well have been the beginning of time.

"I'm not all that complicated."

"You agreed to marry Anvar's brother. That doesn't seem simple."

That cut Zuha. She looked away, and in that moment, if she'd said something in her defense, I would have walked on and never thought about her again. In her wordlessness, however, in that wounded look in her eyes, for a small moment, I saw the reflection of my mother. A few days, at the start of a different journey, that would have been irrelevant. It seemed like everything now.

I sighed even as I decided what to do. "Do you know the story of Musa and Khidr?"

Zuha seemed confused by the quick change in topics. "What?"

"Musa and Khidr, the wise man in green? Musa wanted to travel with him and Khidr—"

"Said that Moses could, if Moses promised not to ask any questions," Zuha finished. "I remember."

"Do you think you can do better than Musa?"

"Sure," Zuha said. "After all, there's no way you're as interesting as Khidr."

I had to shake my head at that. They were flowers from the same garden, she and Anvar. I could see why they recognized each other, liked and loved each other. I, however, was from the desert.

We stopped at Bhatti's office first.

Qais had wrecked the place. Bhatti's desk was smashed, the wood splintered under heavy, relentless blows. Cushions on his chair had been ripped open. Papers and broken picture frames littered the ground, and there was dark green paint splattered all over the walls. It was a disaster.

And it was lovely. It was lovely because there were twenty other people there, with brooms and brushes and hammers and smiles. It was a chance for them to pay their landlord back for all the discounts he'd given them.

"What happened here?" Zuha asked.

"That's one," I told her, reminding her of our arrangement. Khidr had given the Prophet Musa three chances to rein in his curiosity before Khidr parted company with him for good.

She rolled her eyes.

Bhatti's eyes lit up when he saw us together, and he clapped his hands, as if delighted. "Vah yaar, lagta hai Anvar Mian ki kahani mein serious twist aya hai."

I looked at Zuha, but she didn't translate for me.

"There is no need for you to volunteer, my dears. As you can see, here there is house full. So many kind hearts care for this old man. Amazing, no?"

I stayed silent. I didn't want to admit that I hadn't come to help out with the cleanup, but just to check on him.

"I don't see the police here," Zuha noted.

Bhatti glanced at me, very briefly, then said, "The police ask questions."

"Of course," she said. "That's their job. That's what you want them to do."

"Maybe so," Bhatti agreed. "But what if they ask the wrong questions? Or get answers I do not like? Hmm? No. It is much better, I think, to let sleeping dogs snore, as long as no one is hurt." He turned his attention to me. "No one was hurt, right?"

"No one was hurt this time," I agreed.

"For the moment, I fear, that will have to be enough."

To Zuha's credit, she managed not to ask what that exchange was about. As soon as we said our goodbyes to Bhatti, however, she asked, "So where are we going?"

"Two," I said.

She made an irritated sound but didn't say anything else.

I asked her to take me to a post office. Zuha waited in her car as I went in, dug through my backpack and pulled out the envelope I'd addressed to Homeland Security. It was funny, really. This was the most intriguing part of this trip, and Zuha seemed to think it was just a routine chore. She hadn't even seemed curious about what I was doing. Then again, she had no reason to be.

Mailing the letter to seal Qais's fate wasn't dramatic. It didn't immediately change anything. The burdens I carried felt just as heavy as they had before.

I still wasn't free. Not yet. Too much could go wrong. This was a step, nothing more. I had no faith that anything in my life would work out the way I had planned. My will and God's will had too often been at odds for me to believe that, suddenly, He would be on my side.

"Let's walk from here," I told Zuha when I went back to her.

She started to ask why but caught herself, and I showed a little mercy.

"Because, if you can, you should use your feet on a pilgrimage."

I'm not sure that made things any clearer for her, but she wasn't confused for long. This was, after all, her city and as the hills got steeper, my legs started aching, and breathing became a little more work than usual.

"We're going to the Painted Ladies," she said.

I nodded, just as the sloping green park that I'd seen for all those years, in simpler, darker times, came into view. Across the street, a big crowd took pictures of the serene and tranquil houses that I'd come to see.

I heard different languages and I saw different forms of dress on people from all over the world. They'd come from everywhere to visit this one place that had been shown at the beginning of every episode of *Full House*.

These people were like Mama, drawn to a dream of perfect love, perfect understanding and a perfect family that was, I imagined, out of reach for many of them.

Heaven was out of reach for a lot of people too. That didn't stop them from going for Hajj.

These were my mother's people, people with whom she would've belonged, who would have understood her like I never had. It seemed incredibly unfair that I had gotten to come here, and she hadn't.

"Why are we here?" Zuha asked.

"To honor a sinner," I said.

"What do you mean?"

I let out a small laugh. "You've used up all your questions and have failed the test of patience. Like Musa and Khidr, we'll never see each other again."

Zuha frowned. "You're a strange person."

"Yes."

"You know, Moses did get answers to his questions from Khidr, before they said goodbye."

I nodded at a bench. This was true.

As Zuha led me up into the park, on the grass, she began humming the theme song to *Full House*, just like Mama would.

It struck me then, the reason why I'd decided to bring Zuha here with me—why fate or Allah or chance or luck or the universe had made this moment happen. It was a thought that made it impossible to keep walking. I stopped, and Zuha turned back to me.

"What's wrong?"

I stared at this woman who had two men fighting over her, brothers with a bond being tested. Would she marry the wrong one, like my mother had? Was I meant to tell her what would happen if she did?

"Azza?"

"Why did you do it?" I asked without meaning to ask, my voice urgent and raw. "Why did you say you'd marry someone you don't want to marry? It could ruin all your lives. It could ruin everything."

Zuha looked confused, as if thrown by my intensity, but she didn't understand what I was asking or who I was asking it of. Mama, who held the answer I wanted, could not give it to me.

"I . . . I was just angry that Anvar would let it happen, that he wouldn't stop Aamir from—"

"That's a child's answer."

"It hurt me that he would—"

"So you wanted to punish him. That's why you did it. And you did it because you had hope, didn't you? You thought, maybe if you were with him, had an excuse to be around him, if you were in his life, somehow it would all work out. You used Anvar's brother."

There were tears in Zuha's eyes. "It wasn't a plan or anything, I just . . . I thought he would step in. I thought he would finally, for once in his life, speak and say what I needed him to say. I thought, this time, he'd fight for me."

"And if he didn't, he wouldn't be worthy of you anyway. He'd get the misery he deserved."

"It's all so messed up now. I'm sorry. I'm awful and I'm so sorry. I'm sorry for everything."

I went up to her and, ignoring the stares of everyone around us, took her hands. "It's okay. I get it. I'm awful too."

That drew a broken chuckle from her.

I felt the presence of the Painted Ladies behind me.

"Do you love him?"

Anvar would have made a joke. He would've told me I'd already used up my three questions. Zuha, however, was not Anvar.

"It doesn't matter," she said. "It isn't that simple. Not anymore. I told you, I messed it all up."

"You can fix it."

"How do you know that?"

Because you're here, in this place, now, against all odds, with me. Why would Allah make that happen for no reason?

"Because," I said. "I read in a book once that God does not play dice."

"Right," Zuha said, finding her smile again. "He plays checkers instead."

ANVAR

I met Zuha for dinner at Mathilde, a little French bistro near Powell Street station. The candlelit atmosphere, the upscale decorations and the dressy attire of the patrons all signaled that this was a restaurant significantly out of my price range. I tried not to look concerned.

Zuha, for her part, seemed enchanted by everything about the place—the pleasant smell of baked bread, the faint, murmured conversations between the other patrons and the accent of our unnaturally blond waiter.

As he took us to our seats, the waiter smiled at both of us and said, "Charmant."

Zuha blushed, obviously pleased.

"What, are you in a Tolstoy novel or something?" I asked, as soon as our server left to get our drinks—ice cold water for Zuha, a Napa Valley cabernet of a recent year for me.

"He was being nice."

"Too nice."

"You're saying I'm not charming?"

"I would never say that."

Zuha smiled, then looked down at her hands, which had started idly folding and unfolding her napkin. She set it aside deliberately and looked up, as if unsure of what to say next.

"I was surprised you asked me out," I said. "Given that you were dodging my calls."

"I didn't 'ask you out.' This is just dinner. And I wasn't dodging your calls. I just needed time to think. You're still familiar with the concept, right?"

"Of course. I just do it a lot faster than you do."

"You're the worst."

"And yet, you invited me here."

"I got some unexpected clarity. Also, I've got something I want to celebrate."

"Aamir ended your engagement?"

"Can you spare me your stupid assholery for like five minutes?"

I considered pointing out that "stupid assholery" seemed redundant but didn't. "Fine. What are we celebrating?"

"I got promoted. You're looking at the new assistant manager for accounts receivable at Roselin Interiors."

"Just what you always wanted to do with your life."

"We can't all be penniless lawyers."

I had no response to that.

"I'm sorry, Anvar. That was unnecessarily—"

"So what I'm hearing is that you're paying for this meal."

"Yes."

"I wish you'd told me that before I picked the cheap wine."

"Why did you do it?"

"I'm broke."

"Not the wine," she said. "Why did you become a lawyer? All you ever talked about in college was becoming an English professor."

"I discovered I didn't like debating literary minutiae ad nauseam every single day of the week."

"You did that with me all the time."

"I did," I agreed.

The waiter appeared with our drinks. Zuha ordered a filet mignon with sautéed potatoes. I said that I would have the same.

"So why did you call me?"

"Temporary insanity," she said. "Obviously."

"There isn't someone else you'd rather celebrate with?"

She shook her head. Her eyes were disconcertingly earnest.

"So," I said. "No alcohol, no sex, but you're not doing the whole halal meat thing?"

"The beef here is halal. The farm that supplies their steaks . . . What do you care anyway?"

"I'm just trying to measure the depth of your Islam."

"What about you? Are you eating pork now?"

"No."

"But you drink. You're just as much of a hypocrite as anyone else."

"Are you encouraging me to eat pork?"

"You always think you're right, Anvar. Like, always. And you're not. Life isn't that different from literature. There are no right or wrong answers. I'm not wrong to choose to live my life the way I do. I'm not wrong to pick and choose which parts of my faith I'm going to practice and which I won't. At least, I'm no more wrong than you are. You do the same thing."

I watched her take a sip of water before I responded. "I never said you were wrong."

Zuha set her glass down on the table, with a little more force than was warranted. "Not today."

"Are you really going to hold a thirty-year-old man responsible for his opinions when he was twenty?" When she didn't reply, I went on. "Muslims—our generation, in the West—are like the Frankenstein monster. We're stapled and glued together, part West, part East. A little bit of Muslim here, a little bit of skeptic there. We put ourselves together as best we can and that makes us, not pretty, of course, but unique. Then we spend the rest of our lives looking for a mate. Someone who is like us. Except there is no one like us and we did that to ourselves."

She shook her head. "Then we're all doomed to never find our soul mates."

"Some people lead pretty off-the-rack lives. Aamir will be reasonably happy with any proper Muslim girl he marries."

"But not me?"

"Did you ask him who his favorite author was?"

"Of course."

"Was it God?" I said, and Zuha rolled her eyes. "Because the Quran is the only book I've ever seen him read."

"He said he liked Shakespeare," Zuha admitted, that little twinkle of amusement lighting up in her eyes. "I've met a lot of single Pakistani men who like Shakespeare."

"You'll be miserable with someone who doesn't read."

"When Percy Shelley died, Mary Shelley had his heart calcified, wrapped it in his poetry and kept it in a desk."

I frowned. "I'm pretty sure you're wrong about how that went down."

"Really? It doesn't matter. What I'm saying is that two souls probably can't be more compatible than theirs were and yet they had a pretty miserable marriage."

"The Brownings?" I ventured.

"Browning resented Elizabeth Barrett's success because it overshadowed his own work."

"What's your point?"

"Maybe the secret to a decent marriage is just mundane stuff, not passion or even common interest. Maybe it's the color of the baby's poop and the weird mole on your back that won't go away. Maybe there is no such thing as a soul mate."

"You're just flat-out wrong about that."

"How can you know for sure?" Zuha asked.

The answer to that was simple. "I know because I met you."

Our food came and we ate in silence.

"So. Azza seems interesting," Zuha said.

"Sure," I said, as careful as an angel carrying a prayer up to God.

"It's her father who hits her, you know. He's—"

"Wounded," I supplied quickly, happy to push the conversation along in the direction it was going.

"I was going to say monstrous."

"He was captured in Iraq, arrested without recourse. He was tortured. Doesn't that earn him some grace?"

"No. Not for hurting her."

"You're right." I took a deep breath. "But Azza won't go to the police. If the authorities find out who he is—who they thought he was once—then he'll be gone, forever. There's no justice in that."

"This isn't Taleb Mansoor. Her father isn't a client of yours, and he isn't a young, innocent man who is going to get blown up by a drone."

"What would you have me do?" I asked.

"Stop seeing Azza." My expression must have betrayed my surprise. "I'm not saying that because of me. If this is how her father treats her, what do you think he'd do to her if he found out about you? Anvar, she's putting herself in danger. You need to stop."

"Was I ever able to make you do anything?"

Zuha collapsed back into her chair.

"It would have been nice though."

"To have a college girlfriend who blindly did whatever you asked?"

"No," I said. "It would've been nice if you wanted me to stop seeing Azza because of you."

She looked down at her glass and took a sip of water. Then she said, "I don't have the right to ask you that. Not anymore. Just like you don't have the right to ask me to end things with Aamir. We broke who we were a decade ago, and maybe that is forever now."

"It's not fair."

"You're an attorney. Are you even allowed to talk about fairness?"

"It isn't encouraged. It's the Abu Fahd problem though, isn't it? There is no justice in punishment that does not end and is doled out without measure. That's just torment. But that seems to be the way of the world now."

"And how does one survive in an unjust world?"

"That," I told her, "is the only question I do not know how to answer."

Zuha gave me a look that told me my statement was too absurd for words.

"It is, at the very least, the only question I'm willing to admit I don't know the answer to."

"Let me know if you figure it out."

"I will," I told her. "I promise."

I didn't see Azza over the next few days. She'd made it clear from the very beginning that we were not necessary parts of each other's lives. If she hadn't been so bruised the last time I'd seen her, I wouldn't have worried.

I saw Abu Fahd, though. He came by without warning to announce a party to celebrate the fact that he and Qais had agreed on a date for Azza's wedding, which would happen in a couple of weeks. He sheepishly added that he also needed an extra pair of hands to help with the arrangements and didn't know who else to ask.

So I found myself carrying a tray of kabobs back to his apartment from a nearby Afghan restaurant. Abu Fahd walked beside me, carrying a load of groceries, grousing over how little Azza was helping with this event. It was heavy, he told me, this weight on a father alone. He let it slip that he thought Azza would be more helpful if she were actually looking forward to her marriage. I did not know what to say to him, the memory of Azza's ugly bruises difficult to reconcile with this pleasant, almost diffident man.

He looked around us, at the living, eternal bustle of San Francisco, at the billboard advertisements hawking stylish, skinny jeans, at the unceasing variety of goods offered by the storefronts we passed. There was no wonder in his voice when he spoke. "It is difficult in these times, raising children. So many ideas, so many temptations, so many ways of life, akhi. Difficult to get them to choose the right one. Especially my daughter. Always strong willed.

Soon though, she won't be my problem anymore. She will be happy with Qais. He is a good man. A good man."

I didn't ask him if he was trying to convince me or if he was trying to convince himself. "I certainly hope she is happy."

Abu Fahd seemed touched by either the sentiment or the sincerity of the words. "Inshallah. The pen has been lifted and the ink is dry, my friend. No one can escape. We can only hope and resign ourselves to the will of Allah."

Resigning myself to the will of Allah was not one of my many skills, but I didn't say so. My mother had taught me it was best not to argue with piety.

"Silence in the face of wisdom," he said, "is also wisdom of a sort. I like you, Anvar. I can see why Taleb Mansoor trusted you."

"This is the second time you've brought him up. Why does that case interest you so much?"

"Some of my friends knew the boy. We speak of it often. Some thought such a thing would not happen to an American. They haven't forgotten that they were wrong."

I nodded and he went on.

"Come and meet them tonight. They will all love to hear about your heroics in the Mansoor case."

"There were no heroics," I said. "But I look forward to meeting Mansoor's friends."

That was a lie. I had no real desire to talk about my deceased client and, under normal circumstances, I wouldn't have considered going to a celebration Azza obviously didn't want. It would, however, give me the chance to see her and make sure she was fine.

"I would not admit that you weren't a hero at dinner, were I you. One should not disappoint an audience."

"Even if the cost is the truth?"

"When you are telling a story, akhi, you have to be above such trivial considerations."

I waited outside of the apartment while Abu Fahd went in to make sure Azza put on her niqab. It wasn't long before he let me into his sparsely furnished home.

The small kitchen and the old appliances were identical to those in my place. The living area was a little bigger and bedsheets had been laid out on the floor for guests to sit on. There were two other rooms, and Azza stood by one of them. I could tell from her eyes that she was smiling at the sight of me. I bowed my head a little in her direction.

"This is Anvar Faris. The lawyer I told you about, remember?"

"I remember," she said, then turned to me. "As-salamu alaykum."

"Yeah. It's nice to meet you," I said.

"Abu said many good things about you. Are any of them true?"

"They must be." I shrugged. "If your father said them."

The older man seemed inordinately pleased with this remark, but Azza rolled her eyes.

"Help us set up," Abu Fahd said, in the tone of a man expecting an argument. "Then go to your room and stay there. There will be a lot of men here tonight. It is not a place for a young woman."

I was about to point out that this was her home and so the demand being made of her was ridiculous. In fact, as I'm sure my mother—or if she were alive, Naani Jaan—would be quick to point out, it would've been a ridiculous demand even if it weren't her home.

Azza shook her head at me, ever so slightly. Instead of putting up a fight, she walked up to me and took the food I was carrying. Her fingers brushed mine more than was necessary for the transfer to take place.

I helped lay out the food on dishes and watched as Azza made a plate to take back with her to her room.

"I'm fine," she said.

Abu Fahd frowned. "What?"

"If any of your friends ask, you can tell them I will be fine."

"What else would I tell them?"

Azza just nodded in my direction. "Mr. Faris."

"Miss . . ." I started, then drew a blank on her last name, which underscored how profoundly surreal this entire situation was.

"Saqr," she reminded me.

"Right. I'll see you around."

Eventually, guests filtered in until there were around twenty men in that small space. Most were bearded, with hard eyes and skin weathered by cruel winds and a harsh sun. All of them were dressed in shalwar kameez and kept laughing at jokes in Pashto, which I couldn't understand. A few of them smiled at me politely, but it was clear that they were part of a circle I was intruding upon.

By the time we sat down to eat, Abu Fahd had teamed up with Qais to tell everyone that I was the attorney who defended or, more accurately, failed to defend, Taleb Mansoor. The respect that came with that information was palpable. One of the men, reaching for a piece of naan, commented that it was an honor to eat with someone who defended an innocent man.

"I don't know that he was innocent."

"Didn't you tell a judge he hadn't done anything wrong?"

"It didn't come up." They looked incredulous, so I explained. "Whether he was guilty or not wasn't relevant to the case I put on for his family."

An old man glared at me through impossibly thick glasses. He said he'd been a judge once. He spoke in a low, dry voice, which sounded like two pieces of sandpaper brushing against each other. "Justice is no more than finding out if guilt lives. When I gave my rulings, the only thing that mattered, the only thing I took into account, was if a person had done something wrong."

"With all due respect," I said, "that's probably not true. I don't know a lot about Islamic Law, but the punishment for, you know, adultery . . ." I stumbled upon my words a little, when I remembered I was in Azza's home—and whom I was with. I glanced at Qais, and he smiled at me encouragingly. I cleared my throat. I was committed now, though I couldn't help but wonder if Azza could hear me. "What is adultery called in Arabic again?"

"Zina."

"The punishment for which is death by stoning. But you can't just take anyone who you suspect of adultery and stone them. You need a witness."

The old man held up four shaking fingers.

"Right. You need four witnesses to see the actual act. It isn't even enough to see people under bedsheets. It is inconceivable—it certainly was inconceivable at the time of the Prophet—that the punishment would actually be carried out."

I paused as many of the men whispered "Peace Be Upon Him" at the mention of the Prophet. "The process involved in implementing the punishment made it largely theoretical. It was meant to be a deterrent. Plus, the character of the witnesses had to be impeccable, yes? The presence of a proper authority to actually enforce the law was also necessary. All this is due process."

"Technical arguments," the old judge muttered.

"Our food would've tasted very different if I'd made it. Fortunately for all of us, someone trained in a restaurant did instead. Technique is important."

"What you are saying is that these Americans, they disregarded their own laws when they murdered Taleb?" Abu Fahd said. When I nodded, he raised his hands to the heavens in a gesture of both supplication and defeat. "Wallahi, it is a curse to have an enemy without honor."

"They think they have honor," Qais declared in a loud, clear voice. "But they are wrong."

Several men muttered their agreement, while nearly everyone else nodded along, as if the words were widely accepted as a fact.

Qais went on. "They use words, labels, to pretend what they are doing is okay. They fool their people and maybe they even fool themselves."

He sat straight, his eyes bright and shining, a conflagration in his voice. I could feel the fire catching in the minds of the other men. "They wrongly killed Taleb like they've killed thousands. They've made us fear the blessings of Allah. We fear bright days, and the shining sun. We pray for storms now. They killed my young brother with their drones. What crime had he committed? My grandmother burned with him. What crime had she committed? Yet they are afraid of us? We're terror for them, when they come to our lands and, just by saying the magic word of 'terrorism,' justify killing our families? And what does all this blood buy them? What kind of honor is this?"

I had no answer for him. Neither did anyone else.

"Taleb was a good boy," the judge said, finally. "It is a shame you did not say so."

"I didn't know him, and I didn't know what he had or hadn't done. It doesn't matter, don't you see? He could have been innocent, but because he was executed without a trial, we'll never know. That's the tragedy here."

Qais barked a laugh. "The tragedy isn't that the man is dead?"

"There can be more than one tragedy in a case. In fact, there usually is."

None of them seemed at all impressed with me anymore. I guess it made sense. They'd known Taleb Mansoor. They'd seen him grow up. They'd known his mind, and some of them may have known his deeds, whatever they had been. It was personal for them because they felt that the law of man had let Mansoor down.

That bothered me as well. I hadn't known Taleb Mansoor, but I'd thought I knew the law. I'd studied it. I'd truly thought it meant something.

Abu Fahd cleared his throat. "Come. This is a time for happiness, and Qais's thoughts, though true, are not the thoughts a young groom should dwell on. There is no happiness for us in the near past."

"Or in the distant past," the judge chimed in with a morose chuckle.

"And not in the future," Abu Fahd said. "For as Allah says, 'Everyone upon the earth will perish, and there will remain the Face of your Lord, Owner of Majesty and Honor.' Tonight, however, we are here together, and that is cause enough to celebrate."

"Let us eat, drink and be merry, for tomorrow we die." I quoted from a different scripture. "And it shall be well with us."

The men muttered their appreciation.

Qais held up his glass of water in mock salute and drank.

I was the only one who volunteered to help Abu Fahd clean up, so I ended up alone with him after everyone was gone. Azza was still hurt, and I was fairly certain that if I didn't tidy up the place, the job would fall to her.

Abu Fahd insisted that I have some more tea before going home. He preferred to drink it like the Persians do. They place a sugar cube in their mouth and hold it there, letting the tea flow over it when they drink.

"A little sweetness and then a little bitterness. In this way we can understand life," he told me, "through the small things in the world."

I sat on the ground across from him, leaning uncomfortably

against a wall, as he spoke to me of teas. He marveled at the milky pink tea of Kashmir, garnished with pistachios and almonds, and told me that he adored the musky fragrance of a good Darjeeling. He spoke of Ceylon and Shizuoka and of Black Dragons and jasmines. He spoke of memories that were fragrant and warm.

"My father," he said, "he loved good tea. He taught me to love it, to seek it out, to taste the secrets of the land where it is from. Of course, that was a long time ago. Now I make do with whatever is cheapest at the grocery store."

Just like that, I knew more about their family than Azza had ever told me.

"Sounds like he was an interesting man."

"The tea was the most interesting thing about him. He was a soft, uninspiring man who lived a simple, uneventful life. I went to Afghanistan during the jihad, you know, to escape him and his painful mediocrity. By the time I returned to Iraq, he was gone. Strange, is it not, what pleasant things we flee from? You should never forget that the oppression of love is better than the oppression of war. There is no freedom from oppression." He poured himself another cup of the tea. "These leaves have to burn, after all, so that there can be tea."

"That's very poetic," I said, for lack of anything else to say.

He ignored the comment. Picking up another cube of sugar, he held it in his mutilated fingers and turned it around, examining it from all sides. "My father wouldn't have understood the man I became in Afghanistan. I became a hard man, yes, but a man of honor. I never compromised it, except once. The memory of that decision will cause me pain until I die."

I had no idea what he was talking about or why he should say any of this to me. It reminded me, oddly enough, of those long walks I'd been forced to take with my own father, when we'd first come to the States, before he'd found a friend at Joseph Good's ice cream shop. Though Imtiaz Faris and Abu Fahd could not have been more different, I recognized the loneliness that had once been in my father's voice in Abu Fahd's voice now.

So I kept drinking tea, letting him say what he needed to say, because I got the feeling there was no one else he could say it to.

"There was a man in Afghanistan I knew who found out his

daughter was sleeping with a boy in the neighborhood; he shot them both in the head and then he shot himself as well."

I grimaced. That was not at all close to home or at all terrifying. Hindsight, as they say, is perfect, but I probably should've always had a policy of not getting involved with women whose fathers spoke this fondly of murderers.

"You don't like that? It is what a man of honor does."

"I guess I prefer sanity to honor."

"Every man thinks he is sane," Abu Fahd said dismissively. "I am sorry about Qais. He gets angry and zealous and forgets himself sometimes. He has just had to live through a great deal."

"As have you," I said. "From what I've heard."

"He told you that the Americans imprisoned me, did he? Other brothers suffered more than I did, but to be left naked in a cold room, forced to listen to loud, obnoxious music . . . There was no dignity in that. While I was held, my family starved. My son died."

He exhaled forcefully and got to his feet. "Now I am here, among these men, these men the likes of whom looked at me and saw only an animal to be caged and declawed. I live on their land. It has been a strange life. I realize now that it was no small thing, to live and die like my father did, quietly and in his own home. That is a path Allah has closed to me now."

Abu Fahd grunted as he got up off the floor. "My young friend, you should go home and get some sleep. Tomorrow is a new day, for better or for worse."

At around midnight, my doorbell rang. I went to open it, assuming it was Azza, but instead found a young woman and an alarmingly thin middle-aged man I didn't know standing there. They were wearing suits. She was in dark, solid gray, while his suit was a much lighter shade and, unfortunately, made from material that gave it a shiny sharkskin appearance.

Though I didn't know them, there was something about the way they stood and the way they nodded that I recognized. "Officers," I said by way of greeting.

"My name is Awiti Hale," the woman replied. "We just need to ask you some questions. May we come in?"

"No," I told her. "You're fine where you are."

Hale's partner, who hadn't introduced himself, huffed. He might as well have spat out "lawyers" and rolled his eyes, but he didn't.

For her part, Hale seemed unfazed by my response. "Mr. Faris, we're with the Department of Homeland Security and we have reason to believe that you are in possession of information about a credible threat against these United States. We are, sir, fine where we are. You, however, may not wish for this conversation to take place where your neighbors can hear."

I stared at her, trying first to understand what she had said. All the words made sense, of course, but . . . what were they saying? A credible threat? Terrorism? They were here about *terrorism*? That was—

"What the lady is saying, son, is that you really ought to let us in."

"Seriously?" I asked. "This is the routine you guys settled on? You're the bad cop?"

"No," Agent Hale assured me, breaking in, irritation evident in her voice. "That's just how Agent Moray is. All the time."

He tipped an imaginary cap in my direction.

"I'd like to see your badges, please."

That drew a grimace from Moray, but they both complied. They were who they said they were. I stepped back into the apartment a little and gestured for them to come in. There was nothing to hide here, so keeping them out in the corridor served no purpose.

"Finally."

"Thank you, Anvar. May we call you Anvar?"

"Anyone ever told you that you live in a shithole, boy?"

"What you may not call me is 'boy,' " I said.

"Most definitely not," Hale said, glaring at her partner.

The slender man threw up his arms in mock surrender. "Fine. He's aggravating though."

"I'm the one who is aggravating?"

"Most folks get real nervous when people like us show up at their door in the middle of the night," he said. "I like that. It's a warm feeling. You aren't nervous. I don't like that."

"I'm an attorney. I know my rights."

"Don't like that much either. You mind if I take a leak, Counselor? I'd ask you where the bathroom is, but I've got a fifty-fifty shot at finding it on my first go and I'm a gambling man."

Alone with Hale now, I gestured for her to take a seat and sat down across from her.

"Did something happen at the mosque?" I said.

I suspected, as did other Muslims, that mosques were under surveillance. The Republican presidential candidate had discussed it, saying that the government had to "maybe check, respectfully, mosques" and "other places." This suggestion had been met with outrage from his political opponents, but it was an outrage based on the persistent myth of American innocence. Muslims believed they were being watched, even as a national debate about such spying took place. The true question wasn't really whether mosques should be monitored by the government, but whether such surveillance should actually be publicly acknowledged.

Discussions about the national moral fiber aside, this meant that it was entirely possible DHS had some information about allegedly radical activity there. While I certainly hadn't heard anything extreme from the pulpit or among the congregation, I couldn't know what some kid was doing on the internet, or what warped ideology some idiot had decided to adopt on his own.

We were a community haunted by lone wolves.

"Agent Hale, I can assure you that there isn't anything going on there. Not systematically. I've never seen or heard anything militant or suspicious there. The Imam preaches about the importance of smiling at people and about the importance of being clean, about etiquette when using a cellphone—"

"This isn't about the mosque or Imam Sama."

"You've done your research."

A tight smile from her. "We received an anonymous tip regarding potential Islamist activity in your community. It came from you."

"What? No, it didn't."

"Mr. Faris, there is no reason to lie."

"I'm not lying."

Agent Hale stared me down. I folded my arms across my chest.

"Anvar, please, if the tip you sent was accurate, lives may be at risk."

I shook my head. "I didn't call in any tips."

"It was a note."

"I didn't write any notes. By the way, what's your partner doing back there? He's been gone a long time."

She ignored my question. "We know you didn't write the note, sir. But you mailed it. Or, at least you touched it. We were unable to trace the fingerprints on the note itself. They aren't in our database. You, however, went through immigration and, of course, took the state bar. So when your fingerprints showed up on the envelope the note had come in, we had a lead."

I had not touched a letter addressed to the Department of Homeland Security. It was the kind of thing you expected to remember.

"I need some water," I said. "Can I get you some water?"

Hale ignored that question as well. She retrieved a piece of paper from her jacket pocket, unfolded it and slid it over to me.

I recognized the photocopied writing instantly. Hale saw it on my face and gave a triumphant smile. "Who was the author of the note, Mr. Faris?"

"What are you going to do to her?"

"It's a woman then?"

"You already knew that. I'm sure your handwriting experts were able to ferret that out."

"Yes, they were," Hale's partner admitted, walking back into the living room, making a show of drying his hands on his pants. Had I even heard the water run? The fear that my training and knowledge had kept at bay suddenly began to rise. Laws meant something only when people with power agreed to follow them. Otherwise, they were just words.

I'd assumed that the agent would take the time to look through my medicine cabinet or something while he was in the bathroom. I hadn't before considered the possibility that he might plant something there.

That had been stupid. Despite everything I knew, despite everything that had happened with Taleb Mansoor, I was still somehow programmed to trust the authority figures. I blamed my mother.

"We still need you to give us a name. People could die. So why don't you do something for the country that raised you and tell us who wrote the note?"

"Please, Mr. Faris. We need to speak to her."

I thought about it. These two were competent and motivated.

They would, eventually, figure out that Azza was the author of the note. Evading them was not a game I could win. All I could do was control how long it took for them to find out.

Time, as any lawyer who has had to enter billable hours will tell you, is not without value. It is, in fact, the currency of life. Right now, it was the only chip I had to protect Azza's interests. I decided to use it.

I ran a hand through my hair. "You don't need her name. You need to know what she is talking about and who she is talking about. If you bring her in for questioning, or if you show up at her door, you'll destroy her life. Her father will . . . I don't know what he will do. I want to help you, Agent Hale. I just don't want to see her get hurt."

"We do need a name, Mr. Faris."

"I still need some water. You guys want some?"

They looked at each other. Hale shook her head, but Moray nodded. "Sure. Why not?"

I walked over to the kitchen slowly. When had this happened? The day Zuha had come over and found Azza here. I'd picked up an envelope of hers then. That must have been it.

What could Azza know that would interest the Department of Homeland Security?

I walked back to the living room and handed Moray his glass. "I don't know her name."

He rolled his eyes. "Come on."

"I don't know her real name. She calls herself Azza."

Agent Hale started typing into her phone. "Can you spell it? Do you have a last name?"

"Azza bint Saqr," I said, before spelling it out.

"So how do you know this girl?" Hale asked.

"I know her well. Intimately."

"Oh," Agent Moray remarked. "Details please?"

Hale sighed, then tried a different question. "Do you have any idea who her notes could be about?"

"You can ask her yourself."

"Now?"

"No. Not now. I could tell you where she lives and you could go knock on her door with your friend. You'll scare her and you will completely alter her life. Worse, you'll piss off her lawyer, who will instruct her to tell you nothing, and nobody wants that."

Agent Moray frowned. "Who is her— Right, you're her lawyer."

"They gave me a bar card and everything. There is a solution that will get everyone what they want. You'll have to trust me."

Awiti Hale nodded. "We do trust you. We know about your last significant case. You're a patriot."

"She thinks you're a patriot," her partner said. "I think you look at the world and wish it were different. I think reality leaves you scared and confused. I think you're naïve, like a small child."

I ignored him. "I'll talk to her, so that she isn't freaked out. You'll meet her here. I will call you. In one day. You can ask her whatever you need to ask her here."

"In your presence?"

"Why? Were you planning to waterboard her or something?" Hale narrowed her eyes at me and I held up my hands. "Sorry. Just trying to be funny."

"It's a bad habit," Moray said. "Didn't your mama tell you that?"

"Constantly. Yes, in my presence. I won't instruct her to avoid or refrain from answering any questions, though, if they're reasonably calculated to produce probative information. You have my word."

"That's some fancy lawyer speak. Impressive. Fine. We'll do this your way, son, but I can't promise it's gonna end well."

"I know. But that's just a chance we'll all have to take."

AZZA

It would have been nice to tell Anvar the truth, to confide in him and let him know exactly what I was doing and why. But no, I would have to lie to him as well, I'd have to make him believe that Qais was evil and a terrorist, even if only one of those things was true. You never know what someone will do with the truth once they have it.

Trust is always a bad idea. Your family, your friends and, if you ever get married, your husband—always assume they're going to hurt you because they probably will.

In fact, I could use him. Anvar could be very persuasive. He was trained for it. If I convinced him that Qais was a terrorist, he would convince Homeland Security for me.

Lying to him was for the best. It didn't feel good, but I had no option. He was in the middle of it now. I couldn't remember exactly what the Quran said, but I remembered verses that told the world that humans can plan, but God also plans and He is better at it.

Anvar's unexpected involvement seemed like the Hand of God. Maybe He was on my side, for once.

Anvar had brought me to his place. We would meet DHS here.

"We need to talk before you call them."

"Are you okay?" Anvar asked.

"Yes. This is what I wanted. I'm sorry to drag you into it."

"Have you thought about what to say to them?"

I got to my feet and walked away from him.

"Yes. I'm not stupid." I pressed on quickly, before he could reassure me that he'd never thought that. All I wanted was for him to be silent and listen. "Before I tell them anything, I want to tell the story to you, Anvar. I want to tell you the truth."

"You have to tell them the truth too."

I stood by the window, staring out into the dark world. It was time to tell him what I needed him to believe. I needed to weave truth and lies together, until they became indistinguishable.

I'd use pain to do that. If you tell someone a truth that hurts, a personal truth, then it paints over the lie you feed them.

"I'm not a good person. I've done things. Terrible things. You shouldn't feel sorry for me."

"Azza, you don't have to—"

"You won't understand. You haven't seen it. The destruction of your city. War. I saw many things. I'm not making excuses. It's just impossible to explain. The dust and the rubble and the dried blood. What happens to people, what they become. I couldn't tell you and, if I could, you wouldn't get it."

Then I spoke the worst truths.

I told him about Mama and how she had died.

I told him about Abu and how he'd been taken, and the long night that followed.

I told him about Fahd and how I had left him behind.

I felt like I was ripping the story out of my soul, in which it had become intertwined, because of how much it was a part of me, because I had tried not to even think of it, much less speak of it, for so long.

I stared at my reflection in the windowpane as I spoke. It seemed like a face that belonged to someone else. There were tears flowing down the face that was looking back at me, but my voice remained strong. "He begged for painkillers at the end, when I told him I was leaving. He begged me to let him overdose."

"It's not your fault."

"I should've done it. I should have killed him quickly and stayed with him until he passed. Instead, I left him and he died alone."

Anvar walked toward me, to comfort me I'm sure, but I shrank away from him and held myself. He stood where he was, arms dangling uselessly by his sides.

"We met Qais Badami when we left home. He was—no, he is a bad man. He looks nice and he talks nice, you know, and he acts religious, so Abu liked him. They became friends. Abu told him about my desire to leave Afghanistan. One day Qais came to our house when Abu was out. He said that friends of his were organizing a mission in the United States, a mission in which he would hurt a lot of Americans. He could get passage for Abu and myself, by saying that Abu would help carry their mission out. My father would never do that, you know, he would never hurt anyone."

"He hurt you," Anvar noted quietly.

"That's different." I was no longer looking at the girl in the window. I couldn't. "All Qais wanted in return was for me to sleep with him one time. I let him do what he wanted. We had to get out of there—I had to get out. I told myself it was only one night. Abu would never have to know."

"Except he came back," Anvar guessed. "You'd put yourself in his power, and he came back."

How well men understand each other. "I couldn't refuse him, and he knew it. I needed Qais until we came here."

I told Anvar about locking Qais out of the apartment, that Bhatti had made Qais leave and how Qais had finally decided to actually marry me.

"The agents will ask but I don't know what Qais's mission is. I know only that Abu told Qais he doesn't want any part of it. He doesn't want anyone to get hurt. I don't either. That's why I wrote those notes. That is what I'm going to tell them."

I waited for Anvar to say something, but all that followed my words was silence. He was thinking, probably going over the story in his mind, looking for anything that didn't make sense. That was not what I wanted.

For the first time since I'd started telling my story, I turned to look at him. I met his eyes. I didn't flinch.

"That's the whole truth?"

"It's the truth," I said. "What can I get?"

"For what?"

"Tell your friends I want a deal. That's what they do on TV. Cops make deals with people who can give them information."

"These aren't cops. And they aren't my friends."

"Can they protect me?"

"From Qais?"

I shook my head. "No. They're going to take him away. I mean protection from themselves, from the government. I don't want people coming after us, me or my father. We're here illegally. I want to stay."

"Well," Anvar said, "Immigration is part of the Department of Homeland Security. I'll talk to Agent Hale about seeing if we can work out that kind of arrangement. After all, what you're asking for won't cost them anything. You just want them to look the other way. There are something like ten million illegal immigrants in this country, what are two more?"

"Tell them that I have evidence," I said. "Against Qais. I have things of his that will show that he's guilty. If they promise me immunity, I'll show them."

"What kinds of things?"

"I'll tell them when they agree." I nodded toward his phone. "Make the call."

Anvar didn't move. Instead, he sat back down and studied me carefully, trying to decide how to say what he was going to say. Finally, he asked, "Are you going to tell them about your father?"

"What about him?"

"If they find out about what happened to him in Iraq, they'll deport him."

"Maybe," I said. "Or maybe he'll disappear forever this time."

"He hits you, Azza. If they find out who he really is, that'll stop."

Who he really is? Anvar always thought he was so smart, but he was too simple to realize the depths of what he didn't know.

I'd thought about that a lot though. What is a father? Abu wasn't the man who had slept with my mother when I was conceived, true, but he had raised me. He'd often been an awful father, but he had been a father still. That was a debt of a sort.

I'd already thought about the fact that I could be rid of both Abu and Qais in one move, but that wasn't what I wanted. I let out a deep breath, relieved that I could start telling the truth again, if only for the moment.

"He wasn't like this before. Before . . . everything. If I could've saved Fahd somehow, I think he'd still love me like he did once."

"There was nothing you could have done."

"It doesn't matter. We say nothing to the agents about Abu's past. This is about Qais and making sure he never hurts anyone ever again."

Anvar had said there were two agents, but only one, a woman, came to meet us. He invited her in and asked why her partner wasn't with her. She didn't answer him right away. Instead, she sat down in a chair across from me and introduced herself.

Then Agent Hale said, "Take off your niqab."

I looked at Anvar. He started to object, but Hale cut him off. "You've slept with her, so she doesn't wear it in front of you. She doesn't have to wear it in front of me. That's why I asked Moray not to come. I wanted to see her face."

I hoped Anvar would keep arguing, but he didn't. My heart started to beat faster as Agent Hale looked at me, almost unblinking, waiting for me to reveal myself. I'd been counting on the veil. It'd be easier to lie if they couldn't see my face as I did it.

It didn't matter. I'd fooled Anvar. I could fool this woman. I would. True, Anvar wasn't trained to spot liars, not like she was—

"Is there a problem?" Hale asked.

I shook my head quickly and did as she asked. I felt exposed now. Nervous.

Anvar gave me a smile that said everything was going to be fine.

"Tell me everything," Hale demanded.

I told her the story that I'd told Anvar. She took notes as I spoke, even though she was also recording it on what Anvar had called a Dictaphone.

When I was done speaking, Hale said nothing. She just looked at me, weighing my worth.

Did she know that I was lying? I fought the urge to look away from Hale's eyes, to fidget or walk around. I had not come this far to be stopped. No. No, I had to convince her.

"I have evidence," I said. "I'll give it to you."

"What evidence?" Agent Hale asked.

"Qais bought a gun."

"That isn't evidence that supports your claims, Ms. Saqr."

"Wait," Anvar said. "Hold on. Qais did come to me to ask me about the Second Amendment. He admitted to buying a gun, then asked if the right to bear arms included explosives."

For the first time in forever, the agent looked away from me. Her tone got harder than it had been somehow.

"You didn't think to report this to anyone?"

Anvar shrugged. "Report what? It was an entirely theoretical discussion."

"Possibly not," Hale muttered. Then louder she asked, "And you will swear he asked you that? You'll swear it under the penalty of perjury?"

"Of course," he said.

That seemed to be enough for Agent Hale. She turned back to face me, and this time when she spoke, she leaned forward a little. It was all I could do not to fall on my face to thank God. It was a miracle. The Lord of the Universe really was with me.

"What else do you have, Ms. Saqr?"

"Pictures he's taken," I said. "Famous places that he might target. The Golden Gate Bridge. Subway stations. Union Square. And I have maps—"

"How did you come to possess these things?"

"Qais has been trying to get Abu—my father—to go along with his mission. My father is a good man. He refuses all the time, but Qais got him a copy of *Dabiq*."

"What is a *Dabiq*?" Anvar asked.

"An ISIS recruitment magazine," the agent replied. The neutrality had gone from her face.

I reached into my backpack and pulled out the copy of *Dabiq*. Anvar reached for it, but Agent Hale stuck her hand out to stop him.

"Don't touch it."

He nodded and leaned over my shoulder to study the magazine cover more closely. A man dressed in black with a long beard was smiling up at us, heavily armed but apparently carefree. The caption read: WISH YOU WERE HERE.

"What do you think?" Hale asked Anvar.

"I think print media is dead," he said. "As is the guy on the cover, I assume."

Then I pulled out my journals. They were identical, bright pink, with the images of sleeping unicorns drawn on them. Each cover had one word written on it, in a looping, playful font: BELIEVE.

"I wrote down everything I could starting a year and a half ago," I said. "These will be helpful. Right?"

Anvar reached for one, and I expected Hale to stop him again, but she didn't. In fact, as he picked one up, she took the other one.

"Very helpful," Agent Hale said. "With all of this, we've definitely got him."

ANVAR

I flipped through the pages of Azza's journal, trying to avoid getting glitter from the unicorn's horn on my hands as best I could. Entries had been made in a small, neat hand. Azza had mostly used a purple pen, which, combined with the cheery, flamboyant cover, made for a stark contrast with the grim content.

There was no time to read it all in detail, but as I scanned the text, something felt wrong, like the urgent, low howling of the desert wind before the coming of a sandstorm. I searched the words, the thin, almost fragile paper they were written on, trying to discover what it was that was bothering me.

"What is it, Mr. Faris?" Agent Awiti Hale was looking at me, an eyebrow raised.

The journal began with an entry from a year and a half ago. It was about me, about the day Azza had asked me about morality, about choosing between limits and priorities. That had happened just before Aamir's recent engagement party.

In fact, I'd only met Azza around Eid al-Adha. I'd spoken about Mikey and Sisyphus at the mosque. That had happened this year.

Eid had been September 12, 2016. I remembered thinking how fortunate it was that it had not fallen on September 11.

So how did her journal record a conversation between us in 2015, before we'd met?

There was only one possible answer.

The journals were a lie.

Azza had lied to the DHS. And to me.

I glanced over at Azza, in my gaze a question I could not ask, not while Agent Hale was here. She was still as a statue. Her green eyes were wide and fixed on me, unblinking.

My fingers clamped down on the spine of the journal hard, and it clapped shut. The innocent, sleeping, mythical creature on the cover mocked me with its injunction to believe. I turned the book over, so I wouldn't have to look at it.

I took a deep calming breath, trying to force the suddenly rigid muscles in my jaw to relax. Anger wasn't affordable. I needed to be rational. To be a lawyer.

"Anvar," Hale said again. "What is it?"

I needed time to figure out how much Azza—or whatever her name was—had lied about, and what the consequences of those falsehoods would be. So long as I stayed silent, I had options. Once I told the DHS what I'd realized, they would be in charge.

"It is just distressing," I said finally, handing the journal to Hale, "to read everything that's happened to Azza. She's had a difficult life."

Hale tilted her head and gave me an odd look. "But you knew that already, didn't you?"

"Not really. I've never heard the details."

"Are we done?" Azza asked.

The DHS agent frowned, then got to her feet. "I'll be back. I'll have more questions for Ms. Saqr later."

A reprieve. I managed not to let out a sigh of relief. "I'm sure you will."

"I expect your client will cooperate fully with our investigation?"

"We called you, remember?"

"Only after you had no choice left. I'm going to bring this Qais character in, and once we have his testimony, we'll be in touch. Thank you, Mr. Faris."

"I didn't do anything," I said. "It was all my client."

And that, at the very least, happened to be something that was absolutely true.

I leaned against the door as it closed behind me. Azza remained seated, staring down at her now empty backpack. She spoke first.

"Thank you for not telling them."

I tried to control my tone. I didn't want to raise my voice. I fear I wasn't entirely successful. I definitely wasn't able to soften the question I felt I had to ask.

"How could you be so unbelievably stupid?"

"Anvar, I—"

"You never kept a journal, did you?"

She shook her head.

"You wrote the whole thing in the last month or so. You made it seem like you'd been doing it for over a year."

"Yes," she said.

"Why?"

Azza didn't answer.

"Tell me why."

"I need to be rid of Qais."

"So," I said. "Everything you told me was a lie?"

"No." She jumped to her feet, as if driven upward by the force of her denial. "He isn't a terrorist, but everything else, what he did to me . . . I'm not lying about that. I wouldn't."

"Who will believe you now?" I asked her. "You manufactured evidence."

Except me, I didn't add. I did believe her. That was different though. I knew her. At least, I thought I did. I could sense the truth in her voice and read it on her face.

It would be different for DHS. From their perspective, her credibility had been fatally compromised.

"They won't realize," Azza said.

"It took me forty seconds to figure it out. Agent Hale seems very sharp. What happens when they come back and ask you specific questions about what is in those journals? What happens when they question Qais, and he has alibis?"

"But maybe—"

"What happens when they run a fingerprint analysis on that ISIS magazine you said belongs to Qais? Has he ever touched it?"

Azza shook her head.

"Has Qais touched the pictures of his 'targets'?"

"No. I just got them off the internet."

"Azza, they're going to figure this out very, very fast."

She stared up at me. For the first time since this had started, for the first time since I'd met her, really, I saw naked uncertainty in her eyes. It was as if she hadn't ever considered that her plan, which had been terrible by any objective measure, might fail.

"What do I do?"

I had no idea.

"I read about these cases online," Azza said to my silence. "The FBI targets low-IQ Muslims and traps them into getting in trouble, right? They want to catch terrorists so badly, they'll invent them if they have to. They'll want to believe me."

She was right about that. DHS would want to believe her. I was convinced that they had believed her for the moment, but Hale had made her work for it. Azza wasn't giving her enough credit.

When DHS examined the evidence, the thin illusion Azza had manufactured would fall apart. What crime would they charge her with? Obstruction, probably. Lying to a federal agent . . .

There would be no looking the other way about Azza's or Abu Fahd's immigration status. They'd be deported, at the very least.

"What should I do?"

There were no pieces left on the board for me except one, and when you've got only one piece, you have only one option. You move.

"If I were you," I said, "I'd run."

AZZA

Run? That was the best plan he could come up with? I'd been running my whole life.

"I'm not going to do that, Anvar. I can't anymore. I'm tired."

I waited for him to respond, but for once it looked like Anvar Faris had no words to offer. I glanced at the window I'd been standing by hours before, at the waiting dark, always ready to swallow up those who wander into it.

Maybe that was the only home I was ever going to have.

He made a helpless gesture, raising his hands a little, palms out, before letting them drop to his sides. "I'm sorry."

I wanted to stay here, in this city, Mama's city to which she'd never been. Now it seemed like everything I'd done, everything I'd imagined, everything I'd written, had been for nothing at all.

"All I want, all I have ever wanted, is to live," I said. "To live, to be home and to be free. That's not too much to ask. It can't be."

Anvar stepped up beside me. "You can decide to stay if you want. I don't know what happens if you do, but I'll stand for you, no matter what comes."

They would say I was a criminal, put me in jail, then in front of a judge. I'd get either locked up or sent back to Iraq, where there was nothing for me now. Staying was a foolish choice.

"I could go somewhere cold," I said. "I've always wanted to see snow fall. It sounds beautiful."

"It is in the beginning. Then dogs pee on it, people walk on it, drive cars by it, and it just ends up looking like gross sludge."

"I should've guessed. There's nothing beautiful left in the world."

He looked like he wanted to tell me I was wrong, but he didn't. Instead, he said, "I can help you with the details. I have some money."

"No. Wait. Not now. Please. Let's go lie down. Let's pretend like nothing has gone wrong. Can we pretend that things are like they were for a while?"

"Yes," he said. "We can absolutely do that."

ANVAR

We didn't touch, except for our hands, and we stared at the ceiling, as if we were very young, and above us was a field of stars.

"I hate you a little," Azza said. "Not in a bad way."

"It's a good hate?"

"I don't understand you, Anvar." She wove her fingers around mine. "You have all the freedom I have ever wanted, more than most people ever have, but you cage yourself, keep yourself from doing things, taking things, that you want. All of your life is yours, and you just . . . you live like you have no choices, like your fate is written."

I looked over at her, but she wasn't looking at me.

"Only a little time in my life has ever belonged to me," she said. "I stole what happiness I could find in the time I had. Maybe my Lord will forgive me. I have reason to hope. Despite everything, I know that He is Merciful."

I shook my head, amazed.

"After the life you've lived, how can you say that? How can you know that?"

"It's simple," she said. "I know because I met you."

"What are you going to do about Qais?"

The last thing I saw, before Azza's face was obscured by her niqab, was a frown. "What do you mean?"

It was the only detail we hadn't discussed. We'd talked about where to go, how to get there and how to stay off the grid until she could cross the border north. She needed some cash, and I gave her what I could. She was going to leave her phone behind, ditch the niqab and abandon her email accounts.

It could work, even though it was more difficult than it has ever been to be forgotten.

Azza was so calm. Taking a moment to lie still, talk and build an oasis in her mind had strengthened her resolve. It was easy to forget that this was a woman who had walked the world. It was hubris, perhaps, to even think she needed my help.

"They are going to arrest him."

"Good," she said. "That was the point."

"Azza, he's innocent."

"He's *not* innocent."

I stepped back from the sharp edge of her tone. I couldn't see her face anymore, but I'd been in enough arguments to know from the concrete in her eyes and the steel in her voice that there was nothing I could say to make her accept my position.

I tried anyway, refusing on that night to be daunted by futility. "He's innocent of the charges Homeland Security wants to bring against him."

"He did what he did. He should suffer."

"Absolutely. But if they go in thinking they're taking down a dangerous terrorist, knowing he might be armed, we don't know what will happen. If things go sideways, they may not take him alive at all."

"I hope he dies then."

I wanted to tell her that it would haunt her if he did get killed, but I wasn't sure that was true. Azza wanted revenge. Getting it, however, required my silence.

I couldn't tell Agent Hale that Azza had lied, not until Azza had escaped as best she could. It was necessary for her to get as much of a head start on the agents as possible. That didn't mean that my silence had to be absolute. I could warn Qais that he was being hunted.

He could run too.

Even if Azza had no qualms about using the justice system to extract vengeance, I certainly did. Justice and vengeance are different things, though they are often confused. That's what had happened in Taleb Mansoor's case.

"You can't do this. I can't do it. We don't take from the world what we can't give back to it."

"I don't know what that means."

"It means we have to live careful lives."

"Why?"

I frowned. It was not a question I had ever asked, but only because the truth of that proposition had always seemed self-evident to me. Maybe it was an easier thing to understand when you had blood on your hands, even if it was only the blood of a goat.

"Because, Azza, the damage we do to each other, to the world, survives us. In the time we have, we must consider the consequences of—"

"The world will be better when Qais isn't in it. And not just for me. He was the one who destroyed Bhatti's office."

"How do you know that?"

"He hates Bhatti because Bhatti kept him away from me, from what he imagines is his."

Our landlord had called Qais a hyena, but that was not proof of guilt. Not that it mattered. I wasn't saying that Qais didn't deserve a harsh fate, or that his absence wouldn't make society better. That wasn't my position. I was arguing, as I always had, for process.

"We don't get to make that call."

"Then who does?"

It wasn't my night for having answers to the questions she was asking.

I knew how Bariah Faris would reply, of course. My mother would say that only God got to decide the shape of the world. It was a nice answer, perhaps even a true answer, but not a complete one. When you hold a knife in your hand, you're responsible for what you do with it. The will of a higher power doesn't absolve you of the consequences of your decisions. Religion is not morality, despite what Ma might think.

When I didn't answer, Azza stepped closer and rested a hand on the side of my face, forcing me to look into her unreadable eyes. "Don't interfere, Anvar," she whispered. "Let it happen. This is all I have left. I need to hurt Qais. You can't take this away from me. Please."

I turned my head slightly, so I could kiss her palm. I gave her no promise but stopped pushing back. She wasn't going to change her mind, and it was possible I'd never get to speak to her again. I didn't want to waste the last few words we had left.

"Wherever you go, Azza, whatever name you take and whoever you become, I hope that you find everything you're looking for."

She leaned forward and let her veiled lips graze my cheek, before turning away to leave forever.

She did not look back.

I sat with the absence of Azza bint Saqr and tried to see the world as she saw it. It was a difficult thing. I wasn't in the business of vengeance. The lessons I had learned, the words I had been taught, the life I had led, the battle I'd fought for Taleb Mansoor had all contoured my moral lens in a way that made it impossible to see Azza's perspective with any clarity.

I understood her desire to punish Qais. I even shared it. However, it was simply wrong to allow anyone to be condemned for a crime they hadn't committed, especially one as serious as terrorism. There was no guarantee of due process or even survival in a case like this one.

Besides, Azza had concocted her entire scheme with the assumption that Qais's arrest would free her from him, allowing her to continue to live her life with Abu Fahd in San Francisco. That was no longer a possibility. Azza was leaving the city herself. There was no reason, other than retribution, to let the Department of Homeland Security take Qais.

"I am faced," I said to the woman who wasn't here anymore, "with a moral imperative."

Had Azza noticed that I hadn't technically given her my word I wouldn't interfere? I'd go to Powell station. I knew there were pay phones there. There was no way I could call Qais from my cell. It could lead to too many questions from DHS.

Of course, it was entirely possible that he was asleep and would not answer, which meant that Azza might get her wish after all.

AZZA

Abu wouldn't be back until after dawn, so I had several hours to pack. A small carry-on was enough to fit my life. A few clothes, all the money Abu hid under his mattress for emergencies and a toothbrush were all I kept.

Deciding what to take was easy. Thinking about what to leave behind cost me time.

I had to think about what, if anything, to leave Abu. Should I write a letter? For all the writing I'd done in the last month, I had no words of leave-taking for my father.

I couldn't just disappear. Abu would worry. He'd wonder at first where I'd gone. He'd wait for me. Then, slowly, panic would start taking ahold of him. He'd call hospitals and the police. He'd think I'd been hurt or worse.

He'd feel the same way I'd felt, all those years ago, when Abu had been taken. That was too cruel a thing to do to anyone.

There were a hundred thousand things to say and, at the same time, there was nothing to say. Should I write "Dear Abu" when he was neither my father nor very dear anymore? Should I end with "Love, Azza" or "Love, Safwa" or no love at all?

I left him the ring Qais had given me and exactly one word. Goodbye.

I was locking the apartment door behind me when I heard him call my name. I jumped and whirled around, my keys clattering on the ground.

"Abu! Why aren't you at work?"

"Qais called me," Abu said. "The police are after him. He's going to get to safety, and tomorrow, once we have gathered our things, we will join him."

"How did he know?" I demanded, stepping forward. "How could Qais know that?"

I didn't need Abu to answer me though. I knew the truth even as the last question left my lips.

Anvar had betrayed me.

Rage flooded my eyes with hot tears.

Then I realized that Abu was staring at me and at my luggage.

"What are you doing? How are you outside without your niqab?"

I tried to make something up but couldn't. My mind was racing my heart, but my thoughts weren't coherent. All I could think about was the certainty that Abu was going to hurt me. He was going to hit me. It would be worse than it had ever been before.

Then, just like that, it was too late to lie. I saw the burning certainty in the hardening of his gaze, like lava becoming rock. He understood.

"I'm leaving," I said, gathering all the courage I had. "I'm leaving you and Qais and your stupid honor and—"

"You're not going anywhere."

"I am," I said, "I'm running away."

He shook his head. "Safwa, my child, do you not know that in order to run, you have to be able to walk?"

ANVAR

Convincing Qais to run hadn't been difficult. I told him the police had been in the building, asking questions. I'd learned they thought Qais had vandalized Hafeez Bhatti's apartment. Because he was undocumented, I said, he'd face deportation with a conviction.

It wasn't exactly an airtight story. His immigration status wouldn't be reported by the San Francisco Police Department if he were picked up for a property crime. He thought I was an expert though, and he had no reason to mistrust me. When you use the right language, when you use words that seem to be laden with significant meaning—words like "expedited removal" and "extraordinary rendition"—it is easy to make people believe the stories you tell, especially if you know what they are afraid of.

Fearful people are credulous people. That is why entire populations can be manipulated to go along with wars, massacres and atrocities. Qais was only one man.

Yet I worried.

I worried that he might see the flaws in the lies I'd crafted for him or that he might seek a second opinion. Not only was it possible he'd be killed or disappeared, but if he were captured, he might tell Homeland Security I had called him and told him to run. I had no idea how I'd explain that.

I hoped, at least, that Azza was safe. No one was hunting her, at least for the moment. There was a chance that by the time all this played out, she'd be in some remote part of Canada, with a different name, and with some freedom to call her own for the first time in her life.

I tried to sleep, but couldn't. In the deepest part of the night, desperately exhausted, I did something I hadn't done for many years. I stood up to pray in my own home of my own volition.

It didn't help.

Always perhaps, in the court of the King, the Fool is destined to remain unsatisfied.

The worst of it was the guilt. Even though she would probably never know it, I'd betrayed Azza. I'd been absolutely certain that it was the right thing to do. Time, however, erodes certainty like the wind tears away at rock, leaving it jagged and disfigured.

I took out my checkers set and set up the board. I don't know why. There was no one to play against. It helped, a little, to do something familiar, something perfectly under my control.

It helped to remember Naani Jaan, to remember that even though my choices now might have been wrong, there had been someone, once, who'd loved me unconditionally.

Naani Jaan was right about you. You told me she said you play checkers without courage. But it's true about everything you do. You never stand up and fight for what you want or believe in.

You're a coward.

Aamir's words still cut me, threatening to sever the connection I felt then with Naani Jaan's memory.

I got to my feet and began to pace. My first thought, as if I was arguing before a judge, was to say "Objection, relevance." After all, what did this matter just then? It had nothing to do with Qais or Azza. My concerns about what was to come for them, and for me, were rational, given the circumstances. They did not make me craven.

I knocked my knee against the coffee table and a black checkers piece from the last row slid off the board. I picked it up. It was an amazing thing, actually, that little round disk, limited yet full of potential. If it could brave the perils before it and survive, it would be coupled with another just like it, and become royal. It would make a real difference in the world it inhabited.

Or, I suppose, it could sit back, a peasant in the king's row, trapped and made impotent by a desire to play it safe, refusing to move until it was too late to alter the course of the game.

Bhatti had asked me to be brave. It wasn't the first time I'd heard those words.

My father had asked me to do the same, a lifetime ago, when I'd been tasked with killing Mikey the goat. I hadn't told my father then that I wasn't afraid, that I felt something else entirely, on that Eid, as I stood with a knife in my hand.

I'd felt inadequate, like I wasn't meant for the enormously sad charge before me. And I'd been right. If Aamir hadn't spoken God's name then, I would certainly have forgotten to do so and my sacrifice would've been fatally flawed.

Then again, Abraham hadn't been alone when he'd tried to follow God's command either. He hadn't been required to pass the test by himself. His son had been with him.

I took the piece I held, and even though it was wrong, even though it broke all the rules, ancient and modern, that governed the game, I placed it on top of the piece next to where it had been, bestowing a crown on them of which neither one had yet proven worthy.

For a few moments, I stared at what I had done.

Then I called Zuha.

"Anvar? It's six in the morning."

"Can you come over?" I asked.

"Now? Is everything okay?"

"Please. I need you."

There was a pause. I could tell, however, that it wasn't hesitation. It was just Zuha listening to what I'd said and hearing what I'd left unsaid.

"Do I have time to get dressed?"

"I suppose, though my day would be more fun if you didn't."

She sighed. "I'll be there as quickly as I can."

"Thank you," I said, collapsing into a chair and closing my eyes. Finally, I'd found it. Something that I knew, beyond all doubt, was true.

I forced myself to shower, shave and tidy the apartment a little. One must, Bariah Faris always assured me, maintain appearances. I was distracted enough, and tired enough, to not notice that the city still looked like morning hadn't come, until the familiar tapping of heavy raindrops on the windows called my attention to the darkness outside.

When I opened the door for Zuha, I found that the heavens had made her look heart-stopping. Perhaps anticipating a repeat of the bright day we'd had yesterday, she had decided to wear a long cotton maxi dress that must have been both modest and fetching when she had put it on. The rain, however, had left her absolutely drenched, and her dress clung to her with delightfully indecent precision.

I realized that she'd greeted me and was asking if everything was all right when she fell silent and, noticing that I was staring, blushed fiercely.

"I simply love your outfit," I said after I gathered myself.

"Jerk," she muttered under her breath.

I stepped aside to let her in. "I'm the perfect gentleman. I'm the Darcy of brown men."

"Funny. I don't remember Darcy perving on his sister-in-law, Jane."

"Austen never gave him the chance. It's easy to be chaste when you're never tempted."

"And you know all about temptation."

I waved in her direction. "I mean . . . just look at you."

"You're a bad person."

I didn't argue the point.

"I need to dry off and change. Do you have something I can wear?"

I picked out the smallest T-shirt I had. It was green, with the phrase LUCK OF THE IRISH printed on it. I handed it to her along with a white shalwar that was much too long for her. While she was changing, I put some coffee on.

"You look ridiculous," I told her as she marched out of the bathroom. "I prefer it when you are dripping wet."

Zuha shook her head. "You're incorrigible."

"That's a good word."

"I thought you'd like it," she said wryly, then, turning serious, continued, "You all right? You don't look great."

"It's been rough," I admitted, handing her a warm mug she wrapped her fingers around immediately. "I'm glad you're here."

I followed her to the couch in the living room, and she curled up in the corner opposite mine. "Tell me about it."

So I did. I told her about how I'd met Azza and Abu Fahd and Qais, and everything I'd learned about their lives since then. I told her about Azza's plot, Homeland Security's involvement and my decision to tell Qais he'd best run.

Zuha listened without speaking. If she was judging me, she had the courtesy to do so in silence.

"Do you think what I did was wrong?"

She laughed.

"What?"

"This is so like you. Remember that story about how Azar'il— the angel of death—was told that the dinosaurs had to go extinct so Adam could live on the planet, so he flung a meteor at the Earth, setting off a totally unplanned cataclysmic global ice age?"

"Really?"

"So, Jibril goes to him and demands to know what Azar'il thinks he's doing. Azar'il turns to Jibril calmly and asks, 'Why? Did I do it wrong?' Remember that?"

"No." I frowned. "That's new to me."

"It's new to everyone. I just made it up. Anvar, you're so awful at asking for help."

"I called you."

"For comfort and reassurance," Zuha said. "That's not asking for help. What am I supposed to say now? If I tell you there may have been a better way, it'll just make me feel bad about myself and make you feel bad about yourself. It's not fair."

I nodded. "So . . . what was the better way?"

Zuha looked up, as if asking for divine aid. "Telling Agent Hale the truth. Given Azza's circumstances, they may have let her actions go. She would've still been able to leave her father's home, but she wouldn't be on the run from the United States government. Also, the chances of you being in trouble with the Department of Homeland Security would have been zero."

"Too risky," I said. "If the Feds hadn't let it go, if they had failed to have mercy—which, you know, isn't unheard of—Azza could have been in serious trouble. My priority was to protect her."

"Isn't she in serious trouble now? But you're right. Our priorities would've been different. I would have tried to protect you."

Zuha looked down and studied the steam rising from her coffee. The silence was long but comfortable and achingly familiar. It made me think of a trip, years ago, when my family had gone back to Karachi and I'd gotten a chance to walk through our old neighborhood. It was like I had found a piece of myself. I was surprised at how incomplete I'd been without ever realizing it.

"Honestly," she said eventually. "I don't know what I would have done in your place. I do know that I would have called you a lot sooner than you called me."

"That wasn't my decision to make."

"Azza wasn't why you didn't reach out. It never occurred to you to ask your parents or Aamir or me or other attorneys—anyone—to help you. That's who you are. You've always believed your moral character is better than anyone else's. You've always believed that you're smarter than everyone else."

"My 'moral character' is good enough that if you had a sister, I wouldn't have agreed to marry her," I said before I could stop myself.

I waited for her to hit back. She didn't.

"Sorry, I—"

"No, you're right. I should have said no at the very beginning."

"What was your plan, anyway?" I asked. "Marry Aamir out of spite?"

"It wasn't just spite. I mean, he's a nice enough guy."

I snorted my disdain for that notion. "He's a tool from Toolistan."

"If it wasn't going to be you, then what did it matter who I ended up with?"

"That's just about the stupidest thing I've ever heard."

"Didn't you just try to bite my head off for saying you thought you were superior to everyone?"

"I said I was sorry," I protested.

"And I'm sorry I didn't run it all by you first." Zuha snapped her fingers, as if just remembering something. "Oh, wait. You weren't around. The moment there was no sex in our relationship, you dropped me and ran all the way across the damn continent."

"Were you not there when you dumped me?"

"I didn't mean cut me out of your life. Walk by me when you see me in the halls like I didn't exist."

"That is usually what happens when a couple splits up."

"We were more than that." She looked up at me, her voice, her eyes, her expression, pleading for me to hear her, to understand her. "Weren't we? You were my best friend. Then you were gone, without even talking to me, and the next thing I know, I hear about you and some other girl. Then another and another. I felt so replaceable."

I'd gotten to my feet at some point during the conversation.

"That isn't how it was for me."

"I loved you, Anvar." She said it like it was a secret.

It was not a secret, though. I refused to say it like one.

"And I loved you."

"But you broke my heart."

"And I thought you broke mine."

That drew a sad laugh from her, like a bird with a shattered wing trying to take flight. "We're ridiculous. You've got more important things to worry about."

"There's nothing more important. Look, we messed it up, but we can start over. We can give each other a clean slate."

"Don't be a child. There aren't any do-overs. There is no clean slate."

"What then? You're not going to marry Aamir and we'll just go back to being strangers? Or you are going to marry him and we'll pretend everything is fine?"

Zuha stared at something far away, not a place but a time. "It has been fine for years now."

"No. It hasn't."

She bit her lower lip and looked away. "I don't know how this ends."

"I don't either," I said. "But we're going to have to find out."

I watched Zuha's dress tumble wildly around the dryer, as green digits on its timer inexorably ticked down. Once time ran out, Zuha would leave. I might never get another chance to speak with her alone like this again. When her engagement with Aamir fell through, which seemed inevitable, someone else would appear to replace him.

It had to be someone else. Didn't it? It could never be me. It wouldn't be acceptable to our families. It would be impossible to explain to their friends, their society, the people they cared about.

Perhaps this was always how she and I were meant to end. Perhaps the fairy-tale narrative of love's strength, of love's endurance, of love's ability to overcome evil and cruelty and neglect truly is just a fairy tale. Maybe love is just a fragile and breakable thing, which shatters under the weight of misunderstandings, miscommunications and the simple passage of time.

The pleasant, artificial smell of detergents and softeners, combined with the damp air, was making the laundry room oppressive. Despite the rain and the cold, I stepped outside. For the first time in forever, my breath became visible, forming little clouds that disappeared swiftly into the wind.

I'd meant what I said. What was happening with Azza and Qais wasn't more important than what was happening between Zuha and myself. It was more urgent and more dangerous, true, but it was also out of my hands. There was nothing I could do for either of them, and I'd have to see how things went before speaking to Homeland Security again.

All that would be easier with Zuha beside me. The world was prettier, kinder, more comprehensible when she was with me. For years, I had tried to forget this.

I'd willed myself to forget everything—her effortless grace, her good-natured wit, the quick empathy of her soulful eyes, and the tantalizing promise that shone through the light of her personality— a promise that if you were with her, then this year flowers would not die in autumn. It was unbearable that I would have to let her go again.

My clothes were heavy, drunk on too much storm.

I remembered the first time I had danced with her. The first time I felt intoxicated.

The buzzer on the dryer sounded.

I was out of time and I didn't know what to do.

I had tried to face the world alone, and I hadn't been enough. As I went back in to retrieve her dress, I realized I should have called someone for advice about Zuha, just as she'd said I should've called someone for advice about Azza.

I could've called my father. He would have liked that. He probably would've played me a song. Maybe that old melody he had played when, all those years ago, I got home after escorting Zuha home from prom. That night when he had grounded me, there was the memory of a song lingering in the air. I had heard it with him again recently.

Waqt ki qaid main zindagi hai magar . . .

Was that the song he would choose? What would he say after the music died and the singer was silent? Maybe he would say what he had already said.

Don't give this one away. I love this one. This one belongs to me.

I might have asked Hafeez Bhai for some of his street vendor wisdom. Maybe he too would say something that he had already said.

Even if you lose a hundred battles, perhaps Allah helps you and you win the war.

Or perhaps I should have spoken to Abu Fahd.

Everyone upon the earth will perish. . . . Tonight, however, we are here. . . .

And Azza.

You have all the freedom I have ever wanted. . . . I stole what happiness I could in the time I had.

My breath was shaking as it burst out of me.

And my mother? What would she say about it all?

You will roast in hell for what you dare.

Maybe. If so, I would make sure it was worth it.

Be brave.

I began to run, Zuha's dress in my hand, getting wet all over again. I reached the apartment and threw open the door. Zuha was sitting before the checkers board, trying to spin a piece on its edge like a coin. She rose at the sight of me.

"What happened?"

"I realized that I lied to you."

"What?"

"When I said I loved you once." I let go of her dress and it fell to the ground. I walked up to Zuha, winded, and took her warm hands in mine. "I lied to you. I got the tense wrong. But there's still time. You're still here. I can still tell you. There's not a single moment of my life that has not been better because you were with me. And that is all we are. Moments. You and I and everyone. That's what life is. It's just time, and it's ending, Zuha. Everyone is ending. Who really cares what anyone else thinks? We have to steal our happiness in the time we've been given. And you're right. The past is messed up. It's broken. So what? Time doesn't care about that. Time keeps happening and we can do it right moving forward because time's like water, like a river, like the monsoon. It's like the rain. You can't break the rain."

She touched the side of my face. "Calm down. I understand you."

"You do?"

"You're forgetting something though."

"What?"

Zuha pointed up at the ceiling. There was nothing there.

"Mistletoe," she said.

Then she kissed me and kissed me and kissed me again.

The world was new again.

For a divine instant, it was once more the world that God had looked upon after He first created it.

The world He knew was good.

The world before the Fall and before Babel.

The world as it had been before the golden calf was worshipped. Before the Red Sea parted. Before Joseph was thrown into a well. Before the suffering of Job. Before anyone ever claimed that Khidr was dead. Before al-Hajar al-Aswad was forever stained by the sins of men. Before the blood of innocents sanctified the sands of Karbala.

It was a world of light and music and warmth.

I was there. Zuha was there.

And God was there.

It is true that I could not see Him, just as you cannot see Him.

If you listen closely, though, then in the sprouting of new redwoods, in the hoofbeats of wild horses, in the sound of snow falling on distant mountains, in the fingers of lovers interlacing, in the memory of children not yet born, you can hear Him smile.

Then the moment was gone, and I was mortal again.

Zuha stiffened in my arms and pulled away, her eyes fixed at the door I'd left open. She made a sound, something between a gasp and a scream. When I turned around, I saw Azza. She was barely recognizable. Without her usual niqab, her injuries were clear and grotesque. One of her eyes was swollen shut, her nose bent, lip cut and bleeding. There were bruises on her face and arms. She was clutching at her side. Zuha ran over to her and was guiding her to a seat before I could even react.

"What happened?" Zuha asked.

"I was running away," Azza said. "He came home early because Qais told him we had to run."

Qais must have called Abu Fahd.

Because I had called Qais.

"Oh God," I said.

This was my fault.

Zuha said something that I didn't catch. I gave her a blank look and she repeated herself. She was right. Azza needed medical attention and we had to call the police.

"No hospital," Azza insisted. "No cops." Zuha protested, but Azza's eyes were on me. "Please," she begged in a loud whisper. "Please don't."

It was the exact same tone she'd used to ask me not to call Qais. I hadn't listened to her then. There was no way I wasn't going to listen to her now.

"No cops," I agreed. "No hospital. Whatever you need."

"You're out of your mind," Zuha snapped. "Both of you. Look at what's happened."

"I've got to do what she wants."

Zuha saw it then, the guilt that must have been written on my face, because it felt that it was carved on my soul. She knew everything, so she knew I was responsible for what had happened to Azza. Her expression softened a little, but she didn't back down.

"She needs a doctor, Anvar. If she won't go to one, you need to get Aamir here. He won't talk to me."

I made the call. It was short and terse.

Zuha had fetched some ice and was using it to keep Azza's lower lip from bleeding further. She paused her efforts to comfort Azza long enough to ask, "Is he coming?"

I nodded.

"He agreed?" Azza demanded. "No police?"

"I'll convince him," I assured her.

It was easier said than done.

When Aamir arrived, his eyes first found his fiancée, and then her soaked dress on the ground. He managed, however, to give his full attention to Azza. I admired the focus and efficiency with which he worked. It was prettier to watch him practice than to think about how I'd contributed to Azza's injuries.

Aamir was well trained and careful. His largest obstacle was the patient herself, who refused to answer any of his questions.

Eventually, once he was done ministering to Azza, he asked to speak to me in private. We stepped into the corridor and into roaring thunder.

"What the hell happened to her?"

I glanced back at the closed apartment door, then at Aamir.

"You can ask her."

"I need information to do my job. Why did she come to you? She's part of your jihad on virtue, I suppose. You slept with her too?"

"How is that relevant to her current medical condition?"

He shoved out a heavy breath. "Fine. What's her name?"

"You can ask her that too."

Aamir threw his hands up in the air. "What is wrong with you?" He was shouting, which was rare for him, but the weather was loud, and he had to be heard above the crackling sky. At least, that is what I think he would've said, if I'd asked him why his voice was raised. Aamir Faris could lie when he had to, though he'd never admit it. "I'm trying to help you."

"I know." I tried to make my tone conciliatory, tried to convey that I didn't wish to be difficult or unkind. I don't think he noticed.

"And?"

"And you agree that we won't report this to the police?"

"Anvar, she's obviously the victim of a crime."

"She doesn't want to pursue it. Just do what she wants."

"No. The right thing . . ."

I sighed and looked behind him at the furious lightning ripping through the gray noon. The right thing. Always, with Aamir, the world was black and white. I'd wandered into that world myself when I decided to tell Qais that Homeland Security was after him. It was a dangerous place.

If he went to the cops, I wasn't sure what would happen. Abu Fahd would probably get arrested. I already knew that wasn't what Azza wanted. At least, it hadn't been what she wanted before we'd called Homeland Security.

They were another problem. I hadn't heard anything from Agent

Hale or Moray since Azza's interview. How much time did we have before they saw through her shallow ruse? Probably very little, which meant that I couldn't keep Azza here, not for long, and police involvement would complicate moving her.

The real question was simple. Was calling the police the best thing for Azza? It might be, but I didn't think so. Either way, that choice belonged to her. I was determined to honor her wishes, which meant that I had to stop my brother. Unfortunately, I couldn't think of a nice way to do it.

"Fine," I told Aamir, still looking not at him but past him, at the wild sky. "Do what you want. You should be aware, however, that when they ask her to identify her assailant, she will say it was you."

Aamir stared at me. In his eyes, there was little of familiarity and a great deal of contempt. "You're . . . I don't know what you are. 'Asshole' doesn't begin to cover it."

"Do we understand each other?"

His glare was furious and he said nothing. After a few moments, he shouldered past me, back into the apartment.

I remained outside.

He spoke to Zuha loudly enough that I could hear, though I couldn't make out the words. I didn't try. It wasn't a long conversation.

As he walked out the door, he stared me down. "There is a price to pay, for living the way you do. It will come due one day and, on that day, trust me, I will be laughing."

The sun was going down when I woke. Zuha had convinced me to lie down and close my eyes for a few minutes. I was, she argued, too tired to be of assistance to anyone. I'd protested that it was useless, that I was going to be unable to rest. My heart and my mind were still struggling with helplessness and horror. Sleep seemed impossible.

In Pakistan, however, they say that sleep is never impossible. If you're tired enough, it will find you even if you are a prisoner about to be executed, even if there is a noose around your neck. There is some hyperbole there, I'm sure, but the reality that I'd crashed on my couch despite the current circumstances was undeniable.

Zuha came to sit next to me. "I don't think Azza will wake up till morning. Aamir gave her some pretty strong stuff."

I hoped that was true. So far Azza hadn't mentioned my decision to warn Qais, which had resulted in her getting hurt. It was a conversation I'd have to have with her eventually, and in the face of her bruises, I already knew all my high-minded rhetoric about due process and the nature of justice would taste like ash and shame.

"How're you feeling?" Zuha asked.

"Wretched."

"You're not responsible for what happened to her, Anvar. You couldn't have known this would happen."

It was a kind thing to say. However, I wasn't sure if it was true.

Obviously, I hadn't known how events were going to unfold. However, the fact that I'd failed to foresee this possibility was not evidence that I couldn't—or shouldn't—have foreseen it.

"I'm glad you're here," I said, changing the topic.

Zuha gave me a tired smile and she ran a hand through her hair. I noticed then, for the first time, that she wasn't wearing Aamir's ring anymore.

"What about you?" I asked. "Are you okay?"

"It's been a day. Tomorrow will be better though."

"When did you become an optimist?"

"Prom, I think," she said.

"I'd feel a lot better about tomorrow if we had a plan."

"I still think we need to report this to the police and tell Homeland Security the truth."

"If they capture Qais, they may find out that I warned him," I reminded her.

"Will they keep looking for him once they know everything? He's not a terrorist, so what do they care?"

"And what happens to Abu Fahd?" I asked. "Azza doesn't want—"

"I'm not sure," Zuha said gently, "that she's in the best position to decide what should and should not be done with him."

"She is entitled to agency in her own life. I took it away once and look what happened."

Zuha shook her head.

"You don't think she gets to make decisions about her own life?"

"I think she's putting herself in harm's way because of what happened with her brother. She blames herself for her father going over the edge. But that man is still responsible for his own actions. The pain he is carrying in his heart doesn't excuse the pain he's inflicting on Azza."

When I didn't say anything, Zuha added, "That is how monsters multiply, Anvar, spreading their hurt into the world in a cycle of misery that doesn't have an end. Sometimes victims act in a way that deserves censure. The fact that they're victims doesn't exempt them from moral consequences. You don't get to hurt other people just because someone hurt you. That can't be how the world works."

"That's exactly the way the world works. It isn't always an angry man hitting a helpless girl with a belt. Sometimes it happens in the open, like a drone in the sky, raining hellfire on villages."

"Like what I did to Aamir?" Zuha asked. "I made him collateral damage."

I grimaced. That wasn't a pretty thought. "Let's worry about all of that later. Right now, you should get some rest. I'll keep an ear out in case Azza needs anything."

Zuha didn't put up a fight.

"Thank you for . . ." I waved my arms around, gesturing to everything. "For staying and helping."

"I'd say you were welcome, Anvar, but honestly, I didn't do it for you."

Azza woke at around ten in the morning. I couldn't help but flinch when I saw her. She looked worse than she had before. Her bruises were continuing to mature, turning deep red, purple and blue as they started to heal.

"Not a pretty sight?"

"Actually"—I sat down on the bed next to her—"I was just thinking that you look very colorful."

"You're horrible."

I wished that I was carrying something, or holding something, so I'd have something to do with my hands. They just dangled at my sides, awkward and useless.

I saw pills and a glass of water on the nightstand, but Azza shook her head. "Not until you're gone. I want to remember everything you say. I want my mind clear when you tell me why you did it. Why did you warn Qais? I told you not to."

"I didn't know you would end up getting hurt."

"You knew," she said, her tone harsh. "You just didn't know it would happen like this. You knew it would hurt me if he got away."

I hesitated, then offered the only excuse I had. The words felt foreign to me, as if they belonged to someone else, because I hadn't often had occasion to use them myself. "I thought I was doing the right thing."

"You are not God. You don't get to decide what is right and what is wrong."

"I do," I said quietly. "I'm sorry, Azza. I . . . I'm just . . . so, so sorry. But while judgment over other people belongs to God, I get to judge the man in the mirror. What he would become if I'd done what you wanted wasn't something I could live with. It wasn't right."

"That's selfish."

"Yes. I guess it is. But it is all I've got."

Azza gently passed a hand over her wounded face. I noticed that she too was no longer wearing her engagement ring. I guess it was going around.

"Leave," she said.

I didn't argue. I just made my way to the bedroom door. Perhaps she wasn't expecting that because she called out, "Wait. I need something."

"Anything," I said.

"Go see Abu. He'll be worried. I didn't leave a note this time."

"He'll be . . ." I took a deep breath and swallowed the indignation that made me raise my voice. "He's the one who did this to you."

"Yes. Now he's going to be feeling guilty about it. He wanted to leave, to go wherever Qais is, right away, but he felt I was too badly hurt to travel. He still cares about me, Anvar."

I shook my head.

"When you see him, tell him you saw me. Tell him I got on a

bus for the airport. Please. He'll be at the mosque. It's Friday today. Promise me you'll tell him. It is the last of what I owe him."

It also happened to be the least of what I owed her. She didn't say it, but I heard the unspoken words just the same. I took a deep breath, then nodded.

"I'll find him."

Azza looked away from me then, with the air of someone who would never look back.

"Do you think, after everything I've done, everything that happened with Fahd . . . Do you think Allah will forgive me?"

"Absolutely."

"Yet you don't think I should forgive my father? You know that the Prophet said that mercy is not shown to those who do not show mercy?"

"This is different," I said.

"It isn't. Abu Fahd—Fahd's father—is not a bad man. He is just broken and angry, and what I did helped make him that way. What happened—to him, to me, to my brother—none of it was fair."

"No," I agreed. "It wasn't."

"You know, Abu told me that in Afghanistan they say there are no good men among the living. Until I met you, I thought that was true." She looked back at me then, her green eyes full of tears that did not fall. "Even though it went wrong, even though I don't like what you thought you had to do, I'm really glad that happened. I'm glad I met you."

"Are you leaving?"

Zuha stood in the kitchen, watching a pot of tea brew, and she nodded in response to my question. She had put on her long summer dress again. Her chestnut-colored hair was up in a ponytail, her makeup redone. Her eyes still looked tired and exhaustion was evident in her body language. My couch wasn't exactly comfortable.

"I called in sick to work but I need a change of clothes and stuff. I'm going to go after Azza eats something. You're out of coffee, by the way. You want some tea?"

"No. I'm fine. So you're coming back then?"

"Of course. In a couple of hours."

"Thank you. You're a good person."

She smiled a little. "The absolute best."

"I'm heading out too. You can take my keys. Hafeez Bhai can let me in, if I get back before you do."

Zuha frowned. "Where are you going?"

"To the mosque. Azza wants me to tell her father that I saw her get onto a bus. So that he won't worry about her."

"How is that going to keep him from worrying?"

I shrugged. "I don't know. She wasn't clear on that, but I don't really feel like I'm in a position to refuse any of her requests."

"She did seem really fuzzy last night. She was rambling quite a bit."

"Maybe we should have taken her to a hospital."

To her credit, Zuha managed to keep from saying that she'd told me so.

"I'm sure Azza will be fine. She doesn't need a hospital."

"How do you know?"

"Aamir would have insisted that she go to one immediately if it was necessary. Nothing you said would've stopped him."

This was indisputably true.

"Aamir will be at jummah too," Zuha said. "You should apologize. From what I overheard, you were a real jerk to him yesterday."

"He started it," I protested. I'd said what I thought needed to be said to get what I wanted from my brother, but that didn't make it any less awful. "It feels like I've been apologizing to people a lot lately."

"If you don't like it, maybe you should consider not being wrong about everything."

I gave her a reproachful look. "Don't start. This isn't the right time for banter."

"It won't kill you to admit you don't have a comeback."

It was a little amazing how transparent I still was to her, after all these years.

"I'm not taking any chances," I said. "Today is dangerous enough as it is."

AZZA

I didn't know the time. There were no clocks in Anvar's room. I tried to guess how long I'd slept based on the light coming in from the window, but in San Francisco the sun cannot be trusted.

"Are you all right?"

I looked up at Zuha, startled. "I thought you left."

"Not yet. Penny for your thoughts?"

I shook my head. "They aren't worth that much. Just nonsense. The medicines Anvar's brother gave me don't make the world clearer."

"You should still take them. And try to rest, okay? I'll be back soon."

I sat up straighter to ask her something important, but pain shot through my right side and I couldn't remember what I wanted to know. My body did not want to move. Every time I tried, it begged for mercy. Mama told me once that on the Day of Judgment our bodies—gifts from Allah—will testify against us for the sins we've committed using them. I suppose in that sense, mine was getting what it deserved. As they say on American television, snitches get stitches.

I started to laugh at that. It sounded a little less sane than I would've liked, and the hurt in my ribs got worse, but it was nice to remember, if only for a moment, that even though the world was heartless, it was still funny. As long as there were dates in palm trees, God would laugh at us all.

"You're sure you're okay?" Zuha asked. She sounded genuinely concerned.

"Why do you care?" It sounded harsher than I'd meant it. I really wanted to know. But she didn't understand that. The slant of her shoulders became more pronounced. In an instant, she looked exhausted, and her brown eyes lost their spark.

"I'm sorry I hurt you," Zuha said. "I meant what I said the first time we met. I didn't set out to—"

"You didn't," I agreed. "But you Americans never think much about who may get hurt, as long as you get what you want."

We hadn't spoken much yesterday, at least not that I could remember. I'd been falling in and out of sleep, and Zuha just sat with me and tried to make me as comfortable as possible. It was sweet of her and she had absolutely no reason to do it. I should've liked her a lot more than I did.

I couldn't make myself like her, but I could make her feel a little better. That is, after all, what she had tried to do for me.

"You are not one of the problems in my life," I said. It was the nicest thing I could say about anyone just then.

"Azza, I just don't want you to think that I meant to steal Anvar from you."

"That was always going to pass and be lost. It doesn't matter. I should thank you before you go for trying to take care of me."

"You'd do the same for me," Zuha said.

"No," I told her. My voice was tired and, truth be told, I was tired too. "I wouldn't."

"I don't believe you. I'll see you later, okay?"

I nodded, even though I didn't think that was going to happen. I would lie down, only for a moment, and close my eyes, but not for very long. The fact that there were no clocks didn't mean that time wasn't slipping away. Soon I would have to move. It wasn't safe here. I'd have to try to leave before Anvar and Zuha got back. If they didn't know where I was going, they wouldn't be able to tell anyone.

I was about to lie back down when I saw that Zuha still hadn't left. She was standing very still and looking at me with the air of someone risking everything on one throw of the dice.

"I wish he'd told me about you when I first met him again. I mean, I knew there'd been other women." She hesitated, then breathed in resolve, and asked the question that must have been sitting like a splinter in her soul. "Did Anvar ever tell you he loves you?"

And, despite the fog of drugs on my mind, I saw it. A chance for revenge.

I could lie. It would balance out the truth Anvar had felt the need to tell Qais.

I could tell Zuha that Anvar had told me that he loved me. That he told me so all the time, that he'd promised me he was over Zuha, that he'd said horrible things about her when she agreed to marry his brother. It would be such an easy thing to do. All the wonderful blessings of Zuha's life would turn to ash in her mouth. Then she'd get a small taste of the heartache that had been my existence.

Anvar had taken the fate of Qais out of my hands.

With one word, I could take Zuha away from him now.

After all, what reason had I ever had to not set fire to the entire world?

ANVAR

I arrived for Friday prayers before Imam Sama had taken the pulpit, so I was free to peer down row after row of congregants to look for Abu Fahd. He should have been easy to find, given his height.

However, my search was in vain. By the time the Imam cleared his throat and tapped his mike, I'd given up. I sat down facing the door. Abu Fahd either hadn't gotten there yet or was still in a different part of the mosque.

Sama's sermon was about the Prophet Abraham. The Imam described how, furious with the monotheism Abraham was preaching, Nimrod ordered that Abraham be burned alive. A giant fire was constructed and Abraham stood over it, facing his own destruction.

"What was his state of mind in that moment?" the Imam asked. "You know, my friends, the Urdu poet Iqbal asked this question. You see, Iqbal struggled all his life with how to approach God. Can we understand God with our minds or do we have to surrender our reason? Iqbal said that the answer to this question could be found in the moment Abraham leapt into this fire. Jumping into fire is not a rational act. His leap was an act of pure love and surrender to the will of God, and God rewarded him for it by saving him. It was, my friends, an act of true Islam. You cannot approach your religion with your mind. As Abu Bakr said, your inability to comprehend God is your understanding of God. You must transcend reason if you are to experience the divine. The path to Allah runs through your heart alone."

With that, Sama sat down for a moment, then rose again to start the Arabic portion of the sermon. In this lull, I saw Aamir across the prayer hall and went over to him.

He made a questioning gesture with his hand when he saw me.

"Have you seen Abu Fahd?" I asked him in a whisper.

He nodded.

"Where is he?"

Aamir shook his head and pointed to the Imam. Then he gestured for silence. We were not allowed to speak during the sermon, even the Arabic portions we did not understand. I resigned myself to the fact that I would have to wait until the Imam was done. Aamir Faris always did what he was supposed to do.

I had a short window in which he would speak. It would be only a minute, the brief pause between the end of the sermon and the start of the prayer itself. As soon as Imam Sama fell silent, therefore, I grabbed Aamir's hand and pulled him to his feet. He looked annoyed and jerked his hand away. We exited the hall just as the iqama, the last call to prayer, began.

I heard the muezzin start. "Allah hu Akbar."

God is Great.

"Abu Fahd. Where is he?"

Aamir smiled a triumphant smile.

From inside the mosque, the call continued. "Hayya 'ala-s-salah."

Come to prayer.

"Abu Fahd was here. He was frantic, asking everyone if they had seen his daughter. He was worried someone had hurt her. He even had pictures of her with him, one with a niqab and one without it. With those green eyes, though, it was obvious she was the girl from last night. I told him you had her. I told him she knew you well. That I suspected you had an ongoing relationship with her."

"Hayya 'ala-l-falah."

Come to salvation.

I reached over and gripped his arm, wrenching him forward. "You're insane. Why would you do that?"

He yanked himself free once more. "What was I supposed to do? A father was looking for his daughter. I couldn't just let him continue to worry to keep your shameful secrets." That horrid smile never left Aamir's face. "Besides, you will clearly not stop sinning. He has to save his daughter from the hellfire you'll drag her into if you're allowed to continue."

I stared at him. He didn't know. Somehow, he hadn't realized that it was Abu Fahd who'd beaten Azza. He didn't know anything about Abu Fahd's past, the history of his family, what they'd been through or what they had become. Aamir had done what he always did—the right thing, as he saw it. It never occurred to him that he might not have the complete picture, that the world might require more nuance from him than simply picking between virtue and sin.

I wanted to scream at him, to tell him why what he'd done was so reckless, so dangerous, so incredibly stupid, but I shook my head at the impulse. There was no time.

Oblivious to what was happening, and what might yet happen, Aamir went on. "I told you there would be a price to pay, little brother. I just never expected it to come due this soon."

"Qad qamat as-salah."

The prayer was starting.

We ran.

Aamir toward the mosque. I away from it, with the call of "Allah hu Akbar" echoing behind me.

Having once dressed up as Oscar Wilde for the Bay to Breakers race, I knew that San Francisco, with its fifty-odd hills, was not built with runners in mind. It was a fact I rediscovered quickly as I ran home from the mosque. Ten minutes in, my breath was already breaking when I paused to call Zuha for the second time. She did not answer. I cursed and dialed her number again.

When she picked up, her voice was distant. "I'm driving."

"Don't go back to the apartment." I paused to fill my lungs, to let my heart find its rhythm again. Then, putting her on speaker, holding the phone in front of me, I started to run again. "Azza's father is heading there. Stay away."

"I just left her." There was a pause. Then Zuha said, "I can get her out."

"No. I don't want you to get hurt."

There was a small silence, followed by a whisper. "Anvar, I love you."

"Zuha, *no*. Don't—"

She hung up on me.

I cursed. I thought about calling her back, but she wouldn't pick up again. It'd be a waste of time. Instead, I tried to reach Agent Hale. Yes, there would be consequences later, but just then I didn't know who else to call. She didn't answer. I left her a message and raced on.

The door to my apartment was open. It didn't appear to have been forced. It was not broken or splintered. I rushed in, thinking of Zuha, thinking of Azza, calling out their names. I nearly slipped on a checkers piece and, looking back, saw that the coffee table had been upended, and the game board lay, empty, on the floor. There were no moves left to make, I thought, as I flung the door to my bedroom open and saw him. Abu Fahd, sitting on my bed, staring up at me, a revolver in his hand.

I backed away, slowly retreating into the hall. He rose to his feet and followed in a languid fashion. I wanted to turn and run. The front door was directly behind me. I was still gasping for breath, however, and my legs were burning, my calves aching. I would not make it far. Abu Fahd had already raised his firearm and pointed it, not at my head, but at my heart.

The weapon's barrel gleamed like silver and the grip seemed to glow, as if crafted out of pearl. I wondered whether the beauty of the gun was meant to be a luxury for the owner or a courtesy to the victim.

"As-salamu alaykum, Anvar," he said, perfectly calm, perfectly in control.

My heart was wild, though from running or from the desire to run, I could not tell. I failed to manage a reply to his greeting of peace.

"You were sleeping with her."

It was not a question, but I nodded.

"This whole time? You were defiling her this whole time?"

I started to answer, but he didn't give me the chance.

He shot at me. It sounded like thunder sent by God. I ducked my head and threw my arms up in front of my face. If his aim had been true, it would've been a futile gesture. It wasn't. The bullet pinged against something metallic and thudded into a wall.

"Where is she?" Abu Fahd demanded, and I wondered if he had ever meant to shoot me.

"I don't know. I came here looking for her, didn't I? I called out her name," I said. "Don't do this. The police will be here soon."

He didn't seem to care. There was only one thing he wanted. "Tell me where you are hiding her."

"I really don't know where—"

He raised the gun higher, pointing at my forehead. "Do not make me kill you, Anvar. I will. You do not know the things I am capable of doing."

"I know what you are capable of. I've seen Azza's bruises."

"My daughter has no honor, just like her mother. She wanted to break her engagement to Qais. She wanted me to break my promise. A man's word is everything he has in this world. My word is all that I have left."

He shot again. I went to my knees, though again my mind knew attempting any defense was pointless. He missed once more and I was certain now that he was not aiming for me, not yet, because he still wanted to know where Azza was.

I knelt before him. He loomed over me, taller than ever, his revolver pointing down at my head. "You also know nothing of honor. You are like these kuffar, with your clever, twisting words. You made me believe you were one of us who had learned to talk like one of them. No. You're just one of them."

"There is no us, Abu Fahd. There is no them. We're all the same."

"No," he said, almost as if it were the saddest thing in the world. "But it does not matter. No one else is here. It is you and I, here in this place, alone. Tell me. Who will save you from me?"

I cast about for an answer. I tried to find some measure of calm, to summon my ability to focus on forming an intelligent response. The barrel of his gun was hot against my forehead. I smelled something burning. It made it difficult for me to think.

I should be praying. That was what a good Muslim would do.

Then a memory, fourteen hundred years old, passed from generation to generation, rose unbidden in my mind. A man in a desert. A sword at his throat. An enemy asking him the same question. Who will save you from me?

"I say to you what the Prophet would say to you," I told Abu Fahd. "Allah will save me."

He recognized the answer.

He recognized this moment.

The certainty in his eyes shattered.

I could see that he was searching for words. He seemed lost. I knew then, somehow, that he would not kill me. I knew that, in a moment, he would lower his weapon.

Someone screamed my name, then screamed for me to get down. I flung myself to the ground just as Abu Fahd raised his gun toward the door, and the world ignited with the sound of gunshots, a sound that had kept me awake at night many times, in a faraway place in a faraway time. Bullet after bullet tore through the mountain that was Abu Fahd. He slumped against a wall, then fell.

Agent Hale crouched next to me. She was saying something, checking me for wounds.

I couldn't look away from Abu Fahd. There was so much red. Several bullets had hit him dead center, in his gut, but at least one shattered his jaw and teeth. His eyes were still alive and wet with pain. A nearly lifeless hand flopped at his side, maybe searching for his gun. Then, gathering all his will, Abu Fahd raised a disfigured index finger upward at the ceiling. Of course, he was pointing higher than that. He was pointing higher than the sky and the firmament and the heavens. Abu Fahd was pointing at Him.

I knew what he was trying to say. I nodded to show him that I understood. He was trying to muster the last words every good Muslim hopes to say, so the declaration of faith will be his last act in this world, except those words were not written for him, not anymore. He couldn't speak them.

I could speak them though.

"There is no god but Allah, and Muhammad is the Prophet of Allah," I said for him softly, in a whisper, but he heard me. His broken mouth collapsed in a grotesque, limp, sardonic smile. With his last breath, he tried to spit at me, but it resulted in nothing, except a stream of blood dribbling weakly over his lips. Then the old man's hand fell to the ground and he was gone.

"I didn't get a blanket."

I could tell from Agent Moray's blank stare that he did not understand. I didn't care. I stared past him at the flashing lights of ambulances, at paramedics and police officers going about their tasks with calm efficiency, like they understood what had happened and knew how to deal with it. I wished they'd explain it to me. I realized, after a few minutes, that he was asking me something.

"Are you cold?"

"No. It's just that in the movies when something like this happens, they always give out blankets. I'm just letting you know that I didn't get a blanket. I'm lodging a complaint."

Moray looked at me like Satan must have looked at Job, with utter incomprehension. "You're an odd duck."

I didn't respond. I was still watching the competent-looking people going about their business around us. "What are they saying?"

"Those guys? The local police? They're saying it is an attempted honor killing. The kind of thing that goes on in your part of the world."

"California?"

"Have you ever tried not being a horse's ass? You know perfectly well what I meant."

"I do," I admitted. "Have you found Zuha yet?"

"Not since the last time you asked."

"I'm going to keep asking."

"Of course. Why should you, even for a moment, cease to be annoying? Listen, we're going to take you in. You make sure to let Awiti—Agent Hale—know you want to talk to her instead of me. That'll be better for both of us."

"You're taking me in?" I asked.

"That's what I said."

"Aren't you going to tell me I have the right to an attorney, Agent Moray?"

"Why? You know any good ones?" He grinned, waiting for me to acknowledge his cleverness. He scowled when I didn't. "You're not under arrest. You're coming with us voluntarily."

"Yeah. Right."

"I'm serious, son. Hell, we'll even wait on your convenience. Your family is anxious to see you. Especially your mother. So we'll wait for you to be done with her—"

"No. It's fine. I'll come with you now. Voluntarily, like you said." I smiled at the look of surprise on his face. "Trust me. It will be the easier interrogation."

Moray smiled. "Fair enough. And just as a gesture demonstrating how little I like you, I'll be sure to tell her you said that."

"Go ahead," I said. "She'll think it's a compliment."

AZZA

Zuha asked me if I wanted to see the Painted Ladies one last time before we left San Francisco. I shook my head. I was doing, for the second time in my life, what my mother had never done. I was leaving. I didn't want to think about Mama as I did so. I wasn't sure if she would judge me for it or envy me. I wasn't sure if this ability that I had, this ability to fly, which she'd never possessed, made me worse than her or better than her. I just knew that it made me who I was and that, at least for now, was enough.

I couldn't help but remember the day I'd been driven to Basra, by the strange man whose daughter's name I'd stolen.

"If you had a baby, a girl," I asked Zuha, "what would you name her?"

She seemed surprised by the question. "Why do you ask?"

"People say history repeats itself. I was just checking to see if it did."

There were women who would have gone silent in response to my remark, and women who would've been confused and demanded an explanation. There were those who would've thought me bizarre or weird or strange for saying what I had. Some would've even said as much to my face.

None of them would've been able to hold captive and torture the heart of Anvar Faris like Zuha had. She asked the one question that he would have been interested in.

"Does it?"

"It does," I said. "But not exactly."

"Then there's a reason to have hope."

Zuha took me to Sacramento, two hours northeast of San Francisco, to a train station on I Street, which was a squat, long building that looked like it was made from reddish-brown bricks. It probably wasn't. In America, they build things out of wood and then put false faces on them, to make them seem like they are stronger, more durable, than they really are.

I took a deep breath. It was time to go.

I wanted to say something nice to Zuha, something kind. I wanted to offer her deep words of gratitude for what she had done for me.

Without having any reason to do so, Zuha had rushed back to Anvar's apartment and helped me get out before Abu could come find me. Just the thought of what he would've done to me after he found out about my relationship with Anvar was enough to make my soul quiver like I'd sometimes felt California quake. He wouldn't have left me alive. He would have hurt Zuha too, when she tried to stop him from hurting me.

"Thank you."

Zuha shook her head. "I didn't do it for you."

"You did it for Anvar then?"

"No. The choices we make are ultimately always about ourselves, about who we are, instead of other people, don't you think? I did what I had to do to be who I am."

I opened the passenger-side door and got out.

"Good luck," Zuha said before I could close the door.

I smiled for her, squared my shoulders, started limping across the parking lot, ready to begin my journey, to where I did not know.

ANVAR

I didn't have any cell reception in the windowless room they put me in. I kept checking my phone anyway, hoping to somehow get a message from Zuha telling me that she was safe. When the battery ran out, Agent Hale offered to take my phone and charge it.

If any of my clients had agreed to hand over their phones like that, I would have been furious. Faced with the same situation myself, however, I didn't hesitate to comply. I just wanted to hear from Zuha. I didn't care about anything else.

When Agent Hale finally walked back in, she was carrying Azza's journals. She tossed them on the table in front of me.

"They're fake."

I made my eyes wide, gasped dramatically and put a hand on my heart. "Oh no. Gosh. Wow. Really? I can't believe it."

She scowled and sat down. "I assume you didn't know that Ms. Saqr was lying when we spoke to her in your apartment."

"Of course I didn't."

"When did you find out?"

"Shortly thereafter," I admitted.

"And then you, a responsible citizen and an officer of the court, called us to report that we were in possession of fabricated evidence."

"You make that sound like something I should've done."

"Mr. Faris," Hale snapped, her voice an ice pick. "I swear I'll read you Miranda right now."

"I don't need you to read me—"

"Enough. I'm starting to think Moray is right about you people."

"Lawyers?" I guessed.

"Yes," she said. "Of course. Would you please explain why you didn't call us right away to tell us what you'd found out?"

"I was going to eventually."

"Eventually," Hale repeated. "This delay was so that Azza bint Saqr could escape the consequences of her actions?"

"I was going to tell you soon. I wouldn't let Qais Badami be punished for something he didn't do."

"And how did you know we didn't already have his location? While you were sitting on critical information, we could have already been moving in to arrest him. What if something had gone wrong when we tried to bring him in?"

"Do you know what a forced capture is?"

She shook her head.

"In checkers, sometimes you don't get a choice. When you have the opportunity to take an opponent's piece, you must, no matter what the consequences."

"Mr. Faris, are you saying that you simply did what you had to do?"

"Yes."

"Then say that. You don't have to put on a show."

"If I don't, how will anyone know I'm fun at parties?"

Hale sighed and leaned back in her chair. "Just tell me what you know."

I explained how I'd figured out that the journals, and the other evidence, had been manufactured to frame Qais, that Azza had wanted to be rid of him and was using the DHS to make that happen. I told her why Azza had done what she'd done.

"So Abu Fahd came to murder his daughter and found you instead. What happened between the two of you, at the end there, what was that? Just a garden-variety honor killing gone wrong?" She rubbed the back of her neck. "I have to tell you, Mr. Faris, that whole concept eludes me. How can someone want to murder their own child?"

"I don't know. Maybe he wouldn't have killed her. I don't think he was going to kill me at the end there, to be honest."

"That isn't how things appeared from where I was standing. The man went looking for his daughter armed with a gun. I don't see how a charitable inference can be drawn from that behavior."

"If Abu Fahd had planned to kill Azza, it would've been because he thought God wanted him to do it. He wouldn't have called it murder like you just did. He would've called it a sacrifice."

"It is incomprehensible."

"I agree. So what happens now?"

"Now I tell you that you've shown extraordinarily poor judgment through this entire episode. This would have gone differently if you'd trusted your government. I wish you would've trusted us."

"I wish I could have, but I've found my government pretty hostile to my clients."

"Maybe you should represent better people."

I was going to tell her that the right to due process didn't hinge on the value, or perceived value, of the accused, but she knew that, of course. She was just being a federal agent.

When I didn't reply, Hale added, "We'll keep trying to bring Ms. Saqr and Qais Badami in—"

"Wait. Qais?"

"He's in the wind."

I couldn't tell her I knew that, of course, or that I was the one who'd warned him.

"Why do you need to bring him in at all? It's clear he isn't a terrorist."

Hale raised her eyebrows at me. It was an expression of both surprise and amusement. "But he is a criminal. You told me yourself what he did to Ms. Saqr. You also told me he was the one who procured Abu Fahd's weapon for him. He doesn't have a license and the weapon isn't registered. Qais is undocumented too, so there is also that. I guess you were unable to see the whole chessboard, Faris. You missed a trick or two."

"It's not really my game. You'll be looking for Azza as well?"

"Of course."

"Can't you let her go?" I asked. "There's been more than enough damage done. It can stop now."

She shook her head. "You know we can't."

"Okay, well . . . I hope you bring them both in alive."

"As do I."

"If you ever find them, do me a favor. Tell them that I will stand for them. If they want me to, I'll represent them."

"You can't. You're a material witness. Besides, did you learn nothing from the Taleb Mansoor case? What is with you and lost causes, Anvar?"

"It's kinship, I think."

She started to say something when her phone buzzed in her pocket. She reached for it, studied it and then smiled. My heart leapt. She looked up at me.

"One last question."

"What was that text? Did your people find Zuha?"

"Yes. And she says she wants to see her lawyer. Before I let you go, I need you to tell me, did you know who Abu Fahd was?"

"What do you mean?"

"We've identified him now that we have data from his body. Fingerprints, photographs. . . . This man had been held in Iraq on suspicion of being a militant. He was in this country illegally, virtually untraceable, and we'd subjected him to—"

"Torture?"

"Enhanced interrogation. His presence in the States was obviously problematic."

I shrugged. "Not obviously. I mean, you wouldn't have let him go if you'd had any actual evidence against him. In fact, I'm surprised you let him go at all. Innocence isn't necessarily a way out for your prisoners."

"So you knew? How could you not report that a man like that was in our country? He could've been dangerous."

Because we were in his country, I almost said, and were dangerous too.

"It goes like this," I said, quoting one of my father's favorite songs. "The fourth, the fifth, the minor fall, the—"

"The major lift?" Hale finished. "The Fifth doesn't apply in these circumstances."

"Maybe it doesn't," I said with a shrug. "But I've recently been told I'm not a judge, and neither are you."

"So you aren't going to say anything else?"

"Take me to Zuha," I told her. "And I'll say Hallelujah."

—

From Cicero to Clarence Darrow, never in the history of attorneys anywhere has a lawyer been happier to see his client than I was to see Zuha Shah. I sat by her and held her hand as she answered questions posed to her by an agent whose name I never bothered to remember.

Ignoring my instructions and any concern she felt for her own safety, Zuha had turned her car around the moment I called about Abu Fahd and driven back to my place. She had helped Azza escape the apartment, probably moments before Abu Fahd arrived.

"That was very brave," the agent told her.

"Thank you."

"Though it was also very reckless, sweetheart. You should have listened to your man."

I was familiar enough with the narrowing of Zuha's eyes to know that an irritated response was coming, so I squeezed her hand as a reminder of where we were. She gave me the annoyed glare the agent had earned but contented herself by thanking him again, though more sarcastically.

"Your actions did save the life of Azza bint Saqr. As I am sure you already know, Ms. Saqr was an important witness—though now she is a person of interest—so I suppose you did the right thing by preserving her life."

"That's why I did it. To help you guys."

It was the agent's turn to look annoyed. "Are you trying to be funny, Ms. Shah?"

"She isn't," I assured him. "I'm in charge of doing all the jokes. We decided that earlier."

"I can see Agent Moray was right about you, Mr. Faris. I can tell you that I don't have the patience he does with nonsense. So if you would be so kind as to instruct the little lady to give us the location of Ms. Saqr, we'll bring her in for questioning and you two can be on your way."

I smiled at Zuha. "Well, 'little lady,' do you know where exactly Azza is right now?"

"I don't."

"Are you, then, unable to answer the agent's question without speculating as to her whereabouts?"

"Yes."

"As you can see, my client doesn't have the information you require."

"Very droll, Mr. Faris. Ms. Shah, could you please tell me where you last saw Azza bint Saqr?"

"In Sacramento," Zuha said. "At the train station on I Street."

"Did you buy her a train ticket?"

"No."

"Where was she going?"

"I didn't ask. It didn't seem like any of my business."

"Where do you think she was going, Ms. Shah?"

"She's not going to make blind guesses for you," I said.

"Yes," Zuha agreed, her tone all sugar and honey. "I don't want to guess. That'd be reckless."

Zuha and I stood in the darkness together, waiting for her parents to come pick her up. There was no moon and no stars that I could see. My freshly charged phone kept buzzing in my pocket, but I ignored it.

"Is that your mom?" Zuha asked, when the fourth call came through.

I hadn't checked, but the persistence was a bit of a giveaway.

"Probably."

"You should answer."

"I will."

She nodded, and then we fell silent again.

"Are we okay?" I asked eventually. "You and me?"

She turned to face me. "You should've told me about Azza from the start."

"I know," I said.

"She said I couldn't steal you away from her, because you can't steal what already belongs to you. She reminded me that the last time you two were intimate was before you saw me again. Is that true?"

I frowned and thought back, unsure.

Zuha shook her head. "You didn't even realize what you were doing? Or not doing?"

I shrugged. I'd never lied to Zuha, not about anything important, and this seemed like a poor time to start. "No. I really didn't."

"I think that may almost be sweet."

"You're welcome?"

"Don't push it."

I grinned and waited for her to go on. But she didn't. She just looked at me, obviously expecting me to speak.

I didn't know what to say. The simple truth was that I had never loved anyone the way I loved Zuha Shah. I fell short when I tried to find the right words, pretty words, smart words, to express that. It was like Aamir's favorite author, Shakespeare, wrote, you can't force a heart into a throat.

"Well?" Zuha prompted after a while.

"I can't think of anything to say that isn't melodramatic."

"Who cares?"

"I do. It's too complicated to explain and way too sentimental to say out loud. I feel ridiculous even trying."

"Yesterday you did a whole riff on life and time."

"Yeah, but I just said it. I didn't think about it or, you know, compose it. It makes me feel like . . . I don't know, John Donne."

"Seriously? John Donne?"

"Sorry. Were we ever the gushy, word-salad, sweet-nothings people?"

"I guess not."

"So, back to my original question, are we good?"

"It's a little hard to be upset with you after you went and got yourself shot at. A world without you in it . . . Anvar, I can't imagine it."

"Me neither," I said. When she didn't laugh, I reached out and took her hands. "Look, I will say this. Azza said something that's been bothering me. She told me that there is no beauty left in this world."

"Poor girl."

"She's not wrong, you know. Sometimes that is how life feels. It's like there is nothing good, nothing noble, nothing precious left. Everywhere I look there is only pain and struggle and just a shadow over everything. You should know that I never feel that way when I am with you. You're the light of my world. You make the universe beautiful."

Zuha's eyes were as bright then as they had been the first time I kissed her. She stepped up to me and wrapped her arms around my neck. "Why can't you be this sweet all the time?"

"Because it's just not a Donne thing."

She was still smiling when her lips captured mine.

I made my way out into the darkness alone. Zuha's parents had offered to drive me home, but I'd demurred. That option presented more potential awkwardness than I was prepared to deal with just then. I assured them that I was fine, and they left me to my own devices.

I began to walk, not knowing where I wanted to go.

It is strange, wandering in a city you are intimately familiar with, because even when you don't know exactly where you are, you never feel lost. You always know, more or less, how to get back home.

I wondered if Azza had ever felt this sense of security anywhere she'd walked. I doubt she ever belonged to a place in that way. It was a small thing, especially given everything that had happened, but I found myself inexplicably crying over it. I leaned against a dirty wall that smelled faintly like old piss and let myself weep.

Footsteps approached. I tried to stop the tears, but couldn't, which made no sense, because I'd been fine moments before, and with Zuha I'd been glad, even articulate, but now my hands were trembling, and I felt like I needed to sit down.

I heard the scrape and rattle of old shopping cart wheels on concrete. A man pushing a cart loaded with a green coat, a few books and what were probably all his belongings in the world limped up to me. He was almost past me when he looked back. "Spare change?"

I gave him all the money I had on me.

"God bless you."

I smiled and he nodded before pushing his cart away from me. As he faded into the distance, I heard him singing. I couldn't be sure exactly what song he had chosen, but echoing through the empty streets and deserted, shuttered buildings, it sounded like "Ave Maria."

It made me want to go to the mosque. I wasn't sure where else to go. My apartment was a crime scene. I could, obviously, have gone to my parents' house, but I did not feel up to answering their questions.

How would I explain Azza or Abu Fahd or Qais? Though, if I knew Aamir, he would already have gotten them up to speed, having taken care to put himself in the best possible light, of course.

There wasn't a lot of good light to go around. Agent Hale had been right. I'd made mistakes and a man was dead because of them. A man who had broken, under pressures I could not comprehend, much less grasp, in the wrong way, in the wrong place. I suppose I should've been glad that he was dead, because if he were still around, I might not be. However, no part of my heart felt like celebrating.

In the Bollywood movies my father watched when I was a child, when the injustice of the world became overwhelming, I remembered heroes railing at Hindu gods in their temples. Demanding and receiving justice. That was exactly what I intended to do.

Yes, I was alive and Azza was alive and Zuha was alive, and all that was good, but it felt all wrong, like there should have been a different ending, a happier ending, to all the suffering Abu Fahd had caused and endured. God alone could tell me why a man who could've been good had been tortured by the world, until his better nature had finally crumbled like a rock crushed beneath forces it could not withstand. I wanted to demand answers from Him.

It was only when I reached the mosque that I remembered Muslims don't get to do that.

Standing in the prayer hall, in the middle of the night, I was seized by an impulse to scream, to vent my confusion, to make it a real and tangible thing by burning out my voice and turning my throat raw and parched.

However, there was nothing to scream at there. There were no icons or idols and God . . . well, God does not show himself to the likes of me.

So I stood before Him.

I was silent. I did not complain.

I know He saw me. He knew that I was there, in that place, at that moment.

I know He heard the beating of my heart. I know He saw how it was carved.

It was almost enough.

"Wake up, my brother. Wake up."

I opened my eyes. For a moment, I couldn't remember where I was, and then I realized that I had fallen asleep in the mosque. Then my eyes focused on the man who was kneeling before me, a small, grim smile on his face.

"Imam Sama?"

"It is not a good thing to sleep in a place of worship, Anvar. Did no one ever tell you this?"

"Is it time for morning prayers?"

"Not yet. We have to wait awhile for the sun to rise."

"Why are you awake?"

"I came to pray. I could not sleep after Qais Badami left."

I sat up, all thoughts of sleep gone. "Sheikh, do you know where he is?"

The Imam shrugged. "He said that the police were trying to find him because he was illegal. He wanted to see if there was any charity money I could give him because he needed cash."

"Was there?"

The Imam gave me a long stare.

"Sorry," I said. "Not my concern."

"Yes. Well, it is a very sad thing about Qais. He is a good man."

"That isn't what I've heard."

"I know nothing ill of him. Qais was good for the community. Always willing to lend a hand around the mosque. Some of the elderly brothers in homes, you know, with no children to care for them? Qais was helping many of them with their shopping and other chores. A kind soul is gone from among us."

I almost asked him if Qais had been charging those people, or if they'd trusted him with any valuables, but I didn't. Instead, I took a deep breath, trying to find some measure of calm. Incense lingered in the air. It smelled like Arabic tastes. Familiar yet holy, a kiss from a great love.

I reminded myself that the Imam didn't know what Qais had done to Azza. He was just speaking what little truth he knew. I was about to tell him, but just the thought of doing so reminded me how tired I was of telling stories. There would be time enough for that later.

"I don't know, Sheikh. I don't think you really knew him. Maybe we can't ever really know anybody at all."

"That is a cancerous thought, my brother."

"I suppose it is."

"We are responsible only for our souls, not for his." The Imam got to his feet and held out a hand, offering to help me up. "So come. Have you not heard? Prayer is better than sleep."

Imam Sama called my family to let them know where I was. After the dawn prayer, a familiar old silver Camry pulled up in front of the mosque. I was expecting my father. Instead, my mother had come to retrieve me. She was not wearing any makeup and, instead of her usually meticulous hijab, she had a dupatta loosely wrapped around her head. She looked older than I'd ever seen her look.

I took the passenger seat and grimaced.

"How does it still smell like goat in here?"

My mother did not answer as we began to move; instead she chose to ask a question of her own.

"Did they hurt you?"

"No, Mom. They just wanted to ask me some questions."

"I know how that feels."

I chuckled lightly at that and braced myself for a barrage of hostile inquiries.

Instead I got silence.

We drove through the still-sleeping city, my mother focused on the convoluted, hilly streets, where she never felt comfortable driving. Her brow was furrowed, either in concentration or in anger or both. Occasionally, she muttered something about how confusing one-way streets were, or she swerved unnecessarily to dodge a distant red trolley.

"Why didn't Dad come pick me up?"

She pressed her lips together. "I am not a bad mother."

"I don't think you're a bad mother. I do think you're a bad driver."

"Your father said it. He dared say it to me. To me. He dared."

I held my peace.

"Well?" Bariah Faris demanded. "What do you think?"

"I think you did fine, Ma."

"Exactly what I said. You're alive, aren't you?"

"I am."

"You're welcome. Anyway, your father said I should pick you up, so we could talk."

"What on earth are we going to talk about?"

She let out a long-suffering sigh. "This. This thing. This being funny thing you do. It is very annoying."

"Sorry."

"You've always been your father's son, you know that?"

"You never liked him much either, did you?"

A smile tickled the corners of her mouth.

"Don't talk nonsense."

"You can take the 80 from here, Ma."

She nodded and turned on her indicator, preparing to make the turn I'd pointed out.

"Why didn't you tell me about Zuha?"

"You want to talk about Zuha?"

"What else?"

"There is a dead man in my apartment."

"Did you kill him?"

"No."

My mother shrugged. "Then I don't see how that is my problem. My problem is that you've been screwing around—"

"Literally," I muttered under my breath.

"Anvar Faris!"

I held up my hands. "I'm sorry. Of course, I didn't tell you about Zuha, Ma. You would've killed me."

"What? I would have taken a cleaver and made minced meat out of you?"

"It seemed possible."

"Okay. I might have done that, but then Aamir wouldn't have had to go through all this nonsense. Our noses would not have been cut off in front of all our relatives. And the Shahs? Did you consider at all how it would affect their reputation?"

"I don't care, Mom."

"How can you not care?"

"Because a man I knew is dead. His daughter, my friend, is missing. I don't know where she is or how she's going to fend for herself. Mom, you're being—"

Ma took her eyes off the road to give me a warning look. "Don't you—"

"I know. Don't dare. Not this time, Ma. I'm going to dare for once. You want to know why I didn't tell you about Zuha? You want to know why you're not a bigger part of my life? Because you suffocate me. I can't breathe when I am around you. All you care about is God and society and Aamir and what people will say. You don't care about me. You don't care about what I care about. So I don't know how to talk to you. I don't love the things you love, Ma. I've never wanted the life that you wanted for me, but you keep foisting it on me. All I want, all I've ever wanted . . ."

"What? Why will you never tell me what you want then? I did the best I could with you, Anvar. You may not believe me, but I did not want to be disappointed in one of my children. It isn't my fault you turned out to be whatever it is that you are. I didn't want you to be a failure."

"I'm not a failure."

"How? What do you have to show for your life? You don't have a good job. You don't have money. You're not religious. You don't have a good reputation in the community. People won't even talk to me about marrying their daughters to you. So, tell me, Anvar, what is it that you have?"

I looked out the window at the towers of concrete we were going by and shook my head. I'd never before spoken to my mother the way I just had, but she had caught me at a bad time. My soul felt like it had diminished, like the inside of my being had eroded from loss and horror and guilt. I had lost, albeit momentarily, the will to hold back words that had been festering for years.

All things considered, she'd taken it rather well. I had expected her to raise her voice, to yell, to scream. She had not done much of that. She was not, I realized, surprised. She knew this was how I felt. She'd probably known for some time.

I let out a deep breath, trying to calm myself. It was the sound that a fire makes when you pour water on it.

"I'm sorry. I shouldn't have said anything."

"You have no right to say that, you know."

"That I'm sorry?"

"That I don't care for you. You don't have children, so you don't understand. Who was up with you all night when you got a fever, haan? Who taught you to speak? To walk? Who changed your dirty nappies? We didn't have disposable diapers back then, you know, so it was cloth nappies, till you were three and a half."

"Okay. I get it. Like I said, I shouldn't have said anything."

"But you did, and I am telling you that you are wrong."

"I said I was sorry."

"Don't be sorry. Just be wrong. Just sit there with your mouth closed and be wrong."

"Yes, Ma."

"I still expect an answer," she said. "You think you know best in everything. Then tell me, you've lived your life just like you wanted, and what have you to show for it?"

"I found things I love."

My mother sniffed, the sound laced with disdain. "That's it? For all your life, that is all you have to show?"

"What more is there?"

"Everything. Are you crazy, Anvar? You can't eat love. You can't put love over your head when it rains. Love is not an accomplishment. It is worthless."

"I disagree."

"Then I don't understand you."

"I know," I said as gently as I could.

"And you made me miss my exit."

I thought that was the end of the conversation. We would loop around, just as my mother was looping around on the freeway by taking the next exit, and we would just go back to the way our relationship had been before this conversation. We would pretend, as we always had, that we were fine. Indeed, my mother was quiet for a while.

Then she said, "Explain it to me."

"What?"

"I don't understand what you're trying to say. You should explain it to me."

It was an astonishing moment. In my life, I had never heard Bariah Faris admit she did not know something, much less actually ask someone to explain something to her. I sat there for a while, unable get past my surprise, until she prompted me.

I tried to figure out how I could tell her what I was trying to say. In order to make her understand my perspective, I would have to see the world as she saw it. I had to find something in her experience, anything, that would capture what I felt. If I relied on words or images or metaphors that resonated only with my world, she would remain unable to see what I was trying to show her.

"Do you remember when you were teaching me to pray? During namaz, you said, my soul should be full of wonder. Elevated. Reverent. As if I was in the presence of Allah. As if I could see Allah himself."

"I remember."

"Religion has never really made me feel that way. Not in any mosque, not in any prayer. Sometimes when I am reading a particularly beautiful line of prose or I hear a passage of lovely music—"

"Astaghfirullah."

"I know you think it blasphemy, but in those moments, I feel that there is something more, something good, in the universe. The possibility of something being divine opens up for me. That is why I love literature. The human imagination is a miracle, and it is possible that this miracle is a gift from a Creator."

"And what about Zuha?"

"When I see Art, the divine feels possible. When I am with Zuha, the divine feels certain. I've been apart from her for a decade and, in all that time, I tried to do other things, to make a life for myself. Some parts of that life you actually approved of, but the truth is I haven't really been happy. I think she is necessary for me. Do you understand what I am saying?"

"I understand that you are probably going into the hellfire," my mother muttered.

"You know, I'm actually going to start praying that I don't end up in hell, just because I want you to be wrong. I'm going to be the only person in heaven who got there out of spite."

"You're going to start praying? I think that means I am a good mother."

"Yes, Ma. You're fine."

"Good. Don't forget to tell your father."

"My thinking is that the newspaper coverage has very much been poorly done," Hafeez Bhatti told me as he led me through the dimly lit corridors of his apartment complex. "Muslim tries to honor-kill own daughter in San Francisco? I could call it the shit of bulls, my friend, but even that is useful as fertilizer. They know next to nothing about Abu Fahd, but they rush to label him. I told the one reporter who had the sense to come to me with questions that he was no Muslim at the end."

"Maybe you should write a letter to the editor."

Hafeez Bhai chuckled. "I don't think so. It has been a few days, so the hubbub is not so much anymore. No reason to dig it all up again. Though I tried to be a writer when I was a young man. I don't even know how many stories I started but simply couldn't finish. I would always end up telling my wife about what happened and with that went the pressure . . . the drive, you know, to actually be writing. The story was told. That was the important thing."

"You could write now."

Hafeez Bhai snorted. "I am much too wise to write now."

"Humble too." As always, my sarcasm appeared lost on the older man.

"Most humble." He nodded so vigorously that I was afraid he might hurt his neck. "At being humble, I am best. Ask anyone and they will tell you." He stopped and exclaimed, "Here we are."

My landlord had led me to an empty apartment. It was, I think, the farthest he could get me from my old place and still keep me in his building.

"Yes," he told me with his preternatural cheerfulness. "Number 701. Now you have to please keep in mind that the last people, they were not good. Not good at all. Trying to grow the pot and the weed, if you can believe it. I had to kick them out on their bums." Opening the door, he led me in. "They did not take it so well."

I looked at the wrecked apartment. "Hafeez Bhai, you have a talent for understatement."

"Most definitely. I am the best at understatements." He dabbed at the sides of his mouth with his peek-stained handkerchief. "And also overstatements."

I walked through the marvel of destruction that Hafeez wanted to make my new home. The prior tenants had gone out of their way to trash the place. Several of the doors and walls were busted through. Light fixtures had been torn out and electrical wires dangled from the ceiling, limp and useless. Spray-painted racist slurs directed at Bhatti decorated the walls. I stepped over the shattered legs of a broken chair and headed to the bathroom. Predictably, perhaps, the faucets were bent and misshapen, their handles ripped off.

"I hope you didn't give them their deposit back."

Hafeez chortled, and his large belly jiggled in time with his mirth. "What to say? This is what happens when you misjudge people. Anyway"—he slapped his beefy hands together in a thunderous clap that echoed through the nearly empty space—"what are you thinking?"

"How long has it been vacant?"

"A few months. I didn't have the funds to be making major repairs. For you, however, Mr. Anvar Faris Barrister Sir, I will find the money."

"That's very generous, Hafeez Bhai, but you don't have to do that."

He waddled over to where I stood.

"I haven't yet seen how your story ends, yes?" Putting his hands on my shoulders, he added, "I never had a son, Anvar, and I have to say that if I had ever had a son, I would most certainly hope he wouldn't have to be living in this shithole. For you, however, I will make it perfect."

"You look terrible."

"Flattery, my dear, will get you everywhere."

Zuha ignored the feeble joke. "I'm serious. You look like the before picture in an ad for an energy drink." I began to respond but surrendered, instead, to a yawn. "Come on, Anvar, how long are you going to stay at that crappy motel? You're not getting any sleep there."

She was right. The motel was terrible. Unfortunately, it was all I could afford for an extended stay. Besides, while it was true that the paint was loud, the walls thin and the old mattress I tried to sleep on alarmingly lumpy, none of that was what kept me up at night.

"Hafeez Bhai says I can move in within a week."

"From what you've told me, that sounds wildly optimistic."

Also true. I sighed and tried to stretch the kinks out of my back. Zuha, for her part, launched into a now familiar lecture about how I should move back in with my parents for the time being. My mind wandered to memories of dreams stained a dreadful red, which felt like breathing in the horrific metallic tang of blood in every breath.

Zuha snapped her fingers in front of my face, forcing my attention back to the moment.

"Hi," she said.

"I just . . ." I took a deep breath. "I'm a little distracted."

"What are you thinking about?"

"How pretty you are."

"Wow. That was weak."

"I'm a little off my game."

"You haven't taken any of Aamir's calls."

"Yeah."

"He wants to come to the funeral. He wants to know if that would be—"

"It's fine."

"You're sure?"

I nodded. The cold fury I had initially felt toward my brother had started to thaw a bit. Without his interference, without his telling Abu Fahd where Azza was staying and what we had done, it was possible this tragedy would have been avoided. However, the chain of causation was not something I had any wish to dwell upon. I was the one who had listened to Azza and failed to report the violence she had suffered. Then I hadn't listened to her and told Qais to run, which had resulted in her getting hurt. Hell, I was the one who slept with her in the first place. A great deal of the blame was mine to bear.

"And he's off again," Zuha said.

"No. I'm right here. I was just remembering something I heard once. John Greenleaf Whittier wrote: 'Of all sad words of tongue or pen . . .'"

I left the quote unfinished because I could see in her smile that she knew it.

"If you really don't want to go to your parents' place, I've been thinking that you could, you know, maybe crash at my place."

I raised my eyebrows at her and she blushed furiously. A sleepover was skirting dangerously close to the fruit she had forbidden us both.

"I mean," she said, "if you intend to behave yourself."

"No hanky-panky is what you're saying?"

"Hanky-panky? You've been spending way too much time with your Hafeez Bhai. If you start chewing paan all the time . . ."

"It was a serious question."

"It really wasn't."

"Maybe it could have been phrased better."

"You think?" Zuha asked. "But yes. I mean, no. The hanky part is fine. It's the panky stuff that gets us into trouble."

"Maybe you should draw me a diagram, you know, of where it is okay to touch you. Just so there is no confusion."

"Ass."

"Okay. Where else?"

"Fine. Whatever. If you don't want to—"

"No, thank you. I think that would be . . . great. I'm having trouble getting out of my own head when I'm alone."

She held out her hands and I took them in mine.

"Well," she said. "I might just be able to help you with that."

"I think I might vote with the populists this time. They're right about some things. If people like your crazy neighbor can come here and try to kill people, don't you think that's a problem?"

"I haven't seen you in forever," I reminded Jason Backes. "In which time, I nearly got murdered, and that's the first thing you have to say to me?"

My friend, who was loading boxes from his Prius into his food truck, paused, thought for a moment, then shrugged.

"Yeah. Are you going to stand there or actually help?"

"I'm just going to stand here," I told him. "I wouldn't want you to think I'm trying to take your job, being a brown and all."

Jason rolled his eyes. "Hilarious."

"I'm known for it."

"I'm not joking, Anvar. We have to take the country back, you know?"

"From who?"

Jason opened his mouth, then closed it without answering me.

"Do whatever you want. I have to tell you though, it'll be tough to run a halal food truck after there is a Muslim ban in place."

"Come on. It doesn't matter what any candidate for president says. There's never going to be a Muslim ban. The Supremes wouldn't allow it."

"Don't put too much hope in the Court. Liberty lives in the hearts of men and women, and when it dies there, no law can save it."

"Sounds like a quote," he said.

"It was Judge Learned Hand."

"That's a dope name."

"Yeah," I agreed. "Actually, I've thought about names a lot since I became a lawyer. I've thought a lot about the story of Adam."

"Like Adam from the Bible?"

"The Quran's version of his story is a little different. In the Quran, when God decides to create Adam, the angels question Him. Adam, they say, is not as pure as they are. Adam, they say, will bring destruction to the Earth. It's light supremacy." Jason did not react, so I decided to explain. "It's a joke. Because, you know, they're made of . . ."

"I get it."

I shook my head at his lack of appreciation but went on. "Anyway, God created Adam and taught Adam the names of all things. Then He asked the angels to tell Him the names of those same things and the angels couldn't. In response, God commanded the angels to bow before Adam."

"Why?"

"Exactly. Maybe it was to humble them. I was taught it was because mankind is superior to all creatures, including angels. Now,

I think it is because if you control the names of things, if you can master how to twist and turn words, you can control a narrative. I don't think it's an accident that from that point on all the stories in the Quran are about Adam and his children, the human race."

"Okay. That's cool, I guess, but we were talking about who I was going to vote for."

"What I'm saying is that we should be honest about who we are and what we do. We should tell the truth about things, even when it doesn't sound good or feel good or sell well. It's not enhanced interrogation, it's torture. It's not an extrajudicial killing, it's murder. We should call things by their real names."

"This is where you tell me that populism in the United States is racist even though no one admits it, right?"

"I would never presume to tell a white man what is and isn't racist."

Jason scowled. "You were funnier before you were shot at."

"Probably. I'm just saying, look for the truth. Look past the slogans and the spin and what people say their motivations are. Look at what they are actually trying to do, at the world they really want to create, and once you know the truth about them, if you still want to stand with them, to vote for them, go ahead."

"That's it?" Jason demanded, after I stopped talking. "That's all? I thought for sure you were going to try to get me to vote for a liberal candidate."

"Why? You're Californian. No one cares how you vote."

I got to the mosque early. No one else had arrived yet for Abu Fahd's funeral prayer. Except Aamir. When my brother looked up at me, I saw that he was pale, his eyes were red and heavy with exhaustion. It was obvious that he had not been sleeping well either. I was surprised to see him so shaken. Even his typically perfect hair, always arranged with meticulous care, was disheveled. I'd started to believe that was not possible.

He got to his feet when I came in. His expression was anxious and he said, formally, "As-salamu alaykum." I nodded, trying to figure out where to sit. If I sat with Aamir, I might have to talk to him, and I wasn't sure I had anything to say to him just then. Sitting away from him seemed like a cruel rebuff. Before I could make a decision, he spoke again.

"I didn't mean for this to happen."

"I know."

"I did the right thing." I had heard that from him before in my life many times. However, for the first time that I could remember, Aamir didn't say it like a statement. He didn't say it with conviction. He said it like a plea.

"You always do."

That wasn't what he wanted to hear. He pulled his brittle, pained gaze away from mine.

"This isn't how things are supposed to go, Anvar. What Abu Fahd did . . . that isn't what I would've done. It wasn't right."

I wanted to tell him that not everyone was like him, that a man like Abu Fahd was incapable of handling the information that his daughter was sleeping with someone in the same manner Aamir would. I'm not sure what he'd imagined would happen. Knowing Aamir, he probably hadn't thought it through at all. He'd probably done what seemed right to him in that moment. Telling grown-ups when something forbidden was happening had always been second nature to him.

Now he couldn't understand how it had gone wrong, because we were both taught to live in a world where things were black and white. Good prevails over evil. The virtuous act, the upright act, the religiously prescribed act, always brought triumph. I had stopped believing that world was real, so when I stumbled while doing what seemed like the right thing, it hurt but I did not bruise.

Aamir, on the other hand, had kept faith with that worldview his whole life and that was why he looked so shaken. He couldn't understand why something he thought was right had resulted in this much harm.

I remembered the day, long ago, when I looked at the world for the first time and imagined what it would feel like if there really was no God. That was how Aamir felt now. This was his moment of doubt.

I wanted to be as angry with him as I had been when I first learned what he had done. However, that anger had faded quickly, and now that he stood before me, I couldn't summon even the vestiges of the fury that had once gripped my soul.

For once in my life, I was justified in feeling utterly and completely enraged at something he had done. Despite all his advertised excellence, Aamir Faris had made a mistake, a tremendous error, with calamitous consequences. This was my chance to hold him accountable, to show him that he was no different, no better, than I was.

But there was a problem. I couldn't be angry with him because he felt more like a brother to me then, in that moment when we were both broken and imperfect, than he ever had before.

Besides, I too had done something I thought was right—I'd told Qais to run—and had brought pain into the world. It was like Aamir had taken a step toward me, and I had taken a step toward him.

"Listen," he said, "I really don't know how to begin to apologize. I didn't mean for you to ever be in danger, much less shot at. And Zuha could have been hurt too."

"It'll be all right."

"It will?"

A movement caught my eye and I looked up. It was nothing, just a trick of the light, or a trick of a shadow, but I noticed for the first time that there were Quranic verses painted in gold under the mosque's crown molding. At least, I assume they were Quranic verses. It was Arabic, at any rate, and given where I was standing, it was probably not a grocery list.

The shining words ran from wall to wall, uninterrupted, surrounding Aamir and surrounding me, encircling the prayer hall from all sides. I recognized a few of them, here and there, but I had no idea what they meant when they were put together.

"You have to know that I'm sorry, Anvar."

I looked back at my brother. I saw now a part of him that was also a part of me. Somehow, I hadn't seen it before.

"What are you doing after the service?" I asked him.

"Nothing. Why?"

"Let's go for a drive when this is over. We'll get some bubble-gum ice cream."

—

Muslim funerals are simple. There is no beautiful casket. Instead, the body is wrapped in a plain white cotton shroud. There is no elaborate eulogy except the ritual refrain "inna lillahi wa inna ilayhi raji'un." We belong to Allah, and to Allah we return. There is no music or dirge. There is only silence.

Abu Fahd's funeral was simpler than most, in the sense that attendance was low. There were a handful of strangers who happened to be at the mosque, my family, Zuha, Hafeez Bhai and, of course, Imam Sama.

The Imam called for silence and we stood in line to pray for Abu Fahd of Iraq, who once had a name that we did not know.

Qais knew and Azza knew, but neither one of them was here.

What's in a name, anyway?

"Allah hu Akbar."

After the service, my mother was talking to Zuha outside the mosque. They fell silent as I approached. Ma's face was grim, her lips pressed together in a tight line. Zuha wiped tears away with the back of her wrist. When she looked at me, she bit her lip and then hurried past, her hair brushing my shoulder. "Excuse me."

I turned to watch her go and then shook my head at my mother. "Come on, Ma."

"Don't you dare question me."

"What was that?" I gestured toward Zuha's retreating form.

"Don't. You. Dare." When I didn't say anything, she walked up to me and straightened my collar. "And why are you wearing a pant shirt to the mosque? You couldn't find a decent shalwar kameez?"

"It isn't my style."

"Yes," she agreed wearily. "I know all about just how stylish you are. Aamir wore a shalwar kameez. It looks nice."

"I didn't notice."

"We'll talk about it some other time. Today, you should try to make up with your brother. He really is the best person with the best heart."

"I spoke to him, and we'll work on that later today. Listen, Ma, I have to go to the cemetery."

"Yes, yes. Go. Remember to recite the shahada the entire way there. It's important." I nodded and began to walk away, but she called me back. "Do you know where the Quran first existed?"

"What? No, I've never thought about it. Somewhere in Arabia, obviously."

My mother rewarded me with a disappointed grimace. "It existed, of course, first in the mind of God. He knew that one day he would reveal it to his Last Prophet, May Peace Be Upon Him. Don't you dare make that face at me. What I am saying is that just because something is not spoken out loud or told to anyone does not mean that it does not exist or that it is not important. It could be the most important, most holy thing of all." She took a deep breath and leveled her gaze at me. "So even though we have never said it, you must know that both I and your father love you very much. You know that, don't you?"

"Yes," I whispered. "I know."

I slept for a long time. When I got up, I could hear my family moving around downstairs, talking to each other, wondering when I would finally leave my room and come down to join them. I preferred, at least for a moment, to sit by my window and listen to the pattering of rain on glass.

Leaning my head against a wall, I wondered where Azza bint Saqr was, what she was doing and how the world was treating her.

Then my door flew open and Zuha walked in.

"Hey," she said.

"Hi. I'm not sure if they told you . . ."

"You're superbusy brooding."

"I wasn't letting anyone in."

She shrugged. "That's why I didn't ask for permission."

I smiled.

"How are you feeling?"

"I got some sleep. And you're here. Things are looking up."

"They're watching a movie downstairs, if you want to join them. I'm told there will be popcorn."

I made a face. "I'd rather not. Wait. How did you get up here?"

"It turns out that your parents have discovered a marvelous new technology. They're calling it stairs and I think—"

"How'd you get past my mom is what I meant."

"It wasn't hard to give her the slip. I've got the One Ring." Zuha held out her hand. She wore a platinum band with a modest marquise diamond set in it. "Thank you, by the way, I absolutely love it."

"What?"

"The ring is yours. I mean, it's mine, but it's from you."

"Ma gave it to you?"

"I think she was worried you would never get around to it."

"Your conversation with her outside the mosque . . ."

"Was her telling me that, while she thinks we're both unbelievably stupid and, unless we repent, bound to end up in a very bad place, she is not willing to sacrifice her son's happiness for anything in the world."

"That isn't what it looked like."

Zuha sat down at the edge of my bed, opposite me.

"I would have, you know," I said.

"What?"

"Proposed."

"Your mother says you don't know how to do anything. She says she still has to pick out your clothes for you."

"And Aamir?"

"He says he is fine with it. I think it is his way of making amends."

"For being a—"

"Don't start," Zuha warned me.

I didn't start.

"So . . ." she began, before trailing off.

"What?"

"So will you marry me?"

"I don't know," I said. "That sounds like a bad idea."

"It's not. It's the best thing you'll ever do."

THE ENDGAME

I win again.

—Naani Jaan

ANVAR

Donald Trump was elected the forty-fifth president of the United States on a day Ma liked better than did any other Muslim in America. It was as if, for her, Eid had come early.

I was with my parents, watching the news, when the results were announced.

Bariah Faris turned to her husband and said what she had been waiting to say since the day he decided to move our family to the United States.

"I told you. Did you listen? No. You always do what you want. You had your head in the clouds with that Jefferson fellow. All men are created equal, you said. We won't be second-class citizens, you said. Look at what just happened. What did I tell you? He'll find a way, you know, to kick people like us out. He hates people like us, Imtiaz. Don't you dare shake your head at me. He'll do it. You'll see. One day, they will kick us out and your Jefferson won't come back from the dead to help you. Don't you dare tell me I am wrong, Imtiaz Faris. Don't you ever dare tell me I am wrong about anything ever again."

My father watched her stomp off and then offered me a sheepish smile.

"You would think that after all these years, she would know that I am not a very daring man."

"That's not true. You left your home. Crossed oceans. Came here."

He chuckled. "It sounds like a big thing when you say it like that, Anvar. It wasn't all that big a thing, you know. I just wanted to have a little space to myself. Not a lot, you understand, but just a little. Just enough. For a while there, I thought I had found it."

He turned his attention back to the television, to the adoring, cheering crowd greeting their incoming nationalist president.

"When did Americans become so afraid?"

"What do you mean?"

"I understood the business of trying to go back to the safe glory of Islam's past when it came to Pakistan. It came at the end of a long, slow decline the causes of which we didn't fully understand. America is still the most powerful nation in the world. So why are its people so terrified all the time?"

A map of the United States flashed on the screen, splashed with the colors of water and blood. I studied it as I tried to come up with an answer to the question Imtiaz Faris had posed.

"We live on stolen land," I finally said, "in a country built on slavery and reliant on the continued economic exploitation of other people. The oppressor always lives in fear of the oppressed. Americans have always been afraid—of those native to this continent, of Black people, of Japanese citizens they interned, and now of Muslims and immigrants. So the real question, I think, is who is next?"

We watched as, on-screen, the president-elect made his way onto the stage to begin his speech, and Imtiaz Faris let out an exhausted sigh.

"I suppose we have to change the national anthem then."

"You want to take out 'the land of the brave'?"

"No," he protested. "The whole thing has to be replaced."

"With what?"

"With Britney. Remember 'Oops! . . . I Did It Again'?"

On January 27, 2017, a ban on Muslims entering the United States was ordered by the White House. It was disguised as a ban on entry from seven Muslim-majority countries. Interestingly enough, they were almost all countries the United States had recently attacked or droned or waged wars in. None of them, or their citizens, had orchestrated an attack on the United States.

—

On January 28, 2017, protests broke out all over the country, as Americans stood up against the Muslim ban. They stood at airports and in streets, they stood by monuments and before government buildings. My father watched the coverage and seemed caught between the desire to break into tears and the desire to break into a jig.

When the news cut to scenes of attorneys, sitting on the ground in airports, drafting habeas petitions, he looked at me.

"Are you sure you don't want to be a lawyer?"

I don't know what happened to Azza bint Saqr or even Qais Badami. If Agents Hale and Moray ever tracked them down, they didn't tell me. A small part of me wants them found, the part of me that wishes to understand entirely the causes behind the events that so altered my life.

Most of my soul realizes that the cost of those answers would be too high. Most of my soul hopes that Azza found some measure of peace. I sometimes imagine her watching her first snowfall, and I find myself hoping that she thinks it is beautiful.

It's part of growing up to realize that often, perhaps inevitably, we are left with incomplete stories about the lives of other people. It is impossible, therefore, to understand any other being as completely, or incompletely, as we understand ourselves. The best we can do is find some common ground in self-evident truths about how we are, if not the same, then at least similar. We can recognize that our experiences of the world, no matter how various and varied, how tinged with excess or want or joy or sorrow, make us all irredeemably, undeniably, irrepressibly human.

Zuha and I married. It was an extremely small affair. Imam Sama officiated a brief, solemn ceremony in my parents' backyard. A lot of our guests complained that the food, while delicious, was not appropriate for the nature of the celebration. I will concede that having Junk in the Trunk cater the event was an unusual choice.

Hafeez Bhatti didn't get us something off our registry. Rather, he gave us a sterling silver paan daan, an exquisite rectangular box, which is supposed to house all the ingredients necessary for the construction of a good paan. We have yet to find a use for it, though it is by far the most valuable thing we own.

Aamir was soon introduced to an eligible young woman who, my mother made certain, had never heard of me. The spectacle of their union was lavish and grand and, I suspect, exactly what Aamir wanted. My father designated himself the DJ and also found time to dance with Zuha at the wedding.

It was a good night, a joyous celebration of two perfectly scripted lives.

ZAHRA

The sun was still asleep when I left the basement I was renting, a backpack heavy with books on my shoulder. My breath touched the bitter cold around me, became a ghost and then vanished. The dying night was peaceful. The moon was distant but full, and a few stars were shining, waiting to kiss the dawn.

There was a rhythm to my mornings. I opened Mrs. Popova's café for her at five-thirty, and my world filled with the smell of brewing coffee and baking bread. At six, my employer wandered in, still rubbing sleep from her eyes. Four hours later, I went to class.

Before any of that, however, there was Henry. He was a short, thin man, in his early thirties with a nervous smile, and hair that he parted neatly every day, like a schoolboy, but that his toque always messed up a little. Ever since I'd started working for Mrs. Popova, a year and a half ago, he'd become a regular.

More than a regular, actually, because he showed up before I did, before we even opened. On that day, like always, he was waiting for me at the storefront. He waved a gloved hand and offered me his best grin.

"Hi. Hello. It's a good morning, right?"

"It's freezing, Mr. Bowman. What are you doing out here?"

His shoulders dropped a little. "I asked you to call me Henry."

"I forgot."

"I've asked fourteen times."

"I've got a really bad memory," I said.

"That's funny. Have you always been funny, Zahra?"

"No. I just had a good teacher. Let's go inside. I'll get you your usual."

"Sure. Okay, yeah."

I fumbled around in my backpack for the keys, wondering if I should say something else to him. Mrs. Popova was always telling me to give Henry a break. The fact that he was wretched at flirting, she said, didn't mean he'd be bad in a relationship. I needed to either have pity on him, she thought, or end all his hopes.

Where were my keys? I set the backpack down on the ground and knelt next to it, looking through it under the glow of a streetlight.

"Uh . . . so . . ." Henry said. I looked up and saw that he had his phone in his hand. "Zahra is a pretty name."

It had not always been my name, of course, but he didn't need to know that.

"It was my mother's name actually."

"It's nice," he said, then turned his attention back to the screen and read, "Ask her what it means . . . uh . . . I mean—"

I couldn't help it. I laughed. He flushed, his cheeks, already pink from the cold, going almost red.

"Sorry," he said, "I was just . . . I'm not good at, you know—"

"It means flower," I said. I didn't like seeing him struggle.

"Oh. Where does she live?"

"My mother? She died years ago."

Henry looked like he'd stepped on her grave. "I'm so sorry. I didn't mean to bring it up."

"Happens to everyone," I said.

"Your father?"

"I don't know where he is. Last time I saw him was in San Francisco."

His eyes went a little wide. "You've been to California?"

"I've been lots of places."

"I've never left town. What's that like?"

"It's fine. There is nothing beautiful in the world, no matter where you go."

Now he really didn't know what to say to me. His hand twitched, and he was itching, I'm sure, to google for help, but he held off. He looked at me as if he had something to say, but then glanced away, like something unexpected had caught his attention.

"Look," he said. "It's snowing."

Then, as if he'd never seen it happen before even though it happened here all the time, he grinned, as more and more water crystals fell upon us from the sky. They sparkled in the streetlight.

"Isn't it lovely?" Henry asked.

It was.

I could still remember what Anvar had said once, that even though snow was pure when it fell, its short life on the earth made it dirty and gross. He'd been right, in a way, but he'd also been wrong. I saw that in Henry's shy, hopeful, silly, joyous smile as he held out his arms, and looked up at heaven.

Maybe I'd been wrong too. Maybe there was still beauty in the world. Maybe you just had to know when and where to find it.

Acknowledgments

As I begin to write the acknowledgments for this book, I cannot help but think about how the Quran asks, repeatedly, "Which of the blessings of your Lord will you deny?"

I do not deny any of them, but I am unable to count them all. The people who have helped make this book what it is are all blessings. They are also legion. It is inevitable that I will fail to name everyone who deserves mention.

If you feel like you deserve to be on this list but do not find yourself here, know that you were not discounted. You were forgotten. I'm kidding! Seriously though, yes, you were forgotten, but just temporarily, and only because I am human. For that, I apologize.

When I first got edits back from Robert Bloom in the mail, I was convinced he was a magician. The manuscript looked like it had been cut in half. I realized, moments later, that it had simply been printed double-sided. As I read on, it became clear to me that I was dealing not with a magician but with an alchemist. For a writer, the latter is much, much better than the former. Rob, working with you has been the privilege of a lifetime. Thank you for making my words shine.

Melissa Edwards. Am I blinking away tears because I typed out my agent's name just now? Yes, I am, and they are tears of gratitude. I don't have the words to thank her. Melissa, you believed in this book before anyone else in the industry did. You believed in it even when I doubted it. You never gave up on it. I will never, ever forget that. Thank you for making this dream possible.

Speaking of gratitude, if I could take its soul and pour it into a pen (that sounded way sweeter and less grim-reapery in my head), I still wouldn't be able to properly acknowledge the contribution my mentors, Marty Mayberry and Léonie Kelsall, have made to this

Acknowledgments

book and to my growth as a writer. Yes, they made me rewrite the scene were Anvar and Zuha first meet around one thousand times, but I learned a ton. Seriously, Lee and Marty, I'm forever in awe of your generosity and wisdom. Thank you.

Thank you to the amazingly helpful Nora Grubb; to my production editor, Ellen Feldman; my copy editor, Susan Brown; and my proofreaders, Laura Starrett and Jane Elias. Thank you to Mike Collica. Thank you to John Pitts, for his incredible kindness, and to Bill Thomas and the entire Doubleday team.

I'd also like to especially thank Emily Mahon and Samya Arif for their brilliant work on the cover. Honestly, I had no idea what the right cover for this book would look like. Then I saw what you two had done and there it was. You're amazing. Thank you.

Thank you, as always, to Madelyn Burt and Addison Duffy.

Thank you to Zach Watkins, for reading first and being so encouraging. Thank you, Brett Schuitema, for early help with word choice and sentence structure. And thank you, Chloe Moffett, you're a genius. Thank you also, Anne Raven, Elizabeth Chatsworth and Robin Winzenread Fritz and the entire Pitch Wars Class of 2017. You guys are incredible.

A thank you to the artists, singers and poets of Pakistan, past and present. You never cease to inspire me. Keep bringing beauty into the world, for beauty begets beauty, and we are all better for it.

Thank you to Saad Ahmad. Dude, I love you. Thank you to Lendyl D'Souza for being there always. Thank you to Imam Kamran Islam for all the great conversations full of clarity and courage.

Thank you to my in-laws, particularly my parents-in-law, Sameera and Rashid Siddiqui, for being so unfailingly supportive.

Thank you to my mother, Hajra Masood, without whom I would have never learned to love books. Thank you to my father, Syed Manzar Masood, for always being with me, even though he isn't with us anymore.

Thank you to my children, Muhammad and Maryam, for . . . actually, I'm just being nice. You guys didn't do anything to help with this one. Even so, I love you. Grow up well and raise hell.

And to my wife, Saira Amena Siddiqui, for choosing to be the greatest blessing of my life. Your patience, encouragement and insight are everything, and I love you. It is a fact undeniable.

About the Author

Syed Masood grew up in Karachi, Pakistan. A first-generation immigrant twice over, he has been a citizen of three different countries and nine different cities. He currently lives in Sacramento, California, where he is a practicing attorney.